Surprising Lord Jack

Books by Sally MacKenzie

THE NAKED DUKE

THE NAKED MARQUIS

THE NAKED EARL

THE NAKED GENTLEMAN

"The Naked Laird" in LORDS OF DESIRE

THE NAKED BARON

THE NAKED VISCOUNT

"The Naked Prince" in AN INVITATION TO SIN

THE NAKED KING

"The Duchess of Love"

BEDDING LORD NED

SURPRISING LORD JACK

Published by Kensington Publishing Corporation

Surprising Lord Jack

SALLY MACKENZIE

ZEBRA BOOKS
KENSINGTON PUBLISHING CORP.
http://www.kensingtonbooks.com

ZEBRA BOOKS are published by

Kensington Publishing Corp.
119 West 40th Street
New York, NY 10018

All Kensington titles, imprints and distributed lines are available at special quantity discounts for bulk purchases for sales promotion, premiums, fund-raising, educational or institutional use.

Special book excerpts or customized printings can also be created to fit specific needs. For details, write or phone the office of the Kensington Special Sales Manager: Attn. Special Sales Department. Kensington Publishing Corp., 119 West 40th Street, New York, NY 10018. Phone: 1-800-221-2647.

ISBN-13: 978-1-4201-2322-7
ISBN-10: 1-4201-2322-X
First Printing: March 2013

ISBN-13: 978-1-4201-3202-1
ISBN-10: 1-4201-3202-4
First Electronic Edition: March 2013

10 9 8 7 6 5 4 3 2 1

Printed in the United States of America

For Jessica, again.
Thanks for helping me whip Jack into shape.

For Kristen.
Welcome to the crazy MacKenzie clan.

For Kathy K. and Dr. H.
NIH rocks!

With thanks to our church and our local eateries for giving me places to charge my laptop battery when the dreadful derecho of June 29, 2012, knocked out our power two days before my deadline.

And, as always, for Kevin.

Chapter 1

Appearances can be deceiving.
—Venus's Love Notes

Miss Frances Hadley staggered up to the Crowing Cock's weather-beaten door, her legs, backside, and feet throbbing with each step.

Blast it, men rode astride all the time. How could she have guessed the experience would be so painful? And having to walk the last half mile in Frederick's old boots hadn't helped. Damn icy roads.

She took a deep breath of the sharp, winter air. And if Daisy was lame—

She scowled at the door. If her horse was lame, she'd figure out another way to get to London. Hell, she'd walk if she had to. She was *not* going home to Landsford. To think Aunt Viola had been going to help Mr. Littleton with his nefarious scheme—

Oh! Every time she thought about it, she wanted to hit something—or someone.

She put her hand on the door. The drunken male laughter was so loud she could hear it out here. Pot-valiant oafs! At least drunkards were even less likely than sober men to see through her disguise. She almost hoped one of them would approach her. She'd take great delight in bloodying his nose.

She shoved open the door and was hit by a cacophony of voices and the stench of spilled ale, smoke, and too many sweaty male bodies. A barmaid, burdened with six or seven mugs of ale, rushed out of a room to her left.

"Where can I see about a bed for the night?" Frances had to shout to make herself heard. She had a deep voice for a woman, but was it deep enough? Apparently. The girl barely glanced at her.

"See Mr. Findley," she said without breaking stride, jerking her head back at the room she'd just left, "but we're full up."

Oh, damn. Frances's stomach plummeted.

She would *not* despair. If worse came to worst, she'd find a corner of the common room and sleep there. Or perhaps the innkeeper would let her stay in the stables. Even if Daisy were able to carry her, she could not go any farther. Night was coming on.

She went through the narrow doorway. A stout man with a bald head and an equally stout, gray-haired woman were sitting at a scarred wooden table, eating their dinner. Frances inhaled. Mutton and potatoes. Not her favorite dishes, but she was so hungry, the food smelled like ambrosia.

"Tonight's the duchess's ball, Archie," the woman was saying. She waved a bite of mutton at him. "Do you think Her Grace found a match for Lord Ned or Lord Jack this year?"

Archie snorted. "Don't know why this year should be any different than last year or the year before, Madge."

"I suppose you're right. I just—"

Frances cleared her throat. "Pardon me, but might you have a room for the night?"

The man looked over and frowned. "'Fraid every bed is full."

"I see." She bit her lip. Damn it.

"Oh, Archie," his wife said, getting up. "I'm sure we can find something for the poor lad. He looks exhausted."

"I *am* very tired, madam, and my horse is lame." Frances was suddenly a hairsbreadth from groveling. Lying in a real bed would be heaven, especially compared to sleeping on the hard floor with the tosspots in the common room or on straw in the stable.

Mrs. Findley clucked her tongue. "You're likely hungry as well."

Frances's stomach spoke for her, growling loudly. She flushed. She hadn't eaten since breakfast, eight hours earlier. She should have packed something, but she hadn't expected to be so delayed, and to be frank, she'd been too angry to think clearly.

And if she'd had a knife in her hand, Aunt Viola would not have been safe.

Mrs. Findley laughed. "Come, sit with us." She took Frances's arm and towed her over to the table.

"I-I don't wish to intrude. If you could just spare a slice of mutton and a potato, I'm sure I would do very well."

"Don't be ridiculous." The woman pushed her into a chair and started filling a plate with food. "You must be starving."

Frances's stomach growled again, and Mrs. Findley laughed. "Poor boy." She put the plate down in front of her. "Now eat before you fall over from hunger. I'm sure we can find you someplace to sleep."

Mr. Findley was less inclined to charity. "Madge, the only room we have free is the one I save for the Valentines."

"Well, none of them will be here tonight, will they? It's the birthday ball, remember? They won't miss it, no matter how much they hate attending. They're good boys."

Ha! Frances speared a bit of potato with her fork. Jack, the youngest of the Duke of Greycliffe's sons, was far from a "good boy." Aunt Viola was forever holding him up as an example of the evils of Town. A rake of the first order and likely a procurer as well, he was rumored to know—*intimately*—every brothel owner in London.

"I suppose you're right." Mr. Findley turned his attention to Frances. "What's your name, lad, and where are you headed?"

"Frances Had—" Frances coughed. She could use her Christian name—spelled with an *i* instead of an *e* it was a male name anyway—but perhaps she should be cautious about using her family name. "Francis Haddon. I'm on my way to London."

"London?" Mr. Findley's brows shot up and then down into a scowl. "How old are you? You haven't escaped from school, have you?"

"No, sir." She focused on cutting her meat so she wouldn't have to meet his eyes. "I'm, er, older than I look."

Mrs. Findley laughed. "What? Thirteen instead of twelve? Don't try to cozen us, young sir. We've raised three sons. Here it is the end of the day, and you don't have the faintest shadow of a beard."

This pretending to be a man was more complicated than she'd thought. Frances smiled and stuffed a large piece of mutton in her mouth.

"What can your mother be thinking to let you travel alone like this?" Mrs. Findley made a clucking sound with her tongue again.

Frances swallowed. "My mother died a number of years ago, madam. I live with my elderly aunt." Aunt Viola would not be happy with that description, but she *had* passed her sixtieth birthday.

"Well, I can't fathom even an aunt, elderly or not, letting a young'un such as yourself travel up to Town alone." There was more than a hint of suspicion in Mr. Findley's voice.

"My aunt wasn't happy about it, sir,"—Viola had been shouting so loudly it was surprising they hadn't heard her at the Crowing Cock—"but I was desperate to go." She wasn't about to spend one more second under the same roof as that treacherous woman. "I'm to visit my brother. I would have got to London hours ago if the roads hadn't been so bad." She'd meant to stay the night with Frederick, see their man of business in the morning, and then go back to Landsford and wave the bank draft for the amount of her dowry in Viola's face before taking it, packing up, and moving out.

She frowned at her plate. She hadn't yet figured out where she'd go, but she bloody well wasn't going to stay one more night at Landsford. To think Viola had planned to drug her with laudanum, let Littleton into her bedroom, and then raise an alarm so he'd be discovered there by the gossiping servants.

She stabbed a bit of potato so hard, her fork screeched across the plate.

Mrs. Findley wagged her finger at her husband. "Don't glower at the boy, Archie. You're frightening him." Then she turned to wag it at Frances. "And a boy your age should not be traveling by himself. There are bad men—and women—at every turn, eager to take terrible advantage of a young cub like yourself, still wet behind the ears. I'll wager your brother hasn't the least idea how to take charge of you. How old is he?"

Frances blinked. She would like to see Frederick try to take charge of her. If there was any taking charge to be done, she'd be the one doing it. "Twenty-four." They were twins, but she was the elder by ten minutes.

"I don't know, Madge." Mr. Findley was still frowning. "It seems a bit fishy to me. I—"

"Mr. Findley," the barmaid said from the door, "there's a fight starting."

"Damnation." He glanced at his watch. "Right on time, the drunken louts." He looked at his wife as he got to his feet. "I suppose you're right, Madge. None of the Valentines will be needing the room, and I can see you don't want the lad sleeping with the men out there."

They heard a shout and what sounded like a table tipping over followed by glass shattering.

Mr. Findley sighed. "Get the boy settled while I go knock some heads together." He picked up a wooden cudgel leaning against the wall and left to do battle with the drunks.

"Are you ready to go, Francis?"

"Yes, madam." She didn't want to give the innkeeper's wife an opportunity to change her mind. She swallowed her last bite and stood. "Thank you."

"I still don't see how your aunt could have let you travel alone, especially after that dreadful blizzard. The roads were barely passable—well, not passable at all once it clouded up and everything refroze." Mrs. Findley led her out of the room and up the stairs. She looked back, frowning. "You didn't sneak away while she was busy elsewhere, did you?"

"Oh no, madam. My aunt saw me off." With a string of curses.

She looked down so Mrs. Findley wouldn't see the fury in her eyes. Thank God she'd overheard that louse Felix Littleton this morning. If she hadn't stopped in Mr. Turner's store to read Mr. Puddington's letter—if she hadn't dropped the damn man of business's note and had to crawl behind a case of candles to retrieve it—she'd never have learned how Viola had been colluding with the bloody little worm.

Mrs. Findley turned left at the top of the stairs, and Frances followed her down the corridor.

Littleton—she'd recognized his whiny little voice—and his friend, a Mr. Pettigrew, whom she hadn't been able to see but had heard all too clearly, had been laughing about the plot. Littleton had been home these last few weeks, apparently fleeing his creditors, and had been paying her court. He and Pettigrew had sniggered at how easy it was to get silly, old, *desperate* spinsters to lose their hearts.

She felt a hot flush climb from her breast to her cheeks. Mr. Lousy Littleton was flattering himself if he thought she'd fallen in love with him. *Love.* Ha! She was not susceptible to that malady. Yes, she might have begun to fancy herself attracted to the snake—he was very handsome and had been extremely attentive—but her heart had been quite safe.

But why Viola, who'd always told her that men were not to be trusted—and certainly the behavior of her absent brother and father supported that theory—would consent to help Littleton was beyond her. Frankly, she couldn't believe it at first, but when she'd come home and confronted her aunt, Viola's guilt had been written all over her face.

"Here you are, then." Mrs. Findley stopped at the last room and opened the door. "It's—"

They both jumped at the sound of another crash from downstairs.

"Oh dear, I'd better go help Archie. The men can get so obstreperous when they're in their cups, but they'll quiet down in just a bit." She smiled and patted Frances on the arm. "Do sleep well." She almost ran back down the passageway.

Frances stepped into the room, and her feet sank into

thick carpet. Oh! She couldn't track mud and slush in here. She put her hat and candle on a nearby table, closed the door, and leaned against it to tug off Frederick's boots.

Ah. She wiggled her toes in the deep pile and looked around. Red-and-tan wallpaper covered the walls, heavy red curtains hung on the windows to keep out light and drafts, and a red upholstered chair sat by the fire. But the best thing of all was the big mahogany four-poster bed.

Which had likely been used by Lord Jack to entertain countless women. She wrinkled her nose as she jerked off her overcoat and hung it on a hook. As distasteful as the notion was, she was so tired, she couldn't muster much moral outrage. Perhaps in the morning she'd be suitably incensed, but now she just wanted to lie down.

She slipped out of her coat and started unbuttoning her waistcoat . . .

No, better leave that on, as well as her shirt and breeches and socks—all Frederick's castoffs. It seemed unlikely another traveler would arrive so late, but she couldn't take any chances.

She pulled back the coverlet and climbed onto the bed, stretching her aching body over the soft, yielding, wonderful feather mattress.

She was asleep even before her head hit the pillow.

Lord Jack Valentine, third and youngest son of the Duke and Duchess of Greycliffe, jumped behind a pillar in Greycliffe Castle, his ancestral home. It was the last day of his mother's annual matchmaking house party, and Miss Isabelle Wharton, spinster, was scanning the ballroom for prey.

Why did Mama have to be the *ton*'s premier matchmaker and subject them to this annual torture? Everyone called her the Duchess of Love. She even wrote a regular scandal sheet with marital advice—*Venus's Love Notes*—that the *ton*'s females gobbled up like bonbons. It was a wonder he and his brothers hadn't expired from mortification long ago.

"Hiding?" Ash asked from his right.

Damn it, did his brother *want* the woman to find him? He grabbed Ash's arm and pulled him out of sight, too. "Of course I'm hiding. Now that Ned is taken, Miss Wharton is after me."

Ash chuckled. "I noticed."

Ash could laugh—he was safe. Bigamy was illegal. Even though Ash and his wife had been estranged for years, they were still married, much as the matchmaking mothers might wish otherwise.

"It's not funny, Ash. My freedom is at stake here."

His brother frowned. "Jack, no one can force you to marry Miss Wharton."

"I know that." He peered around the pillar. Miss Wharton's mass of blond ringlets bounced with determination as she scoured the room for him. She was charming in a puppyish sort of way—when she wasn't pursuing him like a coursing foxhound. He wouldn't put it past her to try to slip into his bed while he was sleeping tonight.

Gad. He felt a drop of sweat roll down his back. He couldn't take that chance. "Go dance with her, will you? I've got to leave."

"The ballroom?"

"The castle. I'm going to London. Now."

Ash's brows flew up. "Are you mad?"

Miss Wharton was coming closer. "No, I'm not mad, I'm desperate. And London's only an hour or two away."

"Not on a night like this. It's cold and dark, and the roads are likely as slippery as the skating pond."

Ash was probably right, but he'd rather risk travel than

Miss Wharton. "If the roads are too slick, I'll only go as far as the Crowing Cock. Findley always saves that room for us."

One good thing about Ash—he didn't argue with a fellow. He just raised a skeptical eyebrow and asked, "Are you going to tell Mama?"

"Ah." That did not sound like a good idea. "Perhaps you could tell her? Just don't mention Miss Wharton."

"So what am I to say? That you suddenly—in the middle of a frigid night when only the desperate or insane would go out—decided to hare off to London?"

"Just say I had urgent business in Town."

"Mama's not going to believe that."

"I know." Though it was true. There were always women and children in need of his help, but the situation was worse now. A madman the newspapers were calling the Silent Slasher was cutting women's throats, mostly those of Covent Garden prostitutes. Panic was as thick a stench in London's narrow, dark alleys as rotting offal. "But then you can shrug and say nothing. She won't press you." Mama had never tried to get them to peach on each other.

Ash looked at him a moment more and then shrugged. "Very well."

"Lord Jack, there you are!" Miss Wharton's hideous ringlets bounced into view.

Damn. "Ah, Miss Wharton, there *you* are. Were your ears burning? Ash here was just telling me how much he wished to beg a dance from you."

"He was?" Miss Wharton's mouth fell open.

"I was?" Ash raised both eyebrows.

Ash was only engaging in a bit of good-natured brotherly teasing, but Jack surreptitiously administered a well-placed elbow nevertheless.

"Oh yes," Ash said, "so I was. Miss Wharton, will you join me in the next set?"

Ash managed to capture the woman's hand, place it on his arm, and lead her away before she quite knew what was happening. She craned her neck to look back at Jack, but then she was gone. Ash, the splendid fellow, had chosen a set on the far side of the ballroom.

There was no time to waste. Jack slipped out, careful to avoid Mama's or Father's gaze, and ran up to his room. He threw a few things into his valise, grabbed his purse and greatcoat, and ducked down the servants' stairs.

He stepped outside. The cold took his breath away for a moment. A thick blanket of snow muffled the lawns and gardens, while thousands of stars glittered in the cold, clear sky.

He belonged in London, but he loved the country. London was a constant din of coach wheels and horse hooves on cobblestones, drunken bucks singing and shouting. It was dirty and crowded, but the country . . .

The country's quiet peace would be shattered by his curses if Miss Wharton caught him.

He strode toward the stables.

About forty minutes later, he was indeed cursing, but it had nothing to do with Miss Wharton. He'd almost slid off the road for the sixth time.

He should have stayed home and taken his chances, barricading the door to his room or even spending the night on Ash's floor. The fellow snored loud enough to wake the dead, but that would have been better than breaking his—or his horses'—necks on this damn road. There was no chance in hell he'd make it to London tonight.

When he finally pulled into the Crowing Cock, he'd never been so glad to reach an innyard in his life.

Watkins, the ostler, came out to see who was arriving so late. "Lord Jack!" He ducked his head, but not before Jack saw his eyes widen. "I didn't think to see ye tonight."

Of course he hadn't. Everyone for miles around knew tonight was the Valentine birthday ball, the culmination of the Duchess of Love's yearly matchmaking house party. "I've urgent business in London, Watkins, and thought I'd get a start on my journey."

Watkins blinked but didn't point out the obvious: he was only a little closer to Town than he'd be if he'd stayed in the warmth and comfort of the castle.

"The place's right full, milord. Lots o' folks stopped when the chill came on."

"I see that." Even in the cold, the windows were wide open. Light and noise spilled out—the rumble of voices, the clink of mugs. There was little chance he could slip in unnoticed, but perhaps he'd be lucky. All he wanted was to find Findley and go to bed. Dodging Miss Wharton and struggling to keep his horses on the road had worn him out.

He left his cattle in Watkins's capable hands and crossed the yard, pushing open the door—

"Look who's here! Come join me, Jack." Damn, that was Ollie Pettigrew's booming voice. "Dantley's gone off to the privy, and I might never see him again."

Silence descended like a dropped window sash, and the eyes of every man in the room turned to regard Jack.

Bloody hell. So much for avoiding attention.

He strolled over to join Pettigrew, who bore a remarkable resemblance to a large bear, and the hum of conversation resumed. He'd have a quick drink, and *then* he'd find Findley. "What's the matter with Dantley?"

"Ate something that didn't agree with him." Pettigrew pulled out his pocket watch and made a show of consulting it. "Is the ball over already?"

"I left a little early."

"Oh ho! So did you survive another year with your bachelorhood intact?"

Did the man have to be so loud? His damn voice carried to every corner of the room. "I did." Jack smiled at Bess, the barmaid, as she handed him a mug of ale. "Why aren't you there?"

Pettigrew threw up his hands as if to ward him off. "I don't care to risk my freedom at the Duchess of Love's Valentine ball."

Jack could sympathize with that sentiment. "So why are you in the area? I thought you hated the country."

"Oh, I do. I definitely do. Was just down for the day, visiting a friend who fled London when the damn duns started camping on his doorstep." Pettigrew snorted. "Idiot thought he'd marry to keep the dibs in tune rather than hang on his father's sleeve, only the girl got wind of his plans and bolted." He took a swallow of ale. "Just as well. Never met her, but her brother says she's a regular shrew."

Damn, callous blackguard. Anger churned in Jack's gut and his fist itched to plant itself in Pettigrew's face, but he forced himself to laugh. He had to maintain his reputation as a careless rake. It kept society from nosing out his real activities. "He was going to take on a leg shackle? Seems like a permanent solution to a temporary problem."

"Not what I would do, of course, but Littleton was feeling desperate, and the aunt just about dropped the girl into his lap. And really, one female's much like another with the candles snuffed, as you well know."

"Yes." He would *so* enjoy drawing Pettigrew's claret, but he'd have to deny himself that pleasure. Besides it being out of his carefully crafted character, he was far too tired to do a fight justice, not to mention the fact that Findley wouldn't be happy with the resulting mess.

"Littleton had hoped the girl's maternal connections would be a source of continuing funds, but I told him he'd catch cold there. They've never recognized her." Pettigrew grinned. "But don't worry, Felix will land on his feet. His father's sure to cough up more of the ready to tide him over to his next allowance, especially after all the uproar caused by the girl bolting."

As if he cared what happened to the worthless sprig of the nobility. The girl, however . . .

"Where did the girl bolt to?" Surely if she was gently bred she had some relatives to help her.

Pettigrew shrugged. "I have no idea."

"Would she go to her brother?"

"God, no! He just got married. Wouldn't want a shrew in the house with a new wife."

Bloody hell. "Then what of her parents?"

"Mother's dead, father's in foreign lands more often than not. *He* wouldn't care if Littleton married her." Pettigrew leered. "Has only one use for women, don't you know."

Jack gripped his mug tighter and forced himself to leer back. The girl might already be raped or sold to a brothel. "When did this happen?" Perhaps there was still time to save her. "What's the girl's name?"

Damn. Pettigrew's eyes had widened in surprise at his obvious interest. "Might want to have a go at her myself," Jack said quickly, in a practiced, lascivious tone, "especially if she's a virgin."

"Got a touch of the pox, do you?"

He forced himself to smile and let Pettigrew think what he would. Damn, he hated having to masquerade as a heartless rake, but the subterfuge allowed him to move through the worst areas of London without the *ton* constantly speculating about his real interests.

Pettigrew was shaking his head. "Sorry, but really must keep my tongue between my teeth. Littleton wouldn't want it bruited about that he'd caused a spinster to turn tail and run. Doesn't say much about his amatory skills, does it? And

I'm quite sure the girl's not up to your exacting standards. Littleton said she was too tall and far too skinny. Best let her go."

Unfortunately, it seemed he would have to, with no concrete information to go on. He felt a twinge of regret, but he'd long ago come to terms with the fact that he couldn't save every poor girl in trouble.

"Ah, here comes Dantley," Pettigrew said. "Did you fall in, man?"

Ralph Dantley, thin and storklike, burped. "I've got a mind to complain to Findley about his damn dinner." Dantley nodded at Jack. "Hallo, what are you doing here? Shouldn't you be at the duchess's ball?"

Jack did not wish to get into that subject again. He threw back the last of his ale and stood. "I left early. If you'll excuse me, I need to see Findley about a room."

"No rooms to be had, unless a duke's son can make one magically appear." Pettigrew's voice had acquired a sharp edge. "We'll save you a chair in case your exalted position doesn't produce a miracle."

"Splendid." He'd rather sleep in the stables; the animals there would be far more congenial than Pettigrew.

Jack found the innkeeper in the taproom, feverishly filling mugs.

"Good evening, Findley."

"Eh, I'll be with you in just a min—" Findley turned. "Milord!" He grinned—and then his face fell. "Er, we didn't expect you tonight."

"Who is it, Archie?" Mrs. Findley came out of the kitchen. "Oh, Lord Jack!" Her face also lit up and then collapsed. She bit her lip. "Isn't tonight the duchess's and your birthday ball? It's not over already, is it?"

"No, but I need to get back to London." Damn. Perhaps

he *would* be making his bed in the straw. Well, he'd slept in worse places.

Findley snorted. "You won't be going any farther tonight. The roads are awful. But I suppose you know that."

"I do." His arms and shoulders ached with that knowledge. It had been the very devil keeping his horses on the road.

"And you must have missed your supper." Mrs. Findley shook her head. "I'll get you something to eat."

Food had always been Mrs. Findley's solution to any problem, which is why he and his brothers had liked stopping by the Crowing Cock so much when they were young. "I *am* a bit sharp-set."

"Of course you are. Now sit down, and I'll be back in a trice with some mutton and potatoes"—Mrs. Findley's eyes twinkled—"and some apple pie, too." She knew how much he liked her apple pie. She disappeared into the kitchen.

"I'm sorry to come so late and unannounced," Jack said as he sat at the table. "And when you're so busy as well."

"Think nothing of it, milord. We are delighted to see you." The worried look settled back over Findley's face. "It's just that—"

"You've put someone in the room you save for us. I quite understand. With this crowd, it would be foolish if you hadn't." Jack smiled as Mrs. Findley returned with a food-laden tray. "I'll just sleep down here with the others or out in the stables."

"You will not!" Findley was almost sputtering. "The lad will sleep with the hoi polloi. I'll get him up straightaway."

"No, don't evict him on my account." Jack cut into his mutton. Mrs. Findley was an excellent cook. "I don't need a soft bed. I'm not made of spun sugar, you know."

"Oh, milord, it's all my fault Archie let the boy have the room," Mrs. Findley rushed to say, "but the poor thing looked so tired." The woman hesitated, and then forged on, wringing her hands. "I'm sure it is not *at all* what you are used to, but . . . but would you mind sharing? The—"

"Madge! Of course Lord Jack won't share a bed."

It wasn't his preferred arrangement, true, but he'd done it countless times in his travels, and it looked as though that was the only way to save the poor lad from being rudely woken and tossed downstairs. "An excellent plan! That will suit admirably."

Mrs. Findley almost sagged with relief. "Well, he's thin as a whisper, milord. I can't imagine he'd take up much room."

In truth, size didn't matter as much as sleeping habits. Some of the skinniest men made the worst bed partners, whirling like dervishes or snoring so loud they shook the rafters. He'd once ended up with a black eye after sharing a bed with a wizened little preacher.

Oh damn. Mrs. Findley was looking at him hopefully again. What else was coming?

"The boy seems far too young to be traveling by himself, milord. If you're off to London anyway, perhaps you could watch out for him until he reaches his brother?"

Wonderful. Not only would he have a bedmate who likely grunted and squirmed and would poke him all night in the back with sharp elbows and knees, but now he was to bear-lead the lad as well.

"I'd be happy to do so, madam." And he would, once he wasn't so tired. He certainly didn't want another green lad from the country wandering around London alone. He'd much rather take charge of him now than try to rescue him later. He scraped his fork over his plate to get the last bit of pie, wiped his mouth with his napkin, and stood. "Shall I go up now?"

"I need more ale, Mr. Findley," Bess said from the doorway.

"I have a fresh tray for you, Bess. Madge, go ahead and take Lord Jack upstairs."

"No need." Jack said. "I know my way."

"But milord—"

"No, Mrs. Findley, I insist. You're needed here." Jack left before the woman could argue further.

When he reached the room, he opened the door quietly and shielded his candle so he didn't wake the boy. The lad was sleeping on his side, and the covers had slipped down to his waist. Good Lord, he was still wearing all his clothes. Well, not his coat, but his shirt and vest and breeches. Hopefully not his boots . . . ah no, there they were at the foot of the bed.

Red hair curled around the boy's face, and a sprinkling of freckles dusted his nose. He *did* look very young. The light was too weak to see for sure, but Jack would swear the boy's cheeks were free of even peach fuzz.

Frankly, he looked sadly effeminate. He hoped the lad was a good fighter, because pretty boys like him generally got beat up at school. Jack frowned. Or worse.

He put his candle down and stripped off his cravat, shirt, shoes, and socks. *He* wasn't about to sleep in his clothes. He paused with his hands on his drawers and looked at the boy again. On second thought, he'd leave these on.

He sighed and blew out his candle. It looked like he definitely had a traveling companion. Unless the boy was much more imposing awake—which from what the Findleys had said seemed unlikely—he wouldn't last five minutes in Town on his own.

Chapter 2

Sometimes your body speaks a language you don't yet understand.

—Venus's Love Notes

Frances was dreaming. She was lying in the soft grass, listening to a stream burble past. Well, it was really more a torrent than a burble and too loud for a dream. And then it stopped abruptly and the ground shifted . . .

No, it was the *mattress* that shifted. Oh God, now she remembered. She was at the Crowing Cock. The Findleys must have taken pity on some late traveler and let him share her room. The sound could only be that of a man using a chamber pot.

She cracked open one eye. Sunlight leaked around the curtains. Good Lord, it was morning.

Her heart slammed against her rib cage. She'd been completely exhausted, but she'd never slept like one dead before. Had the man guessed she was female? And if he had . . .

Don't panic. She took a quick mental inventory. Her

clothes all seemed to be in their proper places; she didn't feel any different than when she'd got into bed last night. Surely she would if he'd . . . done something.

Men might be officious and overbearing and oafish, but most of them weren't dangerous. The Findleys wouldn't put a violent blackguard in their best bedchamber.

She opened her other eye and turned slightly so she could see her companion.

Zeus, he was naked!

She squeezed her eyes shut immediately, but that didn't help. The image of his tall, lean, powerfully built body with its broad back and wide shoulders was imprinted on her eyelids like a candle flame she'd stared at too long.

At least he wasn't *completely* naked. A pair of flannel drawers covered his narrow hips.

"Don't be afraid, lad. I won't hurt you."

The words were soft, the tone one might use with a skittish horse on the verge of bolting.

She'd like to bolt, but he was standing between her and the door. At least he had a pleasant, educated voice—and he hadn't yet discovered she was female.

He chuckled. "You're acting a bit like a turtle, don't you think? You may pull your head into your shell, but I can still see you."

He was right, of course. She forced her eyes open.

Mistake. He was still virtually naked, and now he was facing her. She'd never seen an almost naked man. Muscles shaped his arms; brown hair sprinkled over his chest, narrowing to a line down his flat stomach to—

She snapped her gaze up to his face. Oh God, if she'd thought Mr. Littleton handsome, she'd much mistaken the matter. Littleton had been merely pretty in a weak, overcosseted way, like a pampered housecat. *This* was a tiger.

Hazel eyes, fringed with ridiculously long lashes, studied her.

She dropped her gaze to the coverlet. His beautiful eyes were far too direct and uncomfortably probing. If she wasn't very, very careful, he'd discover her secret.

"I really won't hurt you."

Ha! That was likely what the tiger said to the . . . what did tigers eat?

Anything they wanted to.

Why the hell wouldn't he put on his clothing? Ah, *finally* he reached for his breeches.

If she tilted her head just slightly, she could watch his muscled legs slide into—

What was the matter with her? He was only a man, a breed she'd never been especially enamored of and now had vowed to avoid entirely.

An almost naked man . . .

That must be the problem. There must be some sort of animal magnetism at work. Perhaps that explained why so many supposedly intelligent women were willing to give their lives over into a man's keeping. With luck, he'd dress and leave quickly.

She pushed herself to sit, feeling slightly more in control in that position.

"The Findleys think you're too young to go up to London by yourself," he said.

"I'm not." Of course, she might not be going anywhere if Daisy was lame. This entire undertaking was one disaster after another.

He lifted a brow but didn't argue the point. "They want me to see that you get safely to your brother."

"What?!" Blast it, she'd squeaked like a girl.

He only smiled. "You *are* young, aren't you? What are you—thirteen? Twelve?"

She wasn't going to discuss that. "I can't travel with you, sir. I don't even know your name."

"Well, that's easily remedied." He stepped closer. His chest was just inches from her now. Was the hair on it soft or wiry? It looked soft—

Damn it, where was his shirt?

"I'm Jack Valentine," he said, and extended his hand.

Oh God, the rake!

She shouldn't be surprised. The man exuded seduction the way most men sweat. He could probably scratch his arse and women would swoon.

He did have a very nice arse . . .

She should *not* be thinking about the villain's bottom.

"It's a hand, boy," he said, speaking in that soft, almost gentle tone again, a tone that made her insides melt. "Take it. I won't hurt you. I promise."

She could well believe whatever seduction he promised wouldn't hurt. He could probably make even the Almack's patronesses do whatever he wanted.

"Frances Haddon," she said, finally laying her hand in his.

He shook it firmly, his grip warm, dry, and strong, and then released her. Her palm tingled. She'd never touched a man's ungloved hand before.

"How did you get to the Crowing Cock, Master Haddon?"

Why wouldn't he put on his shirt? "I rode, sir."

"A long way?"

"Y-yes." She wasn't about to tell him where she'd come from. She did read the gossip columns occasionally, and if she remembered correctly, he knew her cousin. Not that Lord Trent would have mentioned her; he likely didn't know she existed. His grandparents had cut all ties with her mother when she ran away with Benedict Hadley.

He finally moved away to put on his shirt. Thank *God*. She let out a long breath.

Zeus, had he heard her?

He didn't give any indication that he had, but his face was covered at the moment.

Even his stomach was chiseled perfection.

"I came in my curricle"—his head popped out of his shirt—"but we can tie your horse behind and still easily make it to London today. As you can see"—he nodded toward the window—"the sun is out. The roads ought to be good." He wrapped his cravat around his neck and lifted an eyebrow. "Of course, that all assumes you get out of bed sometime."

"I only need to splash some water on my face." She'd like a nice, long soak. Every muscle ached from her awful ride yesterday, even muscles she didn't know she had—she flushed—especially in the area between her legs. But obviously that wasn't possible. She climbed out of bed very gingerly.

He was looking at her as he tied his cravat. Please, God, let her disguise hold. Her thin, unremarkable figure must be good for something.

"You don't want to change?"

Of course she did, but there was no way she could do so with him in the room, even if she had something to change into, which she didn't. "I didn't bring other clothes." She'd been far too angry to think about packing when she'd left Landsford.

She was always cool, calm, and rational. She never lost her temper the way she had yesterday—and she never would again. See where it had got her? In a bedroom—in a bed!—with London's premier rake. Her stomach churned with self-disgust.

And then Lord Jack laughed. Oh! Her stomach suddenly shivered instead. His laugh was so warm and seductive.

Seductive! Exactly.

"As I remember," the dastardly rake said, "young boys aren't terribly concerned about their appearance—another sign that you aren't very old, my grubby young friend. Older youths are generally more interested in soap and water. However, I'm afraid I can't be seen downstairs with such a disreputable-looking whelp."

He came toward her, and she reacted instinctively, jumping back. Unfortunately, she'd forgotten about the boots she'd left at the foot of the bed last night; she stumbled over them and went crashing to the floor onto her already sore behind.

And then to make the situation a complete disaster, she burst into tears.

She slapped her hands over her face and struggled to regain control, but the damage was done. He *must* know she was a female now. And she'd spent the night alone with him in a bed . . . and they were still alone . . . and he was the king of all rakes . . .

She needed to pull herself together immediately and—

She felt a gentle touch on her shoulder.

"Don't cry, lad."

"I'm not crying," she muttered between her fingers. And now he knew she was a complete imbecile as well. Of course she was crying. But she was going to stop. She *was* stopping.

"I know you aren't crying," he said in a strangely bracing sort of way. He'd hunkered down in front of her. "You've no need to cry. You're safe with me."

Ha. She was ruined. It was a very good thing she'd never had any serious intention of getting married. Littleton had just been a momentary aberration. Now if only she could get out of this room in one piece . . .

Lord Jack was rubbing her shoulder. She tried to wiggle free, but then he caught her other shoulder, too, and shook her just a little.

"Francis," he said, "I swear on my honor you're safe." He paused, and then said even more gently, "Did one of the older schoolboys or one of the schoolmasters hurt you? Is that why you're running away?" His hazel eyes were warm with understanding and compassion as he handed her his handkerchief. "You don't need to be ashamed or frightened that I'll do the same thing to you."

What was he talking about? She blew her nose. Whatever it was, he clearly still thought she was a boy, and that was all she cared about. Well, except she didn't want to accept compassion when none was called for. "I'm all right." She flushed. "I just fell on my sore bottom."

His eyes widened, and then he laughed again.

Damn it, that sound did the most ridiculous things to her insides. It was no wonder that he was such a successful rake. His laugh must have women falling at his feet.

Except her, of course. She was made of sterner stuff.

Well, she'd already fallen, but that had been the boots' doing.

"It's very sore from riding yesterday." She didn't want him thinking she was a mewling milksop. She blew her nose again and sniffed. "I don't usually cry."

"Of course you don't," he said, standing and offering her his hand. "Not used to a long day riding, then?"

She nodded. She made a brief attempt to get up on her own, but she was too sore to manage it. So she had to take the hand he was still patiently extending and let him haul her to her feet. He pulled her up as if she weighed nothing.

He was at least six inches taller than she. It made her feel odd—weak and feminine and dependent.

She was not dependent on anyone, certainly not this man.

Except she likely was. If Daisy was lame, she'd need a ride to London. Damnation.

"I can't imagine how you could stand to sleep in your clothes," he was saying, "but at least fix your bedraggled cravat."

She'd been hard-pressed to tie a credible knot the first time; how likely was it she'd manage the feat with Lord Jack watching? Not very, but she went over to the mirror and tried anyway. The result was a lumpy mess.

Lord Jack's expression rapidly moved from surprise to dismay to amusement, ending in a carefully neutral look. He didn't say a word, but Frances felt the need to defend herself.

"You make me nervous."

"Very nervous, apparently." The blasted man was obviously biting back a laugh. "My apologies."

"And the cloth is very limp."

"Indeed it is. Limp cloth makes cravat tying the very devil. I'd lend you one of mine, but unfortunately I don't have an extra. I'm traveling light."

Why was he traveling at all? He must have left in the middle of the birthday ball. Likely there was some scandal involved.

Better not ask. She definitely didn't want him asking questions about *her* reasons for being on the road.

"Let me give it a try"—he smiled at her in an oddly conspiratorial way—"if you don't mind the help, that is."

"Very well." She was never going to be able to tie the cravat successfully herself.

Lord Jack smiled again, as if he knew just how grudgingly she accepted his aid, and stepped behind her. His long, capable fingers made short work of dismantling the linen disaster and retying it into something approaching respectability.

She stood still and stiff. Her heart had started to pound, and she felt slightly breathless, trapped by his body and his arms, surrounded by his heat and scent, as his hands brushed close to her breasts. She should be impatient and annoyed, but this felt more like excitement.

She glared at herself. *Stupid!* She wanted nothing to do with men. She was going to ignore them all once she got Puddington to give her her money.

And in any event, this storm of feeling was all one-sided. Lord Jack thought she was a boy.

"You don't like my efforts, Master Haddon?"

"What?" Her eyes flew up to meet his in the mirror. One of his eyebrows was cocked; he looked both amused and puzzled. She dropped her gaze back to the cravat. "Oh no, it's fine." He'd really worked a miracle with the poor, limp linen.

He gave a theatrical sigh and stepped back. "That's a relief. From the way you were scowling, I was certain you were going to ring a peal over me. Now get your boots on, and we'll go down to see what we can find for breakfast." He grinned at her. "You must be famished, and I'll admit to being rather hungry myself."

"Y-yes." Frances ducked her head and reached for her brother's cast-off boots. She felt a little chilled now that Lord Jack wasn't standing so close. The sooner she got away from the man, the better.

She slipped the boots on and grimaced.

"What is it?"

Damn, he had sharp eyes. Thank heavens she'd be parting company with him in a few hours, sooner if Daisy was healthy. "I seem to have a blister from yesterday. I had to walk my horse for a mile or more." She stood up and winced again.

"Do you want me to look at it?"

"No!" The thought of Lord Jack touching her feet was horrifying; at least she thought it was horror that crawled up her spine. "I'll be fine."

He frowned at her. "Blisters are nothing to ignore. At least you'll be off your feet most of today, but promise me you'll have your brother have a look when you get to London, if you aren't better."

"All right." She had no intention of showing Frederick her feet. There was no point. Even if they were bloody stumps, her brother would expect her to go fetch the surgeon herself. "Did you say something about breakfast?"

Master Haddon is definitely hiding something.

Jack studied the tall, thin figure as he followed him down the stairs. His clothes were of good quality but old, and his boots obviously didn't fit properly. Either his feet had grown and no one had thought to take him to have new boots made, or the boots belonged to someone else. And, frankly, it looked as if the lad had cut his hair himself and in a hurry. It was a good thing it was so curly.

What was the boy's secret? At first he'd been sure the lad had been sodomized—that happened far too often when boys, especially boys that looked like Francis, went away to school. But when he'd hinted at it, as he'd done many times with the boys he'd dealt with in London, Francis had clearly had no notion what he meant.

Perhaps it was just that Francis was afraid of him, which wasn't at all surprising. After all, he'd woken from a deep sleep to find a stranger, a man much larger and stronger than he, in his bed.

Yet that didn't quite ring true, either. Oh yes, Francis was afraid, but he'd wager the boy was less afraid of him than of what he might discover. Which brought him back to the original question: What was the boy hiding?

Well, he'd learn the secret eventually. He'd spent years perfecting his ability to extract the truth from reluctant youngsters; poor Francis was no match for him. And then he'd see him handed over to his brother or he'd return him to his family.

Francis waited for him at the bottom of the stairs. "I'm not hungry, sir. I believe I'll go see how my horse is."

"Nonsense, young boys are always hungry." What was amiss now? Francis looked even paler than he had upstairs.

"Well, I'm not." The boy darted another look into the common room.

It was very, very crowded and very, very noisy. Jack scanned the room, hoping to find a quiet—

"Jack!" Damn, that was Pettigrew, waving from the table he'd been sitting at last night. Conversation paused while everyone turned to observe Jack and Francis. Why the hell did Pettigrew have to be so infernally loud? "We've got two free chairs."

The only two free, it would appear. Jack repressed a sigh. "Come along, Master Haddon."

"No, really, sir. I—"

He grasped the boy's arm. "It's still over an hour's ride to London, and hungry boys, in my experience, are the very devil to travel with. They whine and complain until you want to stuff their cravat down their throat."

Normally Jack wouldn't force the boy, but he knew Francis hadn't eaten since last night, and he was hungry himself. He wanted his breakfast, and he didn't trust the lad not to sneak off while he was having it.

Fortuitously, Mrs. Findley came out of the kitchen just then. "Good morning, milord. I hope you slept well."

"I did indeed, and as you can see, young Master Haddon did not murder me in my bed nor steal my purse."

Young Master Haddon glared at him.

A slight frown appeared between Mrs. Findley's brows. "I hope he didn't disturb your sleep?"

"Oh no. He only snores a little."

Francis tried to jerk his arm free. "I don't snore."

"How would you know? It's *my* ears that were being assaulted."

He could see the boy wanted to argue, but he kept his tongue between his teeth—though only just.

"Now you behave for Lord Jack, Master Haddon," Mrs. Findley said. "He's very kind to take you with him to London."

The boy's jaw hardened even more, but he managed a polite, if stiff, "Yes, madam."

Mrs. Findley nodded and looked back at Jack. "But why are you standing here, milord? Can't you find a seat?" She looked into the common room. "Oh dear. It *is* a bit full, isn't it?"

"Don't worry," Jack said. "Pettigrew has two seats at his table; I'm just having a bit of a time persuading Master Haddon to take one of them."

"I'm not hungry," Francis said, "and I need to check on my horse."

"Nonsense," Mrs. Findley said in a stern voice she'd obviously perfected over the years of raising her sons. "If you aren't hungry now, you will be soon, young man. Go in and sit down. Your horse isn't going anywhere without you."

"But—"

"Go on." Mrs. Findley looked as if she might grab the

boy by his ear. "I'll bring you a nice bowl of porridge and some ham and eggs and toast."

The lad clearly wanted to argue further, but realized the effort would be futile. Mrs. Findley was not going to let him leave without his breakfast.

"All right," he said, sounding more than a little surly, "but I'm not hungry."

"However, I am," Jack said. He smiled at Mrs. Findley. "Thank you for saving me from starvation, madam. Come along, Francis."

Francis grudgingly came along.

"We wondered what the hell had happened to you," Pettigrew said when Jack finally reached the table. "Guess being a duke's son paid off again." He looked at the boy and frowned. "Who's the whelp?"

"May I introduce Master Francis Haddon? Master Haddon, this is Mr. Oliver Pettigrew and Mr. Ralph Dantley."

Odd. Pettigrew's eyes widened slightly and then narrowed.

"Pleased to meet you," Francis mumbled and executed a jerky half bow before dropping rather gracelessly into his seat.

Pettigrew was definitely staring at Francis—and Francis was staring down at the table. "Do you two know each other?"

Francis and Pettigrew spoke at the same time.

"No."

"Never met the . . . lad."

Now why the hell had Pettigrew paused that way? It was almost imperceptible, but from the worried look Francis shot Pettigrew, the boy had noticed, too.

"Where'd you find him?" Dantley asked.

"He was already in the room Mrs. Findley gave me last night."

"Ah, so you two shared a bed." Now Pettigrew's smile was almost a leer.

Bloody hell. Surely Pettigrew didn't think he'd taken any liberties with the boy? Well, he'd plenty of practice dealing with men who were far more offensive than Ollie Pettigrew. He let a threatening note creep into his voice. "Yes. Do you have some objection to that?"

The man paled slightly, and his eyes slid away to study his hands. "No, of course not."

"How did you rate a soft feather mattress while Pettigrew and I had to suffer the bloody night in these damned hard chairs, bantling?" Dantley asked. "Are you a duke's son, too?"

"No." The boy flushed. "I think Mrs. Findley felt sorry for me."

"Well, I bloody well wish she'd felt sorry for me." Dantley shifted in his seat. "I swear I'll never get feeling back in my arse."

Pettigrew snickered, regaining his swagger. "That's because you're such a damned spindle shanks."

"Well, your arse is bigger than most beds, Ollie."

"You mind your manners, Ralph Dantley," Mrs. Findley said, coming up with food and coffee for Francis and Jack. "Don't be giving Master Haddon a bad example. If you'll remember, I know your mother."

Dantley flushed. "Yes, Mrs. Findley."

He turned to Francis once Mrs. Findley left. "I swear you look familiar, Master . . . Haddon did you say your name was?"

Francis blanched and nodded. What the hell was the matter now?

"Don't you think he looks familiar, Ollie? I'd swear we'd met him someplace."

"Where would we have met him, Ralph?" Pettigrew asked, though the oddly cunning expression was back in his eyes. The man was definitely hiding something. "Never say you've taken to spending time with"—he paused significantly—"schoolboys. How old are you, whelp?"

Francis stared at his plate. "N-not quite sixteen."

Pettigrew sneered. "Now there's a whisker if ever I heard one."

Dantley held up his quizzing glass to examine Francis's cheeks. "No, no whiskers, Ollie."

The boy's ears grew red; he looked an uncomfortable mixture of angry, embarrassed, and nervous. And he'd hardly touched his food.

"Finish your breakfast, Francis," Jack said quietly, "and then we'll be on our way."

Francis picked up a slice of toast and nibbled on it.

"So you're taking him with you?"

Damn it, Pettigrew was still hinting at something. Jack would like to call the fat toad on it, but Francis was almost vibrating with tension. "Yes. Mrs. Findley asked me to see that he reaches his brother safely in London."

Dantley snapped his fingers. "That's it! I must know the brother. What's his name?"

A bit of toast must have gone down the wrong way—Francis started coughing rather violently. Jack slapped him on the back and earned a glare for his efforts.

The lad took a sip of coffee and cleared his throat. "F-Frederick."

"Frederick," Dantley said. "Frederick Haddon . . ." He shook his head. "No, I don't know any Frederick Haddons, but I do know a Frederick Had*ley*."

Francis grew even whiter. Jack put a steadying hand on his elbow; it was a measure of how upset the boy was that he didn't try to shake him off.

"Right," Pettigrew said, grinning slyly. "I know the fellow, too. Now that you mention it, there *is* a resemblance. The boy's got the same ginger hair."

"Lots of men have red hair," Jack said. Damn, Francis was almost green now. Was he going to lose what little breakfast he'd ingested?

"Yes, you're right. It must just be a coincidence." Pettigrew smiled as he looked at Francis. "I'm sure Frederick Had*ley* had only a sister—a twin, if I recall correctly."

Chapter 3

Surprises lurk around every corner.
—Venus's Love Notes

Pettigrew knows.

Frances sat in Lord Jack's curricle as it bowled along the road to London. The sun was out, the ice had melted, and she was warm under a heavy carriage fur.

Except for the chill gripping her heart.

She fisted her hands. So Pettigrew knew—or rather, he suspected. He could not be certain. Who would think Miss Frances Hadley of Landsford would dress as a man?

Everyone.

Blast it, she'd heard the damn whispers. She wasn't deaf, though many people seemed to think she was. People had said for years she was mannish, that breeches would fit her better than skirts. But it was all jealousy. She was just smarter and more capable than the local men, and the fact that she didn't bother to hide it put their noses out of joint.

And of course Aunt Viola had seen her set off in Frederick's castoffs. Not that Viola would ever gossip with the villagers, but she'd been screaming so loudly, she'd caused Jeremy, their manservant, and Anna, their maid of all work, to come running, so they'd witnessed her departure as well.

Those two were very fond of gossip.

"Are you certain you've never met Mr. Pettigrew before, Francis?"

She jumped.

Zeus, had Lord Jack noticed? He had bloody sharp eyes.

She looked over at him. Of course he'd noticed. He was studying her as if she was a puzzle he was determined to solve. "You should keep your attention on the road, my lord."

His eyes narrowed, and then he grinned. "Thank you for the driving advice, Master Haddon."

Damn it, her stomach did an odd little flip. He had a dimple, for God's sake.

"I just don't want to end up in a ditch." Not that there looked to be any great danger of that at the moment, but she'd heard Lord Jack had crashed his curricle while racing on ice just a month or two ago. The last thing she needed was to be in an accident. A doctor would immediately discover her bound breasts.

"I shall do my best to keep us on the road."

"Thank you." She returned her attention to the passing scenery.

All right, her eyes, not her attention. Her attention was still focused on the man beside her.

He wasn't dressed as a rake. Not that she knew how a rake dressed, but his plain, serviceable greatcoat, well-worn driving gloves, warm muffler, and beaver hat didn't seem terribly rakish. Of course he was so shockingly handsome, he could be dressed in rags or nothing at all and still be sinfully attractive.

Especially dressed in nothing at all—or virtually nothing—as she'd learned in the Findleys' best bedchamber.

She shifted on the curricle seat. What the hell was the matter with her? She'd never paid so much attention to a man's looks before. Of *course* Lord Jack was attractive. He was a rake. He wouldn't be very successful at seduction if he looked like a toad.

She was not going to fall under his spell like every other silly woman.

"You haven't answered my question."

"W-what question?" Damn. She must keep her wits about her. One false step and the man would pounce on her.

And she should *not* feel a shiver of excitement at that thought.

She was losing her mind. The sooner she was free of the rake's presence, the better.

"You are very cheeky, lad." There was a bit more steel in Lord Jack's voice. "Now out with it. Where did you meet Pettigrew?"

He wasn't going to intimidate her. He was probably used to using his rakish personality or his father's rank to cow people, but she was made of sterner stuff. "You heard Mr. Pettigrew. He said he's never met me. And I've never met him."

Which was perfectly true. She'd been completely concealed by the case of candles in Mr. Turner's shop when Mr. Pettigrew had been present.

"Francis, you'll find I don't tolerate lying." Jack's voice was now sharp as a blade.

"I'm n-not lying!" Blast it, her voice wavered. But she *wasn't* lying, at least not strictly speaking.

She clenched her hands and took a deep breath. She was letting him frighten her. Stupid! She wasn't some timid, dependent, weak female. She'd run Landsford for the last ten years. She could stand up to one rakish lord.

"Perhaps. But you're not telling the truth either. Come

now, empty the bag. I want to know exactly what your connection is to Pettigrew."

The gall of the man. He had no authority over her. "I have no connection. As I said, I've never met him. I wish you would—" She bit her tongue. She may have run Landsford, but she was pretending to be a young boy now. She should not sound so defiant.

There was a very uncomfortable silence, broken only by the sound of the horses' hooves moving steadily over the ground.

"I *will* find out, Francis," Lord Jack said at last. "Don't think I won't. And when I do, it will not go well for you."

He was one to talk about lying. "You said you wouldn't hurt me."

"I didn't say I'd let you ride roughshod over me. I suspect your aunt has spoiled you dreadfully."

"She has not!" Aunt Viola spoil her? If he only knew. Viola had always been a hard taskmaster. She'd insisted Frances do everything perfectly. Frances had had to read and cipher as well as Frederick—better than Frederick, though that hadn't been so difficult. Frederick had never applied himself to his studies. But even when the tutor had praised her, Aunt Viola had always found something she could improve.

Which had been a good thing. And at least Viola hadn't forced her to waste time on useless feminine skills like sewing and dancing.

Lord Jack had apparently decided to leave the question of her connection to Pettigrew for the time being. "Will your brother send someone to fetch your horse?"

"Yes." Now she *was* lying. Frederick wasn't likely to bother himself about something he'd see as her problem. She'd get Daisy on her way back to Landsford.

Poor Daisy had indeed been lame; she'd had to leave her

at the Crowing Cock. Not that Daisy had minded. She'd appeared quite content to stay snug in a warm stall rather than go haring over the rough roads again. And Mr. Watkins, the ostler, had seemed very competent. He said he'd have Daisy back in fine fettle in no time.

"How long are you staying in London?"

"Not long." Only a day or two. Once she had it out with Puddington and got her money, she'd be on her way, but she wasn't about to tell Lord Jack that. The less he knew about her and her plans, the better.

He finally returned his full attention to his cattle, thank God. With luck he'd be content to pass the rest of the journey in silence. Why would he want to talk to her anyway? He thought her a young boy, a lad he'd taken up as a favor to Mrs. Findley. She was no more than a package he was delivering.

She watched the snow-covered fields slip by. The creak of the carriage, the jingle of the harness, the steady beat of the horses' hooves were soothing. They were getting closer and closer to Town.

"Does your brother know you're coming?"

"Uh . . ." Her mind went blank. Damn it, he'd waited to strike until she'd been lulled into letting down her guard. "Not exactly."

"Not at all." He snorted. "You have no idea if your brother is at home, do you?"

Of course Frederick was home. Where else would he be?

Unease gnawed at her gut. Given her horrendous luck recently, he'd probably gone off to the South Seas like their father.

The curricle had slowed. Houses began to crowd the sides of the road; the snow piled here and there was black with soot. Even the air seemed thicker, or maybe it was guilt that was making it hard for her to draw a deep breath.

Lord Jack avoided a slow-moving vegetable cart with a deft pull on the reins. "Where does he live?"

If she told him, he'd probably insist on meeting Frederick, and then he'd learn her gender. But what was her alternative? Frederick's was the only address she had besides that of Puddington's office.

She would just have to be quick-witted, and perhaps fleet-footed, and get to Frederick before Lord Jack did. "He lives in a boardinghouse on Hart Street."

He stared at her. "Hart Street? In Covent Garden?"

"Yes. Watch out for that dog!"

He cursed and pulled back on the reins, narrowly missing the mongrel.

"I don't know how you got such a reputation as a noted whip," she said as she watched the animal run off. Now she understood how Lord Jack had crashed his curricle; hopefully he wouldn't do the same with her as a passenger.

He threw her a glare, but didn't argue. Of course not. She was correct. But she would give him credit for not contesting the obvious. Most men would insist the sky was green if a woman said it was blue.

Though she shouldn't give him too much credit. He didn't know she was a female.

"I take it you've never visited your brother?" he said once he'd got his horses settled down. He sounded as if he was holding on to his temper as tightly as he'd gripped the reins a moment ago.

"No, I haven't. Why?"

He shot her a pointed look. "Because Hart Street is narrow and dirty and full of taverns and brothels and all sorts of riffraff. If you'd come by yourself, you wouldn't have lasted five minutes there."

That didn't sound at all like the sort of place her boring, staid brother would live. "You must be mistaken."

"And you must be daft." His jaw hardened. "You've never been to Town, and yet you think you know everything about the place."

"I know my brother."

"Not very well."

She couldn't really dispute that.

"London is nothing like the country, Master Haddon. There are men—and women—who live to prey on young bumpkins like you. They have absolutely no conscience. They'll take your money or your life—or both—without a second thought." He scowled at her. "You will stay close to my side as though you were glued there until I hand you off to your relative."

Typical male, creating bugbears to try to frighten her into doing what he wanted. "I will not."

"Then I will not take you to your brother's rooms. I'll bring you to Greycliffe House, and he can come fetch you there."

"No!" That would be disastrous. At least if Lord Jack took her to Frederick's, she had some hope of maintaining her masquerade. "I, er, ah . . . you're right." Flattery usually worked. Men liked to think they were superior. "Frederick will probably be annoyed at me for showing up unannounced, but he'll be furious if he has to rearrange his schedule to come retrieve me." She tried for a slight tremor of fear. "I hate it when he's angry."

Perhaps she had some nascent dramatic skills, because Lord Jack's brows snapped down into a deep scowl.

"Does he beat you?" His words cut like steel.

"Oh no." She didn't want him greeting Frederick with his fists. "But he'll give me a thundering scold."

His scowl relaxed a bit. "And you'll deserve every single word of it."

He turned onto a narrow street which shortly opened into a large square. "Covent Garden," he said as his horses picked their way past piles of snow, abandoned potatoes, and scattered cabbage leaves. "We're here at just the right time. In the morning it's a mass of people buying and selling fruits and vegetables and other wares; at night . . ." He looked at her. "You do not want to know what's sold here at night."

She looked at the fine portico around the edges of the square and the jumble of stalls in the middle. The place had the feel of an elegant lady who'd let the ravages of time and the insults of daily life wear her down.

She knew exactly what brought merchants coins at night: idiot men, like her rakish father and Lord Jack, looking for whores.

"I'll leave the curricle at the Nag's Head," Jack said as they left the square. "Hart Street is far too narrow to turn the horses. What number is your brother's boardinghouse?"

"Thirty-four."

"Let's hope that's not a long walk."

Jack pulled up in front of the public house and called to a boy standing outside. "Here, Henry. Watch my horses, will you?"

The boy grinned and hurried over. "Aye, milord."

Jack swung down from the curricle in one fluid motion; Frances clambered down much less gracefully.

She looked around. Could she make a dash for Frederick's place now? No. Hart Street went both left and right. She had no idea in which direction to run, and, after a moment of surprise, Lord Jack was certain to give chase and catch her, dragging her back by her ear. She flushed. That would be beyond embarrassing.

"Take good care of them," Jack was telling Henry when Frances joined him, "and there's a shilling in it for you."

The boy's grin widened. "Aye, milord. I'll watch these beauties well, don't ye worry."

"Splendid. Come along, Francis."

Jack grasped her arm firmly as they started down Hart Street. "Stay close. As I said, this isn't the country."

It certainly wasn't. She would have fished her handkerchief out of her pocket and held it to her nose if it wouldn't have looked too effeminate. Instead she took shallow breaths through her mouth. Thank God it was cold. She'd never have borne the stench in the heat of the summer. She picked her way around the rotting vegetables and horse droppings and a greenish-brown, gelatinous mound she didn't want to examine too closely.

"Hooo, gents. Want some fun?" an old woman called from a doorway. The woman's face was painted and her bodice was pulled so low everyone could see her drooping—

Good God, had she rouged her nipples? They were shriveled up into hard points. She must be freezing. Why wasn't she wearing a coat?

Well, yes, it was obvious why she wasn't wearing a coat, but she was very much fooling herself if she thought displaying her ancient charms would entice a man—

Jack stepped in front of Frances, blocking her view. "Belinda! What are you doing here?"

Good heavens, did the rake consort even with poor, broken-down whores like this one?

Frances's stomach twisted. She was in danger of adding to the filth on the walkway. She hadn't thought any man would take this woman up on her offer. Surely Lord Jack could do much better. But what did she know? Apparently a rake only cared that his companion was female.

The woman made a noise that sounded like a cross between a curse and a squeak of fear. "Lord Jack! I didn't recognize ye."

"Because you aren't wearing your spectacles. Have you lost them again?"

"Maybe."

Jack sighed and shook his head. "I'll get you another pair. Now tell me, why aren't you at the Golden Leg?" A note of frustration had joined the anger in his voice. "You promised to stop working the streets after I persuaded them to take you on as a scullery maid."

This was certainly an odd conversation for a rake to be having with a whore. Well, it wasn't her concern. Now that she knew she was heading in the right direction, she could make a dash for Frederick's boardinghouse while Jack's attention was focused elsewhere.

Frances looked around. Ah, for once a bit of luck—the place was just across the street and down a few doors. This was her golden opportunity.

She moved quickly and quietly.

Belinda shrugged. "This is easier work, milord, and it pays better."

"And?" He knew Belinda. There was more to the tale.

She looked back toward the Nag's Head as if she might flee in that direction. "And I was caught 'elping a gent at the inn, if ye must know. They tossed me out."

Jack expelled a long breath. He knew what "helping" meant—she'd been caught doing some sort of sexual favor.

"Blast it all, Belinda, we've talked about this. You can't be 'helping' gentlemen." He struggled for control. He must remember Belinda had not had the advantages he'd had growing up. She didn't think like he did. None of the denizens of Covent Garden did. If they got an opportunity to earn a bit of money—or to steal it—they took it. They lived in the moment with no thought of the future.

Perhaps because so many of them had very little future.

The children—he had more luck with the children, but even they often sank back into the desperation of poverty and crime.

It was times like these when he thought seriously of giving up and just being the careless, thoughtless, irresponsible fellow he'd been before he'd stumbled over his first abandoned baby right after Ned's son had died in childbirth. "I should find you work in a convent."

If he wasn't so frustrated, the look of horror that settled over Belinda's features would be amusing.

"Not a *convent*, milord." A cold wind whistled down the narrow street, and she shivered, hugging herself tighter. "Maybe a dress shop. I'd like to work in a dress shop. I'm good with a needle, I am."

A dress shop. Where was he going to find a dress shop that would hire the likes of Belinda?

Well, it was worth a try. At least in a dress shop she'd be less likely to encounter men looking for her other skills. "Very well, I'll see what I can do. Where are you staying?"

Belinda looked down and shifted her weight. "Here and there."

Which meant the streets, an especially dangerous choice now that someone was cutting women's throats. He fished some coins out of his purse. "Here. Meg at The Spotted Dog will put you up for a day or two."

"Thank ye, milord." She stuffed the money down the front of her dress as she sniffed. "If Mother Wilton weren't so high and mighty—"

"Belinda, stop. You know you're too old for this line of work."

"Gammon! A woman's never too old fer fun"—she grinned, showing a mouthful of yellowed, broken, or absent teeth—"as I'd be 'appy to show ye or the fine lad who was with ye."

"Was?" He turned. Bloody hell, Francis wasn't where he was supposed to be. He wouldn't have—

He had. The damn, disobedient whelp was over at number thirty-four, talking to what must be the landlady of his brother's boardinghouse.

The tall, bony, white-haired woman who'd finally opened the door after Frances's increasingly desperate knocks glared at her. "What do ye want?"

"I'm here to see my brother, Frederick Hadley."

The woman's glare turned to a scowl. "He ain't here." She started to close the door.

Frances lunged to catch it. "What? But I'm quite sure this is his address."

"*Was* his address. He married and moved out last week." The landlady tugged on the door again, but Frances was stronger.

"Married?"

"Yes, married. And I don't rent to no married fellows. Only single men—and no female visitors allowed. There's enough fornication on this street without my inviting it under me own roof. *Will* you let me close this door?"

"You must be mistaken." The woman could not be referring to Frederick.

"I am not." The landlady sniffed disdainfully. "He took up with some theater trollop. Good riddance, I say—and good day to you." She tugged on the door once more, harder this time. "Let go!"

From the corner of her eye, Frances saw Jack approaching. He did not look at all pleased with her. "Did he say where he was moving?"

"No, and I didn't ask. Now if you don't let go at once, I'll call the bloody watch."

Frances doubted the watch was in hailing distance, but it was clear the landlady couldn't help her, and Jack had almost reached them. She did not want him hearing her real family name.

"Very well." She stepped back. "Thank yo—"

The woman slammed the door in her face.

Jack reached Francis right after the door banged shut. He grabbed the boy's arm and shook it. "What do you mean—"

He stopped. Francis's face was red with anger. "What's the matter? Shall I break the door down? I can force our way in if you need me to do so."

"No. It doesn't matter."

"What do you mean it doesn't matter? Isn't this where your brother lives?"

"Lived. He got married."

Oh, damn. He'd been afraid something like this would happen. "And, er, you didn't know anything about it?"

Francis shook his head.

"I see." Actually, he didn't see. He didn't live in his brothers' pockets, but he couldn't imagine not knowing if one of them was undertaking something so significant as marriage. "But you must have known he was betrothed?"

"No. I had no idea. Frederick never wrote, at least not to me." Francis's jaw hardened. "He should have written. I had a right to know, blast it."

"Yes, you did." Jack led him back to the street. Poor boy. He probably hero-worshipped his brother. There were only four years between Jack and Ash, but he'd admit to doing a little hero-worshipping himself when he was younger, especially when he was this boy's age and Ash was sixteen or seventeen, a man in his young eyes. And there was far more of an age difference between Francis and his brother. Francis likely had never seen his brother's feet of clay.

"Maybe he hasn't had time to pen a letter. Or maybe it got lost. These things happen. Or perhaps he wrote to your aunt and was waiting to tell you in person."

"No, I'm sure Frederick didn't write. He's as bad as our father, always trying to avoid responsibility." The boy glared at him. "Unless . . . yes, that must be it. Puddington must have known; that's why he's been so vague and evasive in his recent letters. And Aunt Viola—she *did* get a letter right before the blizzard, which she was quite secretive about. Damn it, that's why she tried to sell me to Mr.—"

The lad stopped abruptly and shot Jack an extremely guilty look.

"Francis!" Jack took him by the shoulders and made him meet his eyes. Surely he had misunderstood, but if he hadn't, he would be finding the boy's aunt and making it very clear to her that he would not tolerate trafficking in children. No wonder Francis had been afraid of him at the Crowing Cock. "If your aunt was planning to sell you, I will see that she is punished. You don't have to worry that I'll return you to her."

Francis gaped at him. "Oh no. I didn't mean . . . that is . . ."

Children often defended their abusers. He'd learned that over the last four years. He'd had no idea how dark the human soul could be until he'd started taking in abandoned children and helping the poor prostitutes. It sounded as if this aunt was the only family Francis had besides his brother and . . .

"You mentioned your father. I had just assumed . . . is he still alive, then?"

Francis shrugged. "As far as I know. I haven't seen him in years."

So the father would be no help. Damn it, some men should be castrated—but then Francis wouldn't be here. That was what he reminded himself whenever he began to despair. Men—and women—did terrible things, but there was always hope for the children.

"And your mother?"

"Died when I was young—" She coughed. "Younger."

So there was only the aunt and the brother. Or . . .

"Who is this Puddington fellow?"

Oh, damn, now her goose was well and truly cooked. "A, er, family acquaintance. Stodgy old fellow. Knew my father. I'm sure you wouldn't like him."

Lord Jack looked skeptical. "Does he live in London?"

"Yes, I believe so, but I don't know where." That was true; she had only his office address. "Why do you ask?"

"Because now that your brother has moved—and if what you say is true, I refuse to send you back to your aunt—we'll need to find a home for you, at least until I can track down your sibling."

Oh God, that was right. Now that Frederick had gone off, she had no place to stay. It was just like her brother to leave her in the lurch.

"Don't worry." Jack started back toward the curricle. "You can stay with me for the time being."

"What?!" She stumbled, and Jack caught her.

She shrugged out of his hold and kept walking. She couldn't stay with Jack. Sharing a room with the man had been scandalous, but at least it had been at a small, out-of-the-way inn. No one knew of it except for the Findleys and—

Pettigrew, of course. And Mr. Dantley, but he hadn't made the connection between Frederick Hadley and Francis Haddon. Pettigrew had, and Pettigrew would spread the story far and wide.

And Pettigrew lived in London. Had likely been just a little behind them on the road.

The story of her stay at the Crowing Cock was bad enough—well, it was hard to imagine how it could be worse—but if she brazenly lived with Lord Jack in London . . . "I can't stay with you."

"Of course you can. Greycliffe House has a ridiculous number of bedrooms."

"Ah." Well, perhaps it wouldn't be *so* bad. The only other option was to ask him to put her on the stage back to the Crowing Cock, and chances were there wasn't another coach leaving today. And her purse was near empty—she'd have to beg the fare from him. Plus, now that he'd got this idea into his head that her aunt was selling boys . . .

And there was no way she could explain without revealing her gender.

Oh, it was all such a mess.

Well, surely she could keep up her masquerade until tomorrow. Somehow she'd get him to drop her at Puddington's door; she couldn't have him come in and meet the man, because then he'd also discover she was a female. Once she saw Puddington and got her money, all her problems would be solved.

She stumbled again, this time over something she hoped was a mutton bone as they passed a narrow alley, and Jack grabbed her arm.

"Watch where you put your feet."

"I didn't *mean* to trip. I—"

He held up his free hand, his expression suddenly intent. "Shh. Do you hear that?"

"Hear what?" She listened. Jack had sharp ears. It took her a moment to pick up the sound, a faint mewling. "You mean the cat?"

"That's not a cat, blast it." He glanced around. "Bloody hell, where the—"

Frances heard the sound again. "I think it's coming from the alley."

"You're right." He plunged into the dark, dank, narrow space. Frances hung back—the place smelled as bad as a midden—but Jack's fingers were still locked around her arm, so she had no choice but to stumble after him. At least she was wearing Frederick's old clothes—she'd throw them out as soon as she could.

It was a very good thing she couldn't see what she was stepping in. She slipped on something large and mushy, skidding into Lord Jack just as he stopped. His arm went round her, holding her against his body.

A dog, barking wildly, leapt up from a bundle of rags and ran over to jump on Lord Jack. His breeches would have to go on the trash heap also, and they were far finer than Frederick's castoffs.

Jack swore, but not at the dog.

"Stay here," he said and went over to pick up the rags.

The dog transferred his attentions to Frances. There was enough light to see he was of average size and indeterminate origin, with floppy ears and a plumed tail curling over his back. She patted him absently, trying not to think of the fleas and other vermin he might be gifting her with. "Why are you bothering with—oh."

The rags cried.

"Oh my God. It's a baby."

Chapter 4

Lies have a way of coming back to haunt you.
—Venus's Love Notes

"Yes." Jack sounded angry, not shocked or surprised, and he carried the bundle securely as if he'd handled infants before. "A boy—he looks to be a month or two old. He's lucky the dog was here or he would have frozen to death. Come with me."

She hurried after him, the dog following at her heels. Once they were free of the alley, Jack turned right and banged on the first door he came to.

It jerked open, revealing a scowling giant, a man a good handbreadth taller than Jack and weighing at least twice as much. He had a scar over his right eye and a flattened nose that looked as if it had encountered far too many fists.

"What do ye—" The giant's eyes widened as they focused on Jack, and then his face paled as his gaze continued down to the baby cradled in Jack's right arm. "Er, what are ye doing here, milord?"

"What does it look like I'm doing, Albert? I need to speak to your mistress."

Albert's Adam's apple bobbed above his cravat. "I dunno, milord. She's awful busy. If ye come back tomorrow, maybe—"

"I don't care if she's entertaining Prinny himself, she'll see me now," Jack said and pushed past him.

Frances stepped in behind Jack. She didn't wish to be inside this house—she was very much afraid she knew what it was—but she wanted less to be alone on the street.

"Hey, ye can't come in here, ye miserable cur."

Frances scowled, but Albert was addressing the poor dog, not her. He swung his foot. The animal must have had experience with this form of greeting, because he dodged and ran back outside, whining. Albert shut the door.

The baby started crying again—a weak, thin, pitiful sound.

"I assume Nan is in her office," Jack said, striding through the foyer toward a closed door.

"Yes, milord, but—" Albert was almost wringing his ham-sized hands.

"No need to announce me." Jack paused with his fingers on the doorknob, and glanced at Frances. "You stay here."

Frances looked around the garish foyer and felt her flesh creep. The walls were decorated in bloodred flocked wallpaper and overly ornate, vaguely obscene, gold wall sconces, and the paintings had naked—

"And don't look at the artwork."

She jerked her eyes back to Lord Jack. "I'll come in with you."

"No, you won't." He pointed to a straight-backed bench. "Sit there. I promise I won't be long." Then he threw open the door and went into the room.

"Lord," Albert breathed, "the mistress will be mad as a buck. She's been trying fer days to get the Earl of—"

"What the *bloody* hell," a man shouted from the room. "Can't a fellow have a bit of privacy, for God's sake?"

"Now, Ruland, I'm sure—" That was a woman's voice.

"I'm sure I'm leaving, and I'm never coming back, madam."

"Oh, damn," Albert muttered as a fat, balding man with startlingly bushy gray eyebrows came barreling out of the room, slamming the door behind him.

The man glared at Frances, turning his brows into one imposing hedge, as he struggled to button his fall. "What are you gaping at, boy?"

She opened her mouth to tell him exactly what she thought of men, especially men of his advanced age, frequenting brothels but she caught Albert's worried expression before she spoke.

Ah, yes. Perhaps she should hold her tongue. She *was* masquerading as a boy, after all. "Nothing, my lord."

Something heavy thudded against the closed door. Perhaps she was just as happy not to be in that room.

Ruland looked her up and down. "Who are you? You don't look or sound like one of the filthy Covent Garden brats." His beady eyes narrowed. "You came with Jack, didn't you?"

The man must be memorizing her face. "Yes, my lord." She wished she could grab the hideously obscene statue of a pregnant woman and lascivious snakes off the table to her right and bash the lewd lord over the head with it.

"I'll find out who you are, you know"—he finally got his fall buttoned—"and, more importantly, what Jack is doing with you. He'll be sorry he interrupted me."

He tugged on his coat sleeves and turned to Albert, who was holding out his hat and walking stick. "Open the door, you idiot," he snarled as he grabbed his things.

"Yes, milord." Albert bowed as the man departed, then

shut the door and collapsed against it. "Mother of God, now we are in the suds!"

"Why?" For a frightening-looking fellow, Albert was turning out to be no more dangerous than a field mouse. "I mean, it must certainly have been"—she flushed—"awkward when Lord Jack walked in on the man and your mistress, but it didn't look as though . . . he obviously wasn't . . . well, he couldn't have been in the middle of, er, anything, could he?" She was digging a hole; she could feel herself going deeper and deeper. Albert was staring at her as though she were a lunatic. "Isn't he just full of bluster?"

Albert shook his head. "No, lad. Ruland is as bad as they come. Nan thinks he's the one who's been killing all the girls; she was going to try to find out tonight, but then Lord Jack came and ruined it."

"Someone is killing girls?" That's right, she *had* read something in the papers about prostitutes and one or two society women turning up with their throats slashed. She couldn't quite comprehend the tragedy—well, yes, murder was always horrible, but these women had clearly chosen to engage in dangerous behavior, so what could they expect? As she remembered from the papers, even the society girls had been no better than they should be.

But of course Albert and the denizens of this house of iniquity would be concerned. Their lives were the ones most in danger. "Shouldn't your mistress go to the authorities with her suspicions?"

Albert shrugged. "They don't care about a few dead dolly-mops. Nan says they're 'appy to have some of the trash cleaned up. That's why she's looking into it herself."

"Ah." It was a little disconcerting to hear her own theory repeated, but obviously these people understood the risks and their place in society.

"Who's here, Albert?"

"Lord Jack."

Frances looked up to see two women on the landing just above her. They seemed to be about her age and were dressed in gauzy, almost transparent dresses of better quality but otherwise much like the one Belinda, the old drab in the street, had been wearing.

Her stomach twisted. More prostitutes.

She looked at the closed door to the madam's office. When in God's name—if the Almighty could be thought of in such a sinful place—would Jack come out? He couldn't be doing more than talking with the woman, could he?

Her stomach twisted again.

No! No, of course he wasn't. Not with the baby. Even a rake of Jack's reputation couldn't do whatever rakes did, with a baby whimpering so near at hand. And he hadn't looked at all amorous when he'd burst in on the madam.

"Where's that devil Ruland?" the shorter girl asked.

Albert grinned. "He just left."

"Thank God!" she said as the two came down the stairs. She looked at Frances. "Who's this?"

Oh Lord. Frances glanced at the closed door again. Surely Jack would appear at any minute.

"Francis Haddon," Albert said. "'E says Lord Jack is taking 'im to 'is brother."

The girl smiled. "And now you have to cool yer heels, waiting fer Lord Jack to finish his business." She walked closer; Frances stepped back. "Would you like me to help you pass the time?"

Clearly the woman wasn't suggesting a pleasant chat. Frances took another step back and bumped up against the bench. "No, thank you."

The taller one giggled. "I think you're frightening him, Bessie."

Damn it, she wasn't frightened. She just had to maintain her disguise.

Albert lumbered over. "Lord Jack won't be 'appy if ye scare the lad."

"Oh, pish," Bessie said. "I'm just going to make him happy like I do you, Albert."

Albert actually blushed. "'E's only a boy."

"He's taller than me," Bessie said. "Let's see if he's interested." She reached for Frances's crotch.

Good Lord! Frances jerked back, lost her balance, and sat down abruptly.

Bessie laughed. "What? Are you still a virgin?"

"Yes." Frances glared at them. "I am."

"Temper, temper, Nan."

Nan glared at Jack and then bent over to pick up the candlestick she'd thrown at the door. "Why the hell did you have to come tonight, Jack? I had Ruland just where I wanted him."

"With his breeches down around his ankles? I didn't know you had a hankering for the earl."

"I don't." She put the candlestick back on the table with rather more force than necessary. "He's a disgusting, fat, selfish, arrogant blackguard, but I think he might be the Silent Slasher. I was going to try to find out tonight." She glared at him, but he saw the fear in her eyes. "Martha from Maiden Lane showed up dead down by the Bucket of Blood while you were gone."

"Martha? Damn." Martha had been saving to rent a house in the country and had almost had enough money put away. She'd been smart and cautious and had generally avoided the Bucket of Blood due to all the prizefights it hosted.

The bundle in his arms whimpered.

"Oh God, where did you find this one?"

"In the alley next door. Does he belong to one of your girls?"

"Of course not. My girls all take precautions—and the ones who do make a mistake, I send off to your place in Bromley. You know that."

He did know that. Nan might be a madam, but she sincerely cared for the dashers who worked for her and tried her best to run a safe, clean business. "Yes, I know, but I'd hoped to be wrong. This baby desperately needs to suckle. Get me a clean shawl, will you?"

"Only if you promise to buy me a replacement."

"I always do, don't I? Bring me one of the older ones. It'll be softer."

"You should just let him die," Nan said as she went into another room to do his bidding.

Nan said that all the time. He understood her callousness, but he refused to share it. He couldn't, not since Ned's baby had died at birth. He hadn't been able to save his nephew's life or lessen Ned's pain, and he hated how powerless that still made him feel. But collecting even a few of London's discarded children helped. At least he was doing *something* and not standing helplessly by, anger and frustration and gut-wrenching sorrow knotting in his chest.

Thank God he had a gift for making shrewd investments, so he had plenty of funds at his disposal. He'd far rather spend his money on his charity houses than another horse or carriage he didn't need.

"You know I can't do that, Nan."

Nan came back with a bright red shawl—she had rather garish taste. "But you should. The world doesn't need another bastard, and the poor bastard doesn't need to suffer poverty and hunger and cruelty."

Jack knelt to spread the shawl on the floor. "My children aren't hungry, and no one treats them cruelly. They learn a trade when they're old enough, so they can make their way in the world." He removed the filthy rags the baby was wrapped in. The poor infant was very thin.

"You're a dreamer, Jack. You've been doing this . . . what? Three or four years? Soon you'll marry and have children of your own, and you'll forget about this little hobby."

"No, I won't." Any woman he married would have to accept the importance of his Bromley houses. Not that he had plans to tie the knot anytime soon. For one, he'd yet to meet a woman who wouldn't shriek and pull back her skirts or call for her vinaigrette if she were to meet any of his brats. And for another—well, Mama and Father might have made a success of an early marriage, but his brothers had not. He'd wait until he was at least thirty before even considering matrimony.

Nan watched him wrap the infant in her shawl, her arms crossed, a look of resigned pity on her face. "He'll likely die, you know."

"He might make it." Jack wouldn't give him good odds, though. The baby should be kicking and screaming in hunger, but instead he was limp and lethargic. Jack finished tucking the ends of the blanket securely around him and stood. "Tell me about Martha."

Nan shuddered. "She died exactly like the others, her throat slashed ear to ear."

Martha's death put the number of women killed at seven: five prostitutes who lived and worked in the Covent Garden area and two women of the *ton*—Miss Fielding, a daring debutante who'd been rumored to entertain young blades in secluded corners at society's balls, and Mrs. Hubble, a notorious and now equally dead widow.

"Why do you think Ruland's the Slasher?"

"Who else could it be?" Nan grimaced. "The man's as evil as they come."

Nan was letting desperation cloud her thinking. "I grant you he's not pleasant, but I've encountered worse." Ruland had always struck him as a bully—mean, but at heart a coward.

"But think, Jack. He goes to all the social events, and he frequents the brothels."

"That's true of almost every male member of the *ton*, Nan."

Her brows slanted down and she opened her mouth as if to argue . . . but sighed instead. "You're right, of course."

"And what the hell were you doing alone with him if you thought he was the Slasher? Do you have a death wish?"

She shrugged, but wouldn't meet his gaze. "Albert would have come if I'd called."

Nan knew better than that. "Even if Albert had been able to reach you in time—and you're well aware speed is not his forte—everyone, including Ruland, knows you just have to tap the fellow on the jaw and he's down for the count."

Her face grew pale, making the rouge on her cheeks stand out as if she had a fever. "But what if the next victim is one of my girls, Jack? I can't stand by and let that happen. I have to do something."

"I understand, Nan. I'm frustrated, too." Frustrated and furious. "But acting foolishly is not going to catch the villain. I—"

The baby whimpered again. He had to get him to his house for children in Bromley where Ursula, the woman who ran the place, could find him a wet nurse. "I've got to go, Nan, but I'm back in London for the foreseeable future. I'll try to discover the Slasher's identity, but you must send word if you or your girls hear anything."

"Yes, of course I will."

He opened the door and stepped into the foyer to find Francis sitting on the bench, trapped between two of Nan's girls, face red, hands protecting his crotch as if he was afraid he was about to be castrated. Albert stood nearby, looking worried but doing nothing to help.

"I said I am *not* interested." The boy sounded both angry and desperate.

"Bessie, Alice, leave the poor lad alone." Damn it, he should have realized this might happen.

"I told ye Lord Jack wouldn't be 'appy," Albert said.

Bessie dropped her arm over the boy's shoulders. "We were just trying to entertain the lad while you were busy, Lord Jack," she said, leaning over to kiss Francis on the cheek.

Francis wiggled his shoulders and shot his elbow into the girl's stomach; then he snapped his hand back to shield his privates.

"Ouch!" Bessie glared at him.

He glared back. "Go *away*."

Jack opened his mouth to castigate Bessie, but Nan, who'd followed him into the foyer, spoke first.

"Stop that. Both of you, get up. Can't you see the boy doesn't like it?"

Alice stood at once, but Bessie stayed where she was, pouting. "He *should* like it. All men do."

"But he doesn't," Nan said. "He's too young. He doesn't even have a beard yet."

Bessie lifted her hand to touch Francis's cheek, but Francis shoved her away, scrambled off the bench, and strode to the door. "I'm leaving."

"Not without me." Jack collared him before he could

escape and then looked back at Nan. "I'll let you know when I learn anything—and don't take any more risks like you did just now."

Albert opened the door for them. There was the dog, still sitting in front of the building. He jumped up, barking and dancing, as soon as he saw them.

"Quiet, sir!"

The animal clearly recognized the voice of authority. He sat at once, tilted his head, and looked up at Jack hopefully.

"Albert, you must need a dog to help you keep away the riffraff."

"No, milord." Albert peered out at the mongrel. "I don't like dogs. Besides, 'e looks like riffraff 'imself."

"I'm sure he'll improve with a bath, but very well." He didn't have time to argue. Perhaps if he was lucky, the dog would stay at Nan's.

He wasn't lucky.

"He's following us," Francis said as they set off down the street back to the Nag's Head and his curricle. The boy's voice was markedly subdued.

"I see that." The poor lad must be worrying about what had happened at Nan's. Damn Bessie. He shifted the baby to his other arm. Couldn't she see Francis was hardly more than a child? "I'm sorry those women troubled you."

The boy flushed and mumbled something.

Jack cleared his throat. This was awkward, but he couldn't let Francis stew about his feelings. "You . . . well, has your brother talked to you about the, er, changes a boy goes through in becoming a man?"

"No!" The lad's ears turned red and he started walking faster.

"It's nothing to be ashamed of, though I know it can be confusing. When I—"

"Oh, there's the curricle!"

Jack grabbed the boy's arm before he could dart ahead. He remembered all too well the conflicting emotions of that age—desire, shame, confusion, worry, excitement. "Francis, it's all right if you wanted Bessie to touch your cock—"

"Oh!" Francis shouted. "We'd better hurry. I'm sure you should be taking that baby wherever you're taking him. I'll just run ahead and climb into the curricle, shall I? So we're ready to go at once?" He managed to twist free and took off as if all the hounds of hell were after him.

Jack sighed and looked down at the dog. "These are some of the toughest years, you know, when a boy is neither a child nor a man."

The dog barked in apparent agreement and waved his tail.

When they reached the Nag's Head, Francis was sitting ramrod straight in the passenger's seat. He might as well have hung a sign around his neck—DO NOT DISCUSS BESSIE.

Dear God, this masquerade was hopelessly out of control. Lord Jack had almost . . . he'd almost told her . . . it had been kind of him to try to calm a boy's fears, but she wasn't a boy.

She gripped the side of the curricle. She couldn't let him talk about . . . about something so private, but what would she do if he started back in on it when they were going wherever it was they were going?

She should not be going anywhere with the man. He was a despicable rake. He'd been all too familiar with that old whore and that dreadful Albert. And he'd walked right into the madam's office, if that's what the room indeed was, when the woman had been engaged in shocking behavior with that disgusting Lord Ruland. And those girls who'd been talking to her—he'd known their names without an introduction.

He was crossing the street now. He was so big, but he held the tiny baby so confidently . . .

Well, of course rakes would know all about babies.

And now he was coming around to her side of the curricle.

"Here, Francis," he said, "take the infant from me."

Oh God. She looked at the red bundle, her heart thudding in her chest. She'd never held a baby before, and this one was so small. "I can't."

"You have to." His voice was sharp with impatience. "As you said, we need to hurry. The infant can't wait much longer for a wet nurse."

She didn't know anything about wet nurses either. Viola had scoffed at any subject that touched on a feminine skill. But the poor child clearly needed something. She gingerly held out her arms.

"He doesn't bite, at least not yet," Jack said. "Hold him securely."

"Securely?"

"Yes. Support his head—young babies have weak necks. Like this." Jack adjusted the infant's position so his head rested on the crook of her arm.

There was almost nothing to hold, the bundle was so light. She looked down into the tiny face, half hidden in the shawl. Was he even breathing? "Are babies always so small and still?"

"No. This poor fellow isn't well, which is why we need to get him help quickly."

"Oh." The baby's eyelids fluttered and his lips moved slightly; Frances felt a surprising spurt of pleasure. "I think he smiled at me."

Jack grunted. "It was probably gas." He went to retrieve the reins from Henry and give him his coins.

"Ack!" The moment Jack moved away, the dog scrambled up onto the seat next to her. Frances clutched the baby tighter. "Get down!"

Jack glanced back to see what the problem was. "Hey there, sir!"

The dog dropped his head and whined piteously. He looked at Jack and then Frances with big, beseeching eyes, his tail wagging slowly but hopefully.

His hair was matted, he smelled of wet dog and other, even less savory things, and he was likely harboring an entire colony of fleas, but his look of entreaty was so persuasive, Frances couldn't bring herself to argue for his eviction.

"That's Shakespeare, milord," Henry said. "'E was Dick Dutton's, who used to work at the theater, but Dick took off a bit ago. Shakespeare's been living on the street ever since."

"I see. I don't suppose you'd like to be his new owner?"

Henry shook his head. "Nay. Me master'd whip me good if I tried to keep a dog."

Jack sighed and nodded. "I'm not surprised." He came around to vault into his seat and then regarded Shakespeare. The dog's tail moved more rapidly. "Well, I suppose you've earned some reward for watching over the infant, haven't you?"

The tail moved faster, beating against Frances's leg.

"And I assume you have no particular attachment to this somewhat unlovely part of London?"

Shakespeare barked in such a way as to indicate he'd be happy to leave the neighborhood and put a paw on Jack's breeches.

Jack raised his brows, and the dog snatched back the offending body part.

"That's better. Stand clear, Henry; we are off."

They took a narrow street to a wider one and were soon weaving between slower vehicles, heading out of Town.

Jack was traveling quite fast. In fact, the speed was rather alarming. Frances tightened her hold on the baby and the curricle as they hit a bump. "Slow down."

He kept his eyes on the road. "I can't. We need to get to Bromley as quickly as possible."

"It's not going to help anyone if we end in a ditch." She clenched her teeth and gripped the side of the curricle even more tightly, bracing her feet on the floor—and bit back an oath as they barely missed hitting a wagon that pulled out in front of them.

She spared a glance at Jack. He had their lives in his hands, but he looked completely at ease—and he clearly wasn't going to slow his pace. Arguing would only distract him from his driving. She had a strong sense of self-preservation. She held her tongue.

And she prayed.

Once they were free of the London traffic, they went even faster. The wind blew Shakespeare's ears straight behind him and his tongue lolled out so he looked as if he was grinning.

And then it took Frances's hat—she couldn't spare a hand to hold it on her head.

"Don't worry," Jack said, laughing. "We'll get you another."

Frederick's old hat was hardly nice enough to provide a nest for a mouse. "How do you keep yours on?"

"It fits me better." He sent her a sidelong glance. "Frankly, I'm surprised at how poor the quality of country-made clothing is, if yours is any example. While you're in London, we should get you some new things."

Ah yes, she'd visit a tailor with Lord Jack.

Not likely.

It would be nice if she could see some of the London sights while she was here, however, especially since this was sure to be her only trip to Town. If only she could approach her mother's family—

No. She had far too much pride to come crawling to them after they had ignored her so completely her entire life. Her grandparents were quite old and probably not in London, and her uncles . . . well, they'd washed their hands of her, too. And even if they would have recognized her at one time, they'd slam the door in her face now. She was rather a walking scandal.

She glanced down at the baby. Oh dear. The poor infant's face was so white. Her heart started to pound, and she felt a little light-headed. Was it already too late? She couldn't let go of the curricle long enough to touch him and see if he was still breathing.

Why did she care? His mother was only a whore, after all; his father, at best, some irresponsible rake. If this baby lived, he'd grow up to be a pickpocket or worse.

His face—his nose and mouth—were so tiny and perfect. He was just a baby, a poor infant whom no one cared about. She glanced at Jack. Except Jack. For some reason, Jack cared.

She heard a faint noise and looked down again.

Had the baby's eyelids fluttered? She stared, trying not to blink so she wouldn't miss any movement, no matter how slight. Yes! She'd swear his lashes stirred and his mouth moved in a weak little sucking motion.

She let out a long breath. "The baby's still alive, my lord!"

Jack grinned, his eyes on the road. "Excellent. We are almost in Bromley."

"What exactly is in Bromley?"

He shot her a quick glance before looking back at the road. "I'll tell you, but you must swear you won't breathe a word of it to anyone."

How odd. "I promise."

"I've got two houses there, actually. One for women who want to"—he paused and glanced at her—"er, change their professions and another—the one we're going to now—for abandoned children. It's not large, which is one reason I must keep it secret. I couldn't begin to take in all the poor infants who would be deposited on my doorstep if everyone knew about it."

"I see." Though she didn't really. Why would the youngest son of a duke care about helping whores and bastards? There must be something more to it . . . of course. The house must be a way for Lord Jack to hide his by-blows. Though this baby couldn't be his . . .

She shook her head. It was impossible to understand the male mind. Men, as Viola said, let themselves be led around by their cocks. Look at her father, cavorting in the South Pacific. Or worse, Frederick. He'd actually married his theater trollop, who he'd likely dump at Landsford.

Well, if he did leave his wife at Landsford, it was no business of hers. She would not be around to clean up the mess. From now on Frederick could manage the estate and deal with Aunt Viola, who would not be at all happy about the trollop.

Jack slowed the horses, turning them into a long, gravel drive that led to a sprawling country house of redbrick and stone. "Baby still all right?"

She could finally loosen her death grip on the curricle. She stroked the infant's soft cheek. The baby turned—

"Oh!" She jerked her hand back. "He started sucking on my finger."

"An excellent sign. Ah, and here is our welcoming committee."

A stout man with silver hair and an enormous nose came out the front door accompanied by a crowd of little girls and a brown-haired young woman in a severe gray frock. The little girls, dressed in a bright rainbow of colors, ran ahead laughing toward the curricle. If it wasn't February with snow still on the ground, they could pass for a human flower garden.

Not all these children could be Jack's. He might be London's premier rake, but even so, he couldn't have *this* many daughters, could he? Yet each little girl looked as delighted to see him as if she were indeed greeting her own father.

Or so Frances assumed. She couldn't know for certain; she'd never seen *her* father.

Shakespeare leapt up and barked enthusiastically.

"Sit, sir," Jack said, and the dog plopped his bottom back onto the seat, his tail thrashing back and forth. He was ready to jump down into the crowd the moment he was given permission.

"Milord, Milord Jack!" the girls called.

"Look, Milord Jack's got a doggie," a girl with blond braids said. She looked at Frances. "And another boy." This was not said with the same enthusiasm.

"Girls, *please*," the woman in the gray frock said when she caught up. "Lord Jack wants to see your best manners."

"No, he don't, Miss Bea." A chubby girl with a mop of bouncing black curls frowned up at the woman. "He don't want to see our best manners; he wants to see *us*."

"*Doesn't*, Jenny. He doesn't want to see your best manners." The woman laughed, her face softening so that she looked quite beautiful. "Oh dear, you are managing to twist me up." She must be the girls' teacher. She looked to be about Frances's age.

"But you are both correct," Jack said. "I do like to see the girls' best manners, but I most want to see them."

Oh. For some reason a lancing pain twisted in her heart. If only her father . . .

Stupid! She was a grown woman. She didn't need a father. She had done very well without one for her twenty-four years.

"Milord." The stout man finally reached them. He was puffing with effort and his face was red. "We didn't"—he gasped for a breath—"expect you." He took hold of the horses.

"I didn't expect to come, Joseph." Jack climbed down, and the little girls immediately latched onto him, hugging whatever part of his person they could reach. "Hey now," he said, laughing, "I was just here last week." He picked up what looked to be the smallest child, a girl of perhaps three. "How are you, Anna?"

Anna smiled around the thumb stuck in her mouth and laid her head on Jack's shoulder.

"I'm so sorry to disturb your lessons, Miss Weatherby." He smiled at the teacher, and the woman blushed. Of course she did. Jack was looking at her as if he really saw her, his smile warm and personal, not the perfunctory expression of a lord to a servant.

Hmm. The woman was likely far more than a teacher to Jack.

Frances suddenly felt extremely out of sorts.

Chapter 5

The truth always comes out eventually.
—Venus's Love Notes

"Would you take the baby from Francis, Miss Weatherby?" Jack asked. Thank God Bea had come out. All his teachers were good, but not all of them were good with babies. Bea was, not that she could help this infant with what he most needed at the moment. "And tell Mrs. Understadt we'll want a wet nurse immediately."

"Baby?" Bea looked at the blanket in Francis's arms. "Oh dear." She hurried over to take the infant and then frowned at the excited, chattering bevy of little girls bouncing around him. "I . . ."

"Don't worry. I'll take charge of your pupils."

"Thank you, milord." She gave him one of her fleeting smiles and hurried away to find the capable woman who ran the home for him.

It had been a good day when he'd met Bea at the Blue Maiden, one of the better brothels. Ned's wife and son had just died, and he'd been in the deep dismals. Bea had been exactly what he'd needed—quiet and restful. Unfortunately, most men did not value those traits in a bedmate. Three months after their first meeting, just after he'd purchased this house, he stopped by the Blue Maiden as Madam Celestine was throwing Bea out into the street.

Fortunately, Bea was a much better teacher than whore.

"Did you bring us sweets, Milord Jack?" Jenny asked, tugging on his breeches to get his attention.

"Not this time, Jenny. I'm afraid I came out in a bit of a rush."

Jenny, dressed in her favorite blue, smiled up at him. She was six, with dark hair, blue eyes, and an indomitable will, thank God. Her spirit—and her strong lungs—had saved her. A year ago, he'd heard her screaming when Lord Botsley, rumored throughout the *ton* to like little girls far too much, was forcing her into his carriage. She'd even bitten the bastard's hand hard enough to draw blood.

Botsley hadn't wanted to give up his prize, but Jack had persuaded him—with his fists. He'd knocked him unconscious into the muck of a London gutter. Damn, that had felt good.

Botsley had been forced to flee to the Continent a few weeks later, after he'd touched a peer's daughter instead of a whore's, but rumor was he was back in Town. Could he be the Silent Slasher? He'd never killed as far as Jack knew, but his heart was certainly black enough.

Someone—little Eliza—tugged on his other leg. "Can I pet the doggie?"

He glanced back at the curricle. Shakespeare was still sitting on the seat. Francis, now free of the baby, was risking fleas by wrapping an arm around him to keep him from jumping down. He barked and tried to get up when he saw Jack looking at him.

"Not until I know if he has good manners, Eliza. I found him only an hour or two ago in Hart Street."

"Oh." Eliza nodded. He'd found her in Hart Street, too, when she'd been about three. None of the women in Covent Garden had seen the little red-haired girl before, so they'd speculated her mother had abandoned her there after being unable to get her admitted to the London Foundling Hospital. Perhaps Eliza's mother had heard that children left in Hart Street disappeared, and that was all she'd wanted.

He looked down at Eliza's upturned face with its sprinkling of freckles and wondered for the hundredth—the thousandth—time how a mother or a father could abandon their child, especially a child as sweet as Eliza.

"Who's the boy with the doggie?" Jenny asked.

"That's Francis." He looked back up at the lad. "Climb down and come into the house with us, Francis. You must be hungry—we'll have some nuncheon before we head back to Town."

The boy looked reluctant to leave his seat. "What about Shakespeare?"

"He can stay out here with the carriage. Mr. Understadt will keep an eye on him, won't you, Joseph?"

"Of course, milord. Shall I get one of the lads to walk the horses?"

"Yes, if you would. I'm afraid we can stay only half an hour—an hour at the outside—so there's no point in stabling them." He turned back to the crowd of little girls. "And now, ladies, you must be cold, and in any event, Miss Weatherby will have my head if I don't shepherd you all inside, so do come along."

* * *

Frances watched the tall man move off with the crowd of skipping, chatting, laughing little girls. The small one he was carrying—Anna, he'd called her—patted his cheek with her tiny hand, the one not attached to the thumb firmly lodged in her mouth, before putting her head back down on his shoulder.

Was at least one of the little girls his? Anna, perhaps?

"Ye best get down, lad," Mr. Understadt said. "And here, Miss Eliza has stayed behind to see you safely inside."

Sure enough, the little girl with the red hair and freckles was waiting for her.

Frances climbed slowly down from the curricle. Shakespeare jumped down after her and sat at her feet.

"He looks like a very smart doggie," Eliza said. "Does he do any tricks?"

"I don't know. As Lord Jack said, we just met him." Frances looked down at the dog, too—anything to avoid Eliza's far-too-direct gaze.

Why had the little girl stayed behind? Children were unpredictable; they made her nervous. She'd always had trouble talking to them. Unlike Jack. He made dealing with the girls look so natural and effortless.

She frowned. But then perhaps a rake could charm females of any age.

"You'd best be going inside, Miss Eliza," Mr. Understadt said. "You don't want milord to have to come back for you."

"But I'm taking Mr. Francis in." Eliza smiled at Shakespeare and held out her hand. "Do you shake hands, doggie?"

Before Frances could snatch the little girl's fingers back, Shakespeare had put his paw in her grasp.

Eliza squealed with glee. "He *does* do tricks, Mr. Francis! We'll have to show everyone." She patted Shakespeare's head. "Good doggie."

"I'm still not sure Lord Jack will want the dog to come inside, Eliza." Frances looked to Mr. Understadt for confirmation. "I could stay out here with him."

She'd much rather stay out here. It had been hard enough to pretend to be a boy when she'd had only Jack to fool. The incident with the whores had been a nightmare, but at least it had been brief. But if she went into the house, she'd be surrounded by any number of children and their teachers. She'd be discovered in a matter of moments.

Mr. Understadt shrugged. "Seems like the dog's no danger. You go on. If he follows you inside, then that's what he does."

"I don't know. I—" She glanced down, startled. A small hand had snuck into hers.

"Come on, Mr. Francis," Eliza said, tugging her toward the house. "We don't want to miss nuncheon."

Frances gave up and allowed Eliza to pull her along. She would just have to do her best to maintain her charade. Perhaps she could blend into the wainscoting.

Odd. It felt rather pleasant to have Eliza's hand in hers. The little girl was not like other children. She was very well behaved, almost preternaturally mature. And even though Frances knew it was extremely silly, she felt a sort of kinship with her just because Eliza had red hair and freckles like she did.

"Did Milord Jack find you on the street, too?" Eliza asked, looking up at Frances. "That's where he found me."

Dear God, the poor child. "Ah no. I was at an inn on my way to London."

Eliza nodded. "Lots of the big boys and girls go to

London to be 'prenticed to someone. Were you on your way to be 'prenticed?"

"No, I was going to visit my brother."

"Oh." She gave a little hop. "Jenny wants to be 'prenticed to a dressmaker. I don't know what I want yet. I'm only four." She skipped a few steps. "'Course, I don't know how old I am for sure. Milord Jack guesses I'm four." She looked up at Frances. "How old are you?"

"Ah . . ." She did not want to lie to the little girl, but she couldn't tell the truth. Eliza might let it slip when she saw Jack. "Older than four."

Eliza accepted that, moving on to a new topic. "We get to pick a birthday. I picked July first because I like summer. When's your birthday?"

"April fourth." She'd never considered someone might not know his birth date, but of course the baby they'd found today would never know it.

And there was no need for him to know. A birthday was just like any other day. No one had ever made a fuss about Frances's and Frederick's birthday. Still, it seemed somehow wrong not to know such a basic fact about oneself.

When they reached the house, Eliza pulled her through the door and across the entrance hall. It was a surprisingly large, airy place, much pleasanter than Frances had expected.

She heard the scrabbling of nails behind her and glanced over her shoulder. Shakespeare was still following them. Well, if Mr. Understadt wasn't concerned about the dog's presence in the house, she wouldn't be either. Lord Jack could certainly evict the animal if he wanted to.

Eliza brought her to a big, noisy room. There were four large round tables with about ten children and a teacher at each—two tables of girls and two of boys. Eliza ran off to join the little girls sitting with Miss Weatherby, leaving Frances to stand awkwardly in the middle of the floor. The baby was nowhere in sight—Miss Weatherby must have successfully handed him off to Mrs. Understadt. Where was Jack?

"Francis!" Jack called. "Over here!"

He was sitting with the older boys and their tutor, a man about her age. Oh damn. The boys were still children—the oldest looked to be at most twelve—but they had sharp eyes, and their tutor was obviously an expert in dealing with young males. If she wasn't very, very careful, her masquerade would come to a very public, very embarrassing end.

She would keep her eyes on her plate. At least Lord Jack had saved her the place next to him.

"Look! He's got a dog!" one of the boys called.

All the children turned to stare, and some stood up to get a better look, until their teachers bade them take their seats again. But at least they ignored her. She slipped into her seat.

"I'm sorry, my lord," she said. "Shakespeare followed me, and Mr. Understadt said it would be all right if he came inside."

"Well, I'm afraid he's causing a bit of a commotion. Sit, Shakespeare, and behave."

Shakespeare sat down and looked from Jack to Frances and back, his brows tented, his eyes sorrowful.

"I think he's hungry," the boy on the other side of Jack said.

Shakespeare's ears twitched and his tail beat a hopeful tattoo.

Did the boy have Jack's eyes?

No, of course not. He had to be close to twelve, which would have put Jack at fourteen when . . .

She glanced at Jack, and then took a bite of her nuncheon. Was it physically possible for fourteen-year-old boys to become fathers?

She took another bite. The food was excellent—far better than what she was used to at Landsford. If this were a planned visit, she'd think the cook had taken special pains with the meal, but Jack's presence had been completely unexpected.

It would appear Jack was a surprisingly generous benefactor.

"Can he beg for his food?" the boy next to Frances asked.

"I don't kno—"

The boy didn't wait for her to finish. He picked up a bit of meat and showed it to Shakespeare. The dog immediately held up his front paws.

"I guess he can," she said.

The boy gave Shakespeare the treat, which he devoured in two bites. Then he lowered his head as if he was bowing.

Jack laughed. "He *was* an actor's animal. I wouldn't be surprised if Mr. Dutton earned a shilling or two from Shakespeare's performances."

"Can he beg for me?"

"No, for me!"

The boys were leaping out of their seats in excitement. She'd never seen Frederick behave this way when he was a boy.

Of course she hadn't. Viola would have sharply told him to mind his manners—but he never was at meals with them anyway. He was always out in the fields looking at weeds.

These boys had come out of the stews, likely all the children of prostitutes. They seemed very healthy and happy.

Their tutor raised his hand for quiet. "Boys, the poor dog will explode if you all feed him."

"Yes, Mr. Pedley," the boys said in a rather dispirited tone.

"But perhaps he does some other tricks, my lord?" Mr. Pedley asked.

"Not that I know of. Does he do any other tricks, Francis?"

"He shakes hands." Jack was at ease with the boys, too. And they were at ease with him. He must come here frequently.

Visiting a place like this seemed an odd activity for a rake, even if some of the children were his. Her father certainly had never bothered to visit *his* children.

"Splendid." Lord Jack grinned and beckoned a thin girl of about ten over. "Mary, would you like to meet Shakespeare?"

Mary solemnly took Shakespeare's offered paw.

The children called out other tricks, and Shakespeare could do them all—roll over, walk on his hind legs, talk, sing, and chase his tail. One of the older boys offered the final suggestion.

"Play dead, Shakespeare," he said.

The dog's ears pricked up, and he immediately collapsed. The children laughed and cheered.

A few minutes went by. Shakespeare continued to lie on the ground, apparently lifeless.

"How do you suppose we resurrect him?" Jack asked.

The children had started to whisper, and a few of the girls looked as if they might cry. Clearly something had to be done, but Jack did not appear to be the least concerned.

"Shakespeare," Frances said. "Come here."

Nothing.

"Do you want some ham, Shakespeare?" one of the older boys called.

Still nothing.

Little Eliza left her table to stand almost on poor Shakespeare's tail. "Get *up*, doggie."

Those were the magic words. Shakespeare jumped up so quickly, Eliza fell over onto her bottom. She looked as if she might cry—until the dog licked her face. Then she squealed with glee and wrapped her arms around Shakespeare's neck, burying her face in his fur . . . briefly.

"Eew." She wrinkled her nose. "Doggie smells."

"I'm afraid poor Shakespeare is desperately in need of a bath, Eliza," Jack said, standing. "He's not fit company for a lady such as yourself."

Frances got up, too. Thank God they were leaving.

Eliza scrambled to her feet and patted Shakespeare on the head. "Come back when you're nice and clean, doggie."

"Yes indeed." A thin, gray-haired woman who'd been standing by the door for the last few minutes came over. "I do hope you'll bring Shakespeare to visit again, my lord, but now the children must return to their lessons."

The older boys groaned.

Jack laughed. "Indeed they must, Mrs. Understadt, and Francis and I must get back to London." He paused, his brows raised, his face expressionless—except for his eyes. They gleamed with mischief. "I don't suppose you'd like to have a dog?"

Mrs. Understadt smiled. "Thank you, my lord. You are very generous, but I'm afraid this particular animal would be too great a distraction for our students."

The children, particularly the older boys, grumbled, but stopped the moment Mrs. Understadt held up her hand. "However, we look forward to seeing him again—after a bath, of course."

Jack bowed. "Of course."

Mrs. Understadt walked them to the door as the children filed out to class. Jack's smile vanished with the last child.

"How's the baby, Ursula? Did you find a wet nurse for him? What does the doctor say?"

Mrs. Understadt smiled. "He was able to nurse, so that's a good sign. The doctor is cautiously hopeful. Where did you find the poor mite?"

"Leg Alley. If Shakespeare hadn't kept him warm, I'm sure he would have died of the cold."

Mrs. Understadt reached down to pat Shakespeare's head. "That was by far your greatest trick, sir."

Shakespeare barked and wagged his tail furiously.

"I think he likes you, Ursula. You're sure you wouldn't care to have a pet?"

"No, thank you, my lord. The children you bring me are enough for me to handle." She turned to smile at Frances. "And who is this young man?"

Blast it! She'd hoped to make it out the door without drawing the woman's attention.

"My lamentable manners!" Jack said. "Let me make known to you Master Francis Haddon. Master Haddon, Mrs. Understadt."

Frances tried to execute a passable bow.

"I'm delivering the lad to his brother—or at least trying to do so," Jack said. "The fellow moved without leaving his new direction."

"Oh dear, how vexing. We'd be happy to keep Master Haddon with us until you locate his relative, my lord. Mr. Pedley won't mind, and I'm sure the other boys would be delighted to welcome him." Mrs. Understadt smiled at Frances again. "Would you like that, Master Haddon?"

Frances's blood turned to ice. Live in a dormitory with a group of boys and a man close to her real age? There would be no hope of hiding her gender. "I-I r-really think . . . that is, thank you, but . . ." She looked at Jack, not caring that her eyes probably shone with panic. "I do think it's best if I return with you to London, my lord." She turned to Mrs. Understadt. "But I thank you very much for your kind offer."

The ice in her veins traveled to her heart. If Lord Jack decided she should stay, he would leave her here. Mrs. Understadt would probably take her by the ear and drag her into class. In their eyes, she was a child. She had no say in what happened to her.

She had even less power than she had as a woman.

Well, she was not a child. If she had to, she'd reveal her identity. It would be terribly embarrassing, and Lord Jack would be furious at being hoodwinked. Perhaps she could wait to tell Mrs. Understadt in private . . .

No. The woman would be sure to send for Lord Jack the moment the words were out of Frances's mouth, and he would come storming back to drag her home to Landsford. Unfortunately, he did not seem the sort to simply wash his hands of her.

And then, when the villagers and the gentry and Littleton and Aunt Viola saw him with her . . .

Her stomach tightened into a hard knot.

Everyone would whisper about how the scandalous Miss Hadley was in the company of the greatest rake in London—and had been in his company long enough to be ruined several times over. There would be a race to see who could give her the cut direct first.

A large, warm hand grasped her shoulder.

"Hey." Lord Jack shook her slightly. "Don't worry, lad. I won't leave you if you can't like it." He ruffled her hair. "Everything will be all right."

Somehow she very much doubted that.

"Indeed," Mrs. Understadt said. "Lord Jack has eyes and ears everywhere. He'll find your brother, Master Haddon."

And then he'd find out she was Frederick's twin sister.

Blast it, she was beginning to feel as though she was trapped in a room where every exit was locked.

"We'd best be off," Jack said. "It's a pleasure to see you again, Ursula. Send word on how the infant goes on, will you?"

"Of course, milord, though at this point no news is good news. As you know, it will be a while before we can be certain whether the child will flourish." She stepped outside with them. "What do you wish to name him?"

Shakespeare, apparently losing patience with their slow progress, trotted on ahead. Jack grinned.

"I think he should bear the name of his savior, don't you?" Jack said. "William Shakespeare."

Jack set the carriage bowling back down the road to London. That was excellent news about the baby. Sometimes the infants he found were too weak to take the nipple, and when that happened with a baby so young, the outcome was usually not good. But now he felt extremely hopeful about young William Shakespeare's future.

And as to the future of the boy sitting next to him . . . He glanced at Francis. The lad looked distinctly blue-deviled. He hadn't said a word since they'd parted with Ursula.

Well, of course he was down pin. His plans had fallen all to pieces. Yes, Francis should have considered that his brother might not be where he expected him to be, but he was only a boy, and young boys rarely foresaw problems ahead.

Thank God Mrs. Findley had asked him to escort the lad to Town. If Francis had arrived alone in Covent Garden—

It didn't bear thinking of. His boys—the ones they'd just

left—would have managed. They knew their way around the darker parts of London. But Francis was far too green.

"Do you have any idea at all where your brother might be?" Jack asked.

"No."

"Any idea whom he might have married?"

A ray of sunlight glanced along the boy's smooth cheek and soft chin, making him look sadly feminine. Well, a few more years should solve that problem.

But thinking of females . . .

He should put the word out about Pettigrew's anonymous girl, the one who bolted rather than marry Littleton. Perhaps there was still hope for her.

"Not the faintest." The boy's voice was bitter. "The landlady said she was a theater trollop."

That might explain why Francis's brother hadn't mentioned his nuptials. "If she was connected to the theater, the marriage was probably talked about in the neighborhood. I'll ask around. Someone should recognize your brother's name."

Francis's face turned white. Damn.

"Are you all right?" He didn't want the boy fainting and falling out of the carriage.

"Yes. Of course." Francis looked down at his hands. His jaw flexed—clearly, he did not wish to discuss the matter.

The curricle rolled along in silence. They'd reached the outskirts of London, and traffic was picking up. Jack tried to focus on his driving, but it was hard to ignore Francis. The boy radiated tension—and guilt. He was definitely keeping something important from him.

"Francis—"

"Watch out!"

A man stepped almost directly in front of the curricle. Blast! Jack jerked on the reins.

"Ye bloody idiot!" The fellow shook his fist at them. "Watch where yer goin'!"

Jack was sorely tempted to cast aspersions on the man's parentage and intellect, but he bit his tongue. He didn't wish to teach Francis any new words nor waste his breath. The dolt was clearly drunk as an emperor.

Apparently Francis did not approve of his restraint. The boy swiveled around to glare at the man's back. "What a clodpate! Did you see? He didn't look right or left when he stepped off the curb. If you weren't such an excellent whip, you would have flattened him. Why didn't you tell him so?"

Was the lad going to run back and defend his honor? The martial light in his eyes certainly suggested it, but then young boys were often quick to take offense.

"What purpose would that have served? Shakespeare, please!" The dog decided he, too, should share his thoughts with the tosspot, who'd now made it into the public house that had been his goal. "I appreciate your defense, but you are deafening me."

Thankfully, Shakespeare subsided. Francis did not.

"But he was *wrong*."

"Yes, and he was also drunk. Let it go."

The boy's jaw hardened. "If I were a man—" He bit his lip and flushed bright red.

"You'll be a man soon enough, and by then I hope you'll have learned not to take umbrage at every little slight. Save your anger for important things."

Like abandoned children and desperate women.

He'd started his houses because he'd been angry at a fate that had taken his brother's wife and child, but now he took so much satisfaction from them, especially the foundling home. It was humbling, yet inspiring to see how lively the children were, so different from the way they'd been when he'd found them. He always felt so encouraged after he visited. He should—

Good God, would his hearing survive this trip? Now Shakespeare was taking violent exception to a cur on the walkway. "Shakespeare, stop or I swear I shall throw you overboard."

The dog must have believed him, because he gave one parting shot and then resumed his seat, looking rather pleased with himself. Well, he *was* riding in a stylish curricle while the other mongrel was running in the dirt.

It was unfortunate Shakespeare did not look a bit more stylish himself. They'd now reached the shopping district, and Jack could foresee how the tale that he was tooling around London with a mangy mongrel and a young boy would set the gossips' tongues to running on wheels.

Perhaps he would be lucky. Perhaps no one would be out shopping today.

Perhaps the moon was made of cheese.

Lady Dunlee, London's premier gossip, was the first person he saw, promenading with her good friend and equally talented gossip, Melinda Fallwell. Lady Dunlee's eyes widened as she caught sight of them, and her jaw actually dropped. Bloody hell.

She waved. Jack waved back. Best act as if everything was perfectly unremarkable—except the women were already remarking to each other about the odd sight he and his companions presented.

Oh blast. To top it all off, here came Pettigrew.

"Jack!" Pettigrew shouted.

Francis stiffened and drew in a sharp breath. Any passersby who had not yet noticed them stopped to stare. Wonderful.

Pettigrew rode up and turned his horse so he could continue along beside them. He looked a bit nervously at

Shakespeare. "Where did you get the dog? He's not quite the thing, you know."

Shakespeare growled. Francis looked as if he'd like to growl.

Jack quite understood. Pettigrew seemed to bring out the worst in everyone. "See? You've offended Shakespeare." He wouldn't mention Francis's reaction. "I'll have you know he's quite accomplished, though I will admit he could stand to have a bath."

Shakespeare's ears twitched at the word "bath." Damn. He did hope the animal wouldn't put up too much of a protest when he encountered soap and water. Richard and William, his two sturdiest footmen, would not thank him if they got soaked.

"If you say so." Pettigrew didn't bother to mask his distaste; Shakespeare didn't bother to stop growling—in fact, he progressed to a snarl.

Pettigrew ignored him, looking instead at Francis. His brows rose, and his expression turned into something remarkably like a leer. Bloody hell, the fellow didn't have that proclivity, did he?

"Haven't found the"—Pettigrew waggled his brows—"boy's brother yet?"

Or perhaps he was merely drunk.

Shakespeare snarled more loudly, punctuating his displeasure with a few well-placed barks.

"Shakespeare, some manners, please!" Jack said. Pettigrew was still staring at Francis, and Francis was glaring back at him, though the boy's face was very pale.

Perhaps he should encourage Shakespeare to use his teeth to advantage on Pettigrew's person. "Yes, well, it turns out the brother married and moved away. The landlady has no idea where he's gone."

"Married, eh?" Pettigrew was *still* looking at Francis with that odd light in his eyes. "Speaking of marriage, my poor friend Littleton, the one who had the shrewish spinster bolt on him—"

Had Francis just flinched? The boy dropped his eyes to stare down at his hands, his face now completely white. He wasn't going to faint, was he? Jack tried to put a hand on his arm, but Francis leaned away from him.

"—has come to Town to shop the Marriage Mart."

Ah, well, perhaps it was a good thing they'd encountered Pettigrew. If the man was finally willing to share information about the runaway girl, Jack might be able to find her and offer some help. "Has anyone had word that the girl is safe?"

Pettigrew actually chuckled. Bloody hell, the villain had no heart.

"No, but I'm quite sure she's landed on her feet—or perhaps her back."

"Ohh!"

Jack jerked his head around to look at Francis. The boy had one hand over his mouth and the other clutching his stomach.

"I believe we'd best be going." He should get Francis to Greycliffe House as soon as he could.

Pettigrew was already backing away. "Yes. Do take good care of the . . . boy." He waggled his damn brows again and rode off.

If the man wasn't drunk, he was touched in the head. Perhaps he'd had a fall on the ride up to Town.

Jack encouraged his cattle to pick up their pace. He would prefer not to entertain the *ton* with the spectacle of Francis shooting the cat in his curricle. "That came on suddenly."

Francis, having hidden his face in his hands, just nodded. At least Shakespeare, after a "good riddance" bark to Pettigrew, had regained his equanimity.

"Are you feeling better now?"

Francis nodded again.

"Maybe you have a touch of travel sickness. Hold on. We'll be at Greycliffe House shortly."

"Um."

It was odd Francis had taken ill so suddenly. The boy hadn't shown any signs of sickness coming up from the Crowing Cock or on this trip to Bromley. In fact, he'd been fine until they'd encountered Pettigrew.

Hmm. The runaway woman . . . Pettigrew's odd behavior . . .

Oh *God*.

Jack's head snapped round to regard Francis—his long, thin hands and narrow shoulders, his smooth cheeks without even the faintest hint of a beard. He was a pretty boy, or . . .

Of course.

How could he have been so blind? So *stupid*? Back at the Crowing Cock, Francis had looked ill when Pettigrew had mentioned a Frederick Hadley, a man whom Francis apparently resembled and whose only sibling was his twin ginger-haired sister.

Francis—no *Frances*—had some explaining to do.

Chapter 6

There is always a price to pay when one tinkers with the truth.

—Venus's Love Notes

Lord Jack was angry. Frances glanced at him as they turned off the main road. He didn't *look* angry, but she could tell he was. There was a tightness about his face that hadn't been there before. A coldness. He hadn't said a word since they'd left Mr. Pettigrew.

He had guessed her secret.

No, she would not leap to that conclusion. He'd been in her company—she flushed—in her bed, and he'd given no indication that he suspected she was anything other than a grubby schoolboy.

If he had guessed, he'd probably have tried to seduce her. That was what rakes did with women, and one only need read the newspapers to know Lord Jack was a rake of the worst sort: his exploits were recorded in print regularly. Lord J—seen escorting *two* ladies onto the dark terrace at Lady So-and-So's ball. Lord J—glimpsed driving down Rotten Row with the fair proprietress of the Gilded G—.

And she'd seen with her own eyes on what easy terms he was with all manner of light-skirts. He was likely as irresponsible as her father, taking his pleasure wherever he wished, not thinking twice about the women and children he left behind.

Well, no, he wasn't as bad as her father. There was the house in Bromley, and the children who clearly loved him—and for whom he just as clearly cared deeply.

He was probably just annoyed by Mr. Pettigrew, who was certainly an extremely annoying man. Even Shakespeare, who'd been perfectly behaved with the children, had taken Mr. Pettigrew in sudden and extreme dislike.

She must remain calm and keep acting her part. She'd have to stay the night at his family's house, unchaperoned; she didn't wish to be ravished in her bed.

Her stomach shivered.

With *anxiety*. Of course she didn't wish to be ravished. It sounded like a very uncomfortable experience, not that she perfectly understood what was involved.

She would persuade Lord Jack to take her to Puddington's offices in the morning—no, she would ask him to send her in a hackney. Of course! That was the perfect solution; he'd never discover her gender that way. And surely Puddington's offices weren't in a dangerous section of London, so there would be no need for him to escort her.

Now all she had to do was keep up her masquerade for a little while longer, and then she'd retire early and take dinner on a tray in her room. In the morning she'd go off to see Puddington, and that would be the end of Lord Jack's involvement in her life.

She felt an odd twinge of sadness, but she repressed it. The sooner she was free of the rake, the better. His animal magnetism, or whatever it was, was clearly affecting her thinking.

They'd reached a broad square with a lovely fenced garden—more of a park, really—in its center. Jack brought his horses to a stop in front of the largest house, and a footman ran out to hold them, as if he'd been watching for Jack to arrive.

"Welcome back, milord."

"Thank you, Jacob."

Frances started to climb down, but Jack's hand clamped around her wrist like iron. She met his eyes. They were as cold as the day, flat and hard.

"A moment, *Miss* Hadley, and I will assist you."

Oh God! Her heart lurched into her throat. He *had* guessed. What the devil was she going to do now?

He released her and swung himself down to the pavement, Shakespeare on his heels.

She could defy him. She *should* defy him. She was quite capable of getting down by herself, as he well knew. Except her legs seemed to have turned to jelly.

He wouldn't abuse her. She was relatively certain of that, though not completely certain. If she'd had any hope of fleeing—if she could have slid across the seat, picked up the reins, and stolen his curricle—she would have. But she had no idea how to drive a curricle—not that the footman would let go of the horses—and she had no place to flee to.

She was trapped, so she would cooperate for now. She did not care to stoke his anger to any hotter a flame.

He came to her side and extended his hand, his face a pleasant mask. Anyone observing them from a distance wouldn't think twice about the scene—unless they wondered why Lord Jack would be helping a boy descend from his curricle. But if they could see the man's eyes . . .

His eyes promised a very unpleasant interview ahead.

The moment her foot touched the ground, he dropped her fingers and turned to lead the way inside.

She scowled at his back. He had no cause to be in such a pet. Yes, she'd hoodwinked him, but she'd cozened the Findleys, Mrs. Understadt, and any number of other people as well.

But he was a man, and men hated to be made fools of. He was likely berating himself for not seeing through her disguise instead of admitting that she'd done a good job of pretending to be a boy. So she would assuage his male pride. She would apologize profusely, grovel if she had to.

If only she had somewhere else to stay tonight. If she could avoid crossing his threshold at all, she would. There *was* her mother's family. Lord Jack was a friend of her cousin. He would know how to reach them . . .

No. She'd rather risk being ravished in her bed than knock on their door and face their disdain.

She followed Shakespeare through Greycliffe House's front door, and her jaw dropped.

She snapped it shut immediately, but the fact remained she'd never seen such an impressive house, with its high ceilings, broad staircase, and imposing artwork—statues and urns and paintings. A larger-than-life portrait of a Greycliffe ancestor glared at her from the first landing.

Landsford wasn't a cottage, but this house had been built to an entirely different scale.

The butler greeted them with what she would have thought a very unbutler-like grin. "Lord Jack, it is so good to have you home."

Jack grinned back, and she felt a momentary pang. He wouldn't be smiling at her like that again.

"It's good to be here, Braxton."

"And how was Her Grace's party?"

"Painful as always for me, but Mama got one of her dearest wishes. Ned is betrothed to Miss Bowman."

Mr. Braxton's grin widened and his eyes lit. "That is capital news, milord! Her Grace must be beside herself with joy, and of course we are all delighted for Lord Ned." He cleared his throat. "You know, of course, that Her Grace must have already turned her thoughts to your unmarried state."

Jack glanced at Frances and nodded. "Yes, I'm afraid you're right."

Mr. Braxton raised his brows. "I see you have brought along a young person and a dog, milord?"

"Yes. The dog's name is Shakespeare, and he is in desperate need of a bath, as you may be able to tell. I was hoping . . . ah, Richard."

A tall footman, having just come in from the back of the house, stopped. He looked at Shakespeare with a resigned expression. "Yes, milord?"

"Please take this animal off and bathe him."

Richard looked at Jack. "Does he like water, milord?"

"Unfortunately, I have no idea, but I'm sure you'll be able to manage splendidly. He's relatively well behaved and rather talented." He looked down at the dog. "Will you shake hands, Shakespeare?"

Shakespeare offered his paw to Richard and then to Mr. Braxton.

"He's a very bright animal, milord," Richard said, looking somewhat more enthusiastic.

"Yes. Now please take him away and make him a clean animal. You may bring him to my study once he's presentable."

"Yes, milord."

Shakespeare was at first reluctant to depart, but once Richard thought to bribe him with a bit of cheese from the kitchen, he left with good grace.

Mr. Braxton inclined his head toward Frances. "And the young person, milord?"

"Yes." Jack looked at her and then at his butler. "This is Miss Hadley, Braxton. I'm sure I don't need to point out the need for discretion?"

The only sign of Mr. Braxton's surprise was the slight widening of his eyes. "Of course not, milord. I'm offended you should ask."

Jack smiled. "I inquired mostly to put Miss Hadley's mind at ease, Braxton. We'll be in the study. Could you send some refreshments up at once and then Mrs. Watson in about fifteen"—he looked at Frances—"no, twenty minutes?"

"Very good, milord."

"Thank you. This way, Miss Hadley."

Would Lord Jack offer her a piece of cheese or some other enticement to come with him if she proved as recalcitrant as Shakespeare?

She repressed a slightly hysterical giggle and followed him down the grand corridor. Perhaps she should be worried, going off alone with a rake, but suddenly that seemed rather silly. This was the Duke of Greycliffe's London house, after all. It was nothing like the house on Hart Street with the garish red walls and obscene wall sconces. And the butler, Mr. Braxton, did not strike her as the sort who would put up with any ravishment on the premises. A footman would be coming with refreshments almost immediately and perhaps Richard with Shakespeare soon thereafter, and then in twenty minutes this Mrs. Watson. Surely even a skilled rake couldn't conduct a seduction in such a short time and with so many interruptions.

And Lord Jack was far too angry to have any interest in seducing her.

So they would have this discussion in private—not that there need be any real discussion. She would apologize, ask him to procure her a hackney in the morning, and retire to whatever room he'd given her—and barricade her door just in case his rakish tendencies came out with the moon.

She followed him into a huge, wood-paneled study that had to be at least four times the size of hers back at Landsford.

No, not hers—Frederick's.

"Please have a seat, Miss Hadley." Lord Jack gestured to an uncomfortable-looking straight-backed wooden chair in front of a massive mahogany desk.

"You may as well keep calling me Frances." She sat on the edge of the chair. It was just as uncomfortable as it looked.

"Is that your name?" Jack took the upholstered chair behind the desk, of course.

"Yes. With an *e* instead of an i."

A different footman brought in the tea cart.

"Just leave it, will you, William?"

"Yes, milord."

The man scrupulously avoided looking at her. She was beginning to feel invisible, damn it.

"Help yourself to some tea, Miss Hadley," Lord Jack said as the door closed behind the footman. He, of course, picked up the brandy decanter.

"*Will* you call me Frances?" She might like some brandy, too, not that she'd ever had any, but the current situation seemed to call for something stronger than tea. "You've been calling me that since we—"

Perhaps she shouldn't point out exactly when their acquaintance had begun.

Jack had no such compunction. "Yes. I've been calling you by your Christian name since we woke up in bed together."

That sounded very bad. Perhaps she *would* have some tea. She reached for the pot. "It wasn't like that, and you know it."

He just raised his damn eyebrows.

"It was perfectly innocent!"

He poured himself some brandy. "You know that and I know that, but no one else will believe it."

"Because of your reputation as a rake." It was a rude thing to say, but she was suddenly feeling trapped. She tried pouring and splashed a good bit of tea in her saucer, blast it.

His lips twisted into a harsh sort of smile, and his voice sounded slightly sarcastic. "Oh yes, my reputation. Of course I'm a rake. I'm a duke's son. I must be reckless, careless, wild—and definitely dangerous. And I'm well known to frequent London's worst stews. So, yes, no one will believe I'd spend five minutes in bed with a female without having my wicked way with her."

Damn. Her stomach suddenly felt as if she'd swallowed a cannonball. She put her cup down; she couldn't manage even a sip of tea. Oh, why, if she'd had to share a bed with a man, couldn't the fellow have been an anonymous old curate?

"But the hard truth is no one would believe any man could spend the night in bed with a woman without far more than sleep occurring, Miss Hadley. My being Lord Jack just means the story will spread like wildfire."

"But *nothing* happened." Blast it, if she was going to be pilloried, she should at least have committed the sin.

Her treacherous body stirred with interest . . .

No! She did not want to have anything to do with men . . . with a man . . . with Jack.

"That is immaterial. What's important is what everyone *thinks* happened."

"But—"

"Come, Miss Hadley—*Frances*—I can't believe that's not the case even in whatever little hamlet you call home."

"Er . . ." Of course the annoying man was right. When

Squire Adams's youngest daughter had been found at night in a gazebo, her dress disarranged and the arms of the second son of a baronet around her, Aunt Viola had begun speculating at once about how soon after the wedding the baby would arrive.

"You see? You are well and truly ruined, unless . . ." His eyes brightened. "I don't suppose by some miracle you really are twelve?"

"N-no." For a moment, she was tempted to lie, but that would be foolish. Now that he knew her identity, there was no hope of concealing anything from him. He was just the sort to ferret out every last detail of her life.

"Damn." He frowned. "My pardon."

"Oh, don't stand on ceremony at this late date, my lord." She was impressed that he'd limited himself to *damn*.

He glared at her. "I would never have treated you with such familiarity if I'd known your gender, Miss Hadley."

Oh, good God, now he was on the high ropes.

"Was Pettigrew right—your brother is your twin?"

"Yes."

"So how old are you, if I may be so bold as to ask? It's a little difficult to tell in your current guise, but since your brother is of age to marry, I assume you are, as well."

He was not going to like her answer. "I'm twenty-four."

"Ah." He closed his eyes briefly, and then took a swallow of brandy. "I see. Then I'm afraid there's no hope for it. I'll have to marry you."

"What?!" She felt as if she'd been punched in the stomach. Marry the biggest rake in London? Oh no, she was not going to marry a rake like her father. And in any event, surely that was like amputating an arm to cure a hangnail. "I don't want to marry you."

"And I don't want to marry you, but I don't have a choice, do I? No one else will have you now that I've ruined you."

"You *haven't* ruined me. I'm perfectly fine, and I—"

"Miss Hadley, you have already acknowledged that the fact you are still a virgin—" He raised a lascivious eyebrow. "I assume you *are* a virgin, not that it makes a great deal of difference to the case."

"Of course I am." How dare he think otherwise, even for an instant? "Not that it is any of your concern."

The rake merely nodded. "As I say, the fact of your virginity is completely beside the point. You—and I—can both announce it until we are blue in the face, but society thinks it knows differently, and once society has made up its mind, no amount of protestations will convince it otherwise. Believe me, I know."

She forced herself to take a deep breath. Jack was being a typical male, seeing only one solution—the most obvious one. There were always alternatives. "If you will simply put me in a hackney coach in the morning, I will go see Mr. Puddington and get the funds I came to London to procure. You need have no more to do with me. After all, hardly anyone saw us together, and those who did thought I was a young boy."

"You are forgetting Pettigrew."

"Pettigrew?" She was most certainly not forgetting that unpleasant man.

"Yes. Oliver Pettigrew, the fellow we ran into today in Cheapside, who met you at the Crowing Cock, who knows we shared a room—and a bed—there because I told him. He's clearly concluded that you're my mistress."

"That's disgusting!" She felt dirty just thinking the toad had been contemplating her. "The man's mind is a dung heap."

"Come, Miss Hadley, wouldn't even you be suspicious if you heard an unrelated man and woman shared a bed at an inn?"

She wanted to say no, but of course the answer was yes, so she simply said nothing.

Jack nodded. "Just so. And furthermore he's also identified you as Frederick Hadley's sister, Littleton's runaway bride. I'm sure he'll lay your bolting at my door." Jack took another swallow of brandy. "He'll be able to dine out on the story all this Season and perhaps next Season as well."

Blast it, if Pettigrew were in the room right now, she'd pour the contents of the steaming teapot over his head.

Jack frowned. "Why *did* you run from Littleton? Your aunt couldn't actually have been selling you to him."

"Not literally, of course." She remembered all too clearly how her stomach had knotted as she'd crouched on Mr. Turner's floor and heard Littleton and Pettigrew talk about her. Bloody scoundrels! "Aunt Viola somehow convinced the man that she could ensure I'd accept his marriage offer or she'd arrange things so he could compromise me."

She almost wished she had come face-to-face with Mr. Lousy Littleton. She'd have been delighted to treat him to the sharp edge of her tongue. "Not that I would have married him under any circumstances, of course."

"Of course." Jack clearly knew better than to contradict her; he merely raised his damn eyebrows again. "Why would your aunt do that? Does she think the man would be a particularly good match for you?"

"No." She was certain Viola had been motivated by nothing more than a desire to look to her own comfort. "I think she must have got a letter from Frederick and knew he'd married. Her 'payment' for handing me over to Littleton with my dowry was that he take her, too, and let her live at his estate."

"I see. Well, that makes an even stronger case for our marriage, I'm afraid. You clearly can't go home, even if your reputation wasn't shredded."

"I don't care about my blasted reputation." She leaned

forward. She had to get through his thick male skull and make him understand. "Pettigrew can talk all he wants. If I'm not in London, it won't make any difference."

She could *not* wed Lord Jack. She'd seen how her mother's life had been ruined by marrying a rake. Each new rumor of infidelity had taken a little more of her mother's happiness until the poor woman had died of a broken heart when Frances was seven. Her father—all men—were irresponsible miscreants who treated women little better than animals, and produced children only to abandon them. Jack's Bromley house was proof of that. Those children would not be there if they had fathers to see they were cared for.

She'd rather live without a reputation than die her mother's slow death of despair.

Jack opened his mouth, but she kept talking.

"I came to London to get my dowry money from our man of business. I plan to find a cottage somewhere and live by myself." She scowled. "I've managed the family estate for years with no help from my father or brother. Damn it, I'm the elder twin. In a sensible world, the estate would eventually be mine." She knew it was a stupid thing to say to a duke's son, but she couldn't help herself. "And I'm much more qualified to run the place than Frederick is."

"I'm sure you are. Many landowners are terrible stewards of their inheritances, but that doesn't change the rules of primogeniture." He smiled. "Frankly, I wouldn't want to trade places with my eldest brother. I'm much happier with my freedom."

Aha! Finally something he might understand. "And that's exactly what I want—my freedom. I will get my money from Puddington and sink happily back into obscurity in some little corner of the country."

"Good *God*!" Jack slapped the desk so hard a penknife

sitting on the blotter jumped—as did Frances. "I swear you are being purposefully obtuse. Rumors never stay in London. Someone always has a friend or a relative that writes home with the juiciest tidbits—and I promise you, these tidbits are very juicy indeed. Zeus, forget about personal correspondence. All one need do is read the newspaper gossip columns."

Oh. Well, yes, she'd certainly read the newspapers.

"And, as I can see you know, the papers delight in covering any scandal that has my name attached to it. People think me a rake, but they've never—until now—had such hard evidence of my complete dissipation."

She could believe that. The man was clearly a master of subterfuge. He hid his children's house in Bromley, didn't he? And his house for prostitutes. "But—but I plan to find a small cottage in some very remote village."

"No village in England is remote enough, Miss Hadley—trust me on that. And usually the smaller the place, the more the gossip rules all conversation. There's nothing else to do but talk about your neighbors and pass judgment on them. Would you really wish to have everyone shun you?"

"Well . . ." It did sound very unpleasant, but Jack was just trying to browbeat her.

"No, you would not." Jack glared at her so she couldn't look away. "And this is not just about you. My reputation is at risk here, too. No one has ever—yet—accused me of debauching an innocent, and I do not propose that they start now. You *will* marry me, Miss Hadley."

He'd been saved by Mrs. Watson.

Jack poured himself some more brandy and stared at the closed study door. He could have kissed his inestimable housekeeper. She'd arrived right after he'd pointed out the obvious to Frances—not that the prickly woman saw it as obvious, of course—and just as Frances was drawing breath to argue further. Thank God Mrs. Watson had taken her off to find some female attire, or he might have completely lost control and strangled her.

Of course now that he knew Frances—Miss Hadley—was female, he'd noticed how long her legs were. Fortunately her coat covered her derriere, so he couldn't also admire her arse.

He should not be looking at—he should not be able to see—such details of her person.

And her voice. It had been a little high for a man, but it was low, and very alluring, for a woman.

Someone scratched on the door, and he braced himself. Damn, was Mrs. Watson back so soon? Likely Frances had loped off, and he'd have to go out again to search for her. "Come."

The door swung open and a much cleaner Shakespeare trotted in, followed by Richard. Jack got up—he'd only been sitting at the desk to intimidate Frances, a trick that clearly hadn't worked—and came over to greet them.

"He hardly looks like the same dog, Richard. Thank you. Do I owe you an increase in your wages?"

Richard grinned. "I'd like to say yes, milord, but the dog was quite well behaved. I wouldn't have guessed it when I first saw him, but he seems no stranger to soap and water."

"Excellent! You put my mind at rest. Did you happen to feed him as well? Not that he should be hungry; he ate an amazing quantity only a few hours ago."

"Really, milord? He acted as if he was starving down in the kitchens. Cook quite took pity on him—and I must say we all enjoyed his tricks. Did you know he can beg?"

"Oh yes. He's quite talented. I believe his previous owner taught him how to work a crowd."

Richard nodded. "That would explain it, then. I also

took him outside to attend to his business. Is there anything else you need, milord?"

Patience? Luck? A miracle? None of those things was in Richard's power to deliver. "No, thank you. That will be all."

Jack regarded Shakespeare as Richard left. "Have you no shame, manipulating my kitchen staff in such an outrageous fashion?"

Shakespeare yawned and spread himself out before the fire.

"Apparently not." Jack grabbed the decanter and sprawled in one of the wing chairs nearby, hooking a leg over its arm. "This might be a full bottle night, my furry friend."

Shakespeare turned his head and frowned at him.

Jack sighed. "You are assuredly correct—drunkenness solves no problems, it just makes more. But damn it, Shakespeare, I do not want to marry Miss Frances Hadley." She might have long legs and a voice that called to mind the Sirens of Greek mythology, but she also had an independent, quarrelsome disposition.

Yet even if she was a model of womanly decorum—which sounded sort of nauseating, actually—he wouldn't want to wed her. He'd seen the disaster his brothers had made of their early marriages. "I'm only twenty-six, Shakespeare, and the third son. I have years before I need to consider settling down and starting my nursery." He snorted. "I've enough of a nursery already out in Bromley."

True, none of those children was his, but they still took a lot of thought and energy, and he wasn't about to give them up. Hell, most women of the *ton* would have an apoplexy just hearing about his Bromley house; they'd be as likely to visit it as to invite a night-soil man in for tea.

Miss Hadley hadn't seemed to mind his children, though. Well, she'd been trying too hard to keep her own secret to complain about a few bastards and a prostitute here and there.

He took another swallow of brandy and sank deeper into his chair, thinking about his children. Frances had been right; some men *were* irresponsible idiots—blackguards, really. He'd wager her father was of that ilk.

He wouldn't desert her like her father apparently had, but he did not want to chain himself to her for life either.

"If only I'd stayed at the blasted birthday ball, Shakespeare. Then I wouldn't have stopped at the Crowing Cock and encountered the troublesome woman." He'd be blissfully unaware of her existence—and he most certainly would not be sitting here talking to a dog.

But if he hadn't stopped at the inn, what would have happened to Frances? Somehow he doubted she'd let a little thing like a lame horse keep her from her goal, but the thought of her wandering the stews of London by herself was frankly horrifying.

"And we mustn't forget Miss Wharton, Shakespeare, much as I'd like to. You will hopefully never have the dubious pleasure of making her acquaintance, but she's the reason I fled my home in the middle of the night. At least Miss Hadley isn't trying to trap me into marriage."

No, she'd managed that trick without any effort at all.

Blast it, there must be some solution to this problem other than stepping into parson's mousetrap. Getting a life sentence for a completely innocent series of events was ridiculous.

He took another swallow of brandy. But no one would believe any of it was innocent. His damn reputation! It was completely unmerited. Well, at least now. He might have been a bit wild in his salad days, but for the last couple of years he'd lived like a monk.

Even a monk would be condemned for spending the night in a woman's bed.

"But, Shakespeare, I thought she was a *boy*!"

Shakespeare raised his brows, his large brown eyes saying most eloquently that he understood completely.

"And I'd wager most of my investments that Pettigrew has already spread the story far and wide."

He was trapped like a fox at the end of the hunt, the hounds surrounding him, ready to tear him to pieces.

"Pettigrew said Miss Hadley's twin thinks her a shrew, Shakespeare, and in my limited contact with her, I have to agree. She is extremely overbearing, a regular virago. I have no desire to play Petruchio and try to tame her." He shuddered. "I'd likely be beat about my head with her reticule, if she has such a feminine accessory."

Shakespeare gave him a reproachful look.

"Yes, I know you like her, but you're a dog." Still, Eliza had also liked Miss Hadley, and Eliza didn't like many people. She'd even trusted Frances enough to hold her hand.

But Eliza didn't have to marry the woman and live with her until death, which might come awfully quickly if he really did tie the knot.

"Look at it from my point of view, old boy." Jack counted on the fingers of the hand not holding his brandy. "One, I'm only twenty-six years old. I am far too young to marry. Both my brothers married young with disastrous consequences. Two, I hardly know the woman. Three, I don't like what I do know." That was not entirely true, but it made no difference because . . . "Four, she doesn't like me, largely due to the fact, I suspect, that five"—he held up his thumb—"she doesn't like men in general."

He was not going to put down his brandy to enumerate any more reasons. Five was more than enough. Even Shakespeare agreed. He'd laid his head on his paws, conceding the argument.

"I should wash my hands of her. If she thinks she can

live happily in a cottage by herself somewhere, who am I to gainsay her?"

But that was the brandy talking. Miss Hadley couldn't possibly know how vicious and pervasive London gossip was. He wouldn't be surprised if it reached all the way across the ocean to the Colonies. There was certainly no hope of escaping the whispers anywhere in Britain.

It was one thing to not seek company; it was quite another to be forcibly excluded from it.

"I can't let her do it, Shakespeare." He hated to see women hurt; he hated even more to be the cause of their pain. Yes, he'd had only the best of intentions—he didn't fault himself in the slightest—but his intentions were of no consequence. Her name was going to be linked to his, and because of that, her reputation would be blackened—as would his, at least among the people whose opinion he valued. "I can't let her go back to the country thinking her life will go on as blissfully as she imagines."

Shakespeare barked twice and beat his tail on the hearth in an encouraging fashion.

"But she won't let me help her." No amount of brandy could cloud his thinking on that point. Miss Hadley was completely disinclined to listen to sage male counsel. He'd wager she'd rather have sticks shoved under her fingernails first. There must be some way—

Of course! He got up and went back to the desk. Shakespeare stretched and padded after him.

"Miss Hadley may not listen to me," he said, pulling a sheet of paper out of the drawer and picking up a pen, "but she will not be able to withstand my mother. Much as I hesitate to admit it, Shakespeare, I need the Duchess of Love."

Chapter 7

Sometimes your only recourse is to surrender.
—Venus's Love Notes

"What is it, Mr. Dalton?" Venus, Duchess of Greycliffe, forced herself to smile at the butler—it helped keep the annoyance out of her voice. She thoroughly enjoyed her annual Valentine house party—this year more than ever, with three matches, one of which was Ned's—but it *was* exhausting. The last guest had finally departed, and Ned had ridden over to the vicarage with Ellie and her parents. Even Ash had left. All she wanted was to put her feet up and relax. She'd retreated to her private sitting room to be alone.

Well, not *completely* alone. Her husband was sprawled on her chaise longue, reading. He'd glanced up when Mr. Dalton entered, but had gone back to his book once he'd ascertained the butler hadn't come in search of him.

"This just arrived for you, Your Grace." Mr. Dalton held out a silver tray bearing a letter. "One of Lord Jack's servants brought it."

A letter from Jack? Her heart jerked and started to thud so hard she could barely breathe. Her vision narrowed to that white rectangle. Jack had left just last night—why was he writing now? Or was the letter written by someone else on his behalf? Had the boy crashed his curricle? Was he injured or . . . worse?

"I'm sure it's nothing serious, Your Grace," Dalton said quickly. "I did ask, and the man said Lord Jack was well."

Her breath rushed out. "I see. Thank you." She took the letter and was happy to see her hand trembled only slightly.

Dalton went off, and she looked over at Drew. He'd sat up, his finger marking his place in his book.

"What does the letter say?"

Yes, she should find out, shouldn't she? She broke the seal. "It says . . . oh! Oh my goodness. Hmm."

"Out with it, Venus. You're suddenly scowling at that poor sheet of paper, but I cannot imagine anything Jack would write that could possibly provoke such a reaction."

"Well, then you need to be more imaginative." She was not going to let some scheming, grasping hussy force her son into wedlock. "He—wisely, I suppose—committed very few details to paper. However, somewhere between here and London, he acquired a young woman and needs us to come to London with all possible haste. I think perhaps he's afraid he may need to marry her."

"What?" Thucydides's *History of the Peloponnesian War* hit the floor with a thud. "That's ridiculous. Jack's no saint, but he's not a careless rogue."

"Oh? My friends tell me he has quite a scandalous reputation." And she was quite sure her friends spared her the worst of the talk.

"Idle chitter-chatter. The *ton* loves to gossip, and if they don't have any details, they will make them up. You know that."

"Yes." That was certainly what she'd hoped. "But I also

know Jack is a bit secretive about his London dealings. Just consider that ridiculous taradiddle Ash told us about Jack having 'urgent business' in Town. What business could he possibly have that was so urgent he needed to set out on such a cold, icy night?"

Drew raised one of his eyebrows. "Well, I suspect—as I'm sure you do, too—that the urgency this time was caused by Miss Wharton. But Jack does have projects in Town, though there's nothing the least bit scandalous about them."

Venus narrowed her eyes. "You know something that you haven't shared with me?"

"Yes." Drew bent over to rescue Thucydides and put him on the table. "I am a damned duke. I hear things."

"But you're supposed to share everything you know with your wife—at least things that pertain to our sons." Venus felt—well, she wasn't sure how she felt. "Don't you trust me?"

"Of course I trust you, but this is Jack's secret. I only know by hearsay, and I don't know all the details. He will tell us if and when he wants to."

"But you *must* give me a hint!"

Drew regarded her, clearly deliberating. She pressed her lips together. As much as she wanted to, teasing him would only make him refuse to say another word.

Finally, he sighed. "Very well. I will only say that I believe he's involved in helping young women and children." He shrugged. "Perhaps this female is one of the ones he's assisting."

Venus felt a flutter of pride. She'd always hoped there was something solid and responsible under Jack's laughter and recklessness. She'd spent many a sleepless night worrying about him. At best he seemed rather careless. At worst—well, she did not care to be the mother of a rake.

She studied the letter again and shook her head. "No, I don't think so. He says so little, but . . . no. He clearly needs our help to avoid parson's mousetrap."

"Let me see."

She handed him the missive, but there was nothing to decipher. "If it was summer, I'd suggest we leave immediately, but with night coming on . . ."

He scanned the letter, brow furrowed, and then handed it back to her. "And the cold and the possibility of ice. No, we'll have to wait until morning to set off."

"I'll tell Mr. Dalton. Mary and Timms can start packing our things so we can leave as soon as the sun is up."

Drew groaned. "And here I was so happy to see the backs of our London guests. I don't know that I can stomach another dose of the *ton*—and a much larger dose, at that—so soon."

"You know you can. You'd do anything for your boys."

"Damn boys."

Venus smiled. Drew might grumble and complain, but it was very true—he *would* do anything for his sons, as would she.

"If Jack is concerned he'll be forced to marry, there must be some gossip involved. We don't want to add to that, so we can't make it look as though we are rushing to his aid. But we've never come up to London so soon after our Valentine party—and everyone knows only wild horses would drag you to Town a moment before you needed to be there." She tapped her finger against her lips—and then smiled. "Of course! We will announce Ned's and Ellie's betrothal."

"Oh, I'm sure our recently departed houseguests have already done that."

"*And* introduce Ellie to society."

Drew grimaced. "Except for that one ball gown you had

Mary make for the birthday ball, Ellie's wardrobe is . . ." He cleared his throat. "Won't Ellie need to see a lot of dressmakers before she can take her bows?"

"But where better to visit dressmakers than London? I will send word to Ellie's mother at once, and of course tell her we will foot the bill. After all, Ellie is betrothed to our son."

"Yes, and I think it would be wisest if she was very quickly married to him. The *ton* may be a great collection of idiots, but each one of them has learned to count to nine."

Venus nodded. She was quite certain Ellie had not slept in her own bed last night. "Ned can get a special license, and they can be married next week at Greycliffe House. I'm sure Ellie's parents will come up to Town for that." She grinned. "Oh, there is so much to be done!"

She was no longer feeling the least bit tired.

Mrs. Watson was not a magician nor could she spin gold from straw. Miss Hadley appeared in the small dining room wearing an oversized gray frock—clearly one of the servants' dresses—with a high neck, not-quite-long-enough sleeves, and an incongruous yellow ruffle tacked to its hem. And Jack would swear he'd glimpsed the scuffed boots she'd been wearing all day peeking out from under her skirt.

"You don't have any tall maids," Frances said, clearly noticing his startled expression at the ruffle. She scowled. "I told Mrs. Watson I could just come down in my breeches—it isn't as if you haven't seen me in them—but she wouldn't hear of it. She said you'd have her head."

Miss Hadley's tone was defensive and rather accusatory.

Jack snorted. "Mrs. Watson has been housekeeper here

since before I was born. I assure you she's far more likely to scold me for not behaving as she thinks I ought than to worry about my displeasure. But she is quite right. You can't wear the breeches." Though in her formless frock and short, ragged hair, Miss Hadley still looked like a young boy, albeit one forced to wear his older sister's clothing.

She did not provoke the slightest tremor of male interest in him—a depressing state of affairs if he was indeed going to be forced to marry her.

He gestured to the table. He'd told Braxton they'd serve themselves. The conversation was going to be awkward enough without having servants listening in. "Come sit down. I hope you don't mind that I've ordered only a light meal. I usually take a tray in the study or my room the first night I'm back in London."

"I would have been happy eating in my room," she said, taking her seat. "Where's Shakespeare?"

"I left him sleeping in the study." Jack frowned and looked toward the door. Should he have woken the animal and brought him along? Shakespeare had seemed well behaved, but . . . "I do hope Mr. Dutton taught him proper, er, manners along with all his other tricks."

"I'm sure he did. Shakespeare must have shared the man's quarters, don't you think? I can't see how he could have roamed the streets, as a general rule."

"Very true. Let's hope your theory is correct." He would check on him after dinner and ask Richard or William to take him out again. He reached for the decanter. "Would you care for some Madeira?"

"Yes, thank you." She leaned forward as soon as he moved to pour his own glass. "I'm determined to go see Puddington in the morning. You could come along if you like—I'm sure he'd be very impressed to see you and would be more likely to cooperate. And then once I have my money, I can be on my way."

He wished he could do as she asked. She'd ride out of his life, and everything would return to normal. If no one had seen them at the inn, he'd be tempted.

Whom was he trying to fool? Even if they hadn't been seen, he couldn't pretend the last twenty-four hours hadn't occurred. He couldn't ignore Miss Hadley's shock and dismay at her brother's surprise marriage, and he couldn't let her turn herself into a hermitess.

And in any event they *had* been seen.

Miss Hadley might believe nothing had changed, but she was wrong. Everything had changed. He had no choice—unless Mama found him a way out of this mess.

"No."

Her brows snapped down. "What do you mean, no?"

"No. It's a simple word—one of the first words children learn, I believe."

She looked as if she'd like to pick up the fricassee of turnips sitting by her elbow and dump it over his head.

He smiled to take the sting out of what he had to say. "We went over this in the study. I will not let you try to vanish into the countryside. Your reputation is quite ruined, but more importantly from my point of view, my reputation will be ruined if I allow you to do as you suggest." He picked up the carving knife. "May I offer you a slice of beef?"

"I am twenty-four years old, for God's sake. If I wish to live in disgrace, I can damn well do so."

"Don't shout. And it is I who doesn't want to live in disgrace." He gestured to the beef. "One slice or two?"

"One, thank you," she said through her teeth.

He tightened his hold on the knife in case she chose that as a weapon in place of the turnips.

She took a deep breath. "I do not understand why you are being so pigheaded."

He laughed as he took some beef himself. "Perhaps I am merely taking my example from you. Could you pass the turnips—after you help yourself, of course?"

She slapped a spoonful on her plate and pushed the bowl in his direction. "Why won't you help me? You must want to be free of me."

He did, but it was too late for that. Unless Mama came up with some brilliant plan, he'd never be free of her.

"I *am* helping you. I've sent a messenger with a note to my mother. She should arrive in the morning." Mama would know if there was an honorable escape for him that didn't involve meeting Miss Hadley at the altar. She was the Duchess of Love, after all, not of marital misery. "Would you like a muffin?"

"Your *mother* is coming?" Her jaw dropped, and her eyes grew so wide they really did look as though they might start from their sockets.

"I expect so." If she didn't want a muffin, he did. They were one of Cook's specialties. "I can't swear to it, of course. She *might* throw my letter in the fire, but knowing Mama, I'm willing to wager a tidy sum she'll leave Greycliffe Castle at first light and tell John Coachman to spring the horses."

"Ohh."

That sounded unpleasantly like a moan. Miss Hadley *was* a bit green about the gills.

Blast it, she wouldn't be desperate enough to try to sneak off during the night, would she? She must know that would be futile. And it was dangerous, too, especially while there was some maniac roaming the streets, killing women. He would have a word with Braxton about securing the doors.

He reached for the dish of buttered prawns. "I'm sure Father will come as well—he hates London, but he won't let Mama travel by herself. My brother Ned and Ellie, his betrothed, might accompany them, but that's less certain."

Miss Hadley had dropped her head into her hands.

"Do try Cook's buttered prawns. They are quite good."

She looked up at him. "Are you mad?"

"No, they really are extraordinary."

"What?"

"The prawns."

She actually slapped her hand on the table. "I am not talking about the bloody prawns."

"Miss Hadley, your language!"

He could almost hear her teeth grinding. "Good *God*, you are the most annoying, infuriating, unbearable man I have ever encountered."

"I find that hard to believe. Most people think me very accommodating."

"Most people are idiots." She took another deep breath. "This situation can be resolved very easily if I just go to see Puddington in the morning. You do not have to involve your family. I'm sure they will not thank you."

He took a generous helping of prawns. "Well, you're wrong there. My mother likes nothing better than to meddle, especially if there's any chance she can do a bit of matchmaking."

"Matchmaking?" Miss Hadley surged to her feet. "There will be no matchmaking." She just about spat the last word.

"Miss Hadley, please sit down. You haven't touched your food."

And now he sounded like an old nursemaid, but at least the woman resumed her seat, though she didn't pick up her fork. Instead she leaned toward him, her face red, her finger stabbing at him.

"I am not going to marry you or anyone else—ever. Can you get that through your thick skull?" She pressed her lips together and looked away for a moment, nostrils flaring.

She was most definitely a shrew. He could *not* marry her.

His stomach twisted and he put down his fork, laden with prawn. If they didn't marry, she'd be a social outcast because of him, even though it wasn't his bloody fault.

But then life didn't care about such things, did it? Look at the baby they'd found in the alley. Poor little William Shakespeare. His mother and father had got off scot-free, while the baby had almost died through no bloody fault of his own.

"You're just like everyone else," Miss Hadley said, pressing the heel of her hand against her forehead as if she had the headache. "Of course you're like everyone else. You're a duke's son."

"Er, most people aren't dukes' sons."

Her head snapped back up, and she glared at him.

Well, it was somewhat amusing to bait her. And perhaps she'd improve once she got over her pet at having her will thwarted. She'd been relatively congenial when she'd been masquerading as a boy.

And surely Mama would find a solution that didn't involve matrimony. She was very clever that way.

He smiled and picked up his prawn-laden fork again. "Your dinner is getting cold."

She ignored him. "You think all my problems will be solved if I can just get some *man*"—she might as well have said flesh-eating devil—"to marry me. Some bloody male who will get me with child and then leave me."

Ah yes, the larger problem of Miss Hadley's negative

sentiments toward the male of the species. "Not some man. Me. And I would never leave you."

"Oh."

She flushed a startling shade of red, and he suddenly had a far too graphic image of being between her long legs—

Good God, he wasn't blushing, too, was he?

"Miss Hadley—Frances—you don't have to be concerned that my mother will force you to do anything you can't like." He smiled in a friendly, comfortable, careful way, the way he smiled at the poor girls or young children he found on the streets. "I often find Mama maddening, but she *is* rather wise. I wrote her because I know she's the best person to find a way out of this mess that will cause the least damage to your reputation."

"I don't care about my reputation."

"Truly?"

"Y-yes." Her gaze wavered though. She looked down at her plate, picking up her fork to push some fricasseed turnips around.

"Frances, you saw only my foundling home today. My other house in Bromley is for girls who want to break free of the streets and learn a trade other than the one they've been forced to practice on their backs."

Frances sucked in her breath. "Are you saying I'm a, a—" Her face lost all its color.

"No, of course I'm not saying that. What I am saying is that none of those women set out to be light-skirts. Many were born into good families. Some were in service, but a few were gentry. Some lost their virtue to villainous employers, and some gave it to a man they loved who might even have promised marriage, but in every case, once they lost their reputations, they lost everything. Their families turned them out, and their friends turned them away."

"But I haven't done anything. I'm still a vir—" She flushed.

"And how are you going to prove that? We've gone over this before. Pettigrew will tell everyone we spent the night in the same room. The Findleys, who will probably be shocked and angry at your deception, will confirm that to anyone who asks. And the fact is, we *did* spend the night together."

She was even redder now. "Yes, but *nothing happened*."

He leaned forward. It was important that she understand. "Frances, people will already be shocked that you dressed as a boy and traveled by yourself. Just having that come out will put paid to your reputation."

He saw in her eyes that she knew he was correct.

But then her chin went up. "It's not fair. Yes, I made a mistake—a few mistakes—but I didn't do anything *that* dreadful."

Many people would think what she'd done to be exactly that dreadful, but it was time to give her some hope. "I'm sure my mother will be here in the morning. If anyone can get you—can get *both* of us—out of this social quagmire, she can. So may I suggest you eat something to conserve your strength?"

She took a grudging bite of beef. "You're not in any sort of mess. No one expects men to keep their virtue."

Well, yes, men weren't expected to be virgins, but there were other sorts of virtue. "We are expected to maintain our honor, however."

She snorted. "You're more likely to be ostracized for cheating at cards than taking advantage of some foolish girl from the country."

Unfortunately, there was much truth to what she said. "Perhaps, but I would consider myself dishonorable—as would my family and friends—if I ignored your plight."

"I don't know why," she said bitterly. "It's a plight of my own making."

Best not agree with that. "Let's not worry about it now. As I say, my mother is very capable; I'm willing to wager a good sum that she'll be able to find an answer to this problem. In the meantime, it might help if you tell me a little about your family." Might as well take on the major problem. "Where is your father?"

Oddly enough, she blushed—and then speared a turnip more forcefully than necessary. "I believe he's in the South Seas. He's a naturalist, studying the flora and, er, f-fauna." Her blush deepened, and she shoved the turnip in her mouth. Then she attacked her poor, defenseless beef. At least she was eating.

"Have you heard from him recently?"

Her knife screeched across her plate. "No."

"Oh." Communicating with someone so far away would be difficult in the best of circumstances—there weren't any mail packets going to and from that area—but this was clearly not the best of circumstances. "When did he leave?"

"I don't know, and I don't care." She stabbed at him with her fork to emphasize her point. "He left my mother when she was increasing with me and my brother. Apparently she wasn't very attractive with the huge belly he'd given her. And then he forgot about us."

He heard the familiar pain of an abandoned child under her anger. "That's despicable."

"Yes, it is, isn't it? And my mother never said a word against him. Can you believe it? She always told us he was a brilliant botanist, traveling all over the world, and that's why he was never home, but I saw how she cried when she read the newspapers. So once, when I was about six, I picked the paper up after she'd fled to her room in tears."

She put her knife and fork down too carefully. "Even then I was a good reader. And I was smart. When I read that scandal column, I finally understood. My father wasn't traveling the world; he was traveling London brothels, from one whore to another with an occasional detour to an accommodating widow."

Bloody hell! If Hadley senior were present, he'd gladly rearrange his face for him. Far too often he'd seen the same look of defiance and carefully cultivated indifference that was in Frances's eyes in the eyes of the children he collected from the stews.

Frances shrugged. "He must correspond with Puddington in some fashion, because the man keeps assuring me he's not yet dead. Not that it makes a great deal of difference to me. My brother will inherit the estate, even though I've been the one running it all these years." Her mouth tightened.

She'd mentioned that before. "How many years have you had charge of the place?" Frances was only twenty-four, after all.

"Ten. Warwick, the old estate manager, dropped dead in his office when I was fourteen, but he'd already shown me everything I needed to know. I'd always been interested in what he did—unlike my brother. Frederick was too busy studying the weeds in the fields to think about planting any crops."

"Good God, Puddington let you act as the estate manager when you were only fourteen?" The man was either shockingly lazy or completely incompetent. No one would allow a child to run a property. "I would have thought he'd insist on hiring a new manager."

Pride flashed in her eyes. "Oh, he did, but within hours of arriving, the man managed to offend my aunt, and she sent him packing. When Puddington got wind of it—I assume the fellow came whining to him—he rode down and realized I was quite capable of handling things, though I'll admit in the beginning he thought it was Aunt Viola who was in charge."

"That's very impressive," Jack said—and saw Frances's first genuine smile. It lit her face and made her look almost pretty.

He leaned back, done with his meal. "But you've only told me about your father's family. What of your mother's relatives?"

Frances's expression tensed. "What of them?"

"I would have thought they'd have taken more of an interest in you and your brother."

"Oh no. They cut the connection when my parents married. They did not approve of my father."

He could well believe that. He didn't approve of her father. "So they never visited?" Poor Frances. He couldn't imagine living a life so devoid of family.

"Not that I remember."

"And you've made no attempt, now that you are grown, to contact them?"

"No. If they had no use for us, I have no use for them."

Spoken by someone with a surfeit of pride.

"May I ask who your maternal relatives are?"

She hesitated and looked down at her wineglass as if it was suddenly very interesting. "Their family name is Sanderson."

"Sanderson?" Good God, it couldn't be . . . but of course it was. It made perfect sense. "You're Rothmarsh's granddaughter, aren't you?"

She tilted her chin. "Yes, I am. So you can see the problem. The marquis was not happy his daughter married a mere mister."

She had *far* too much pride, just like her mother, if his friend Trent was to be believed.

“Do you really think his reservations had anything to do with your father’s lack of title?”

She glared at him and shrugged. “Isn’t that the way of it?”

“No, it’s not.” He struggled to keep the frustrated anger out of his voice. “The marquis and marchioness and their family wanted you in their lives very much.”

She almost sneered at him. “Come, Lord Jack, how can you possibly know that?”

“Because your cousin Robert, Viscount Trent, has told me so many times.”

Chapter 8

Sometimes it pays to listen to an older and wiser woman.

—Venus's Love Notes

Frances choked down another bite of toast. She wasn't hungry, but she had to eat, just as she had to wear the same hideous dress she'd worn last night along with Frederick's old boots.

She closed her eyes, a leaden feeling settling in her stomach. She'd look like a clown. What would the duke and duchess think of her?

They were here. She'd heard a commotion half an hour ago and glanced down from her window to see an elegant traveling coach pulling up. Two couples got out, one older and one younger—Lord Jack's brother and his brother's betrothed must have come as well. She'd watched them walk inside, talking and laughing.

They'd looked happy. They'd come to save Jack from a colossal mess, and they were laughing.

They wouldn't be laughing when they met her, unless it was at her outlandish appearance.

She pushed aside her breakfast and grabbed her borrowed stays.

Why the blazes did she care what the duke and duchess, or Jack's brother and soon-to-be sister-in-law, thought? She'd never before been concerned with people's opinions, especially opinions of how she looked. Fashion plates and the ladies' magazines were for silly girls whose only goal in life was to catch a husband.

The stays had been made for someone twice her size. She tried to tighten them, but it was hopeless. She should just take them off, but then she'd feel naked, and they did take up some space in the voluminous dress. The garment hung like a sack on her—a short sack, saved from immodesty by the ruffle the housekeeper had made from an old curtain last night, which also served to hide Frederick's boots . . . somewhat.

She stood and forced herself to look in the mirror. Oh, hell. All she needed was a jester's hat and the ridiculous picture would be complete. Well, perhaps her frightful appearance would convince the Duchess of Love that she was a wildly unsuitable match for her son.

She grimaced at her repulsive reflection. Even if Jack's mother thought she was perfect for Lord Jack—which of course the duchess wouldn't—she was *not* going to marry the man. He might be handsome and charming and even kind occasionally, but he was still a rake. She refused to repeat her mother's mistakes.

Oh God, no. There was no need to borrow her mother's errors; she'd made more than enough of her own. She pressed her fingers into her forehead. What the bloody hell was she going to do? If only she could turn back the clock—

But she couldn't. She dropped her hands and reached

for the comb, dragging it through her poor, shorn locks. Perhaps Jack's mother *could* find a way out of this mess; it just had better not involve marriage. She would rather live a pariah, shunned by even the little children, than give her life over into some bloody man's keeping.

She slammed down the comb. It was hopeless. Nothing could be done to make her the least bit presentable. She turned quickly and hit her shin on the bedpost. Damn! It didn't hurt so very much, but it still caused her eyes to water.

Clearly she needed to gather her composure before she went downstairs. She'd just sit on the window seat for a few moments and take in the view before descending to her doom.

The park in the center of the square looked so peaceful. The snow in the road was rutted and dirty, but in the park it was still pristine. A couple with a dog—ah, that was Shakespeare, so the man and woman must be Jack's brother and future sister-in-law—were making their way over the slush to the park gate. If only she could be out there instead of in here.

She rested her head against the cool glass. It wasn't her dress that bothered her so very much—though it did bother her—it was what Jack had told her last night.

He wasn't right about her mother's parents, was he? He'd said her cousin had told him the marquis and marchioness had come to Landsford after she and Frederick were born, but that her mother and Aunt Viola had turned them away. That neither Viola nor Frances's father had written to tell them when her mother died. Well, her father had been in South America then—or at least that's what Viola had said—and hadn't found out for months, not that he would have cared, but Viola should have sent a note to her mother's family. They'd learned of it from Littleton's father, of all people, long after her mother had been buried in the Landsford graveyard.

Jack assured her they all would be overjoyed to meet her.

She pressed her forehead harder against the glass.

They wouldn't be, of course. If her cousin was correct in his story—and he very likely wasn't—everything had changed. Now she was dragging her own scandal with her.

They'd likely think she was just like her father.

Shakespeare and his human companions had disappeared into the park, hidden by the pine trees. She should go downstairs. There was no point in delaying any longer.

She took a few deep breaths. Yes. She should go. She would go . . . in just a few more minutes.

Venus took a sip of tea and considered her youngest son. He was sitting in the chair across from her in the blue drawing room, leaning back, one leg crossed over the other, a smile on his lips—the picture of a relaxed, composed gentleman.

He was on edge. She could tell. He had shadows under his eyes, and he was clutching a very large mug of coffee.

She tightened her hold on her teacup. She would *not* let some conniving female ruin his life. If the woman thought Jack was a target because his mother was the Duchess of Love and so would promote marriage no matter what, she was in for a very rude surprise.

"Ned and Ellie took off in a flash, didn't they?" Jack said, his foot jiggling. Another sign of nerves. "And they took my dog." His lips turned up, but the smile didn't reach his eyes. "Shakespeare is a very fickle creature."

Venus shrugged. "They are violently in love, and the dog needed a walk."

To think she'd been in alt after the birthday ball and Ned's betrothal—until the servant had arrived with Jack's letter. Less than twenty-four hours to feel all was well with her world.

That wasn't completely true. She'd been worrying about Ash, of course. Unfortunately that worry was as constant as breathing.

She reached for a slice of seedcake. One problem at a time. "When did you acquire this dog? I don't remember you mentioning it when you were home."

"Just yesterday, actually. He's quite talented. Does all sorts of tricks."

"I see." Did the dog belong to the woman he'd acquired yesterday as well? Of course he didn't say—he was too busy listing all the dog's talents. Well, she'd long ago learned that silence was often the best approach when she wanted to discover something. Eventually, if one was patient, one's sons would get around to the main point.

Patience was a very difficult virtue to master.

Drew, sitting in the wing chair by the fire, grunted and frowned at his newspaper. Oh dear. She'd considered hinting that he should leave her alone with Jack, but Drew didn't always take hints, and she'd been afraid pushing him out of the room would have been a mite too obvious. Now he was clearly going to distract Jack from discussing why he'd sent for them.

"Another debutante was fished from the Thames last night," Drew said. "Apparently one more victim of the Silent Slasher."

Jack put down his mug and leaned forward. "Who was it?"

"Darton's second daughter, Lady Barbara."

"Ah. She's been rumored to be having an affair with one of Darton's footmen."

"Yes, the footman's mentioned here."

"There you have it—that must be who the villain is."

Venus took a sip of tea. This was all quite horrible, but it wasn't getting them any closer to discussing the more important matter—the villainess who was trying to trap poor Jack.

Drew shook his head. "No, it wasn't the footman."

"Why do you say that? He's the obvious choice," Venus said. If girls would just follow the rules—well, some of the rules . . . or at least only break them carefully, with men they knew to be honorable and whom they were going to marry—much trouble could be avoided.

"Because Darton had become suspicious and told the butler to keep the man busy. The butler swears the footman was polishing silver all night."

"Well, thank God for that," Jack said. "If he hadn't had an alibi, the mobs might have hung him and then realized he wasn't the Slasher when some other poor girl showed up dead. What else does the paper say?"

No one cares about the blasted murder! That was what Venus wished to say—no, shout—but she merely reached for some more seedcake. She would put on another stone if they didn't get to Jack's problem soon.

"Let's see." Drew consulted the paper again. "The earl had stayed home while his wife and daughter went to the Duke of Chesterman's ball. No surprise there. The man's always been a bit of a hermit."

"As if you're not." *Why* wouldn't Drew focus on Jack's problem? He could ask the question bluntly; men were far more direct with each other than they were with women, particularly mothers.

Drew snorted. "I would prefer to avoid the *ton*, but I do attend the dratted events when I'm forced to, don't I?"

"Yes, you do—and I very much appreciate it." She would appreciate it more if he would get Jack to talk.

"As you should."

"The article, Father?"

One would think Jack would *want* to discuss the reason why he'd sent for them with such urgency. The way this conversation was progressing—or not progressing—he might just have wished their opinion on a new waistcoat.

"Ah yes. So it says Darton thought Lady Barbara would be coming home with her mother, of course, but instead the girl told her mother she felt sick and would leave early with Mrs. Black—who knew nothing about the matter. Apparently Lady Barbara has been running this rig for a while—pretending to leave with someone and then meeting up with the footman. Unfortunately this time things went badly awry."

Drew put the paper down. "The article ends with the author wondering if there is only one Slasher, since the society women end up in the Thames and the prostitutes are abandoned where they fall."

"Good heavens!" Venus said. She had seen the previous accounts in the papers but hadn't been overly alarmed. London was the city. One expected a certain amount of crime. But if things were truly out of hand . . . "Surely there aren't men with knives and bloodthirsty motives hiding around every London corner?"

"I don't think you need worry there are multiple Slashers, Mama. Where the fellow disposes of his victims varies, but the manner of the murders is identical. All the women had their throats cut in exactly the same way. And all had questionable reputations."

"There's nothing questionable about a prostitute's reputation!" Venus said. "Everyone knows she doesn't have one."

Jack looked annoyed, but he only shrugged. "I'm almost certain it's the same man. It's just easier to abandon a body on the ground in the stews than outside a Mayfair mansion."

Drew nodded. "So do you think it's some religious fanatic?"

"I don't know."

This had gone on long enough. Venus wished to get to the reason for Jack's letter before the reason appeared in the drawing room, which could happen at any moment. "If I might suggest a change of topic?"

Jack and Drew jerked their heads toward her as if they'd momentarily forgotten her presence.

"Yes, of course," Drew said. "Not at all the sort of subject for female ears."

She snorted. "My dear duke, I am not some delicate hothouse flower that needs to be shielded from the harsh world, as well you know. I am happy—well, happy isn't quite the word. I am glad to be made aware of such a danger, but I'm far more interested at the moment in discovering why Jack requested our presence so precipitately."

Sometimes patience had to be abandoned. She looked at Jack expectantly.

He looked as if he'd rather keep discussing corpses.

"Yes, Jack," Drew said, "why did you have us dash up to Town? I was just enjoying having the last of the *ton* out from underfoot at the castle, and now here I am in the middle of the main infestation."

Jack was a brave boy. He took a deep breath and smiled. "Yes, well, I do thank you for coming. The problem is—"

"Me."

Venus turned to see a . . . person standing in the doorway.

No, on closer inspection it was definitely a female. Tall and thin with wild red hair that looked like it had been cut by a blind monkey and wearing the most hideous dress she'd ever seen. And, good heavens, were those *men's boots* on her feet?

Jack had gone to stand by her in a rather protective manner. Interesting.

Venus forced herself to smile while her stomach sank. "Hallo, dear. I'm sure my son will manage the introductions in a moment."

She should have stayed in her room.

Lord Jack introduced her to his parents, and she made her curtsies.

No, she couldn't hide away like a scared little mouse.

"Please, come sit down, Miss Hadley," the duchess said. She had a pleasant, almost reassuring voice, but her brown eyes, which were rather too much like Jack's, were frosted with suspicion.

"Thank you, Your Grace." Frances perched on the edge of her chair. She refused to cower, but her knees were shaking badly. Fortunately, today she had a skirt to hide them.

"I'm sure you will think us very silly, Miss Hadley, but Jack has not yet got around to explaining why he wrote asking us to come to London." The duchess looked from Jack to the duke. "Some people were too busy discussing current events."

"Important events, Mama," Jack said, seating himself next to Frances. "There's been another woman murdered, Frances, a member of the *ton*. You and Mama and Ellie—all the ladies—must take extra care until the killer is caught and brought to justice."

"Yes, yes," the duchess said. A hint of exasperation had crept into her voice. "We will be on our guard. But now get to the point, Jack. What is the trouble you need our help with?"

Frances was not going to let Lord Jack muddy the waters. "It is all my fault, Your Grace," she said before Jack could speak. "I've been trying to convince your son that I just need to see my family's man of business and get the funds owed me. Then I can be on my way, and he can wash his hands of the scandal."

Jack glared at her and opened his mouth again, but this time it was his mother who spoke first.

"If there's a scandal involved, dear, Jack can't wash his hands of it."

"Exactly." Jack nodded. "I—"

He was going to tell the story all wrong. "No, I—"

"Miss Hadley, *will* you let me speak?" Jack's voice had an edge to it.

"But you will make it out as if you have some fault in this, and you do not." She appreciated his not laying this completely on her doorstep, but taking any responsibility himself was wrong.

"I will not." Jack looked as if he wished to grab his hair and tear it out in fistfuls. "Don't you realize that sometimes people can be entirely blameless yet still find themselves in trouble?"

Of course she realized that—it just wasn't the case in this instance. "But I'm *not* blameless."

"I believe," the duke said in a calm, authoritative tone, "we will make more progress understanding the situation if you would let Jack tell the tale in his own way, Miss Hadley. When he is done, you can add anything you think we should consider." He smiled at her. He had a very nice smile.

"Yes, of course. I'm sorry. I'm sure you're quite right." She bit her lip and sat back.

Jack gave her a pointed look and then proceeded to share the basic facts of the situation. "So you see," he concluded, "the main problem is that Pettigrew knows Miss Hadley is a female."

Frances couldn't hold her tongue a moment more. "The *main* problem is I dressed as a boy."

The duke laughed. "No, Miss Hadley, I'm afraid Jack is correct. Getting caught is the issue." He sent the duchess an odd glance. "You could swim naked in a pond, and if no one saw you, there would be no scandal."

The duchess suddenly flushed. "Er, yes. That's very true." She smiled at Frances with a little more warmth. "It was quite daring and resourceful of you to venture up to Town in breeches, Miss Hadley. Your plan would have worked very well if the roads had been better."

"It would *not* have worked well," Jack said sharply, glaring at his mother. "It was madness. Fra—Miss Hadley had no idea where her brother lived."

That wasn't true. "I had his address."

Jack turned his glare on her. "Which is in an exceedingly dangerous part of Town—*and* as it turned out, wasn't your brother's address any longer."

"But I didn't know that."

"Exactly." He raised his brows in a very annoying manner. "And what, pray tell, would you have done when you discovered that truth and found yourself alone in the stews without any place to turn?"

She pressed her lips together. The bloody man was correct. She would have been in a very uncomfortable position.

"In any event," the duchess said, "there is no blame to assign here. You didn't intend to embroil Jack in scandal, Miss Hadley. You were asleep when he arrived, after all. And Jack had no idea you weren't what you appeared to be."

"But—" Of *course* she was at fault. Why didn't Jack's mother see that?

"No, my dear." The duchess blushed again. "The duke is quite right. Something can only be a scandal if you get caught out."

"Which we did," Jack said.

"You don't yet know that for a fact, do you?" the duke said. "Being caught—yes, I suppose that's a given. But there's the remote possibility Pettigrew decided that silence was the honorable course in this case. I suggest you and I go off to White's and see if he has indeed been spreading the story."

Jack sighed. "An excellent idea, but I went to the clubs last night." He darted a glance at Frances and then shrugged. "The word is already out."

"Ohh." Frances slapped her hand over her mouth. She hadn't meant to moan, and she certainly hadn't wanted the duke and duchess to hear her.

"I see." Jack's father smiled at her somewhat regretfully. "That does put a different complexion on things."

"It only means we move to the next step." The duchess picked up the teapot. "Would you care for some tea, Miss Hadley? A nice cup of tea can be so soothing."

Frances wasn't sure she agreed with that, but she nodded anyway. "The next step?" she asked, taking the cup from Jack's mother.

"Yes." The duchess was actually grinning.

"Watch out, Miss Hadley," the duke said. "I can see my dear wife has a plan!"

"Of course I have a plan." The duchess took a sip of her tea.

Frances would swear the woman's eyes, far from being icy, were now twinkling over the teacup. She glanced at Jack. Damn. His expression had grown wary.

"What is it, Mama?"

"Have some seedcake, Miss Hadley," the duchess said. "It's very good."

"Mama." Jack scowled at his mother.

Frances cautiously took a slice of seedcake. There was

no reason for her to think the duchess could find a way out of this, but somehow she did think it. Whether she would like the solution remained to be seen. She took a bite of cake.

"Obviously the first thing to do is to get Miss Hadley some new clothes."

"Argh!" A bit of seedcake went down the wrong way; Jack leaned over and pounded on her back. Frances held up her hand to get him to desist and took a swallow of tea, burning her mouth. "Ack!"

"What is it, Miss Hadley?" the duchess asked while the duke tried to muffle his laughter and Jack made an odd growling noise. "Do you actually like that frock you're wearing?"

"No, of course not." She should be kind. "Though Mrs. Watson did the best she could."

"I don't doubt it, but you can't go about like that."

"I'm not going about anywhere except to Mr. Puddington's offices and then back to Landsford, Your Grace." And then—well, she didn't know where she'd go after she had it out with Aunt Viola, but it wouldn't be London.

"Landsford!" the duke said. "That must mean you're . . ."

"The Marquis of Rothmarsh's granddaughter!" The duchess put down her teacup and clapped her hands. "Excellent."

Oh, damn. Frances wanted to sink into the carpet. She definitely did not want her mother's family dragged into this.

"And Whildon's niece." The duke was smiling as well. "The earl is a particular friend of mine, Miss Hadley. And Trent's one of your circle, isn't he, Jack?"

"Yes. I looked for him at White's last night, but didn't see him. I'm sure he and his family will wish to help Fra—"

"No." Frances's stomach tightened into a hard knot.

"No." Jack had said her grandparents and the rest of her mother's family hadn't turned their backs on her, but she didn't wish to put that theory to the test. Better not to know for certain and leave the faint possibility alive that Jack was right.

The duchess's forehead wrinkled in puzzlement. "No what, dear? Of course your mother's family will close ranks around you. Their support—and ours—will quickly put any unpleasant tittle-tattle to rest."

"I don't believe they will wish to have anything to do with me, Your Grace." Oh, why was she even trying to fool herself? She had twenty-four years without even a single letter from any member of her mother's family as proof of their feelings. The fact of the matter was they *had* turned their backs on her. "The marquis and marchioness disapproved of my father because he didn't have a title, and completely washed their hands of my mother when she married him."

She heard Jack growl again, but she chose not to look at him. She couldn't ignore the duke's expression, however. His eyebrows shot up.

"I don't know who told you that, Miss Hadley," the duke said. "I recall events much differently."

"You do?" Damn it, even she heard the pitiful hopefulness in her voice. *Stupid!* She did not care about her mother's family. She'd done very well without them for twenty-four years.

"Yes indeed, though I will admit Lady Diana's parents weren't happy with her choice of husband. Whildon told me on more than one occasion about the colossal rows they had over your mother's infatu—" The duke cleared his throat. "I mean your mother's strong attraction to your father."

"But if my father had been a peer—"

The duke didn't have to raise his hand or say a word; the slight hardening of his expression was enough to cause Frances to fall silent.

"His lack of a title had nothing to do with it, Miss Hadley. I'm sorry to have to tell you it was his lack of character that caused Rothmarsh and his family to argue against the match—and I agreed with their assessment. Your father was handsome and dashing—brilliant, really, when it came to botany. But—and I hope you don't mind my saying this—he was also cocky and self-centered and a rake. Rothmarsh was not of the opinion that rakes could be reformed, and he certainly didn't want to have his precious daughter risk her happiness trying to see if she could prove him wrong."

Ah yes. Rakes couldn't be reformed, could they?

Frances kept her eyes on the duke, though she was tempted to look at Jack. She could feel him watching her. He might not be quite as bad as her father—he did seem sincerely attached to the children at his foundling home, even the ones who weren't his own—but he was still a rake.

The duke smiled. "Your mother was the baby of the family and the only girl, Miss Hadley, so everyone doted on her. This might have been the single time her parents opposed her." He gave Frances a suspiciously bland look. "According to Whildon, she was a trifle headstrong."

Headstrong? That was not how she'd have described the sad, sullen woman she'd known. Her mother had been a ghost long before she'd died. "But then why did they never visit, Your Grace, or even write?"

"Again according to Whildon, they did visit, Miss Hadley. They arrived after a long journey to discover they were grandparents—your mother had never told them she was increasing—and that they were not welcome at Landsford. Lady Diana apparently slammed the door in their faces, and they had to stay the night at an inn. They never got more than a glimpse of you or your brother."

"Oh!" the duchess said. "How horrible! Poor Lady Rothmarsh."

That *was* harsh, but also rather unbelievable. She'd never seen her mother get angry, and the woman had certainly had plenty of cause to do so with her husband's never-ending raking. Likely Rothmarsh and his wife had exaggerated. "Still they never wrote a single letter to try to mend matters, Your Grace."

"Oh, I believe they wrote many letters, Miss Hadley, but Whildon said they were all returned unopened. He was very irate about the situation. I remember quite clearly the day he came into White's ranting about it, wanting to ride down to Landsford to shake some sense into his sister, but he said his father forbade him from doing so. Lady Diana was an adult. If she wished to cut herself off from her family that was her choice."

"Weren't they afraid Hadley might be abusing Miss Hadley's mother?" Jack asked, sounding rather angry for some reason.

"No, because they knew he wasn't at Landsford. The man's exploits were covered rather completely in the papers."

Of course the Duke of Greycliffe would side with his friend. "But that makes no sense, Your Grace. Why would my mother send her parents away and return all their letters?" She'd always assumed her mother had stayed at Landsford because she'd had nowhere else to go. There was likely far more to this story than the duke knew.

The duke smiled gently. "Whildon thought, perhaps, that Lady Diana was too proud or too stubborn to admit she'd made an error and ask for help."

"Oh no. I'm sure that wasn't the case."

But . . .

One of her earliest memories—she could have been only four or five years old—was of running down a garden path at Landsford to tell her mother Frederick had snatched her doll. She'd tripped and fallen just a few feet from where her mother sat reading. She'd wailed, but her mother had just looked at her.

Don't waste your time crying, Frances, she'd said. *You're a big girl. Get up and brush yourself off. Learn to help yourself.*

"Whildon told me his parents last wrote when you were sixteen, Miss Hadley, offering to sponsor your come-out. At least this time your aunt opened the letter—and sent them back a very strongly worded note telling them no, and furthermore, in case they had so far failed to discern it, they had no place in your life."

"Aunt Viola never said anything about it to me." It was true her aunt had used to make a point of getting the post, and Frances did suspect her of hiding a letter from Frederick . . .

No, it was too incredible. "Lord Whildon must be mistaken."

Of course he was mistaken. He was a man. He'd probably overheard a few comments and assumed a great deal. And then, being male, had insisted his version of things was the truth.

"Well"—the duchess put her teacup down with a decisive click—"I know of only one way to find out what your mother's family thinks, Miss Hadley, and that is to ask them. I shall send a note to Rothmarsh House at once." She smiled at Frances. "The past is what it is. We need to concern ourselves with the present and the future."

Blast it, she did *not* want to go crawling to her mother's

family for help. "I'm afraid the present is worse than the past, Your Grace, given the scandal I'm embroiled in. I still think it would be better if I returned to the country."

"Oh no. That would be fatal." The duchess offered Frances some more seedcake, which she declined. The last piece had not gone down well. "If you do that, people will assume you had reason to flee. However, if you stay here and go about with our support—and, I firmly believe, Rothmarsh's support, as well—we shall put this unpleasant gossip to rest in a twinkling."

"Mama is never wrong about these things," Jack said.

"Exactly!" Her Grace actually grinned.

Frances felt as if she were drowning. Why were these people so determined to drag her into London society? There must be some excuse she could use to get free of them—of course. It was weak, but perhaps it would work.

"I can't stay here, Your Grace. Daisy, my poor horse, went lame on my journey, and I had to leave her at an inn along the way. I need to go back and fetch her."

"Oh, don't worry about that." The duchess dismissed her excuse with an easy wave of her hand. "We'll send a groom down to bring her to London or take her back to Landsford, whatever you like. Though taking her to Landsford might be the best plan. I can't advise riding a horse in Town that's not used to London, and in any event you need to let your aunt know that you are safe. She is probably beside herself with worry."

It was hard to imagine Viola being anything other than furious. "But . . ."

Apparently the duchess was done with listening to Frances's ineffectual protestations. "The first thing to do is to get you a new wardrobe," Her Grace said. "I must take Ellie, our son Ned's betrothed, to the dressmaker's anyway; it will be no problem at all to take you along as well. In fact, I'm sure Ellie would be happy for the company. I must tell you her wardrobe is almost as sad as yours." She examined Frances again. "Well, that would be impossible. Hmm. Now that I think about it, I believe we should have Madam Celeste come here."

"But . . ." Why wouldn't Jack's mother listen to reason?

"You would be wise to capitulate now, Miss Hadley," the duke said. "My wife is very tenacious and, much as I do hate to admit it, generally right."

"Yes," Jack said. "That's why I wrote to Mama, Miss Hadley. I have complete confidence that she'll bring us about."

"And please remember this does affect Jack's reputation as well as yours, my dear," Her Grace said. "You must take pity on him and help him maintain his position in society."

Jack nodded. "Yes, Miss Hadley. You'd be doing me a great favor if you will do as Mama asks."

"But . . . oh, very well." With Frederick married, she needed to plot a new course anyway, and if the cost of her new wardrobe depleted the estate and Frederick's future funds, well, she couldn't find it in herself to care very much.

Chapter 9

When venturing among the ton, *courage is as necessary an accessory as the proper gloves and shoes.*

—Venus's Love Notes

Jack looked up from the newspapers he'd spread over the desk when he heard someone come into the study. "Ned—and Shakespeare!"

Shakespeare barked a welcome and came over to allow Jack to scratch his ears. It had certainly taken him no time at all to make himself at home in Greycliffe House. "Where's Ellie?"

Ned sat in the chair across the desk from him. "Where do you think she is? Braxton was on the watch for us and snatched her from me the moment we got back from walking Shakespeare. He said an army of dressmakers is waiting for her in one of the sitting rooms."

"Not an army—Madam Celeste and two of her assistants plus countless bolts of fabric. It took Richard and William three trips to the carriage to bring everything in."

Ned frowned. "I don't know why Mama is in such a hurry."

"Well, you have yet to meet Miss Hadley, but, trust me, her need for a new wardrobe is rather an emergency—and she is not terribly cooperative. We will just have to hope Mama's presence will keep her from leaping out a window or stabbing Madam Celeste with her own scissors." Jack grinned. "And much as I'm sure Ellie would prefer to spend her time with you, you have to agree she could stand to have a few new things besides that lovely red dress she wore to the birthday ball."

Ned's cheeks turned almost as red as the dress. "Ellie is beautiful whatever she wears."

"Of course." Jack stretched; his shoulders and neck were tight from being hunched over. "When is the wedding, by the by?"

"I'm off to get a special license shortly. The plan is to wed as soon as may be."

Since Jack was quite sure Ned and Ellie had anticipated their vows—and would likely continue to do so—the sooner they tied the knot, the better. "Are you going back to the castle for the ceremony?"

"No. Mama suggested we get married here, and Ellie and I thought it a good idea. One wedding in Greycliffe Castle chapel was enough for me." Ned grimaced. "And since Mama seems to think it's important Ellie be introduced to society, we'll spend a week or two in Town."

"Splendid. I confess I'm hoping Ellie may be able to serve as a friend to Miss Hadley. The woman is a bit, er, prickly, and to add to the mess, there are likely some unpleasant stories circulating about us."

"Stories? What kind of stories?" Ned's brows snapped down. "What have you done?"

"I haven't done anything, damn it." Trust Ned to jump

to that conclusion. "We are merely the victims of a set of unfortunate circumstances."

"Hmm."

If Ned accused him of being careless, he was going to push the blasted desk over on him.

Instead his brother nodded. "Of course you can rely on me—and I'm sure Ellie as well, though I suspect Mama will bring the thing about in short order. Where's Father?"

Jack was surprised at how relieved he felt that Ned supported him. "Out doing his part to discredit the malicious tales."

"Good." Ned finally looked down at the newspapers strewn over the desk. "Have the stories shown up in the gossip columns, then?"

"No. Or at least not yet. Or not that I've seen." Damn, he hadn't checked, but if the men at White's had been talking about it last night—

He flipped to that section of the morning paper. Bloody hell.

"Yes." He handed the paper to Ned.

"*'Lord J——, just returned to Town, has already shocked the* ton *by driving through our fine metropolis with Miss H——, who was dressed in* breeches. *Is this the new fashion in the country? And what can our dear D—— of L—— think of the rakish Lord J—— sharing a bed at an inn with the scandalous Miss?'*"

Ned put the paper down and stared at Jack. "Even you wouldn't do something so outrageous."

"What do you mean, *even you*?" Maybe he didn't want his idiot brother's support.

Ned frowned and opened his mouth as if to say something—and then obviously thought better of it. Perhaps his newfound love had made him more aware of emotional undercurrents—or perhaps he'd noted Jack's fisted hands, itching to punch him in the face. "Why don't you tell me what actually happened?"

Jack sighed. That was the devil of it, wasn't it? "Unfortunately, the account is true, only I sincerely thought Miss Hadley was a boy. She'd disguised herself to come up to London and, er, discuss some issues with her family's man of business." *Discuss* wasn't precisely what he suspected Frances intended to do. Demand, browbeat, shout—those were likely more accurate verbs.

"Ah." Ned cleared his throat. "I see."

"No, of course you don't see. It's a damnable coil, really. I'm hoping Mama can sort things out, but if she can't, I'll have to marry the girl."

Ned's hand shot across the desk to grasp his. "Don't marry someone you can't love." His grip tightened before he released Jack. "We'll find a way to fix this. Is the girl a complete hoyden?"

"No!" Frances was strong-willed, hardheaded, and argumentative, but she wasn't a hoyden.

Shakespeare, who'd settled down by his feet, lifted his head and whined at his sharp tone.

Jack struggled to modulate his voice. "She was just desperate and somewhat misguided." She'd been completely mad, but he had to admire her pluck.

"If she's been parading around in breeches, she certainly is misguided." Ned sounded quite shocked. No surprise, that. A woman in breeches would not suit his brother's notion of proper behavior.

It wouldn't suit anyone's notion, which is why they were in this mess.

"Yes, well, she really didn't do anything wrong—"

Ned's brows almost climbed off his forehead.

"—and definitely doesn't deserve to be shunned, which she will be if I don't marry her, assuming Mama can't bring things about."

Ned gave him a brotherly punch in the arm. "Buck up, Jack. Mama's sure to work her usual miracles. If the Duchess of Love takes her up, everyone will, won't they?"

"I do hope so. And it should also help that Rothmarsh is her grandfather."

Ned let out a long, low whistle. "Yes indeed, though I can't imagine why Rothmarsh's granddaughter would be coming to London in breeches."

Jack straightened the newspapers. "There was a falling out in the family. Miss Hadley has never met her mother's relatives."

"Hmm. That could be a bit of a problem."

Everything related to Miss Hadley seemed to be a bit of a problem.

"Well, I'm sure Mama will work that out as well," Ned said. "So what are you doing perusing these papers if not searching the gossip columns?"

"There's actually a problem larger than my endangered bachelorhood in Town at the moment: an anonymous killer is at large. The papers have dubbed him the Silent Slasher because he cuts his victims' throats, but no one has ever heard a scream or any sound of a scuffle."

Ned stared at him for a full minute and then surged to his feet. "Zeus, I hate London. It's too big and anonymous." His eyes clouded with worry. "I'm taking Ellie back to the castle in the morning. We can be married by her father at the vicarage and then go off to my estate."

Damn, that would not be a good thing. "But if you do that, people will think you left because you disapproved of Miss Hadley."

Ned started toward the door, clearly eager to begin making arrangements for his return to the country. "I'm very sorry for it if that's the case, but Ellie's safety must take priority."

Jack rose, too. "But Ned—"

"What about my safety?" Ellie asked, almost colliding with Ned in the doorway.

At the sound of Ellie's voice, Ned's expression changed. His eyes lit up and his lips pulled into a wide grin. He looked completely, utterly, madly, in love.

Jack felt a sharp jab of envy and a touch of . . . what?

Dread. He did not want to marry Miss Hadley and be forced to endure a loveless union for the rest of his life.

"We are leaving London in the morning, my love," Ned said, taking her hand.

"We are?" Ellie shot a puzzled look at Jack. "Why? We just got here." She smiled up at Ned. "Madam Celeste will be quite distressed. She's making me an outrageous number of dresses."

"She can send them to us in the country." Ned brushed his lips over her fingers. "And why are you suddenly so interested in clothes?" His expression turned markedly lascivious. "You won't have much need of them."

Clearly, Ned was not referring to the country's more limited range of social events. Ellie's cheeks turned bright red, and she jerked her fingers out of Ned's grip. "Behave yourself, sir. You are putting poor Jack to the blush."

Ned laughed. "Am I, Jack?"

"Definitely."

The envy and dread twisted together in Jack's gut to form a heavy lump. He not only didn't love Miss Hadley, he didn't feel the slightest whisper of lust for her.

Of course he didn't. She looked like a young boy.

He did like her, though. She was prickly and independent and foolhardy, but she was brave and determined, too. She'd made it through all the ugliness of Hart Street—the dirt and stench and Nan's brothel—without a single case of the vapors. And she'd taken his foundling home in stride.

She needed him at the moment. He just hoped he could help her without having to marry her.

"We can't go home now," Ellie said. "We'd be leaving Miss Hadley in the lurch."

"Mama will take charge of her, Ellie. And Jack says she has relatives in London who will stand by her as well."

"Yes, but the duchess was just saying how poor Frances has no female cousins." Ellie smiled and put her hand on Ned's arm, shaking it a little. "I think she needs a friend."

"Yes, well, that may be. It is kind of you to think of Miss Hadley's welfare, but we are still leaving in the morning."

"But why? You still haven't told me why."

Ned frowned at her. "Because Jack tells me there's a lunatic at large, murdering women."

"Oh?" Ellie looked at Jack. "How many people has this person killed, Jack?"

"Eight. Five prostitutes and three female members of the *ton*."

"And do you think it's too dangerous for me to stay?"

"Jack," Ned said, a distinct warning in his voice.

"I can no more tell you what to do than Ned can, Ellie, but I will say Mama is staying."

Ned growled. Jack ignored him.

"As long as you don't go wandering off into the dark without Ned at your side—"

"No chance of that," Ned said.

"—you should be perfectly safe."

"Splendid."

"Ellie—" Ned was clearly readying an impassioned argument, but Ellie put her finger on his lips.

"Ned, your mother has everything planned. I'm the first daughter-in-law she's been able to bring up to Town, and I think she's looking forward to presenting me to the *ton*. And I'm looking forward to seeing some of the London sights and going to my first London ball with the handsomest man in the room at my side." She grinned at Jack. "No offense, Jack."

He bowed. "None taken. I'm delighted you find my ugly brother attractive."

Ellie laughed, and then looked back up at Ned. "And I wouldn't mind having someone else who's new to the *ton* by my side, Ned."

"*I'll* be by your side," Ned said, looking very disgruntled.

Ellie rested her head briefly against his shoulder. "I know, but it's not the same. Not only are you a man, you're used to being, if not the center of attention, then the focus of much interest." Ellie suddenly looked a little pale. "You're used to having people stare at you."

Ned snorted. "*Ton* parties are nothing more than a crush of annoying, gossipy, overdressed nincompoops—my mother's Valentine party magnified a hundred times. I believe you are making a great deal over nothing."

"See? I told you you wouldn't understand."

Ned scowled at her. "What don't I understand?"

Ellie patted his arm. "Let's stay, Ned, at least for a little while. If things seem truly alarming, we'll leave then, all right?"

Ned's scowl deepened, and then he capitulated. "All right. But you must promise to stay close to me and not do anything foolish."

Ellie leaned into Ned. Her voice took on an intimate, husky tone. "Oh, I promise I'll stay *very* close to you."

It was clearly time for a change of subject.

"Where is Miss Hadley, Ellie?" Jack asked.

Ellie smiled at him. "She's still getting fitted. She has truly nothing to wear, so Madam Celeste is making up two dresses immediately. And of course she needed her hair cut as well."

"Isn't it short enough?" Jack couldn't imagine Miss Hadley's hair trimmed any shorter.

"Yes, but one of Madam Celeste's girls, who's very good with her scissors, shaped it so it looks a bit more, er, planned. In any event, it will still be a while before she is ready, which is why the duchess set me free." Ellie laughed. "I think Her Grace feels she needs to stay in the room or Miss Hadley will bolt."

Jack sighed. "She very likely would."

"Surely I don't need another walking dress," Frances said. It was one thing to dip into Frederick's funds; it was quite another to completely bankrupt him. Madam Celeste was talking about walking dresses and carriage dresses and habits and ball gowns, not to mention chemises and stockings and gloves. She looked at the fabric piling up on the sitting room sofa.

Perhaps it *would* be better if she returned to the country. The gossip couldn't be that dreadful, could it? More likely it would be a case of out of sight, out of mind. She would sink back into anonymity like a pebble thrown into the center of a pond. There might—might—be some brief, small ripples, and then all would be quiet and smooth again.

"Nonsense," Her Grace said. "Of course you need another walking dress. You need many other dresses." She smiled with what appeared to be sincere delight. "This is just to get you through the first few days."

"But . . ." There was no possible way she could wear so many clothes, and they would be useless once she left London. It was a shocking waste of money. "I have clothes at home." *If Viola hasn't shredded them.*

Madam Celeste's face flushed, and she popped the pins out of her mouth. "Oh, mademoiselle, you cannot wear country dresses in Town. Eet would be une grave erreur. Très, très grave. Everyone, they will laugh and turn their noses up at you." The woman turned beseeching eyes toward the duchess. "Tell her, Your Grace, s'il vous plaît. Tell her eet would be une catastrophe."

The duchess laughed. "Madam Celeste is quite right, Frances. You can't wear country clothes in Town." She raised her brows. "But I think you know that."

She did know it. And truthfully, if she let herself consider the matter, much of her clothing would cause comment even in the country.

She'd never gone to any social gathering other than church services. She had no time for such things or any interest in their main purpose, which was catching a husband. She didn't know how to make small talk or sing or even how to dance.

Oh God. And Jack's mother was proposing to drag her to all manner of society events, some of which were sure to include balls.

"Will you just finish up that dress, Madam Celeste? Miss Hadley and I need to have a little chat."

Frances heard the duchess's words faintly over the pounding in her head; she felt Her Grace take her arm and lead her out of the sitting room and into a smaller room across the corridor.

"What's the matter, Miss Hadley?"

"Ah." She swallowed. "Ah." What could she say?

The duchess was looking at her calmly, as if she had all day to stand there and listen to her sputter.

"I don't have the money to pay for all these dresses," she finally managed. It wasn't the real problem, but it was the one she was willing to discuss. "I mean, I assume the estate will cover some of it, but I—"

The duchess patted her arm. "Miss Hadley, please. Don't worry about cost. I'm quite certain Rothmarsh will be delighted to pay for all your things."

"Ah." This was even worse. It was only supposition that

her mother's family would want anything to do with her, and here she was going to introduce her scandalous self by presenting them with a sheaf of bills? "I really don't think that's a good idea."

The duchess sighed and led her over to a small settee. She pushed her gently to sit and then sat next to her. "My dear, may I call you Frances?"

"Um." Apparently she still couldn't form a coherent sentence, so she simply nodded.

Her Grace held Frances's hand in both of hers. "I remember talking to Charlotte—that's Lady Whildon—about the pleasures and the . . . well, I guess you might say regrets of having only sons. We both love our boys, you must understand, but we're a little sad not to have the fun of a daughter's come-out: the dresses and shoes and all of that." She paused and looked at Frances as if she expected a response.

"Er," Frances said, nodding. "Quite."

"Ash's wife and Ned's first wife had no interest in coming up to London, so you might guess my excitement at having you and Ellie here now, doing all of this." She gestured back at the sitting room and Madam Celeste.

Frances flushed. "But I'm not . . . you have Ellie, of course, but I'm not—"

The duchess held up her hand to stop Frances from heaping more excuses on her head. "I distinctly remember Charlotte telling me how sad Lady Rothmarsh was when your aunt wrote refusing her offer to sponsor your come-out. I know the marchioness will be thrilled to have this second chance to see you grace London's ballrooms."

Oh God. The marchioness would see her stumble through all those ballrooms. She'd—

Frances blinked at the duchess. She hadn't considered . . . "My grandparents are in London?"

"Yes, of course."

Panic and something else—excitement?—battled in her chest. "Aren't they rather old?"

The duchess shrugged. "They are past seventy, but still quite spry. I sent word telling them you're here and that your wardrobe needed a bit of refurbishing."

"They know I'm here?"

"Yes, of course." The duchess looked a bit puzzled. "I told you I was sending a note to Rothmarsh House."

Yes, Frances remembered Her Grace saying that, but she hadn't thought Rothmarsh House actually meant *Rothmarsh*. Her grandfather.

"We certainly don't wish to keep it a secret, my dear. I expect—"

Someone scratched on the door.

"Come in," the duchess called. "Oh yes, Mr. Braxton. What is it?"

The butler bowed and extended a silver plate with a folded note. "This came from Rothmarsh House, Your Grace."

"Splendid. I expect this is Lady Rothmarsh's reply." Her Grace broke open the seal. "Yes. We are invited to dine with them tomorrow." She smiled at the butler. "Please send our acceptance, Mr. Braxton."

"See?" the duchess said, turning back to Frances and handing her the note. "Your grandmother is *very* excited. She plans to have the entire family over, which will be a bit confusing for you, I'm afraid, but it will be for the best. We want to be sure the *ton* knows all your relatives accept you."

"I-I see." Frances stared down at the somewhat wavery writing on the vellum. This just got worse and worse.

"We will also have to locate your brother and his new wife. Oh, not in time for tomorrow's dinner, of course—that would be too difficult. But we should find them soon. Rothmarsh and his family will want to meet them as well, but we also want to be certain they don't somehow add to the problem. Have you given any thought to where they might be?"

"No." *Why* hadn't Frederick told her he was getting married? And if the landlady was right, and his wife was a trollop . . . well, there was nothing at all she could do about that. "I have no idea, though I suppose my aunt might know." Hmm. Frederick had not got along with Viola at all. He must have told her he was marrying, but likely did not give her his new direction. "Or maybe not."

The duchess gave her a long look. "Pardon me for saying so, Frances, but I'm a little suspicious of your aunt's motives. It seems clear she never shared any of Rothmarsh's communications with you."

Yes, it was very odd, and after Viola's treachery with Littleton, Frances had to conclude that her aunt could only be trusted to do what benefited her aunt.

"Is there anyone else we can ask?"

That was an excellent question. Who would . . . of course! "If Frederick told someone, it was probably our man of business, Mr. Puddington."

"Excellent! At least that gives us a place to start. Jack can escort you to see this Mr. Puddington as soon as possible. In the meantime, you can write to your aunt to let her know you are safe with us." She smiled. "I think it would perhaps be best if we didn't invite her to join you, however; don't you agree?"

"Yes." She definitely did not want Viola here, and wouldn't even if her aunt hadn't betrayed her. Now that she was away from her, Frances saw even more clearly how very critical and, well, gloomy her aunt was—like a depressing, dark rain cloud; especially compared to the duchess's sunny disposition.

And this plan would serve her purposes very well, too.

She could finally confront Mr. Puddington about her dowry.

Her Grace stood. "Splendid. Now we should go back to Madam Celeste and let her finish your fittings."

"Ah." Frances didn't get up. There was still the main problem—she didn't know how to dance.

Well, she could always take her place with the other wallflowers. She might even invent a physical impairment to explain her situation.

"Is there something else, dear?"

She should tell the duchess so she wouldn't try to get her to do something she couldn't. "Well, yes. I, er . . ."

Her Grace waited patiently, her expression pleasant and politely inquisitive. "Yes? You . . . ?"

There was no way to say this except baldly. "I don't dance."

Of course Her Grace wouldn't let it go at that. "You don't? Why not?"

Frances flushed. She must be the only twenty-four-year-old woman in England who had never learned to dance. "Because I don't know how."

The duchess's brows did shoot up briefly, but instead of laughing at Frances, she smiled.

"Then Jack can teach you. He's a very accomplished dancer."

Chapter 10

Family is so important.

—Venus's Love Notes

"So what do you think of Miss Hadley, Drew?" Venus asked, climbing into bed beside him.

He looked up from the *History of the Peloponnesian War*, peering at her over his spectacles. "She seems very nice." He went back to reading.

"Yes, but what do you *think* of her?" She wormed her way under his arm to lay her head on his shoulder.

"As I say, she seems nice enough." He sighed and closed the book, putting it on his nightstand with his spectacles. "More to the point, what do *you* think of her?"

Drew was very perceptive—he knew she wished to talk. She ignored his somewhat longing glance at Thucydides. "She is not at all what I expected. I was afraid she'd be impudent and, well, common. Out to sink her talons into poor Jack. But she's not like that at all." She snuggled closer to him. "She needs our help."

He pulled her up so she was half lying on his chest and cupped her face. "Do you think she would make Jack a good wife?"

"I don't know. Perhaps. I certainly won't rule out the possibility." She turned to kiss his palm. "But she *is* quite prickly."

He chuckled. "I noticed." He stroked his fingers through her hair. Ah. It felt so good.

But there would be time for that later. Now she must consider Miss Hadley. "It sounds as if she's lived a terrible existence, Drew. Can you believe she's never learned to dance?"

How did a young woman of the gentry reach Frances's age and not know such a basic social skill? Even in the vicarage in Little Huffington, even with parents whose noses were perpetually stuck in Greek or Latin tomes, she and her sister had learned to dance.

Drew brushed a stray hair out of her face. "I'm not surprised. I asked Whildon about her background when I saw him at White's. From what he told me, as far as his family can ascertain, Miss Hadley has never mixed with society."

"Never? How sad. So she and her aunt just sit home all the time?" Drew was massaging her neck now. She felt like purring.

"Apparently. Miss Hadley manages the estate, and the aunt complains—at least according to Whildon, who had it from the Earl of Addington. Addington has an estate in Landsford's vicinity and has never liked the elder Miss Hadley. Calls her supercilious and argumentative."

"Oh dear." This just got worse and worse. It was hard to see how a flower could spring from such a dung heap.

Well, no, flowers did grow out of dung, if the proper seed was planted. But was Miss Hadley the proper seed? It wouldn't do for Jack to marry a virulent weed.

"And what of her paternal grandparents?" Perhaps there was hope in that quarter. Grandparents could have a very positive effect on children, as she was eager to demonstrate if her sons would only gift her with some grandchildren. "Did they visit Miss Hadley at all when she was growing up?"

"I'm afraid not. The grandfather was a botanist like Miss Hadley's father. He sailed off on some plant expedition when Hadley was only a year or two old and never came back. The grandmother died about a year before Hadley married Lady Diana."

"Oh." Her heart sank. So Frances's father had followed in his father's footsteps. And she wouldn't be surprised if the unpleasant man, marrying just a year after his mother's death, had been looking primarily for a housekeeper to replace his equally unpleasant sister. "And the brother? What do you know of him?"

"Not much. He's in London, and Whildon did make an effort to reach out to him when he first heard he was in Town, but got soundly rebuffed for his pains." Drew shrugged. "Rothmarsh finally decided to stop beating his head against that particular wall. With three married sons, he has plenty of grandsons to keep him and his wife busy."

Venus could not repress a sigh. "It would be very nice to have even one grandchild."

Drew chuckled. "Unless I much miss my guess, Ned is working on that for you right now."

"Yes." She should be scandalized at what she was just as certain was going on in Ned's—or Ellie's—room, but she could only feel happy and excited. She'd even put the two in adjoining bedchambers so they didn't need to creep up and down the corridor. "It's so good to see Ned happy again, but we do need to get those two married very soon."

"Ned's getting a special license." Drew twirled a lock of

her hair around his finger. "Dare I say he's not the only one interested in conjugal—or, in his case, pre-conjugal—relations?" He raised his brows. His face had that familiar, intent, rather hungry look.

They had things to discuss first. "Getting back to Miss Hadley—"

He looked resigned. "Must we?"

"Yes." She kissed the base of his throat, the bit of his skin that was closest to her lips. "Just for a little longer. Do be patient."

"I've been patient." He looked over at Thucydides. "Can I read a bit more while we discuss Miss Hadley?"

"Don't be silly." She sat up. This was serious. "Do you think there's any chance Jack will be compelled to marry her?"

"No, not with the Duke and Duchess of Greycliffe and the Marquis and Marchioness of Rothmarsh supporting her as well as the Earl and Countess of Whildon and her other uncles and cousins. It would be social suicide to cut her." He managed to look rather haughty and a little bit dangerous. "Being a duke *does* have some rewards, you know."

"That's what I thought." A match was always better if it wasn't forced, and besides, she was far from convinced Miss Hadley was a suitable match for Jack. In fact, at the moment, she was almost persuaded a marriage between them would be a disaster. The girl needed far too much work.

"There may be some high sticklers who won't accept her," she said, "but we can ignore a few spiteful old cats." She shrugged—and noticed Drew's eyes had fastened on her breasts. Anticipation started to simmer in her belly.

Soon, but not *quite* yet.

"I shall also find Miss Hadley some other marital

choices in case a wedding does become the only way to salvage her reputation."

Drew's eyes widened. "I hesitate to question the Duchess of Love, but have you looked at her? A man would have to be blind or desperate to court her."

She slapped him gently on the shoulder. "Drew! Don't be unkind."

"I'm not. I'm being truthful."

Men were sometimes so shortsighted. "Just wait until you see her in her new clothes. You won't recognize her."

"Hmm. Perhaps. I will admit you transformed Ellie with that red dress, but there is another problem here."

"Another problem? What can that be?"

"Miss Hadley must *wish* to be courted. You can make her look like Helen of Troy, my dear duchess, but if she snarls at every man who approaches her, she'll send them away as quickly as if she were Medusa. I don't believe the girl likes men."

Drew had a point. "Well, she doesn't have much reason to, does she? Her father and brother certainly haven't endeared her to the breed."

"True, though at least with regard to Hadley senior, she's probably fortunate the fellow's absent. People can only speculate what he's doing in foreign lands; if he were in Town, we'd all know."

"He's that dreadful?"

"Yes." Drew's lips curled in distaste. "Don't you remember? A day didn't go by that his name wasn't mentioned in the scandal sheets. He's a thoroughly dirty dish."

"I see." Drew was not one to exaggerate. If he said the man was dreadful, he was. "It does sound as if Frances's father is best left abroad. Why did he pursue Frances's poor mother, do you suppose? I have to confess I missed all that. I must have been too busy with the boys." Jack would have been only one when Frances's mother and father wed, which meant Ned was three and Ash, five.

She'd put aside her matchmaking efforts when she'd been a young mother—her boys had taken all her energies. They'd had a nurse, of course, but Venus hadn't grown up with a nurse herself and so didn't wish to delegate the care of her precious sons to anyone else. Though she'd definitely needed the nurse's help. Little boys could be very exhausting.

She smiled. But she was ready now for grandsons—or granddaughters. That was the beauty of grandchildren. One could hand them back to their parents when they—either the grandparents or the grandchildren—became fussy.

"Conceit, vanity, pride, sheer competitiveness," Drew said. "All the men were trying to win Lady Diana's hand that Season. She was a marquis's daughter, but also very beautiful. The toast of the Town."

Yes, she could understand that. She'd seen her boys fight over something none of them really wanted just to be able to say they'd won. "But why did Lady Diana not see his true colors?"

"Ah, well, Hadley *was* very handsome and charming. But Whildon thinks what really pushed his sister to elope was the family's vocal dislike of the man. If they'd just held their tongues and let time take its course, he thinks Lady Diana might have broken with the blackguard. But she had never been told no before and did not like the experience. It got her back up and likely made her stubbornly insist on having Hadley."

"How sad." It just showed what she'd always believed, that there was no more important decision than that of choosing one's spouse. And she must be careful, too, not to warn Jack against Miss Hadley. He was quite capable of jumping to the girl's defense and perhaps acting as rashly as Lady Diana. "Did you notice how protective Jack was of Miss Hadley when we met her?"

"He was?" Drew stared at her blankly.

"Yes." It was amazing how unperceptive men could be about some things, even her dear duke.

"If you say so." Drew sighed, and then raised his brows in a hopeful fashion. "Are we done talking now?"

She laughed and leaned forward to kiss him. "I suppose we are."

"Splendid!"

In a twinkling, her nightgown parted company with her body, and Drew's nightshirt ended up on the floor. Miss Hadley's situation was completely forgotten.

Drew had been very patient, after all.

Jack checked his pocket watch surreptitiously while he waited in the drawing room with Father and Ned for the ladies to come down.

He did not have time for Rothmarsh's blasted dinner party. He needed to be out talking to people—to Nan and the other madams or to the men at the clubs. *Someone* must have seen or heard something that could help him identify the Silent Slasher.

"I don't see why Ellie and I need to go to this party," Ned said, glaring at Father.

"Your mother wishes it. And what would you do instead?"

Ned flushed. "Have a quiet dinner here."

Right.

They probably *would* have a quiet dinner. It was what they'd have for dessert that was the problem—not that they weren't doing that every night anyway. Jack half wished Ash was here so he wouldn't be the only one sleeping alone.

Well, Miss Hadley was sleeping alone, of course, but that was different.

To think he'd spent an entire night at the Crowing Cock with her without guessing she was a woman. She'd been a pleasant enough bed partner—no thrashing or sharp elbows or even much snoring. But if he'd known she was female—

It would have made no difference.

She did have very long legs and a very attractive—

No. He should not be thinking of Miss Hadley in bed.

"Remember, Ellie is making her bows, too," Father said. "Up until now, our annual Valentine's party has been her only contact with the *ton*. It will be good for her to get her feet wet at this small gathering."

Ned still looked unconvinced. "I would much prefer to go home to Linden Hall, especially with that murdering maniac on the loose."

"And I'd much rather be at the castle, even without the consideration of a murderer at large," Father said. "But your mother will have no part of that. And in this case I have to admit she is right. I do believe the risk to the ladies is minimal, and much as I hate to admit it, it does pay to be acquainted with some of the *ton*, especially Rothmarsh and his family. They will help Ellie's debut immensely."

"And, as I told you before," Jack said, "people talk, especially in the days after Mama's house party. It's a very good thing you and Ellie are appearing as a betrothed couple—you will spike the gabble-grinders' guns."

Ned grunted. "I don't see why they're interested in me at all."

Ned was being purposefully obtuse. "You're a duke's son and, for the last four years, unattached. Of course the *ton* is interested in you."

"Then they must be *very* interested in you."

"Oh, they are, but I'm here most of the time. They can see me; they don't have to speculate."

Though they did anyway. They were gossiping wildly now about his supposed relationship with Frances. Some hint of his charity houses must have surfaced as well, for the most recent tales had him with ten children by Miss Hadley as well as a sizable harem murderously jealous of his new interest. All of which made no sense at all, of course. Miss Hadley could hardly be a new interest if she was the mother of his numerous supposed progeny, not to mention she was far too young to have so many offspring. But reason was not engaged when tongues wagged so furiously.

And no matter how ridiculous, the talk was damaging to poor Miss Hadley.

He stole a glance at his watch again. Perhaps if the dinner didn't last too long, he could go looking for information about the Slasher afterward.

"Jack is right," Father said. "The unknown is far more interesting than the known. Stay for a few weeks, go to a variety of events, and then once the old cats have had their fill, go home."

Ned blew out a long, annoyed breath. "Very well, I shall try that, but if there's the slightest indication Ellie is in danger, we are leaving." He looked at the door. "Where *are* the women? It's taking them forever. I can't—ah."

"Impatient, are you?" Mama said, laughing as she entered the drawing room with Ellie. "Miss Hadley will be down shortly. Mary wanted a few more minutes to work on her hair."

Jack bowed to Ellie. It was still a shock to see how pretty she was now that she'd finally stopped hiding herself in hideously ill-fitting, fussy dresses. "You look beautiful," he murmured. "Not that you care what I think."

Ellie laughed. "Of course I care, Jack." She grinned. "Just not very much." Her eyes had already moved on to Ned, who was gazing at her with an embarrassingly besotted expression. She hurried to his side.

Jack checked his watch again. Miss Hadley didn't have that much hair—what could be taking the extra time? Not that getting to Rothmarsh House earlier meant they'd be done earlier, but he could hope.

"Are you sure Miss Hadley will come down if you aren't there to push her, Mama?" he asked. Mama was standing by Father—who also had a vaguely besotted expression. Damn it, the man was too old for such things.

Mama laughed. "Oh, I think so. You know Mary. It would take a woman even braver than Miss Hadley to defy her."

Mary had been Mama's maid for as long as Jack could remember; she was used to dealing with strong-willed females. Still, Miss Hadley was a special case. "Perhaps you should—"

"Ah, here she is now," Mama said. "Do come in and join us, Miss Hadley."

Jack turned.

Zeus! Lust slammed into his chest . . . and lower organs.

Miss Hadley looked nothing like a grubby young schoolboy now. An emerald-green dress highlighted her creamy skin. It hugged her small breasts, skimmed her hips, and tumbled down to hide her long, slender legs.

He wished his coat would hide his suddenly overly enthusiastic greeting.

He forced his eyes up. Mary had indeed worked wonders with Frances's hair. Soft red curls, threaded with green ribbon, framed a face . . . that was white with terror. Her wide green eyes gave it its only color.

"Frances," he said, stepping forward and taking her gloved hand. It trembled in his grasp.

Would she want him to compliment her? Or would she snap his head off if he tried?

Anger was better than fear. "You look lovely."

She blushed—and then scowled at him. "I couldn't look much worse than I did, could I? I thought Mary would never be done."

"Well," Mama said, clapping her hands, "now that we are all here, we should be off. Frances and Jack, come with me; Ned and Ellie, you take the second carriage."

Jack offered Frances his arm; she clutched it tightly.

"Don't be nervous," he murmured.

"I'm n-not n-nervous." Her chin was up, her jaw was tight, and her eyes were still wide with panic.

He felt a sudden flood of fierce, protective tenderness.

Ridiculous. Miss Hadley was perfectly able to take care of herself once she got over all this newness.

"Your grandparents are not so alarming," he said, following his parents out to the carriage. "Rothmarsh can be a bit loud and blustery, but he has a kind heart, and Lady Rothmarsh is very sweet. She *is* prone to hugging, though." He'd been enveloped in the marchioness's soft, perfumed clasp more times than he cared to count.

Frances wrinkled her nose. "I am not a hugger."

"I didn't think you were." He handed her into the carriage and took his seat beside her as she adjusted her skirt. It caught under her for a moment, outlining her thigh—

He adjusted his legs. Damn, things—well, one particular male thing—had been far more comfortable when he'd thought Frances a boy. However, looking on the bright side, he could now imagine consummating a marriage if he had to wed the woman.

Actually, he could imagine doing a lot more, in far too intimate detail.

He shifted his legs again. He needed to think about something else.

"Have you told Miss Hadley who will be at dinner tonight, Mama?" he asked as they jerked into motion. It seemed a good idea to prepare Frances for the crowd she'd be meeting. The Rothmarsh family could be somewhat overwhelming, and Frances was on edge enough as it was.

"No, I don't believe I have. Let's see . . . there will be your grandparents, the marquis and marchioness, of course, and I'm certain their three sons—your uncles—and their wives will be present: the Earl of Whildon and Lady Whildon, Lord and Lady Ambrose, and Lord and Lady Geoffrey. And then there are your cousins. Whildon has three sons, Lord Ambrose four, and Lord Geoffrey two, none of which is yet married, which I suppose, at the moment, is fortunate as wives would certainly add to the confusion, wouldn't they?"

"Y-yes."

Perhaps having Mama list all Frances's relatives had been the wrong approach.

"Don't worry about remembering names," Father said. "No one expects you to keep everyone straight, and frankly, the cousins all look alike."

"Ah."

Were his parents *trying* to terrify Frances? "And of course we'll help you," Jack said.

Mama laughed. "Of course we will, but you won't need any help. Everyone will be so delighted to meet you. You're part of their family—that's all that matters."

"Y-yes." Frances was sitting bolt upright, her gloved fingers clasped tightly in her lap. "I d-don't have m-much experience with family."

Mama leaned across the carriage to pat Frances's hands. "I know, dear. But don't worry. It will be fine—you'll see."

The coach rocked to a stop, and poor Frances jumped two inches. She looked desperately at Jack as the footman let down the stairs. Father and Mama climbed out, but when Jack started toward the door Frances grabbed his arm.

"I can't go in there," she hissed.

"It can't be worse than dressing as a boy to come to London," he whispered back. "You managed that; you can manage this."

She jerked her head once from side to side. "No." Her breath was coming short and fast. "They'll all be *staring* at me."

He couldn't deny that. "They probably will at first, but then they'll stop. And I'll stay by your side as long as you need me."

Her grasp tightened. She might leave bruises. "You promise?"

"Yes." If she needed him, he would not desert her.

Mama looked back at them. "Are you two getting out of there tonight? Ned and Ellie have arrived; we should go in."

Frances made a small noise that sounded like a whimper and pulled back.

"Of course, Mama," Jack said, squeezing Frances's hand in what he hoped was a reassuring manner. "We're coming right now."

What was the matter with her? She'd almost turned into a sniveling, sobbing blancmange back there in the carriage. It had been a very near thing whether she'd get out at all, and now she was clinging to Lord Jack's arm as if it was the only thing holding her upright as they followed everyone up the stairs. He must seriously doubt her sanity.

She glanced up at him.

He was so bloody handsome. He'd been very attractive in his regular clothes or—she flushed—almost no clothes at all, but he was breathtaking in evening wear. No wonder he was such a successful rake. Women must trip over each other to pursue him.

He smiled at her, and she felt an odd fluttering in her belly.

She whipped her eyes ahead to study the duke's back. She was insane. When had a male *ever* improved a situation? She should not have this idiotic feeling that Lord Jack was the one solid thing in the tempest of anxiety and confusion that raged inside her.

She tightened her grip on his arm.

But what if the duchess was mistaken? What if Lord and Lady Rothmarsh hadn't written any letters? What if they'd invited her here just to sneer at her? They must have heard the rumors; they knew what a complete hoyden she was—as disreputable as her father.

This was a huge mistake. She should leave now. She could get back to Greycliffe House some way . . .

And how would she explain her sudden flight?

"It really will be all right, Frances," Jack whispered. His breath tickled her ear.

"What?" She jerked her head away; if she turned toward him, their lips might have—

She was sick, that was it. She must have some bizarre brain fever.

"You are holding my arm so tightly, you've about cut off my circulation."

"Oh! I'm so sorry—"

"The Duke and Duchess of Greycliffe," the butler announced. "Lord Ned and Miss Bowman; Lord Jack and Miss Hadley."

She was going to see her grandparents now. There was no escaping it.

Her fingers tightened again—and she noticed Jack

flinch just a little. She forced her grip to relax. Both Ned and the duke were tall. She couldn't see past them—

Someone shrieked.

"That's Lady Rothmarsh," Jack murmured. "Prepare to be hugged."

The duke and Lord Ned stepped aside, and a tall, thin, white-haired woman dressed in a dark blue gown rushed toward her.

"Frances!" she said. "Oh, Frances."

And then the woman—it must be her grandmother—wrapped her arms around her, and she was breathing in lily of the valley, hugged fiercely by soft, wrinkled arms.

Her arms went round her grandmother of their own accord, and she hugged her back in dazed self-defense.

She couldn't remember ever being hugged. It felt good. Very good. She'd thought she'd feel smothered, but she didn't. She'd thought she didn't like being touched. But this . . . there was something here she hadn't realized she'd been missing.

Surely her mother had hugged her when she was a baby, though then again, her mother had likely been overwhelmed with twins.

"Let me look at you," Lady Rothmarsh said, taking a step back, her hands moving to Frances's shoulders.

Lady Rothmarsh's face was soft and wrinkled, and she had green eyes like Frances's.

"Oh, you are so much like your mother. Sebastian, doesn't she look just like Diana?"

The tall, broad-shouldered man with thick white hair standing just behind Lady Rothmarsh nodded. He looked a little like Frederick. His eyes were damp, and his voice had a slight catch. "That she does, Imogen."

Lady Rothmarsh's eyes started to water as well. "I never

thought to see this day." She sniffed before pulling Frances back into a tight hug. "I am so glad you're here, dear."

"I-I'm glad to be here."

Surprisingly she thought maybe she was.

And then Lady Rothmarsh let Frances go to search her pockets, taking out a handkerchief and blowing her nose.

"We've waited far too many years to meet you, Frances," Lord Rothmarsh said, taking her hand and kissing it. "Welcome—and now come meet your uncles and aunts and cousins who also wish very much to make your acquaintance."

It was a good thing no one expected her to remember names, Frances thought later as she looked down the table at dinner. She had so *many* new relatives and, except for her three aunts, they were all male.

She didn't know what to feel besides overwhelmed. Everyone was talking, laughing, teasing each other. She'd never experienced anything like it. At Landsford, she'd taken to having her meals on a tray in the study while she worked on estate affairs. It was more efficient . . . and her aunt's constant carping tied her stomach in knots.

She glanced down the table at Lady Rothmarsh. Her grandmother was smiling at her, a sort of wonder and joy in her eyes. It was impossible to miss how happy her presence at this table made the woman.

How could her mother and Viola have cut her off so completely from this part of her family? She'd missed twenty-four years of dinners and birthdays and all manner of celebrations. She would have missed *this* dinner, if Jack hadn't dragged her out of the carriage.

He might be a rake of the worst sort, but she'd have to be thankful to him for this, at least.

"Where is your brother, Frances?" Lord Rothmarsh asked. "I believe he is in London, too?" The marchioness had dispensed with any formality and seated Frances next to the marquis.

"I'm not sure where he is, my lord. When he married and moved from his boardinghouse, he didn't leave his new direction."

"Ah, well, I'm sure Lord Jack can find him. He's very resourceful, isn't he?"

"Yes. And I plan to ask our man of business tomorrow. He may know Frederick's whereabouts, my lord."

Lord Rothmarsh frowned and put his large, blue-veined hand over hers. "Please, don't *my lord* me, Frances."

"But what am I supposed to call you, my, er, sir?" That was certainly wrong.

He smiled. "Grandpapa."

Frances's mouth opened, but she couldn't get anything to come out. Call this impressive, elderly lord *grandpapa*?

The marquis patted her hand. "I know this is all new to you, my dear, but my wife and I would be very happy if you could bring yourself to call us grandmamma and grandpapa like our other grandchildren do."

"I . . ." She looked into his eyes and saw an almost painful yearning.

"Please, Frances? Your mother was our daughter." His voice broke, and he glanced away for a moment. When he looked back, his eyes were wet again. "You are very like her."

"But I'm not her, your lo—" She saw pain flicker in his eyes and swallowed. "Gr-grandpapa." Saying the word felt odd, but if it made the elderly man at her side happy, it seemed like a little thing to do.

"We know you aren't Diana, Frances, but you remind us of her and all the happiness she brought us." He smiled. "And the arguments, too. Your mother was a wonderful, bright, determined woman—as I'm sure you are. We'd like to get to know you, if you'll let us." He nodded at the noisy group around the table. "We would like you to be part of our family."

Part of a family—of this big, noisy, happy family.

A deep, gut-wrenching longing rushed through her like a sudden windstorm.

"I'd like that, Grandpapa."

Chapter 11

But family can also be very difficult.

—Venus's Love Notes

Frances tugged on her gloves as she descended the stairs. She didn't want to keep Jack waiting when he'd so kindly offered to take her to see Mr. Puddington.

She turned at the landing and saw him standing in the entryway. He looked up—he must have heard her—and smiled.

Her foolish heart gave a little leap.

Damn it, what was the matter with her? She no longer knew herself.

She was tired, that was all.

"Good morning, Frances."

"Good morning, my lord. I hope I haven't kept you waiting."

"No, I just got here a moment before you." He helped her on with her cloak, and her silly heart fluttered at his nearness, at the brush of his hands on her shoulders, the scent of his shaving soap. "My curricle's outside. Shall we go?"

"Yes indeed." The sooner she put some distance between them, the better.

When they arrived at his curricle, he offered her his hand.

She didn't want his help. "I can climb in myself, you know."

He raised his brows. "Ah, but not, I think, in this lovely dress."

He was correct. The dress was beautiful, but breeches gave her more freedom. It was too bad ladies couldn't wear them.

His hand grasped hers, firm and strong, and her damn heart just about jumped into the carriage on its own.

She was *definitely* not herself.

Jack went around to climb into the driver's seat, and the boy holding the horses scrambled up behind.

"You have a tiger now?" The child was about twelve, dressed neatly but not in livery, and looked vaguely familiar.

"For the time being. Sam, make your bows to Miss Hadley."

Sam grinned and bobbed his head. Ah, now she knew where she'd seen him—at Jack's house in Bromley.

"Hello, Sam." She turned back to Jack. "I'm sorry that I've not thought to ask before—how is the baby?" She *had* thought to ask; she'd just been afraid of the answer.

Jack grinned. "Amazingly enough, it looks like he's going to be fine."

"Oh, thank God."

He set the horses into motion, and she turned to study the passing scenery—far safer than admiring the man sitting next to her.

She was so tired because she'd tossed and turned all

night, furious with her mother and aunt for keeping her from her grandparents and other relatives, and overwhelmed and touched—and a little frightened—by their welcome.

Her grandparents couldn't *really* love her, of course; they just loved the idea of her. She was their second chance with their daughter. Once they got to know her and discovered how contrary she was, they wouldn't be so enthusiastic. They'd be relieved when she disappeared back into the country.

"Did you sleep well?" Jack asked.

"Yes." She was not about to share her turmoil with Jack. He was *not* her safe harbor: He was a whirlpool that would suck her down to disaster. She knew better than to rely on a man, especially one who was a rake. She'd accept Jack's help just as long as she needed it, and then she'd move on.

And yet . . .

No and no. She could not think she had any future with Lord Jack.

Jack turned off the main road, navigated through a series of narrow streets, and stopped in front of a nondescript, rather sad-looking building. Sam jumped down and went to hold the horses.

There wasn't a soul in sight, if one didn't count the black cat that had just darted down an alley. "It seems a bit deserted."

"Don't worry, Puddington is expecting us." Jack hesitated. "Frances, before we go in, I want to explain about Sam."

"Yes?" She looked down at Sam; he grinned up at her. What in the world could there be to say about Sam?

"I didn't bring him to Greycliffe House primarily to be my tiger, though he's useful enough in that role today. I brought him to look after you."

"What?" Her brows snapped down. "Why do you think I need a boy looking after me?" The idea was both ridiculous and infuriating.

"Well, he's not to look *after* you, of course. More look out for you."

"And why would I need that?"

Jack's eyes were suddenly bleak. "Belinda was found dead this morning, her throat cut."

"Oh." The old whore. The blood rushed from her head, and she felt a little dizzy. Belinda had been soliciting them just a few days ago in that doorway on Hart Street, and now she was dead. It was horrible, but why did Jack think it had anything to do with her? "Belinda was a . . . that is, she lived a dangerous life in a dangerous neighborhood."

"Yes, but the Slasher isn't killing only light-skirts, Frances. Three society women have been murdered as well—women who had questionable reputations, a category into which I'm afraid you now fall."

"I see." Damn it, much as it galled her to admit it, Jack was right. "But I'm smarter than those girls. And I'm not looking for any sort of assignation, so I won't be going off into a secluded place with some man." Unless the man was Jack—

No, not then, either.

Jack was frowning at her. "Frances, overconfidence leads to carelessness, which leads just as surely to disaster. If Nan is correct, and Ruland is the Slasher, he's surely figured out by now that you were the 'boy' with me that day at the brothel. He was not happy when I evicted him from Nan's office. If he's looking for his next society victim, he might well look to you."

Her stomach twisted. Yes, he might. He'd certainly been angry enough to do her an injury when he'd seen her at the brothel.

She must have turned white, because Jack laid his hand on her arm.

"I hope I'm overreacting, Frances, but we can't take any chances. Sam knows to keep a sharp eye out, especially when I'm not with you, and get help if you need it." His hand slid down to grasp hers. "You can do your part by remaining alert and not going anywhere alone. If you do that, you should be fine. I'm trying my best to discover the Slasher's identity. Once he's caught, we can all rest easier."

"Yes. Of course." She swallowed. Belinda was dead; her throat cut, and Ruland . . . "I'll be careful."

"Splendid." He smiled at her—and her damn heart started fluttering again.

Stupid! She watched him come around to help her alight. Jack had just told her her life was in danger, and all she could think about was his dimple.

If she didn't leave London soon, she'd be staying for good—in Bedlam.

Puddington's offices were up a narrow flight of stairs. Jack had Frances precede him so he could catch her if she stumbled, but the position also gave him an excellent view of her derriere and well-turned ankles—which reminded him forcibly of the long legs he'd so recently seen encased in breeches. And *that* thought had a very predictable effect on his anatomy.

He stayed behind her, shielding his misbehaving anatomy with her skirts as they entered the offices.

Puddington's clerk—a painfully thin, stooped fellow with a large nose on which perched a pair of spectacles—stood when he saw them. He looked to be around Jack's age, but his hairline was already receding, perhaps to escape the towering pile of papers on his desk.

"May I help you, sir?" he said, looking right past Frances.

"I believe we have an appointment with Mr. Puddington." Did the clerk not realize his life was in danger? Frances's chin had gone up; she was clearly on the verge of explosion.

"Yes," she said, biting off the word. "I am Miss Hadley, and this is Lord Jack."

Comprehension of a sort dawned. The clerk's face glowed. "Oh yes, of course. Please excuse me. Mr. Puddington has been eagerly awaiting your arrival, Lord Jack. It's not often we have a man of your rank visit our offices. Please, come this way."

He turned, leaving his back exposed. The fellow was exceedingly lucky Frances didn't have a knife in her purse or he might have found it protruding from between his shoulder blades.

"Do not, I beg you, box him about the ears with your reticule," Jack murmured.

Frances glared at him.

The clerk opened a door. "Lord Jack is here, Mr. Puddington," he said, and then stepped aside for them to enter.

Frances's face was now red with fury. Poor Puddington. If the man knew what was coming, he'd hide behind his desk.

Puddington was as mutton-headed as his clerk.

"Lord Jack," he said, bowing and waddling over to greet him as they stepped into his office, "such a pleasure to meet you. I've heard about you, of course, but I never expected to see you in my humble place of work."

"Mr. Puddington," Frances said, her voice as sharp as a whip.

It got Puddington's attention. He looked at her, his eyebrows raised. "Yes?"

She was almost vibrating with anger now. "Lord Jack was kind enough to act as my escort this morning, but your business is with me."

Puddington, the cabbagehead, laughed, wiggled his

damn eyebrows, and leaned over to whisper to Jack, "Quite fiery, ain't she?" He chuckled. "I have to say, I didn't believe the rumors—the girl always struck me as a bit of a cold fish, don't you know?—but I guess they're true. Well, you're here with her, aren't you?" He grinned. "I assume you wish to discuss the marriage settlements?"

Fury, colder than Jack had ever felt, flooded him, and his mind became clear and sharply focused as it did before he faced a fight in the stews. He could kill this soft, flabby fool in any number of ways, all quick and simple and painless—well, painless for him, not so painless for Puddington.

But first he had to keep Frances from beating him to it.

"This is not about marriage settlements, you bloody blockhead." Her hands flexed as if she were within ambsace of wrapping them around Puddington's neck.

"Miss Hadley, such language." Puddington looked at Jack. "Say something, my lord."

Jack smiled coldly. "What would you like me to say?"

Puddington was not a complete idiot—he realized he was in danger. He stepped back so quickly he caught his heel and stumbled, landing on his desk and upsetting his pounce box, scattering sand all over his papers. "I just thought, given the rumors, that you'd come to discuss the f-financial arrangements."

Jack said nothing; he just watched the sweat bead up on Puddington's forehead and run down his fat cheeks.

"Well, you thought wrong." Frances stabbed her index finger at him. "I have come to discuss obtaining my dowry *because I do not intend to marry anyone ever.*" She struggled to take a calming breath. "And to see if you know Frederick's direction," she said with slightly less venom.

Puddington ran a finger around his cravat as he slipped his handkerchief out of his pocket. He mopped his forehead. "Frederick's direction. Yes, I have that. I'll just get

Swigert to jot it down. Please have a seat. I'll be back in a moment."

"You'd best hurry," Frances said. "We do not have time to waste."

"No. No, of course not, my lord, Miss Hadley." Puddington bobbed a quick bow and bolted out of the room, likely looking for the nearest chamber pot.

"I think you frightened him," Jack said as Frances sat on the edge of one of Puddington's chairs. The heel of her right foot bounced up and down on the floor. She was still very angry.

She snorted. "I suspect your presence had more to say to that."

He took the chair next to her, facing Puddington's disorderly desk. "Has he always been such an idiot?"

"Yes." She glared at him. "Though no more idiotic than most men."

He stretched out his legs and weighed his words. He was more than a little hesitant to say anything—Frances was fiercely independent and, at the moment, blindingly angry—but he didn't want her to feel she was alone any longer. "It cannot have been comfortable dealing with him by yourself all these years. I hope you know you can rely on me to help in any way you need, including bashing the lobcock over the head."

Something flickered in her eyes, and a faint smile flashed over her lips before she looked down to fiddle with the strings on her reticule. "Thank you."

Puddington bustled back into the room just then. "Here you go, Miss Hadley." He handed her a slip of paper. "Frederick is off on his honeymoon, but he should be at this direction next week. Your father felt, of course, that as a married man, Frederick should live in a better place than Hart Street."

Oh, damn.

Frances had been in the process of putting the paper with her brother's location in her reticule, but her hands froze at Puddington's words. She looked up. Her face was suddenly white; her eyes . . .

All the fire that had been there moments ago was doused. She looked like the children did when he found them wandering the streets, lost and alone.

"My . . . my f-father?" She cleared her throat. "You've spoken to my father?"

Puddington lowered his bulk carefully into his chair. "Oh, not recently, of course. He hasn't been in London for at least a year." The man smiled briefly. "Slips in and out of Town when he does come. Doesn't want Rothmarsh or Whildon to get wind of his visits. Bad blood there, you know." He righted the pounce box and dusted some of the sand onto the floor. "I received a letter from him two or three weeks ago with instructions about Frederick's housing."

"So he's not in the South Seas?"

Devil take it, Frances's lovely voice cracked. If her damned father were in the room now, he'd tear the man's heart out—except the miscreant clearly didn't have that particular organ.

Puddington shook his head. "Hasn't been there for five years or more."

"So where *is* Hadley senior?" Jack didn't try to hide his anger.

Puddington threw him a nervous glance. "Somewhere in South America. Frederick will know better than I when you catch up with him. They correspond regularly about botany and such—or as regularly as distance and infrequent mail packets permit, that is."

From the corner of his eye, Jack saw Frances flinch.

"So Hadley never felt the need to visit his estate when he was in England?" Jack tried to keep his voice even. He wouldn't mention Frances. How the blackguard could fail to see his daughter or even write her a letter was impossible to fathom. Unless . . . could he have written, and Frances's aunt kept his letters a secret, just as she'd hidden Rothmarsh's correspondence?

No. The aunt might have hidden a letter, but she couldn't have hidden a visit. There was no justifiable reason Hadley hadn't come to Landsford. It was only a few hours' ride from London.

"But why would he visit?" Puddington smiled at Frances. "Miss Hadley was doing a satisfactory job managing things, especially for a female." He winked at Jack. "As Hadley said, it kept her busy and out of trouble, eh?"

The bloody bounder. He saw Frances's hands grab the chair arm. Good. A little fire was coming back to her eyes.

"Now, Miss Hadley," Puddington said, tugging on his waistcoat and turning to Frances, "about your nonsensical request for your dowry. I'm afraid it's really not possible to advance you the money. And in any event, not that Lord Jack needs any extra funds—everyone knows he's rich as Croesus—you don't want to go to the altar completely empty-handed."

Frances leaned forward. "Didn't you hear me?" She pronounced each word distinctly, as if Puddington was a halfwit. "I. Am. Not. Marrying. Lord Jack." She paused to take a deep breath and then hissed, *"I am not marrying anybody!"*

Puddington reared back, shock and distaste warring on his fat face. "But your reputation, Miss Hadley! Think of your reputation." Puddington tugged on his waistcoat again, but it was a hopeless endeavor. There was far too little cloth to cover his expansive middle.

He took a breath, obviously gathering his courage, and looked at Jack. "My lord, much as it pains me to say it, what about Miss Hadley's reputation? I'm certain her father and brother would wish me to point out the stories are quite damning." He squared his narrow shoulders. "*Quite* damning. The chance of Miss Hadley finding anyone to marry her after you are through with her is miniscule."

"I am not marrying anybody," Frances repeated forcefully.

Jack leaned forward and looked straight into Puddington's jowly, trembling face. "Miss Hadley does not have to do anything she does not wish to do."

"But, my lord—"

"You and Miss Hadley's relatives need not worry." He was quite certain the only thing the blackguards would concern themselves with were the marriage settlements. "My mother and Miss Hadley's grandmother have things well in hand. Who do you think would dare argue with the Duchess of Greycliffe or the Marchioness of Rothmarsh, not to mention the duke and the marquis?"

"Er . . . Well, of course . . . That is . . ."

"No one." Jack smiled in the way that made people—even some of London's worst villains—squirm. Puddington was no exception. He turned an interesting shade of green.

"My mother is the best of women, Puddington, but she does not suffer fools gladly, and my father most assuredly will not allow anyone to criticize his wife. I assume Rothmarsh feels the same way."

"Ah. I did not mean to imply—"

Jack went on as if the man hadn't spoken. "My brother's betrothed has just come to London and is making her bows as well, so Miss Hadley has graciously agreed to accompany her to all the Season's social events."

Frances made an odd little noise, a cross between a gasp and a giggle. She had clearly reached her limit.

He stood. "I believe we've accomplished all we can hope to at the moment. Do you agree, Miss Hadley?"

Frances nodded.

"Then, good day, Puddington."

He offered Frances his arm. She took it and walked with him out of the office, head high, looking neither right nor left, eyes focused on some invisible point in front of them. He felt her tension as she gripped his arm, and saw it in the stiffness of her gait, the brittle way she held her head steady. She was going to come crashing down like a tower of blocks at any moment.

He didn't speak—even one word would have been too much. When they reached the street, he helped her into the curricle and went round to climb into his seat.

Frances would not want anyone to observe the loss of control he was certain was coming; she wouldn't want him to witness it, either, but he was not about to let her weather this storm alone.

The snow had melted; it wasn't so very cold. He would take her to a quiet part of Hyde Park where they could leave the curricle with Sam and walk a bit.

Her father was *not* on some South Pacific island.

Frances sat in Lord Jack's curricle—she couldn't quite remember how she'd got there—and clutched the side of the carriage.

He'd been in England, in London, and he'd seen Frederick. He even wrote to her brother regularly. But he'd never come to Landsford. Not once. He hadn't seen her since her birth. If she passed him on the street, he'd not know it. *She'd* not know it. He could be any of the men strolling along the pavement right now—

No, Puddington had said he was in South America.

She drew in a deep, shuddery breath.

"Hold on," Jack said. "Just a little longer now."

She blinked. They had just passed the place they usually turned to reach Greycliffe House. "Where are we going?"

"To walk in Hyde Park. It won't be crowded now, but we'll take one of the less popular paths to ensure we won't be disturbed."

Was Jack mad? "I don't wish to go for a walk." She swallowed. "I-I have the headache. Please turn around."

"I'm not surprised you have a headache—*I* have a headache. Puddington is a complete horse's arse."

Jack was not turning around; in fact, he'd just driven through the park gate. She should demand he change course, but she didn't have the energy to argue with him. It was too hard to keep from bursting into tears, damn it.

She was not going to let her father turn her into a watering pot like he had her mother. *She* didn't love him. Absurd! She disliked him intensely. He was a bloody rake, a heartless rogue, a—

Oh God, she *was* going to cry.

"Here we are." Jack pulled the curricle to a stop, and Sam ran to grab the horses' bridles. In a moment Jack was beside her, extending his hand to help her down.

She stayed in her seat, her fingers clutching the side of the curricle. "It's cold. I don't want to walk." She wanted to go back to Greycliffe House, close the door to her room, throw herself on her bed, and let the blasted tears flow until they were gone.

Her father had been in London and had not taken the time to travel the short—the very short—distance to Landsford to see her. Not one single, bloody time.

And why the hell did she care? He was a brainless, disgusting animal, just the man who'd impregnated her mother—just a studhorse. She'd done very well without him.

She bit her lip and squeezed her eyes shut. She hated crying. It was such a weak, feminine thing to do. It was what her mother had done all those years when she'd sat at Landsford, reading the London scandal sheets.

"Come, Frances," she heard Jack say.

He was still holding his hand out to her. He looked calm and determined, as if he'd stand there for as long as it took her to decide to get out of the curricle. Clearly, he was not going to drive her back to Greycliffe House until they had this bloody walk. She might as well get it over with.

She let him help her down. It was cold, though not bone-chilling, and quiet. There wasn't another soul in sight. She took his arm, and they strolled along a slightly rutted path. She had to mind where she put her feet to avoid turning an ankle, but at least it was dry. Most of the snow was gone; only patches remained in the shady areas.

"We should bring Shakespeare here," Jack said.

"Yes." His choice of the plural pronoun gave her a funny, warm feeling in the pit of her stomach. She'd never been part of *we*—she'd always been only I.

Which she still was. Jack was a rake, and consorting with rakes was disastrous. She of all people knew that. Look at her mother. What had her grandfather said at dinner? That her mother had been bright and determined once. And see what loving Benedict Hadley had done to her. Turned her into a sullen ghost. Frances was *not* going to make her mother's mistake.

But what was she going to do? Unless a miracle occurred, Puddington wasn't going to give her a single farthing.

"Is Madam Celeste coming back to measure you for more dresses today?" Jack asked.

"Yes. This afternoon. I can't imagine how I could possibly need so many dresses, but your mother says I do."

He laughed. "If Mama says you need them, then you need them."

"Oh no." The duchess was very kind, but she was wrong here. "They are a terrible waste. They are far too fine to wear in a country cottage."

He frowned down at her. "You are not going to be living in a country cottage."

Too true, given Puddington's damnable pigheadedness. Perhaps she could apply directly to Frederick—

Blast it all! Here she'd run Landsford for years, keeping the property prosperous, and now she had to come crawling, hat in hand, to her irresponsible, couldn't-care-less brother for funds. It was infuriating and insulting. Damn, blasted, bloody, useless males.

And if she couldn't get the money, what the hell was she going to do? Live the rest of her life with Viola and Frederick's trollop wife?

Panic fluttered in her chest, but she beat it back. She would manage somehow. She always had.

"Frances, about your father—"

Oh God, she did not want to speak about her father! She rushed to talk over Jack. "But even if your mother is right and I do need the dresses, I'm afraid I just can't afford so many."

Which was true. Much as she'd like to bankrupt the estate, she couldn't in good conscience do so. *She* wasn't irresponsible. She knew Madam Celeste's dresses must cost a fortune, but she'd not yet been able to find out exactly how much. It might be rude to ask, but she was going to do so today—and insist on getting an answer.

Jack shrugged. "Don't worry about it. I'm sure your grandparents will stand the expense—or else my parents will."

She stumbled, and he caught her.

Did the man think she had no sense of propriety at all? Well, perhaps he did, since she'd come to London in such an improper fashion, but he was very much mistaken. "I can't sponge off my grandparents, and I certainly can't sponge off your parents."

"But you're not sponging, Frances. You would make your grandparents—and my parents—very happy if you would accept the gowns."

She poked him in the chest to emphasize her words. "Are you mad or do you think me a complete greenhorn? It would be totally inappropriate—and greatly add to the scandal—for your parents to buy my clothing. And as to my grandparents footing the bill—"

Oh God, her grandparents. Even though she'd just met them, she'd miss them when she left. But it would be for the best. They had a wonderful, large, scandal-free family. They didn't need her, and would soon discover they didn't want her. "I can't imagine they really wish to spend a small fortune on a girl they've spent only one evening with."

Jack covered her finger where it pressed against him. "But they want to spend more time with you, Frances. You saw how happy they were at dinner last night."

She tried to retrieve her hand, but he wouldn't release her. "I'm a moment's entertainment, that's all."

"No, you aren't. You're their blood—their family."

Zeus! She jerked free and took a step back. "Oh yes. Just like I'm my father's blood? *His* family?"

What if her grandparents turned their backs on her, too? It would be even worse now that they'd met her. Better to turn *her* back on them. "I'm leaving London as soon as I can."

She whirled away from him, took a step toward the curricle—and tripped over a rut. Damn. She tried to recover, but her ankle twisted. She threw her hands out to break her fall—

Jack's arm snaked around her waist and hauled her up against his rock-hard chest, turning her so her breast was against his. For a moment she was surrounded by him, by the rough fabric of his greatcoat and the strength of his arms.

She'd never been held this close to a man. Hell, she'd never been held by a man at all. Jack's shoulders were so broad. She didn't see the trees or the grass or the snow; she saw only Jack.

Her stomach felt hollow and shivery. She looked up at his chin, his lips—

He held her away and shook her just a little.

"Frances, your father is a complete bounder, and I'd like nothing more than to teach him that lesson with my fists. I do not understand how he can live with himself. But you cannot let him rule your life like this."

What the hell was the matter with Jack? "I'm not letting my useless father rule my life."

"Yes, you are. Don't you see that? You're angry that he never came to visit you and that he's been corresponding with your brother. That's perfectly understandable. But you need to understand that his failure to seek you out is his loss. Truthfully, I'd say you were fortunate not to have made his acquaintance."

She tried to shrug, but his hands kept her shoulders still, so she glared at him instead. "I understand my father's limitations. He's a man. That's the way men are."

His grip tightened, and he scowled at her. "That is *not* the way men are. I'm a man, Frances, and I'm not anything like your father."

The odd feeling in her stomach exploded until it felt as if she was one hollow, shivery mass. She wanted to believe him—

But she couldn't. He was a rake. He was a master at charming women.

She forced herself to step back; he dropped his hands and let her go.

"Thank you, Lord Jack. Now please take me back to Greycliffe House."

Chapter 12

Dancing in the ballroom sometimes leads to dancing in the bedroom.

—Venus's Love Notes

Jack and Frances entered Greycliffe House as a phalanx of housemaids, armed with mops, brooms, and buckets, passed through. Jack looked at Braxton and raised his brows.

"Her Grace is getting the house in order, milord," Braxton said resignedly.

"I see." He usually fled to one of his clubs when Mama was in a cleaning mood, but he didn't want to desert Frances. "In that case, is there somewhere we can hide—I mean, be out of the way?"

"I believe I'll go up to my room." Frances took a step toward the stairs.

Braxton cleared his throat. "If you please, milord, Miss

Hadley, Her Grace would like you to join her in the music room. Lord Ned and Miss Bowman are already there."

"The music room, Braxton?" What could Mama be planning?

"Yes, milord. She has engaged a musician to play the pianoforte so you can practice dancing."

"Dancing?" What the hell—

He saw Frances stiffen. Panic flashed over her face before it shut down into an expressionless, guarded mask. Except for her eyes. She couldn't hide the misery darkening her eyes.

Damn. What was the problem?

"I'm afraid I'm exhausted," she said, backing toward the stairs. "Please give my apologies to Her Grace."

Jack closed the gap between them and took Frances's arm. "I'm sure you'll perk up, Miss Hadley." He looked at Braxton. "Have some tea and cakes sent in, will you?"

"Very good, milord. William delivered a tray half an hour ago, but I suspect it would be wise to take in another."

"Indeed! If my brother's had half an hour to make inroads in the provisions, they're sure to need replenishment."

"My thought exactly, milord." Braxton bowed and went off to give Cook the message.

"I'm tired," Frances said. Her tone was an odd cross between a hiss of anger and a whine of fear. "I wish to go to my room now."

She tried again to move toward the stairs, but he wouldn't let her.

"I assure you there's no escaping my mother, Frances. If you don't appear in the music room now, she'll send someone to drag you down, or she'll postpone whatever she has planned for later. Best get it over with." He took her other arm, turning her so she faced him squarely. "I think you're more afraid than tired."

She glared at him, jaw clenched, nostrils flaring. "I'm not afraid."

"Then what is the problem? Mama may be overly enthusiastic, but she's not dangerous." Unless one was a young, single male intent on remaining that way.

Frances looked away. "Very well, if you must know, I can't dance."

"Pardon?" He must have misheard. "Did you say you can't dance?"

"Yes, damn it." She glanced at him and then away again. Her face was bright red.

He frowned. He didn't understand. "But you aren't deaf or blind or lame."

That brought her eyes back to his. "Of course I'm not, you dunderhead. It's not that I'm physically incapable; it's that I don't know how." Her jaw hardened. "I told your mother that."

He'd never encountered a woman Frances's age who hadn't been taught to dance, but now that he considered the matter, he shouldn't be surprised. Nothing in Frances's upbringing had been what one would expect. "And what did she say?"

Frances's shoulders hunched. "That you were an excellent dancer and would teach me."

He laughed. Trust Mama. "Well, I'm not sure I could hire myself out as a dancing master, but I believe I know all the steps. And Ned and Ellie will be there to help if I turn out to be a complete failure."

"Don't be ridiculous." Her voice was tight with embarrassment. "I should just go back to the country. I don't belong here."

She did belong here, but there was no point in arguing about it. She wouldn't listen to him. She was too upset.

Better to stoke her anger.

"I didn't think you were such a coward that you'd run home with your tail between your legs at a little thing like learning to dance."

Her head jerked as if he'd hit her. "I'm not a coward."

"No? I think you are. I think you're afraid to face a ballroom of people."

"I'm not."

"And even more, I think you're afraid to admit the world isn't exactly as you've decided it is."

"That's ridiculous." Her eyes were flashing now.

"Is it?" Suddenly his own anger and frustration were pushing him on. "Mostly I think you're afraid to admit that not all men are bloody bounders like your father."

Her hand flashed up, but he stopped it before her palm could connect with his cheek.

"You *are* a bounder, damn it."

He certainly felt like one at the moment. He should apologize, but the words stuck in his throat. He watched tears well up in her eyes. He wanted to wrap his arms around her and hold her, but he knew she'd knee him in the groin if he tried.

"Perhaps I am." These were not the words he should be saying. "But at least I won't turn my back on you. I won't leave you when you need me."

She sniffed—in disdain but also, he'd wager, because she was too proud to pull out her handkerchief. "I don't need you."

She was lying, and they both knew it. At least she no longer looked as if she was going to cry.

He smiled. "Then who's going to teach you to dance?"

She shook her head, but she was smiling a little, too. "All right, I give up. I'm sure your mother *will* hunt me down if I don't come now." She laid her hand on his arm. "Let's see what sort of a dancing master you are." She grimaced. "And what sort of a student I am."

He led her toward the music room. "As long as you apply yourself, you'll be an excellent student. It's the teacher's duty to see his charges learn, so if by some strange turn of events you don't become an able dancer, you can lay all the blame on my doorstep."

"Well, that will be amusing at least. I suspect you don't fail at many things."

"Exactly!" He opened the door and whispered in her ear as she went past. "And I don't intend to fail with you."

"Oh, there you are!" The duchess beamed at Frances. Did she look a little relieved, too? "Did you have any luck locating your brother?"

"Yes, Your Grace. Mr. Puddington told us where to find him once he returns from his honeymoon." Just as Jack had suspected, only a few fragments remained as evidence that cakes had ever been in the room. Lord Ned dusted something from his lap as he stood to greet them, and Shakespeare hurried to investigate. He sneezed and trotted over to be petted—apparently the crumbs were too small to interest him.

"This is Miss Addison," Her Grace said, indicating a white-haired woman who was just putting down her teacup. "She will play the pianoforte so you can learn a few steps, Frances, and Ned and Ellie can brush up on theirs."

The carpet had been rolled back and elaborate marks chalked on the floor.

"I *know* how to dance," Ned grumbled, "as does Ellie."

"But I'm happy to have the chance to practice." Ellie glared at Ned and then turned to smile at Frances. "I've never danced in a London ballroom. I'll confess I'm a little nervous."

A little nervous was nothing compared to what Frances

felt. Full-blown, breath-stealing panic was more like it. And also something else at the thought of being Jack's pupil—an odd, fluttery feeling, akin to what she'd felt at the park.

She must be getting sick.

"I truly don't mind being a wallflower, Your Grace," she said, patting Shakespeare.

"Nonsense. There will be no talk of wallflowers. You can't go to a ball and not dance, Frances. Dancing is invigorating"—the duchess smiled at Jack—"and an excellent way to flirt, isn't it, Jack?"

"I am not given to flirting, Mama."

"You certainly have women throwing themselves at your head."

Jack flinched. "Through no fault of my own. The ladies of the *ton* can be excessively silly."

"As can the gentlemen," the duke said, coming into the room with a slice of seedcake. William was behind him, bearing fresh tea and a plate with the rest of the cake.

"Splendid!" The duchess took the duke's arm. "We are all here. Now if everyone will take his or her place, we can get started."

"But Frances and I would like some tea and cake," Jack said.

"After we've gone through a few dances. We don't want to keep Miss Addison waiting any longer." The duchess smiled at Frances. "I do hope you aren't too hungry, dear, but at least Ned will be dancing, too. The cakes should be quite safe."

"I'm not hungry at all, Your Grace," Frances said. The thought of eating made her stomach churn even more. That would just complete the dreadful morning, if she cast up her accounts here on the music room floor.

"I expect you will be, though, after a few vigorous

country dances. Now if—hmm." The duchess looked at Shakespeare, who was watching William put the cake-laden plate on a table. "Perhaps the cakes aren't so safe. William, put the plate up on top of that cabinet by the mantel, will you? We don't want to tempt the poor dog into misbehavior."

"Yes, Your Grace." William moved the plate; Shakespeare treated the duchess to an exceedingly mournful look.

"Now, Shakespeare, you will just have to wait until Jack and Frances are ready for some tea. You've already had more than you should. Cake can't be good for you."

Shakespeare lay down, put his head on his front paws, and regarded the duchess with large, pleading brown eyes.

"Oh dear. Perhaps one—"

"Be strong, my dear duchess," the duke said, popping the last bit of his cake into his mouth and dusting his hands. "Do not let Shakespeare's acting skills persuade you to ignore your better judgment."

"Yes," Jack said. "You'll spoil the dog if you do. And the sooner we get this dancing over the sooner I can have *my* cake."

The duchess sighed. "Yes. It is always best when one is firm with animals."

The duke laughed. "Have you ever been firm with one of your pets, my dear?"

"Of course I have."

Ned snorted. "Not with Sir Reginald."

The duchess dismissed this with a wave of her hand. "Reggie is a cat. Cats are vastly different from dogs. Now come, take your places. Frances, you stand between Ellie and me on that triangle there."

"What have you done to our floor, my dear?" the duke asked, standing on a circle across from the duchess.

"I have marked out the steps to help Frances learn them, of course." She smiled at Frances. "We will go through everything slowly several times, and then Miss Addison will play for us. Let's start with turn your partner. Take Jack's hands, Frances, and we'll begin."

At first she thought she could manage it; the basic steps were simple enough. But putting them together was confusing, and it didn't help that she was so very distracted by Jack's touch. Her nerves must still be frayed from her meeting with Puddington. Everything—the strength of Jack's fingers, his closeness, the act of moving together—affected her. She was having trouble breathing; remembering steps was out of the question.

"Clockwise, dear," the duchess said when Frances bumped into her for the fourth time. "Move clockwise."

"I'm so sorry, Your Grace. I hope I didn't hurt you?"

"No. No, I'm fine."

Frances would swear the duchess winced.

"Perhaps Frances will do better with music, Mama," Jack said.

"Or perhaps I'd do better as a spectator." She forced herself to smile. "You must all be covered in bruises."

Lord Ned started to nod, but Ellie trod upon his foot. "Ouch."

"Don't give up." Ellie ignored Ned's wounded expression. "I think you're doing quite well."

Which was a plumper of enormous proportions, but Ellie smiled so kindly when she said it, Frances actually felt encouraged.

"You're thinking too much," Jack said. "Relax. Once you have the music to guide you, you'll find the steps come easily."

"Yes." The duchess nodded, though she looked more

than a little doubtful. "Music will likely solve the problem. Miss Addison, if you would be so good."

Miss Addison struck the opening chord.

"Though perhaps a little slower than normal," Her Grace said, "if you will."

Music did help, somewhat. By the time they'd gone through the dance three times, the last time at full speed, she was only making a few missteps, though the last one had sent her full up against Jack just as the music was ending.

It was like hitting a wall—a warm, male, far too attractive wall.

She felt sure her entire body turned as red as her hair. "Oh, excuse me."

Jack's eyes held an odd, somewhat hot light, but he laughed. "No damage done."

Her Grace was smiling—in relief, no doubt. "I think that's all for now. You've made excellent progress, Frances."

"Thank you, Your Grace." She must look a sight. Her hair was coming out of its pins, and she felt very . . . damp. She took out her handkerchief to blot the sweat from her face. Her feet hurt, too.

"So do Frances and I finally get our tea and cakes, Mama?" Jack asked.

"Yes, I think you've definitely earned some refreshment. Let's—"

Crash!

They all spun toward the fireplace to see what had caused the noise. Shakespeare was jumping down from the chair by the cabinet, and the cake plate was in pieces on the floor, slices of cake strewn everywhere.

"Oh dear," the duchess said. "Well, I suppose it's time for nuncheon."

* * *

"Do you think Frances will be ready to dance at Ned's and Ellie's wedding ball?" Drew asked as he untied his cravat. He and Venus were in their room, preparing to retire for the night.

"Of course." Venus sat down at her dressing table and fumbled with a hairpin. At least she hoped Frances would be ready.

Drew raised his brows before pulling his shirt over his head. "The wedding is only four days away. It will take a miracle to make Miss Hadley safe on a dance floor." He dropped his shirt on the carpet and sat down to deal with his footwear. "She'll be crushing toes and colliding with people left and right. Our ballroom will look like a battlefield."

"Jack will work with her. I've got Miss Addison coming every day until the wedding."

"For twenty-four hours a day?" Drew dropped his stockings on top of his shirt. "It will take Jack every waking moment and then some to transform the girl from a dancing disaster into an even moderately competent partner. I think her wallflower idea might be a good one."

"You are too harsh."

He snorted. "I believe you have the bruises to prove my case."

"I do not." Though she hadn't checked her shins yet. "Oh, Drew, what are we going to do about the poor girl?"

He came over to help her pull the rest of the pins from her hair. "What? The Duchess of Love is asking my poor advice?"

She tried to frown at him but got distracted by the sight of his naked chest. He was in excellent condition for a man his age—well, for a man any age. Mmm. And his fingers moving through her hair felt wonderful.

But they were speaking of Jack and Frances. "Perhaps I am. I think Jack may like her."

"I'm sure Jack does like her. Jack is a very friendly fellow. He likes most people."

"That can be a fault, too." She frowned up at Drew. "Do you think he's not very discerning?"

Drew picked up her brush. "Actually, I think Jack is one of the most discerning people I know." He pulled the brush through her hair.

"But the rumors." She closed her eyes and felt her tension begin to drain away with each long stroke. She forgot when she was in the country how bad the rumors were.

Surely she could not have raised a rake . . . could she?

"From what people say, one wouldn't think Jack was at all discriminating in his tastes. Lady Dunlee has whispered to me on more than one occasion that he frequents some of the worst brothels."

"You can't listen to what Lady Dunlee and the other old cats say, Venus. You know how much people like to spread half-truths and even complete fabrications."

She frowned at him. "There's no smoke without fire."

"No, my dear duchess, sometimes there *is* smoke without fire. Think of your breath in the cold or the steam rising from boiling water." He smiled. "Sometimes what looks like smoke isn't smoke at all."

She twisted around to face him. "You think the rumors stem from Jack's charity work?"

"I think many of them do." He shrugged and turned her back so he could keep brushing. "Jack is no saint, but he's no scoundrel, either."

He put the brush down and began unbuttoning the back of her dress. Clearly, he was not going to say another word about Jack's activities. She would have to try a different tack.

"What does Whildon say about Frances?"

Drew pulled her up so he could reach the rest of her buttons. "What can he say? He's just met her." He paused to kiss the back of her neck. "He has a lot to say about her father, though."

Miss Hadley's father—now there was a man she'd like to kick in a very sensitive area. "A man who could desert his children like that is beyond despicable."

He finished the buttons and tugged her dress down. "I'm afraid it's worse than that—well, worse for Miss Hadley."

"Worse? How could it possibly be worse for Frances?" She stepped out of her dress; Drew swept her hair off her back and over her shoulder so he could work on untying her stays.

"Whildon discovered that Hadley has been in London from time to time over the years, as recently as last fall, and has been in regular contact with Miss Hadley's brother."

"What?" Venus swung around to face him. She felt as if ice water had been poured over her head. "And he never visited Frances?"

"Never." He turned her back so he could finish with her stays.

"That's horrible. Can you imagine a father behaving in such a fashion?"

"Unfortunately, I can."

Unfortunately, she could, too. There were far too many blackguards among the men of the *ton*.

"Whildon further discovered—he was talking to Stephen Parker-Roth, a young plant hunter who's around Jack's age—that Frances's brother is quite open about wanting nothing to do with his mother's family." Her stays dropped to the floor next to her dress. "Whildon says

Frederick doesn't care a jot about the *ton*." Drew laughed. "I have to agree with him there."

"But you are a duke. You can afford not to care. A mere mister . . ." She shook her head. "But even a mere mister should care about his family. He should meet them if for no other reason than to see if he wishes the connection."

Drew put his arm around her and led her toward the bed. "Likely the boy is driven by loyalty to his father—Lord and Lady Rothmarsh have made no secret of the fact they can't abide Hadley senior—but he's also socially awkward. Parker-Roth told Whildon that Frederick is a brilliant botanist but has very few friends. And he's just married a woman from the theater."

Venus gasped. "A prostitute?"

"No. Not even an actress, I believe. But you can see why the man might think Rothmarsh wouldn't accept her."

"Yes. Oh dear. And if Jack marries Frances, he'll be stuck with this unpleasant fellow as a brother-in-law."

Drew had his hands around her waist to lift her onto the bed, but stopped and frowned at her. "I thought you planned to repair Miss Hadley's reputation so Jack wouldn't feel compelled to meet her at the altar."

"Yes, but if Jack likes her—"

Drew put his finger on her lips. "Liking her doesn't mean he wishes to marry her."

She pushed his hand away. "I know that." Sometimes Drew could be such a cabbagehead. "But sometimes liking turns to love."

Drew looked extremely skeptical as he lifted her onto the bed. "Sometimes lusting turns to love. I'm not so certain about liking."

"I am. Admit it, Drew. Lovers have to like each other."

"Sadly, my dear duchess, I must inform you that you are wrong. Lovers merely need to lust for each other. I've known people who dislike each other intensely when they aren't in bed together." He pulled off his pantaloons and climbed in beside her. "Lovemaking can be an intensely selfish activity."

"Not if it's *love*making."

Drew inclined his head. "But *love*making is an extremely rare activity." He directed his gaze at her lips. "One I would dearly like to engage in, if I have your permission?"

Venus grinned, all at once feeling nineteen again. She loved Drew so much. Even after all their years of marriage, she thrilled at being in his bed and in his life. "Very well."

"Splendid. Then let us get rid of this very annoying shift. I don't know how you came to wear it to bed."

Venus happily raised her arms to allow him to pull the garment up and over her head.

"This is hopeless," Frances said. "I'm never going to learn to dance."

Jack was about ready to agree with her. They'd practiced almost constantly—or at least it felt that way—but dancing with Frances was still like trying to herd a wayward sheep. Well, when it wasn't like dodging a charging bull. His toes were throbbing from their most recent encounter with her foot. Thank God she was no longer wearing her brother's boots.

Even Miss Addison seemed to have lost patience; her playing was getting faster and sharper.

"Let's take a short respite. Miss Addison, would you like some tea?"

"Yes, thank you, my lord. That would be very pleasant." Miss Addison stood slowly and gave Frances an annoyed look. "My old bones were getting a mite tired from sitting on this hard bench."

Frances stiffened. "There really is no need to torture

everyone any longer," she said. "You know what they say: you can't teach an old dog new tricks."

Miss Addison started to nod in agreement but stopped when she caught Jack's glare.

"Speaking of dogs, I'm sure Shakespeare could use a walk. Why don't you relax for a half hour or so, Miss Addison, while Miss Hadley and I take a turn around the square?"

"Very good, my lord." Miss Addison smiled hopefully. "I'm sure we'll all be in better fettle after a bit of a rest."

He certainly hoped so. "Go get your coat and bonnet, Miss Hadley, if you will, and I'll meet you by the front door."

"This isn't going to help," Frances grumbled as she left.

Her face still looked mulish when she joined him a few minutes later, but at least Shakespeare's enthusiastic greeting caused her to smile.

She went on the attack as soon as the front door closed behind them. "When will you admit this is a waste of time, my lord? I'm too old to learn to dance."

He snorted. "You're twenty-four, not eighty-four."

Shakespeare tugged on the leash, trying to drag Jack across to the park.

"It appears we are crossing the square; please take my arm."

She put her fingers on his sleeve. "I'll grant you I'm not an octogenarian, but I might as well be. Most girls learn to dance when they are only fourteen or fifteen—or even younger. It is too late for me."

"No, it's not. You're just too stubborn to try."

She whipped her hand back to her side. "How can you say that? I've been trying until everyone—including Miss Addison—is ready to scream in frustration *and* pain. I'm sure you must have several bruised toes. Even Ellie, who is a saint, deserted us today."

He opened the gate to the park and allowed Frances and Shakespeare to precede him. "That's because the wedding is tomorrow, and Madam Celeste wanted to check the fit of her dress once more—as well you know." He shook his head. "Mama is in such a dither, she's driven Father and Ned to hide out at White's."

"Where you'd like to be as well."

He couldn't deny it, but he wouldn't admit it. "I have our dancing lessons."

"Which are like trying to teach the Thames to run backward. I'll never learn to dance."

The woman was maddening. "Certainly not if you keep insisting you won't. It's not such a hard skill to acquire. Why, I'll wager even Shakespeare can dance." He looked at the dog sitting impatiently at his feet, waiting to be freed from his leash. "*Can* you dance, Shakespeare?"

Damned if the dog didn't get up on his hind legs and hop about.

"Well done." He patted him on the head, removed his leash, and watched him take off after a squirrel.

Hmm. Perhaps that hadn't been so well done on his part. He'd just demonstrated that Frances was less talented than a dog. "You *can* learn to dance, Frances, if only you'll allow yourself to believe it's possible."

She snorted, though he thought he heard a little hiccup, too, as if she might be on the verge of tears. "I'd rather just sit on the sidelines."

She was lying again.

Why was she so difficult?

Shakespeare treed one squirrel and took off after another.

Because she was afraid, just like the children he rescued from the streets. She could run an estate by herself, but she couldn't navigate a dance floor. She was proud, and she was risking very public embarrassment.

But she was also lonely. He'd swear under all her obstinacy, she had a deep longing for life. He just needed to help her see that.

"Dance with me, Frances." He took her hand and smiled. "Show me you're as clever as Shakespeare."

She frowned at him, and he felt sure he was going to get slapped soundly, but then she laughed.

"You are absurd."

He tugged on her hand. He knew she was at least a little attracted to him. Or maybe it was his attraction to her he was feeling, because he certainly was feeling that.

Trent had often accused him of having an unnatural fascination with lost souls. And he'd often wondered himself why he, the third son of the Duke of Greycliffe, who had wealth and a loving family, who wanted for nothing, would feel this need to work with those whom no one wanted. Yes, the death of Ned's son had started it, but that hadn't been enough to sustain him through the months of frustration and disappointment, the various aspersions cast on his name, and the false rumors about his philandering. He hated being forced to pretend to be someone he wasn't.

But there had been great satisfaction, too, especially when he visited the children at his foundling home. He was doing something important.

Perhaps that was it. As a third son, he wasn't even the spare—he was the spare's spare. Redundant. But his work gave his life meaning. The whores and abandoned children needed him. He was making their lives better, at least for a short while, and sometimes, with some of the children, he hoped forever.

Frances was nothing like the women and children he

helped, but her loneliness and her fierce courage called to him in a way he couldn't ignore.

And it didn't hurt that she had big green eyes, flawless skin, a voice that made him think of bedrooms, and a slender, delightfully endowed figure—a figure he'd closely encountered numerous times recently while trying to teach her to dance.

"Dance with me," he said again, lower, deeper. He would seduce her into his arms if he could.

He smiled. As Mama had said, dancing was an excellent way to flirt.

Frances glanced around nervously. "Here? But what if someone sees us?"

"No one will. The nurses have taken their charges in for naps, and the trees will hide us from anyone peering from the neighboring windows." He took her hand and led her farther into the park—and she went, if not quite willingly, then without protesting.

Fortunately there was a healthy squirrel population; Shakespeare would be busy for as long as needed.

"But there's no music."

"I shall hum." He turned to face her. "We will start with the waltz." He started untying her bonnet. He couldn't waltz with a bonnet poking him in the face.

Her eyes widened in alarm, and her fingers flew up to stop him. "Oh, I don't think—"

"Relax." He gently shook off her hold and finished with the ribbon, lifting her headgear off and placing it on a nearby bench. "Let's just have fun." Had she ever had fun? He offered her his other hand. "Trust me."

That was the heart of the problem, wasn't it? Whom had she been able to trust in her life? No one but herself.

He would convince her to trust him.

She hesitated, but then gave in. "Oh, very well, but this is ridiculous."

He didn't waste time arguing. He began to hum and then to dance.

"You're a bit flat, you know," she said.

"Quite likely. I've been told I can't carry a tune. You'll be delighted with Miss Addison's efforts when I take you back inside."

"I don't think she approves of me."

Frances was moving easily with him now that she wasn't focused on getting the steps right. He urged her a little closer—closer than would be permitted in a ballroom. But it was just the two of them—and Shakespeare and the squirrels, of course.

"And why do you care what Miss Addison thinks?"

She stumbled slightly. He caught her. Their bodies were almost touching.

"I don't care."

He could smell the light, clean scent of her hair and skin.

"It's all right if you do," he said. He wished it was summer, when they'd have on far fewer layers of clothing. "No one likes to be disliked, but we all are, by someone."

Did she feel it, this heavy, dark, insistent thrum? Did she know what it was?

He did—all too well. But he hadn't felt it in a long, long time, and he'd never felt it with a marriageable woman.

Marriageable? Good God. Mama was supposed to save him from having to marry Miss Hadley. He was far too young to wed. Ash and Ned had made mice-feet of their early nuptials. And Miss Hadley didn't even like him much.

The throb of attraction wasn't persuaded. If anything, it intensified. His brain was arguing with his body, and his body was winning.

Well, he might as well enjoy the sensations for the

moment. His thinking would clear once he wasn't in such close proximity to the woman.

He smiled and led her through a turn. "You will find it hard to believe, but even I am disliked by some people."

Her eyebrows went up theatrically. "Really? How shocking."

Good, she was teasing him—and she was dancing very well, even without music, since he couldn't talk and hum at the same time.

"And you aren't devastated by that knowledge?" Her tone was still mocking, but there was a thread of sincerity there, too.

"I am not, because I am liked by the people I care about."

And he cared about Miss Prickly Hadley. He moved them deeper into the trees. What he was going to do was very stupid, but he didn't care. The heavy beat in his groin was begging him to do *something* to satisfy it.

This would hardly do that. In fact, it would likely make the pain greater. If he was lucky, Frances would slap him soundly, and that sting might distract him from this deeper ache.

"Though there is one person I find I care about very much, but whom I suspect doesn't like me at all." They were in the most secluded spot in the little park, completely alone except for the birds and squirrels and Shakespeare.

"Really? And who might that be?"

Did she know her body was moving so closely, so well with his? Could she hear the seductive note that had crept into her beautiful voice?

Her mind probably didn't know, but her body did.

"You," he murmured. He stopped, bent his head. "I care about you."

And then he brushed her lips with his.

Chapter 13

A kiss can be a window into your love's heart, if the glass isn't too fogged by heavy breathing.
—Venus's Love Notes

She'd never been kissed before. She'd never wanted to be kissed. In truth, she'd never thought about kissing at all.

Jack's lips were dry and firm. They skimmed over her mouth with the slightest friction, but the effect was devastating. Heat pooled low in her belly and her chest ached.

He lifted his head. His hazel eyes were warm and lazy and fearfully intense.

A thread of panic whispered through her stunned brain. He would see all the way to her soul if she didn't look away. But she was like a mouse entranced by a snake. She couldn't move.

Gently, he pulled her closer until her body touched his from breast to thigh. Her bones turned liquid; she had to lean against him, unable to stand without his help.

This was a *very* bad idea. She should push away from him immediately. She knew he would let her go.

But need and wonder and curiosity silenced her good sense. She *wanted* to find out what would happen next.

His mouth came down again. It touched her forehead and her temple and her cheekbone. Her lips ached for it to touch them, too, and she sighed with relief when it finally did.

And then the heat in her belly exploded into a raging furnace, and what little caution she had left evaporated. She slid her hands around his back, straining to bring him even closer. A hard ridge pressed into her stomach; she wanted it lower, pressing against the part of her that ached the most.

She was turning into someone she didn't recognize, but she didn't care.

And then Jack raised his head. She made a small sound of distress and displeasure and tightened her arms, but he loosened them and stepped back.

"It's time to take Shakespeare inside, Frances. Miss Addison must be wondering what has become of us."

Miss Addison? Who was . . . oh yes, of course! The elderly woman playing the pianoforte. How could she have forgotten her name for even an instant?

"Yes." She cleared her throat, and her befogged brain cleared, too. Good God! She'd been clutching Jack, pressing against him. "Yes indeed."

She suddenly understood why women allowed themselves to be seduced. Something in men's kisses turned their minds to mush. Well, now that she was aware of the danger, she would guard against it.

The next morning, the day of Ned's and Ellie's wedding, Frances stood in the blue drawing room with Shakespeare, waiting for Ellie to come down. She hadn't slept well—she'd kept dreaming of Jack and waking hot and uncomfortable, the coverlet in knots. Now she was trying hard not to look at him.

"What can be taking the women so long?" Ellie's father asked no one in particular. He was standing by the hearth, dressed in his clerical robes, *The Book of Common Prayer* in his hands. He looked happy, proud, and perhaps a little nervous.

Ellie was still upstairs with her mother and the duchess. They'd invited Frances to join them, but she hadn't wanted to intrude. She didn't belong, not really. Yes, Ellie had asked her to be her witness, but that had been because none of her sisters could come, being busy at home with their families.

"Last-minute preparations, I'm sure," the duke said. "You're married; you know how women can be when they are dressing for a special occasion." He grinned. "And I suspect my dear duchess has been weeping all over your daughter."

The vicar grinned back at him. "As has been my wife." He glanced over at Ned. "Tears of joy, of course."

Her mother would never cry at *her* wedding . . .

Damn it, what the hell did it matter? She was never getting married. And her mother had done far too much crying, all because she'd made the grave error of wedding a rake.

Ned laughed. "Of course." He looked eagerly at the door for what must have been the hundredth time.

But what if this wedding *were* hers—hers and Jack's?

Frances bent down to scratch Shakespeare's ears and hide her blush. Blast it, she was going insane. She was *not* going to make her mother's mistake.

The sooner she talked to Frederick about getting her funds and finding that cottage, the better. Jack had sent a letter to Frederick's new rooms, asking her brother to call on them at his earliest convenience.

"I don't know," Jack said. He was standing on the other side of the vicar with Ned. "Poor Ellie might have finally come to her senses and realized tying herself to my dull-as-ditchwater brother was a mistake."

Ned punched him in the arm, and Jack laughed—the sound drew her as the Sirens' songs had drawn sailors to their deaths.

He was so handsome in his black evening wear and snowy white cravat. Her silly heart started dancing an idiotic waltz like the one they'd danced in the park. Her eyes dropped to his mouth, and she watched his lips curl into a lazy sort of smile. Oh. She met his gaze—it was intent, hot, and . . . laughing. He winked.

She jerked her eyes back to Shakespeare.

Thank God Ellie arrived then, looking beautiful in a white dress with red ribbons and a fine lace veil.

"I hope we didn't keep you waiting too long," the duchess said, walking arm in arm with Ellie's mother. Mrs. Bowman's eyes and nose were red, and she carried a crumpled-up handkerchief in her right hand, but she was smiling. "As you can see, the delay was well worth it. Not that Ellie doesn't always look lovely, but she looks especially lovely today, don't you think, Ned?"

Ned nodded, his smile almost blinding.

"You *are* a beautiful bride, Ellie," the vicar said, before straightening his glasses and opening his prayer book. He cleared his throat. "Shall we begin?"

Frances left Shakespeare to go stand beside Ellie.

"'Dearly beloved, we are gathered together here . . .'"

Ellie was almost glowing with happiness. Had Frances's mother looked this happy when she'd married? She'd been only twenty-one and had left her home, her family, and her friends for the man she must have loved beyond all reason.

Or had she simply been young and rebellious? Had she

regretted her decision almost immediately, realizing that kisses and a handsome face were not enough?

Ned took Ellie's right hand in his and recited after the vicar. "I, Edward Walter Valentine, take thee, Eleanor Ursula Bowman, to my wedded wife . . ." His voice was so strong and confident.

Had her father sounded confident, too? Had he ever intended to keep his vows?

Jack looked uncharacteristically serious, paying strict attention to the vicar's words. What sort of husband would he make?

It might be comforting to have a partner, to not be so alone . . .

But men always left, didn't they? Or at least they left her. Her father. Frederick.

"'With this ring I thee wed'"—Ned slipped the ring on Ellie's finger. "'With my body I thee worship . . .'"

Oh! Hot need shot through her, and her eyes went unwillingly to Jack's. He had the same hungry expression he'd had in the park when he'd kissed her.

Frederick had best come back and give her her money before she did something dangerously stupid.

Jack stood by a pillar near some open windows and surveyed his parents' ballroom. Ah, there was Miss Wharton. He'd been dodging her all evening again, but at the moment she was dancing with Stevenson, a tall, thin, hook-nosed boor. He almost felt sorry for her.

As expected, Ned's and Ellie's wedding ball was a shocking squeeze. Hundreds of elegantly clad bodies crammed into a space that would better accommodate half—or even a third—their number. Clearly, no one lucky enough to receive an invitation had declined. They all wanted to see the Duchess of Love's London-averse second son. And if Ash, whose odd marital situation had fascinated the gabble-grinders for years, were here as well, Father would have had to station armed guards at the doors to keep the *ton* out.

At least Frances didn't have to worry about making a mistake on the dance floor—there wasn't room to take a misstep. And she'd done fine when he'd had his set with her. Who was she dancing with now? He searched the moving mass of people.

Pettigrew. Odd. He'd have thought Pettigrew would have steered clear of Frances. Besides the fact that the fellow usually came to Mama's gatherings just to eat the lobster patties, he'd been the author of Frances's disgrace. If he'd kept his lips sealed, Frances might have been able to slip quietly back to the country.

Which would have been a very good thing. An excellent thing. Jack's life would be so much simpler if Frances weren't in it. He wouldn't have had to play dancing master; he would have been able to spend more time searching for the Slasher.

And he wouldn't have had his sleep disrupted by extremely inappropriate, erotic dreams.

Hell.

Yes, she was making his life hell. She was contrary and argumentative and completely infuriating.

And she had soft lips and a strong will and indomitable courage and she needed him.

And maybe he needed her. He certainly felt an unpleasantly empty feeling at the thought of her leaving.

Well, there was no point thinking about it. She was here, and she would stay here.

So why was Pettigrew dancing with her? Perhaps he regretted his actions and was trying to make amends. That was good. It should help quiet the gabble-grinders.

The man was more lumbering than lithe, but Frances seemed to be managing as his partner. She had a slight crease between her brows, and her lips were moving as if she was talking herself through the figures.

Those lips . . .

He shouldn't have kissed her yesterday. He'd known it at the time, but he'd been powerless to stop himself. She'd looked so pretty, with her green eyes and pale skin and her short red hair almost glowing in the sunlight. She'd reminded him of a disgruntled pixie.

He shouldn't have kissed her, but he'd like to do so again very soon. That first time she'd been hesitant and tentative—but not afraid, thank God. Not prudish. She'd obviously never been kissed before. But the second kiss . . .

He shifted position, shielding a suddenly obvious part of his anatomy behind a handy potted palm. The second kiss had been rather chaste, too, but his reaction had not. If he hadn't immediately escorted Frances back into the music room and Miss Addison's, er, deflating presence, he might have taught her an entirely different form of dance.

He'd spent far too much time during Ned's wedding imagining what *his* wedding night would be like if Miss Hadley was his bride. She was so passionate about everything else, how could she not be equally fearless in bed?

"Which young lady has put that grin on your face, my friend? Not my newfound cousin, surely?"

Damn! Thank God for the palm, or Trent would be commenting on more than his smile. "Trent! What do you mean by sneaking up on me?"

"There was no sneaking involved. A herd of elephants could have stampeded by you and you wouldn't have noticed."

"I think I would have noticed elephants in my parents' ballroom."

Trent laughed. "It looks like my cousin is dancing with an elephant right now. Have you ever seen Pettigrew capering about like this before? I thought he only came to these things for the food."

"I was surprised to see him dancing, too, but thought perhaps he was trying to help mend Frances's reputation, since he was the one who started the rumors."

Trent snorted. "You're giving the man far too much credit. If it isn't edible, it's not memorable as far as he's concerned."

"You may be right." Pettigrew was now stumbling through an allemande, an action that looked horribly familiar. "You know, I think I *have* seen him dance recently, but the sight was so hideous, I blocked it from my memory."

"I just hope my poor cousin minds her toes. It would be a shame to have her lamed so early in the evening."

"Yes." Jack flinched as Frances did a little hop to avoid being trod upon. Compared to Pettigrew, she must feel quite accomplished.

A cold burst of air came in through the windows and Trent sighed happily. "If I'd realized you'd found the one cool spot in this infernal room, I'd have come over sooner. By gad, this place is stifling with all the candles and the people packed in cheek by jowl." He wrinkled his nose. "And a great many of the guests need to discover the joys of clean linen and regular bathing."

"True." Frances was now being careful to keep her arm fully extended whenever she had to clasp Pettigrew's hand, better ensuring a safe distance between her feet and his. It was a very good thing she was tall.

But perhaps Trent had sought him out with news. Jack glanced around and dropped his voice. "Any luck finding witnesses to the murders?"

Trent's brows snapped down into a scowl. "No, and it's damned frustrating. You'd think someone would have seen something. Someone *must* have. We just haven't located that person yet."

Jack nodded. "I didn't think we'd find anyone to come forward about the killings in Covent Garden, but I was hoping we'd have more luck with the society girls. The damn gossips are busy enough about everything else. You've asked the servants, of course?"

"Several times." Trent started to run his hand through his hair, but stopped himself before he disordered his carefully arranged locks. "You know how busy they are at these things. I'll wager none of the Greycliffe staff can tell you tomorrow who left this party with whom. If the woman wasn't struggling or in some way bringing attention to herself, why would anyone notice?"

That was, unfortunately, too true. "So did you talk to Mrs. Black, the woman Lady Barbara said she was getting a ride home with from the Chesterman ball?" If he hadn't been so damn busy with Frances, he'd have talked to Mrs. Black himself.

"Yes. She was extremely upset that her name had been mentioned in the newspaper accounts and insisted she knew nothing about the matter; that she'd left early—and alone—because she had the headache."

"Hmm." Jack nodded. "It's quite possible Lady Barbara was on the watch for any early departures so she could spin a plausible tale for her mother." Damn it, he felt so helpless. He looked out over the crowded ballroom. Was the murderer one of the men present? "Who do you think the Slasher is?"

"Ruland and Botsley seem the most logical choices. Both were at the events from which Miss Fielding, Mrs. Hubble, and Lady Barbara disappeared, and both were absent after the ladies left. Both frequent the stews, and both are heartless, soulless scum—but merely being human vermin doesn't prove either of them is the murderer. And no one can definitively place either of them with the women." Trent let out a long, annoyed breath. "If only we could find a witness."

They were back to that. "Nan's certain the killer is Ruland, but she's got no evidence either. She just doesn't like the man," Jack said. "I'd put my money on Botsley. Ruland's a bully, but not, I think, capable of killing."

"But you have no evidence of that."

Jack nodded. "True."

"Blast!" Trent's jaw clenched. "The devil of it is we may have to wait for another poor girl to be murdered, and even then we may not be any closer to catching the bounder."

"I know." Jack should be working on finding the Slasher, not standing in a ballroom. "I have boys shadowing both Botsley and Ruland, and Nan is trying to watch out for the Covent Garden girls. We'll just have to keep our eyes and ears open and hope we catch the scoundrel before he strikes again." Not a very satisfactory course of action.

"Speaking of scoundrels, I see Ned's brother-in-law has arrived."

"What? Oh, damn." Sir Percy was just entering the ballroom. It had been a little over a week since Ned had thrashed him at the Valentine party, but it looked as if most of the bruises had faded—or been covered with powder.

"Should we add him to the list of suspects?" Trent asked. "I wouldn't put murder past him."

"No." Jack didn't like Percy either—hadn't liked him even as a child—but he was certain the man wasn't the Slasher. "Percy's a bully like Ruland, but I doubt he'd kill anyone. And in any event, he was at Greycliffe Castle with me when Martha was murdered."

"Right—the Duchess of Love's annual Valentine house party. Happily, I've managed so far to escape the guest list."

"A shocking oversight! I'll be sure to suggest your name to Mama for next year's gathering."

Trent looked a bit alarmed. "You wouldn't really stab me in the back like that, would you?"

Jack laughed. "Of course not."

"Good, because I know where I can get copies of the Duchess of Love's *Love Notes*, and if I ever find myself invited, I'll tie you to a tree and read you every last word she's written."

"I'd like to see you try. Who do you know that has copies of that miserable rag?"

Trent grinned. "My mother."

"Good God! Your mother needs to read my mother's advice on love?"

Trent grimaced. "I have no idea why she has them, nor do I wish to contemplate that question."

"Now you know how I feel."

"Ah, Jack, so good to see you again." The voice came from slightly behind his right shoulder.

Damn! Why was Percy seeking him out? He turned to look at Cicely's—Ned's first wife's—brother. "Hallo, Percy. You look, ah, much recovered." Percy was definitely using powder to mask his lingering bruises.

Percy smiled stiffly and nodded to Trent. Trent, the coward, nodded back and fled.

"Yes. I'm much better, thank you." Percy inclined his head toward where Ned and Ellie were talking to another couple. "I confess I didn't expect the nuptials, though I suppose your mother has been trying to get Ned to marry Ellie ever since Cicely died."

What was Percy implying? "We all miss Cicely, of course, but we're glad Ned could finally move beyond his mourning. He and Ellie have known each other forever, so their marriage should not be surprising at all."

"Perhaps." Percy let that go. "What *is* surprising is that

Ash didn't come to Town for the ceremony. It's an easy ride from the castle to London. I hope he's well?"

Percy didn't hope anything of the kind, and Ash wasn't at the castle. "Oh yes, Ash is disgustingly healthy. He just had another commitment."

Percy's brows rose. "Something more pressing than his brother's wedding? My, my. You do know the *ton* will likely attribute his absence to a case of sour grapes. It's no secret Ellie has favored Ash at your mother's parties."

Likely Percy would encourage that sentiment, as ridiculous as it was. "The cabbageheaded members of the *ton* will think what they will—facts and logic have never stopped them before. Don't cause trouble for Ash, Percy."

"I wouldn't think of it." Percy smiled, making Jack think, as always, of a snake. "But enough about your brothers; tell me about yourself. I've heard such interesting rumors about you recently, much more interesting than the usual fare."

The set was coming to a close. Jack glanced over to see how Frances was managing with Pettigrew. He should warn her to avoid Percy—nothing good could come of any conversation between them.

"Yes," Percy said, obviously following his gaze. "Rothmarsh's granddaughter. Everyone says you played a very interesting role in her journey to Town. And she's staying here, rather than with her grandparents. How . . . convenient."

Pettigrew was leading Frances away, likely to the refreshment room. She did not look happy about it.

"I would greatly enjoy adding to Ned's handiwork, Percy—good job hiding the bruises, by the way—but unfortunately I have more important matters to attend to at the moment. Do try not to be more of an idiot than usual, will you?"

Jack strode off to rescue Frances.

Chapter 14

Strive for your heart's desire.

—Venus's Love Notes

Thank God! Frances tried to hide her relief as the orchestra played the last note. She'd survived her dance with Mr. Pettigrew without permanent injury. Now she wanted to get free of the unpleasant man as quickly as possible.

Mr. Littleton was here, too, but thankfully he'd limited himself to a few pointed glares. He hadn't tried to approach her.

"May I escort you to the refreshment room, Miss Hadley?" Mr. Pettigrew asked. "You really should try the duchess's lobster patties. They are the best in London. In fact, I will even say they are the best in all of England."

"I'm afraid I'm not hungry, Mr. Pettigrew."

"Some lemonade then? There's nothing better to quench a lady's thirst than lemonade—and nothing better to raise a thirst than dancing."

Clearly the man was not going to take no for an answer.

She *was* a little thirsty, and she didn't want to give Mr. Pettigrew the impression she was afraid of him. "Very well. Thank you, sir. That would be pleasant." She allowed him to lead her out of the room.

She could not like the man. He was Mr. Littleton's friend and had done nothing to dissuade him from trying to trap her into wedlock. On the contrary, Mr. Pettigrew had laughed and encouraged the little weasel. She'd swear he'd taken great delight in holding his knowledge of her identity over her head at the Crowing Cock and then in Jack's curricle, and she'd be willing to wager he'd taken even greater delight in spreading the tale far and wide.

But even if she were meeting him now for the first time, she would not care for him. He was so big, she felt as if she were being escorted by a large bear. She hadn't noticed at the Crowing Cock—likely because she'd only seen him seated—that he was tall, though probably not as tall as Jack. But he was a good seven or eight stone heavier, with big bones and an even bigger belly.

She felt small—and not in a good way—at his side.

And his smell! She'd detected an unpleasant, sour odor when he'd asked her to stand up with him, but the exertion of the dance had made the stench many times worse. He was clearly—overpoweringly so—not a proponent of frequent bathing.

She started breathing through her mouth.

Mr. Pettigrew leaned closer as they left the ballroom and murmured, "How did you get the duchess to accept you?"

His garlic- and onion-laced breath momentarily stupefied her. "Pardon me?" Would he notice if she held her handkerchief over her nose?

"The duchess." His gaze sharpened. "How did you get her to take you in after you'd slept with her son?"

Zeus! She felt as if she'd been hit in the stomach. She struggled to fill her lungs with air and keep her hand from slapping the slimy scoundrel senseless. Pettigrew's insulting eyes suggested that something of a more salacious nature than two people slumbering in the same bed had occurred.

She wanted to defend her virtue and tell him that her stay at the inn had been completely innocent, but arguing that point would be like waltzing on quicksand. The fact was she *had* slept with Lord Jack.

Perhaps the best plan was to ignore the subject completely.

"I don't believe I've seen Mr. Dantley here tonight. Is he well?"

He blinked, and the peculiar intensity in his eyes vanished. "He had to go home. His mother's ill, and so he's been in the country more than in Town recently."

"I'm so sorry. I hope it is nothing serious?"

They stopped by the pitchers of lemonade. "I don't believe it is," he said, pouring a glass and handing it to her. "His mother tends to hypochondria."

"Ah." She took a sip, scouring her mind for another conversational topic.

Unfortunately, Mr. Pettigrew beat her to it, choosing one almost as distasteful as his initial selection—not surprising as Mr. Pettigrew himself was extremely distasteful.

"I assume you saw that Littleton's here?" He turned away to procure a glass of champagne—clearly not his first. "You'll be happy to know his father fished him out of the River Tick, so he has a little more time to look around him for a wife."

Mr. Pettigrew's appearance would be much improved by a glass of lemonade dashed in his face. "I am *not* happy to know it." Good Lord, so Littleton was going to try to trap some other unsuspecting female? Despicable! "Frankly,

Mr. Pettigrew, your friend needs to learn economy, not cozen some poor girl into throwing her life away by marrying him."

He looked down his large nose at her. "That's an interesting thing for you to say. I'm sure you'll be wishing you hadn't run from him, madam, as no one will offer for you now. Rather a soiled dove, aren't you?" He had that annoyingly intent look in his eyes again. "It's shocking Rothmarsh recognized you, but then I suppose I shouldn't be surprised. Everyone says your mother was wild. The dam bred true, eh?"

She would *not* throw her lemonade in his face. She did not wish to cause a scene in the Duchess of Greycliffe's refreshment room, but, oh, she would so like to see him covered in the sticky liquid. She would offer him a handsome helping of her opinion instead—

"Does Rothmarsh know your brother married a Covent Garden nun?"

She choked on her lemonade. What was this? "A nun? Oh no, I don't think—that is, I've yet to meet my brother's wife, but I can't imagine . . . I mean, where would he have found one? Are there nuns in England?"

He stared at her. "I meant a prostitute."

She stared back at him. The man *must* be drunk to so totally forget his manners. Well, she would struggle to hold on to hers. "As I said, I've not yet had the pleasure of meeting my brother's wife, but I believe my father approves of the match." After all, upon his son's nuptials, he'd instructed Puddington to have Frederick move to a better apartment rather than cutting him off without a sou.

Mr. Pettigrew snorted and took a swallow of champagne. "He would."

Dear heavens, this conversation was only getting worse. The damnable thing was, she couldn't really disagree with Mr. Pettigrew on this particular point. She sipped her lemonade and looked around the refreshment room. The only guests present at the moment were young men availing themselves of the duchess's lobster patties. None of them looked like hero material, willing to sacrifice even one bite of lobster to rescue her.

Not that she needed anyone's help. She would just finish her lemonade and rescue herself.

"Let's take a stroll in the gardens," Pettigrew said. "It's uncomfortably hot in here."

The man was a candidate for Bedlam. Yes, it was very warm, but why would he think she'd want to spend one moment longer than she had to in his objectionable company?

Good God, surely he didn't think she was a wanton from whom he could steal a kiss, or worse? The thought of his garlicky lips on hers, his large sweaty body so close . . .

Ugh!

"No, thank you."

He frowned and opened his mouth as if to argue, but this time she spoke quickly. "Do you intend to stay in London long, sir?" Please let him have friends in Yorkshire—or better, Scotland—that he was planning to visit for an extended period.

He shrugged. "Oh yes. Like Lord Jack, I spend almost all my time here. The country is dreadfully dull."

"Did I hear my name?"

Splendid! Jack had finally torn himself away from the flock of females fluttering around him in the ballroom. She'd swear every woman under the age of forty had singled him out for a smile and a bit of conversation. And of course he'd been happy to oblige them all.

She turned and smiled up at him. But he was here now. He would make her escape look like a normal, unhurried departure.

Another, warmer emotion flooded her when Jack smiled back.

Damn it, she should not be feeling this way. In a few weeks—a month or two at the most—she would have left London. Lord Jack would be only a memory. He might be a necessary companion now, but he was a very short-term one.

"I was only saying we both prefer London to the country," Mr. Pettigrew said.

Jack looked thoughtful. "I don't know that I prefer Town. There's just more here to keep me busy."

"Yes indeed. Far more." Mr. Pettigrew offered a rather wooden smile. "And when I'm in London, I don't have to listen to my father drone on and on about sheep."

"You'll inherit those sheep one day, you know," Jack said.

Mr. Pettigrew grimaced. "I know."

So Mr. Pettigrew was like her brother, taking his good fortune for granted and completely ignoring any corresponding duties. "Do you have any siblings, Mr. Pettigrew?"

Perhaps some of her annoyance showed in her tone. Jack gave her a quelling look and shook his head slightly.

"Just an older sister."

An older sister who, in a more enlightened world, would be the heir instead of this lazy, irresponsible, beetle-headed man. "I see. So—ouch!"

Lord Jack had trod upon her foot. She glared at him, but he ignored her.

"If you'll excuse us, Pettigrew, I believe my mother wishes to speak to Miss Hadley."

"Of course. Don't let me keep you. And please tell the duchess how much I enjoy her lobster patties." Mr. Pettigrew bowed and headed toward the buffet.

"You're lying," Frances hissed as she walked back to the ballroom with Jack. "Your mother doesn't want to see me."

"On the contrary," he murmured as he nodded at an old woman with a forest of puce plumes on her head, "I'm certain she'd like to point out that antagonizing Pettigrew is a useless and very unwise thing to do."

"I'm not afraid of him."

"I'm not saying you are. I'm just saying you should be more prudent. Gifting him with your opinion on primogeniture will not make him any more responsible, but it may well anger him, and an angry man is far more apt to relish spreading damning stories. I—oh, blast."

"What—oh." Lord Ruland was coming toward them. "Was he lying in wait for us?"

"Probably. He's another it would be unwise to antagonize."

"I *know* that. Can't we dodge him?"

"That would only delay the inevitable," Jack muttered and then Lord Ruland was within earshot.

"Lord Jack," Ruland said, "and Master—" His beady eyes slid from Frances's head to her slippers, and his thick, furry eyebrows arched insolently up toward his bald head. "Or, should I say, *Miss* Haddon? But I don't believe that surname is quite right, either. What is your name, my dear?"

It would have been far more polite for Ruland to ask Jack to present him rather than refer to their awkward first encounter, but she already knew the earl was not one to be overly courteous. Well, she was not going to let him intimidate her. She looked him in his nasty little eyes. "Miss Frances Hadley."

"Miss Hadley is Rothmarsh's granddaughter, Ruland," Jack said, moving forward just slightly so he seemed to be sheltering her from the man, "and my mother's newest protégé."

"Ah yes, now I see the resemblance. When you are wearing skirts, Miss Hadley, you look very much like your mother."

So the man had known her mother. She shouldn't be surprised. Likely many of the men his age had.

His lips curved up in a very unpleasant smile, and her palm itched to slap him.

"But the gossip about you is even more interesting than it was about her when she eloped," he said.

"I'm sure you realize that it's never—" Jack paused. He was still smiling, but his eyes were suddenly hard. "—*wise* to listen to gossip."

Lord Ruland was either very brave or very stupid. He looked blandly back at Jack. "Ah, but one of the most interesting details I witnessed myself, didn't I?" He switched his attention back to Frances. "I wonder if Lord Rothmarsh knows his granddaughter was capering about a brothel in breeches?"

"I was *not* capering." That was a rather stupid thing to say, but it just burst out of her.

Jack had been looking like a thundercloud, but he laughed then. "Of course you weren't. Now if you'll excuse us, Ruland?"

Jack led her over to where the duchess was standing with Lady Rothmarsh. She forced herself to look ahead, but she'd swear she could feel Ruland's nasty eyes burning holes in her back.

"Are you enjoying your wedding ball?" Not that Jack really needed to ask. Ned was holding up a pillar, scowling at Ellie, who was dancing with Trent's youngest brother, Peter. Trent was partnering Frances in the same set.

"No, I'm not. I'm more than ready to take Ellie upstairs to b—" Ned cleared his throat and his cheeks flushed. "To go to sleep. It's been a tiring day. Ellie's exhausted."

She didn't look exhausted. She looked happy, happier than Jack had ever seen her, as if she'd just got her heart's desire. Which she had. She was finally Ned's wife.

What would it be like to have a woman love you so wholeheartedly?

If Frances . . .

But Frances wouldn't. And he was too young to consider marriage anyway. With the exception of Mama and Father, early marriages rarely prospered. Look at Ned's first marriage. Look at Ash's.

He would just keep using the accommodating women at the brothels and wait until he was thirty or so to take a wife.

But what would it feel like if the act was more than a physical release . . .

"Ellie looks like she's enjoying herself," he said. His eyes slid back to Frances. Her expression was far more serious, as if she was still counting her steps.

He'd been very lucky she hadn't bitten him when he'd kissed her in the park yesterday. Likely it was only her surprise and shock that had saved him.

What was *her* heart's desire?

Him?

Good God, he was insane. Her heart's desire was for England's laws of primogeniture to be amended so she could inherit Landsford.

"Yes, damn it, I think Ellie *is* enjoying herself." Ned blew out a long, unhappy breath. "I suppose Mama is right. We should stay in London for a while. Ellie should have her chance to experience the parties and shops and to see the London sights before she becomes a m-mother." He turned rather pale.

Ah, so Ned was worrying about that already, was he? Jack wasn't surprised, but there was nothing he could do except remind Ned again that not all women died in childbirth—which would be a waste of his breath.

"Of course Mama's right," he said instead. "She's always—or almost always—right." He clapped Ned on the shoulder. "And you could stand to have some fun, too, before you ensconce yourself at Linden Hall again."

Ned glared at him. "How can I enjoy myself when I know there's a deranged killer on the loose?"

Poor Lord Worry. "So far the Slasher has limited himself to prostitutes and a few unwed women of the *ton* with sullied reputations. Ellie's married now. She should be completely safe."

But Frances . . . the damnable rumors made her sound like exactly the sort of woman the Slasher preyed on. He looked around the room to find Ruland—

Ruland must have left—or else he was keeping Pettigrew company in the refreshment room. And Botsley was far too dirty a dish to be invited to Mama's ball.

"How can you predict what the lunatic will do?" Ned sounded both angry and frustrated.

"I can't. And while I think it's highly unlikely Ellie's in danger, I have taken the precaution of having one of my boys shadow her whenever she goes out."

Ned frowned. "What do you mean, one of your boys?"

His family knew nothing of his London charities, and he certainly did not want to explain it here in the noisy ballroom. "One of the boys I employ. His name is Robin. I'll introduce you tomorrow."

"You should have consulted me first."

"Why? I knew you were worried—" Damn, Ned had stiffened. He was too sensitive—but then, Jack *had* teased him for years about his propensity to fret. "And you're right to be concerned. I think Frances is most at risk, so I have a boy following her, but then I decided I might as well enlist another to keep an eye on Ellie. Didn't you want me to take any steps I could to keep Ellie safe?"

"Yes, of course I want you to do what you can. I'm sorry. I'm just . . ." Ned shook his head and looked at the dancers. "I don't much care for London. It's too damn crowded."

Jack tried not to smile. Ned was too damn anxious to have his wife to himself in a comfortable bed with a securely locked door. There was a reason for honeymoons.

He was surprised at how much he envied his brother.

Ah, but he must remember not all marriages were blissful. Look at Ash's. If Ash's marriage had failed when Ash and Jess knew each other so well, how could he hope a union with Frances would have any chance of success?

"I cannot believe all the lobster patties are gone," Drew grumbled as he served himself some paper-thin slices of ham. The refreshment room was deserted at the moment.

Venus patted his arm. "You know many of our guests come for the food as much as the dancing."

"More for the food," Drew said, adding a couple of rolls to his plate.

"And Cook's lobster patties are much admired." She should be starving, but with the big wedding breakfast and all the excitement, her appetite had departed. She took a meat pasty.

Well, and perhaps she'd have one of the ratafia cakes—or two. They were very small.

They took their things over to a table largely hidden by a few exuberant potted plants. The servants knew to set the room up so that such a refuge was available. It was so pleasant to be able to take a few moments of solitude even when one was having a lovely time.

"The ball is a great success, isn't it?" she asked as Drew held her chair for her.

"Of course. Your parties always are." He sat across from her and raised his glass of champagne. "To your superlative hostessing—and matchmaking—skills."

Venus held up her glass in response, but her heart didn't lift as well. "I don't feel like much of a matchmaker tonight."

Drew's brows shot up. "How can you say that? This should be your night of triumph. Your years of planning and plotting have come to fruition—Ned has married Ellie. One of our sons, at least, is happily wed."

"Yes, but what about Jack?" Venus looked down at her plate and sighed. None of the food looked appealing.

"What about Jack?"

She picked up the pasty—and then put it back down. "I cannot decide about Miss Hadley."

Drew was a man. Nothing affected his appetite. He chewed the large bit of ham in his mouth and swallowed before replying. "What do you need to know to decide about Miss Hadley?"

"Whether she's right for Jack, of course."

He snorted. "I think Jack will decide that." And then he put *more* ham in his mouth.

How could the man eat at a time like this? "But she seems so angry and defensive."

"It sounds as though she's had an unfortunate upbringing with no parents and a very odd aunt." He looked at her plate. "Are you going to eat both of those cakes?"

"No, I suppose not."

Drew didn't wait for her to change her mind; he snagged one immediately.

"I don't think she's the girl I would choose for Jack."

Drew paused, the cake halfway to his mouth. He put it

down and leaned forward to take her hands. "Venus, you are a wonderful matchmaker, but you are not infallible. Remember how we thought Jess was perfect for Ash?"

"Yes." Her heart felt even heavier. She was ready to give up her other cake as well.

Drew's face grew more serious, and he squeezed her fingers. "Don't despair over Ash's situation. Perhaps he and Jess will reconcile. At least he's finally gone to see her. But whether they reconcile or not is *their* business. Our job is to keep silent, which I think we've largely managed to do." He shifted in his chair. "Well, at least about Jess herself, if not completely about the need to address the problem. There is the succession to consider."

Venus nodded. She had tried very hard not to blame Jess or disparage her in any way, but the whole situation made her angry. Why hadn't Jess made the effort to solve whatever the problem was? She must know men were hopeless when it came to such things. They were wonderful in many ways, but addressing emotional issues was not one of them. They tended to bluster and growl—at least in her experience. She squeezed Drew's hands. But once a problem was solved, it was as if it had never happened. They didn't bear grudges.

"But getting back to Jack, you need to trust him to make his own decision in this. We can only be sure he knows he's under no obligation to marry Miss Hadley—that her reputation will survive without a wedding ring. Then we must leave things up to him." He released her hands and sat back, taking up his cake again. "You can trust Jack. He has a good head on his shoulders."

"But what about his curricle-racing and other careless behavior? What about all the rumors of his raking?"

"Unimportant. Stop thinking about the stories you've heard and think about the man. You know he had a hand in getting Ellie and Ned together. Jack sees and understands a lot." Drew grinned. "He's your son—though I don't believe he has any aspirations to matchmaking."

She smiled, suddenly feeling as if a huge weight had been lifted from her shoulders. "Perhaps you're right." She picked up her pasty and took a bite. It was delicious.

"Of course I'm right." Drew eyed her plate again. "So what about that other cake?"

Venus shielded it with her hand. "I'm afraid you'll have to go get one for yourself, my dear duke. This one is mine."

Chapter 15

Sometimes a knee to the groin is the only answer.
—Venus's Love Notes

Jack was in the library after Mama had banished him from the red drawing room. She'd accused him of glowering at her guests.

"Who wouldn't glower?" he asked Shakespeare, who was resting in the sun by his feet. "The damn bucks and gossips gathered there are the largest collection of nodcocks it has ever been my bad luck to encounter."

Shakespeare cracked open an eye and wagged his tail somewhat halfheartedly in support.

"Did Billy wear you out?" Billy, the boot boy, had taken Shakespeare on a morning romp.

The dog yawned and rolled over, presenting his belly to be scratched. Jack obliged.

It had been a week since the wedding ball, a week of one interminable social event after another. Now Mama and Ellie and Frances were once again "at home" for whatever nincompoops wished to stroll through the front door. Ned and Father had fled to White's; Jack had been seriously tempted, but he'd decided he'd better stay at Greycliffe House.

"You don't think Frances will dump her teacup on one of those coxcombs in the drawing room, do you?"

Shakespeare barked twice, but whether he agreed that Frances would restrain herself or wished to encourage her to misbehave, Jack couldn't tell.

He didn't think Frances would do something so outrageous, but one never knew with Frances. She'd looked on the verge of explosion on more than one occasion this week. At least Ellie's presence seemed to have a calming—or perhaps the better word was *restraining*—effect on her.

Someone scratched at the door, and Shakespeare jumped up, suddenly alert.

"Come."

The butler entered bearing a small package wrapped in paper and twine. "This just came for you, milord."

"Thank you, Braxton." Jack took the bundle, keeping it out of Shakespeare's reach. "Who delivered it?"

Braxton frowned and absentmindedly patted Shakespeare. "A boy, milord. He says his name is Jeb, and that he has a message for you. I left him by the back door." Braxton sniffed. "He has an unfortunate odor."

Jack grinned. "I don't suppose I could persuade you to deposit him in the red drawing room, could I?"

Braxton choked back a laugh. "No, milord, you could not."

"Too bad. Well, show the boy in. I think I can survive the stench, though I'll keep my handkerchief at the ready, just in case."

"Very good, milord." Braxton left to fetch Jeb.

Shakespeare seemed to comprehend that staying in the library was going to be more interesting than following Braxton. He sat and tilted his head, looking up at Jack.

"I'm quite sure it's nothing to eat, Shakespeare." Jack turned the package over in his hands. It was about the size of his palm and had some weight to it. Was it from Nan? Jeb was the boy he'd assigned to watch that area of Covent Garden.

He carefully cut the twine with a penknife and pulled back the paper, revealing . . . a gold watch. Why the hell would Jeb bring him a gold watch?

The door swung open and Jeb came in. Braxton was correct; Jeb stunk with that distinctive odor of young boys, some mix of sweat and dirt that was extremely pungent. Shakespeare yipped with delight and trotted over to sniff the interesting scent more thoroughly.

"It's Shakespeare!" Jeb grinned. "Shake, Shakespeare."

Shakespeare promptly sat and offered his paw.

"Jeb," Jack said, once the greetings were completed, "where did you get the package you brought me?"

Jeb's smile vanished. "It's from Nan, milord. She told me to tell you the Slasher killed her girl Bessie early this morning."

"Damn." How many more girls would die before they caught the bloody devil? "But why a pocket watch?"

"That's the good news, milord. Nan said Bessie must have fought like one possessed. She screamed so loud Albert heard her inside. Woke him from a sound sleep, she did."

"Wait—why was she outside at all?" Nan was the most concerned of all the brothel madams. "I thought Nan had told all her girls not to go out after dark."

"She did, milord, but she said there was never telling Bessie anything. The girl did as she pleased. Albert had locked all the doors after the last customer left—the lower windows, too—and went to bed. But Bessie must have worked a deal with some fellow to get paid directly—more money for her since Nan wouldn't get her cut. She climbed out an upper window and down a drainpipe."

"And the man was the Slasher."

Jeb nodded. "Poor Bessie had her throat cut, but Albert got there quick. Didn't even stop to put breeches on. He heard someone pounding down the alley, but it was too dark for him to see anything, and he stopped to help Bessie." Jeb looked down at Shakespeare and patted him. "Wasn't no helping Bessie, but he did find that watch clutched in her hand. Nan thinks it must be the Slasher's, so she told me to bring it to you."

Jack nodded, excitement surging through him. Finally, they had a clue. The answer to the Slasher's identity might lie on the desk in front of him. "Well done, Jeb." He tossed the boy a shilling. "Tell Nan you delivered the package, and I'll let her know if I discover anything."

"Yes, milord." Jeb patted Shakespeare one last time on his way out.

Jack snatched the watch up before the door had closed and examined it. One side was smooth, but the other—

"Aha!" There on the front of the watch cover was a monogram, engraved in flowing script. "Initials, Shakespeare! H, E, and B. Now we've got the bounder!"

Shakespeare put his paws up on the desk and barked enthusiastically.

"It must be Botsley, but let me check his Christian and middle names." He grabbed the *Debrett's* off the bookshelf and brought it back to the desk, flipping to the index and then to the page with Botsley's pedigree. "Yes, here it is—Hugh Edgar Botsley. I knew it." He should have hit the bloody blackguard harder last year when he'd pulled Jenny away from him—hard enough to send him straight to hell. If he had, ten lives would have been saved. Why—

A vague memory—well, hardly a memory even—flitted just out of reach. What was Ruland's surname?

He flipped back to the index to find Ruland's page . . .

"Bloody hell! I can't believe it."

Shakespeare whined and covered his head with his paws. Jack would have laughed if he hadn't been so frustrated. Ruland's name was Henry Edward Benton. What were the odds that both his suspects would have the same initials?

"Maybe there's something else here, Shakespeare." The gods couldn't be so cruel as to give him such a clue and no way to use it.

He popped the cover open to reveal the watch's face. Nothing fell out—no little note or identifying memento. He looked on the inside of the cover. There *was* something engraved there, but he was not going to get his hopes up again. He took the watch over to the window to examine the engraving in the sunlight.

The inscription was in Latin, but easy to translate. "'Death to all enemies.'" Jack looked down at Shakespeare. "Rather violent, but appropriate in this case. Do you suppose it's the family motto? No, that would be too easy."

And indeed, it was too easy. He checked both Ruland's and Botsley's pages in *Debrett's*. Ruland's family motto was rather arrogant: Always right; and Botsley's, sanctimonious: Virtue before all; but neither was the least bit bloodthirsty.

"Damn it, Shakespeare, the answer *must* be here. If only—"

Someone scratched at the door again.

"Yes? What is it?"

Braxton looked in. "Mr. Frederick Hadley has called, milord, asking for you." He sniffed; the butler clearly did not approve of Frances's brother. "I put him in the yellow parlor."

"Thank you, Braxton." Braxton most definitely did not care for Hadley; the yellow parlor had the most uncomfortable furniture in the house and likely in all of London. "I'll be there directly."

Jack closed the watch as Braxton left, and slipped it into his pocket. Then he glanced at Shakespeare. "Care to meet Miss Hadley's brother? I warn you, Braxton disapproves of him, and I confess I'm not anticipating I'll like him much, either." The man had treated his sister shamefully. Not telling Frances he was marrying was bad enough, but keeping from her the information that their father had been in England numerous times was unconscionable.

Hadley was pacing the parlor when they arrived. Not surprising—Jack wouldn't sit on any of this furniture either. He'd long thought it more appropriate for a torture chamber.

"Mr. Hadley," Jack said, allowing Shakespeare to precede him before closing the door.

Shakespeare trotted over to sniff Hadley's breeches.

Hadley frowned as he patted the dog. "What is Shakespeare doing here?"

"Ah, so you know each other." Frances's brother had the same red hair as his sister and looked just as mulish. He also looked as if he found his surroundings extremely distasteful—and not just because of the uninviting furnishings. The man's lip curled into a sneer as he surveyed Jack.

Jack's fingers curled into fists, but he forced them to straighten out. He would be wise to take the advice he'd given Frances when that drunkard had stepped in front of the curricle on the way back from Bromley—don't take umbrage at every little slight. Save your anger for important things.

It remained to be seen whether Hadley's presence would be important enough to merit a thrashing.

"I take it you met Shakespeare when you both lived on Hart Street?"

"Yes. He's Dick Dutton's dog. Where's Dutton?" Hadley's tone suggested Jack had murdered the man to steal his dog.

Shakespeare objected to Hadley's manner. He growled, hackles rising.

"Yes, the man is rude, Shakespeare," Jack said, "but he is our guest at the moment. We must be at least moderately polite."

Shakespeare looked at him as if to ask for an exception to the rules of courtesy. When none came, he obligingly stopped making threatening noises and came back to sit by Jack's feet.

Hadley had the grace to blush faintly. "Pardon me. I just . . ." He shrugged. "Yes, I met the dog when my wife worked at the theater." He shot Jack a dark look. "So where is Dutton?"

"I don't know. The man apparently loped off and left Shakespeare behind."

"That's odd. Maria, my wife"—again the dark look that dared Jack to criticize—"never said anything about Dutton planning to leave."

"So he was still at the theater when you married?"

"Yes. He was one of our witnesses." Hadley rocked on his feet, clearly impatient to depart. "Look, I'm only here because my wife insisted. Can't make enemies of a duke's son, she said, even if he is a rake and procurer. But I don't care if you're Prinny himself. I don't have time to waste, so why not get to the point. Why do you want to see me?"

"I don't particularly, but I thought you'd want to see your sister." Jack smiled unpleasantly. "Especially as I am a rake and procurer. You might wish to ascertain her safety."

An odd look, a mix of anger and pain, flitted over Hadley's features before they settled into a scowl.

"Well, I don't. I don't expect you'll do anything dastardly under your father's roof and your mother's nose, and if you have seduced Frances, well, that's her problem. I'm sure she's more than capable of handling the situation. In truth, if the rumors are correct and she's been attending all these society events, decked out in new finery, she's quite fallen on her feet, hasn't she?" He picked his hat off the table. "So if you'll excuse me—"

The door opened behind Jack. Probably a good thing—a moment later and he would have been a terrible host and knocked Hadley to the floor. He turned to see who had so boldly interrupted them.

It was Frances, of course.

"Frederick!" Her jaw dropped. Shakespeare trotted over to greet her, and she patted him absently.

"Hallo, Frances." The scowl deepened, turning slightly sulky. Hadley did not put his hat down.

"Did Braxton fetch you from the drawing room?" Jack asked.

Frances was still staring at her brother. "No. I got bored—I mean, tired—and left your mother and Ellie with the idiots—er, visitors. I asked Braxton where you were, and he said you were here with my brother." Her brows snapped down into her own scowl; the resemblance between the siblings was quite striking. "Why didn't you come get me when Frederick arrived?"

That was a good question. Had he wished to see what sort of danger her brother posed—danger to her peace of mind—so that he could protect her somehow?

He couldn't protect her from this. He could just be here

to pick up the pieces. "I was going to after I'd made Mr. Hadley's acquaintance, but since you're here now, I will leave you two alone."

"No need for that," Hadley said, starting toward the door. "I was just going."

"Oh no, you're not." Frances moved to block his path. "You're not going anywhere until you agree to get Mr. Puddington to give me my dowry and"—she took a deep breath—"you tell me what's going on with our f-father."

Hadley's jaw flexed, his expression stony. For a moment, Jack wasn't certain whether the fellow would go or stay—and which would be the better outcome. But finally he put his hat back on the table.

"Very well, we'll talk. I suppose it's time."

This did not sound good. "Shall I stay, Miss Hadley?"

Frances kept her eyes on her brother. "No, of course not."

"Very well. I shall be nearby if you need me." Jack was relatively certain Hadley wouldn't hurt Frances physically. Emotionally—well, that was another story. "If you'll excuse me then?"

Neither of them looked at him as he and Shakespeare left the room.

"Why didn't you tell me you were marrying?" Frances stayed where she was, a good ten feet from her brother. She recognized him, of course, but at the same time he looked like a stranger. She hadn't seen him for, what? Six years? He was no longer a boy, all arms and legs and sharp angles. She wished—

She didn't wish anything. She was angry. His failure to tell her about his wedding and subsequent move had put her at great risk. And he'd never told her about their father. Of course she was furious. But . . .

Frederick was her *twin*. Shouldn't she feel something for him other than anger? Jack seemed so close to his brother—

She could not compare. Jack and Ned were the same gender. They understood each other. And they had the benefit of attentive parents.

Frederick was scowling at her. "I wrote to Viola. I assumed the poisonous old witch would tell you. You and she are so damn close."

"Close?" How could Frederick say such a thing? "I'm not close to Viola." *Especially after her treachery with Littleton.* "I never was."

He snorted. "Oh, come on, Frances. She doted on you. You were the perfect child. You could do no wrong."

Was her brother insane? "Viola did *not* dote on me." Viola hadn't held her back, that was true. She hadn't had any nonsensical notions of what was proper for a female to learn, so she'd let Frances take lessons with Frederick in Latin and mathematics and anything else he studied—and hadn't forced her to do silly, feminine things like sewing and painting and dancing.

Well, all right, learning to dance would have been good. And Viola hadn't tried to keep Frances from managing Landsford. But her aunt had never been happy with her efforts, no matter how hard she'd worked.

Frederick's mouth twisted with scorn. "Oh no? Viola was forever telling me how smart you were, how you learned to read before I did, how you could add and subtract faster than I."

Well, what did he expect? She *was* smarter than he. All their tutors had said so. They—and Aunt Viola—had often teased Frederick that a girl could best him, and yet that had never motivated him to work harder.

It was on the tip of her tongue to tell him exactly that, but suddenly she remembered Jack teaching her to dance.

Neither he nor his family had ever once hinted at how socially backward and inept she was compared to even the youngest debutante. If they had, that would likely have killed her very small desire to learn the blasted steps.

"Viola never praised anything I did," Frederick was saying. "If she'd tried, I swear she would have choked on the words." He shoved his hands into his pockets. "It was the constant criticism, the never-ending belittlement, the bloody scorn that ate at me. Father said she was just as bad when he was growing up—and she was forever harping about how Landsford should have been hers, since she was the elder."

She'd begun to feel some compassion for Frederick, but his mentioning their bloody father stopped that cold. Damn it, whatever Frederick had suffered at Viola's hands was nothing compared to the way their father had ignored her. "Well, Landsford *should* have been Viola's." Viola would certainly have been a better steward of the property than their bloody father.

"No, it should not have been." Frederick gave her a look of disgust.

Idiot male. "A woman is just as capable of running an estate as a man."

"And a second son is just as capable as a first son," Frederick said, "but the law says it's the oldest male who inherits."

"Then the law should be changed. It's not fair."

Frederick actually rolled his eyes. "Frances, primogeniture *isn't* fair. Is Lord Jack whining because he won't inherit Greycliffe's vast holdings?"

"N-no." Jack *could* have envied his brother Ash . . . But the situation was not the same at all. "He's a man. He can do anything he wants."

"No, he can't. He can't become the next Duke of Greycliffe, can he? Not unless both his brothers die without sons."

Frederick was being purposely obtuse. "Jack doesn't want to be the duke."

"No? Or perhaps he's just smart enough not to want what he can't have. Just as you should be." He threw his hands up in the air to emphasize his point. "Damn it, Frances, stop trying to be a man, and be a woman for once, will you?"

Oh God. She felt as if she'd been hit in the stomach. Is that how he—how everyone—saw her: as a woman trying to be a man?

Is that how *Jack* saw her?

But if she hadn't been willing to take charge and do what the world considered unfeminine, the estate would have been much the worse for it. "You and our father were happy enough to allow this *woman* to run Landsford all these years. You never once looked at a single estate ledger, Frederick."

"Because you wouldn't let me near them. Why do you think I took up botany? It got me out in the fields away from you viragoes."

He thought her a virago? He lumped her in the same category as Viola? She closed her eyes briefly. She was angry; that's what this painful feeling was.

She tried to marshal her composure. There was no point in continuing this argument. "In any event, Viola did not tell me you had wed. She was too busy trying to trick me into marrying Felix Littleton."

"Really?" Frederick's eyebrows rose. He looked moderately interested. "Why'd she do that?"

"From what I could sift out of all the invective she threw at me, you were going to kick her out of Landsford, and she wanted to ensure herself a comfortable home. The price for her assistance was that Littleton allow her to accompany me and live at his estate."

Frederick snorted. "Viola would have got a rude surprise there. Littleton's estate is hardly more than a pile of rubble. But I am surprised she was so ready to sacrifice you." He shrugged. "I suppose she must have realized Father would never approve your daft idea of taking your dowry money and renting a cottage."

"You knew about my plan?" Bloody hell, how long had the damned men been discussing her?

"Of course I did. Puddington, Father, and I all had a good laugh about it."

They'd been laughing at her? Embarrassment, hurt, and anger warred in her chest. Anger won.

Damn it, she was going to strangle Frederick.

She fisted her hands, digging her nails into her palms. No. She could not stoop to that level. But hell, she'd gone to all this trouble, come to London and exposed herself to Lord Jack's fatal charms, and everyone had been *laughing* at her. Puddington, her brother.

Her father.

Her father was a rake, a bounder, a blackguard. She didn't care what he thought of her.

So why did she still feel so hurt?

"And I'm not going to toss you out on the street, of course," Frederick said, "but as I wrote to Viola, now that I'm married, I'm planning to come back to Landsford, and frankly, I don't think my wife will care to have you—or Viola—in residence." He looked down, straightening his coat sleeves. "I've discussed the matter with Puddington and Father. We've found a tidy little house just outside Bath that you and Viola can remove to."

Oh! This was too much, these jingle-brained men deciding her life for her. "I don't want to live with Viola." Nor did she want to live near Bath, where all the old hypochondriacs went to drink the waters.

He shrugged. "I completely understand that, but I'm afraid there's no other solution. You can't live alone. It just isn't done, and now that I'll have a family, I can't have you sullying my name." He glared at her. "You've already done enough of that with this demented—and scandalous—run up to Town."

"Sullying your name?" She hadn't thought she could get any angrier.

"Yes." Frederick looked so blasted supercilious. "Frankly I'm shocked the duchess let you cross her threshold after you dressed as a boy and slept in the same bed as her son. And Rothmarsh! He's so damn high in the instep he virtually blackballs our father from all of society, yet he welcomes you, a girl who's little better than a light-skirt."

"Nothing happened at the Crowing Cock!" She took a deep breath. She would not shout. She would not hit Frederick. She would not.

But, oh, how she itched to do so.

"Right. You spend the night alone in bed with London's premier rake, and you still have your virginity. Bloody hell, Frances, I know you always thought me slow-witted, but I'm not that much of a knock in the cradle."

"It's true, damn it."

Frederick just lifted a mocking brow.

Jack had told her no one would believe her, and of course Pettigrew had not, but it was beyond maddening to face it in her own brother.

Well, he was a fine one to talk.

"I don't see how I can sully your name—*our* name," she said. "Our father ran off with our mother and then deserted us—or deserted me—and likely has half a dozen bastards all over the globe—"

Frederick opened his mouth as if he was going to object, but Frances rushed on.

"—and *you* married a prostitute."

His face turned purple, and he stalked up to her until he was only inches away. She could see a vein throbbing in his forehead.

She'd admit to being a little afraid, but she was also still very, very angry. She held her ground.

"I never want to hear you say that again." He bit off each word. "Maria worked at the theater as a seamstress. She was never ever a—" He swallowed. "She was never what you said she was. She's a lovely, quiet, *ladylike* woman—nothing like you. And if you want to know the truth of it, I didn't tell you I was getting married because I knew you'd be mean and hateful and cruel to Maria, and I would not and will not tolerate that. Do you understand?"

"Yes." She would not have been cruel to Frederick's wife. Of course she wouldn't have. "I—"

Frederick spun away from her, grabbed his hat, and shoved it on his head. "I don't want to hear another word from you. Good day. I will find my own way out." He slammed the parlor door behind him.

"I . . ." Frances stared at the closed door for a moment, and then the tears she'd been holding back overwhelmed her. She collapsed onto the most uncomfortable settee she'd ever encountered, buried her face in her hands, and sobbed.

Jack had retreated to the library and was trying to concentrate on puzzling out the Slasher's identity, but his mind kept drifting back to the yellow parlor.

"Do you think any of the knickknacks will survive Miss Hadley's meeting with her brother, Shakespeare?"

Shakespeare put his head down on his paws and arched his brows in a worried fashion. Clearly he'd not give that possibility good odds.

"At least there's nothing there that Mama particularly values. I don't understand why she doesn't just throw it all out and start over. Perhaps the Hadleys will do us a favor and splinter one or two of the chairs."

He looked up at the clock on the mantel. How much

longer should he leave them alone? He'd told Braxton to listen for any sounds of violence. Frances was safe . . . wasn't she?

The door swung open; Jack and Shakespeare sprang to their feet. "Yes, Braxton?" The butler did not look happy.

"Mr. Hadley has just left, milord, so far forgetting himself as to slam the parlor door in his departure."

"And Miss Hadley?"

Braxton pulled on his waistcoat, an alarming sign of how upset he was. "Not seeing Miss Hadley emerge as well, I took the liberty of listening at the keyhole."

"And?" Jack wanted to strangle someone, and Braxton was the handiest candidate.

The butler's eyes widened in alarm, as if he comprehended the direction of Jack's thoughts. "I'm sorry to report, milord, that I believe I heard Miss Hadley crying."

"Bloody hell!" Jack brushed by Braxton, intent only on getting to the yellow parlor as quickly as possible. If Hadley had laid a finger on Frances—if he'd even brushed her dress with a fingernail—Jack was going to twist the swine's head off and ram it up his—

Well, first he should talk to Frances. She likely wouldn't care for him mutilating her brother without her consent.

He should never have left the two of them alone.

He paused at the parlor door, took a deep breath—and heard a sob.

He'd thought he couldn't feel angrier, but he was wrong. Scalding hot fury cascaded through him, actually blinding him for a moment. All he could see were his fingers wrapped around Hadley's throat—

He struggled for control. If Hadley *had* hurt Frances, the last thing he should do would be to storm into the room angry. He'd learned that from dealing with the women and children he'd brought out of the stews. Emotion begot emotion, and anger—even if on someone's behalf—begot anger and fear. What Frances needed most was a calm, nonjudgmental listener.

Shakespeare butted Jack's leg with his nose and looked up, clearly asking why he was delaying.

He took another deep breath, forced his muscles to relax, and opened the door. Frances looked up from her perch on the settee.

"Go away." She sniffed. "Leave me alone."

He approached cautiously. Shakespeare, the coward, turned tail and deserted him.

"Are you all right?" He didn't see any bruises or cuts.

"Yes." She sniffed again and tried to wipe the tears off her face with her fingers.

Liar. "Then why are you crying?"

"I-I'm n-not." Her voice quavered.

He offered her his handkerchief. She glared at him, but then snatched it out of his fingers.

He sat down slowly next to her on the settee, careful to leave some space between them.

"Your brother didn't touch you, did he?" He struggled to keep his tone level and conversational.

She paused, his handkerchief held over her nose. "What do you mean?"

"Did he put his hands on you?" He had to keep his expression neutral as well. "Did he hit you or push you?"

She frowned at him and then blew her nose. "No, of course not. Why would you think such a thing?"

A hard, tight knot loosened in his chest, and he exhaled slowly. Thank God. "Your brother was very angry. I didn't think he would do you an injury—I would never have left you alone if I had—but I was afraid I'd been wrong when I saw you crying."

"Well, he didn't touch me." She raised her chin. "I should like to see him try."

Damn. It was a horrible time for such a lesson, but he

couldn't allow her to think even for a moment that she could defy a grown man. It was too dangerous, especially given that the Slasher was still at large.

"Don't fool yourself, Frances. If a man wants to hurt you, he will. Men are bigger and heavier than women, and they usually know how to fight."

"I can defend myself."

"Have you ever had to?"

She sniffed in disdain this time. "No, but I'm smart. I can outwit—*what* are you doing?"

He reached across the small space separating them and grasped her wrist. "I'm giving you a very small taste of what it's like to be trapped. Go on. Break free."

She glared at him and then jerked her arm back—or tried to. He held her still with very little effort. Her jaw hardened, and she twisted and pulled, again without success. "Let me go."

He did and then watched her rub her wrist.

"You hurt me," she said.

"No, you hurt yourself trying to get away. Now just imagine if I'd *wanted* to harm you. You would have been in very serious trouble."

Her chin went up again. "I would have screamed."

In one fluid movement, he grabbed her wrist again and pulled, pinning her against him and covering her mouth with his hand.

"Mphft!" She wiggled and grabbed his fingers. She tugged and squirmed harder. *"Mphft!"*

He put his face down by her ear so she would be sure to hear what he had to say.

Mmm, she smelled of lemons. Her lips under his fingers were so soft, and her body felt very good against his. It would feel even better if he could pull her onto his lap and silence her with his mouth instead of his hand. But she'd been crying and deeply distressed just moments ago. He would have to exert some self-control.

And he had a very important—a *deadly* important—lesson to teach her. "A man might very well anticipate that you'd try to call for help and stop you just like this," he murmured. She'd stopped struggling; she must be listening, but he'd keep his hand over her mouth a moment longer to ensure she didn't interrupt. "Never be overconfident. Never underestimate your opponent. Do you understand?"

She made a muffled sort of growl that he took for assent.

"Good. You must stay alert. Keep to lighted areas with other people, and if you do find yourself alone, know where safety is and be ready to run for it." Was she still listening? He'd hold her quiet for just a little longer.

"If a man should manage to grab you, act immediately—don't hesitate. Jerk your elbow back as hard as you can into his stomach; kick, bite, scream. I have Sam shadowing you, so if you make noise, he'll hear. Can you do that?"

Frances showed him she could, but he had anticipated her reaction and let her go before she could do him any damage.

"Well done, but in a real attack, you need to move faster and with intent to injure."

She narrowed her eyes. Good. Anger was better than tears. "Shall I try again?" she asked.

He smiled, but this was nothing to make light of. "It's unlikely you'll be sitting next to the man when he attacks." He stood and offered her his hand. She looked at it as if it were a snake, but finally gave him hers, and he pulled her up to stand in front of him.

"If he grabs only one arm,"—he suited his action to his words—"hit him with the heel of your other hand in the face or under the chin so his head snaps back." He held his other hand up at chin level. "Come on. Try it."

"Must I aim for your hand?"

He grinned. "This time, yes."

He made her practice until she was putting her weight into her efforts. Then he grabbed both her arms and pulled her up against him.

She was breathing hard from her exertions; her scent—lemons and woman—was stronger. It went straight to his head like wine on an empty stomach.

Her body, though tall, was so much smaller and finer than his. She looked up at him, passion in her eyes. Her lips were parted and so close . . .

Was he insane? The passion was *anger*, turning, as he watched, to uncertainty. He didn't want to see fear as well. She'd been crying when he'd come into the room, for God's sake. She'd been through enough this morning.

"Can you free yourself now?"

She twisted and wiggled, doing dangerous things to his self-control. He moved his hips backward slightly so she wouldn't be alarmed by the rather pointed evidence of his reaction.

He forced himself to focus on the lesson he had to teach, not the one he wanted to.

"If he traps you like this," he said, "you must scream and jerk your knee up between his legs as hard as you can. When he doubles over in pain, slam your fists or elbows into the back of his head to knock him down; then run as fast as you can to other people. The key is to act quickly. Don't hesitate and don't hold back."

She blinked. Hadn't she been paying attention?

But then she smiled. "Yes, I think I have it. Would you like me to demonstrate?"

That would be especially painful in his aroused state. He dropped his hold on her and stepped back a safe distance.

"No, I don't believe that will be necessary."

Chapter 16

Love is maddening, confusing, frightening—and wonderful.

—Venus's Love Notes

Venus found the duke in his study. "Oh, good, you haven't left for White's yet." She closed the door behind her and almost danced over to his desk. She hadn't been quite this happy—or happy in quite this way—for four years.

Drew stood and his eyebrows rose as well as he watched her approach. "You have good news?"

"The very best." She reached him and wrapped her arms around his middle. "Ellie thinks she's in the family way."

She watched joy light his face—but then he frowned. "Does Ned know?"

That was the problem, wasn't it? She rested her head on Drew's chest. "Yes. I'm sure he suspected, since Ellie's been feeling unwell in the mornings and has been far more tired than usual, but now that it's been two weeks since her courses . . ." Venus sighed. "Ellie told him this morning before she told me."

Drew rubbed the back of her neck. "How did he take it?"

"As badly as you'd expect. Ellie said he turned white as a sheet and left their room without saying a word."

"Zeus!" Drew led her over to the settee. "Not the best way to react to such news. And how did Ellie take his lack of enthusiasm?"

"I'm sure she was disappointed, but she understands." Venus sat down. "Well, if anyone would understand, it's Ellie. She got him through Cicely's death, didn't she?"

"Yes, she did." Drew sat next to her and laid his arm along the settee's back.

"But she's worried about him."

"I don't doubt it. Where is he now?"

"Braxton said he retreated to the library with a brandy bottle."

"Damn. Not, I'll wager, to toast the good news. Would you like me to talk to him?"

"Yes. Give him a little time, and then please do try, not that I think anything will come of it." Ned worried about many things, but Ellie's pregnancy would take him to new heights—or depths. "It's going to be a long nine months."

"It is." Drew smiled and touched her hair. "But let's at least take a moment ourselves to celebrate the news. I know how you've been looking forward to a grandchild."

"As have you."

"Indeed I have." He pulled her up against him and kissed her.

She kissed him back. She was so thankful to have him. No matter what sorrows entered her life, she could face them all as long as she had Drew at her side.

She rested her head on his shoulder, her hand on his chest. His heartbeat was slow and steady. His calm helped her regain her own.

Surely nothing would go wrong this time. God could not be that cruel.

But, as they all knew too well, God didn't make any promises. Sometimes things *did* go wrong—horribly wrong. There were no guarantees in life. She bit her lip. "I do wish this was a story whose ending I already knew was a happy one."

Drew gave her a little shake. "Now don't *you* start worrying, Venus. You know we have to act as if everything will be fine, for Ellie's—and Ned's—sakes. And things will be fine. Most mothers and babies live through childbirth."

"I know." And she knew at heart Drew was just as concerned as she was.

"Worrying will only make you—and all of us—miserable. It will have no effect on the outcome." He smiled. "As I believe you've told Ned on more than one occasion."

She grimaced. "I can be very annoying."

"But very wise." He leaned back on the settee. "Now, speaking of wisdom and interesting developments, what do you make of Jack and Miss Hadley? My admittedly poor male powers of observation lead me to think Miss Hadley has warmed toward Jack, and that he is not totally averse to her—a good thing, since no other male besides the Pettigrew boy has had the courage to approach her." He shrugged. "Not counting Percy. Percy is just out to make trouble, as usual."

Venus smiled. For once Percy was a bright spot in her thoughts. "Have you noticed how Percy will leave Frances alone whenever Miss Wharton is present? I have high hopes for that match."

"If you say so."

"Oh, ye of little faith." She kissed him again and then frowned. "But as for Jack and Frances . . . yes, I think you are correct. There is some interest there."

"And you aren't happy about it?"

"I don't know." She just could not decide if Miss Hadley would be a good wife for Jack. It was so much simpler making matches for people who were not her children.

"You aren't thinking of pushing her toward Pettigrew, are you? He's been hanging around her skirts since the wedding ball."

She'd noticed that, too, and she'd considered encouraging the match, but something about it had not felt right—and she'd learned to trust her instincts. A match that looked perfect on paper when one listed all the important items—income, beauty, wealth, interests—often failed miserably when the two parties met. The intangible *something* that was as important as it was elusive was missing. "Oh no. He's far too young."

Drew's brows rose. "He can be at most two years younger than she. I'll wager he's older than I was when I wed you."

"Yes, but . . ." She shook her head. "There's just something about him I cannot like."

Drew contemplated an invisible speck on his pantaloons and nodded. "You may be right about that. Remember the scandal with his sister and the half-pay officer about five years ago?"

"Yes, now that you mention it, I do. Ophelia was only seventeen, wasn't she? It happened just before her come-out, which her parents then cancelled, of course."

"Of course. Pettigrew senior caught them before they reached Gretna Green, but they'd been on the road for two days. The girl was quite ruined."

"But we can't hold the sister's sins against Mr. Pettigrew. He could have been only sixteen at the time. Poor boy. As I recall he had to go with his father to bring Ophelia back. And she never forgave him, though why she should be so angry with him was a mystery. Everyone said they'd been quite close before then."

"Perhaps too close."

Venus stilled. Drew couldn't mean . . . but the tone of his voice indicated he might. "Oh?"

"There may be nothing to it, but once Pettigrew began showing an interest in Miss Hadley, I asked a few questions—obliquely, of course."

"Of course." Drew could be very discreet when the occasion warranted.

"Everyone agrees Pettigrew and his sister don't get along—or even speak."

"But that describes Frances and her brother as well."

"Exactly, which is why I didn't find it terribly alarming. But everyone also agrees they'd once been inseparable."

"Oh dear. I do hate it when families have a falling out." Ash and Jess had been inseparable, too, in their youth, and now they seemed permanently separated if not on their way to divorce. She cringed at the very thought of that, but of course she'd support Ash in whatever he chose. And maybe divorce would be better than the current unresolved situation.

". . . *intimately* inseparable."

"What?" That would teach her to let her thoughts wander. "What did you say?"

"You should pay better attention."

"I'm sorry. I got thinking about—" No, she wouldn't mention Ash. Drew would only tell her their son's marital problems weren't her business. "I was thinking about, er, separations."

Drew gave her a speaking look. He knew exactly what she'd been thinking about, but he mercifully didn't comment. "I was saying that Cranburt, who lives not far from the Pettigrew family, hinted that Pettigrew and his sister may have been involved in an unnatural relationship."

Venus's stomach lurched, and she feared for her breakfast. "And you are just now telling me this?"

"I just learned of it last night. Cranburt was deep in his cups and wasn't explicit—I'm only reading between the lines. He's also been known to play fast and loose with the truth, *and* it's common knowledge he detests Pettigrew's father over something that happened when they were both in school. So I only mention it as a caution. It's probably just as well Miss Hadley not develop a tendre for Pettigrew."

"Yes indeed." She should put a word in Frances's ear—but what should she say? Frances likely didn't even know such a thing was possible—and it might not be true. What a horrible tale to spread if it had no basis in fact.

Drew shrugged. "But getting back to our real problem—tell me how we can keep Ned from worrying himself sick about Ellie and the baby, and driving us all mad as well."

"Congratulations, Ellie," Frances said. Ellie was hovering outside the library as Frances came down the corridor to take Shakespeare for a walk. "I hear you're increasing." The news of Ellie's pregnancy—and Ned's worried reaction—were all the servants could talk about.

"Thank y-you." Ellie's smile wavered, and she bent quickly to pat Shakespeare. She did not look elated.

"Are you feeling quite the thing?"

"Oh, I'm f-fine except for when I first get up in the morning." Ellie looked at the library's closed door.

"Were you going to get a book? Don't let me detain you."

Ellie shook her head quickly. "Oh no. N-Ned's in there. He—" She bit her lip. "He wishes to be alone." She blew out a long, disheartened breath. "He's, er, concerned about the baby and me. His first wife died in childbirth, you know, and, well . . ." She tried without complete success to smile. "It's understandable, but I was hoping—"

Being on edge like this could not be good for Ellie or the baby. "Would you like to come with me to walk Shakespeare? We are just going to the park in the square."

"I would love that. Let me get my bonnet and pelisse."

"Don't hurry. We'll wait for you in the entryway."

"I promise I won't be long."

Ellie darted up the back stairs; Frances and Shakespeare continued on to the front of the house, passing the yellow parlor on their way.

Damn.

It had been two weeks since her brother's visit, and she *still* cringed every time she passed that room—and not because the furniture was so very uncomfortable.

When she approached the front door, Sam, her shadow whenever she went out, popped up from the chair where he'd been kicking his heels.

"I can take Shakespeare out for you, madam," he said, petting the dog's head. He was very fond of Shakespeare.

"Thank you, Sam, but I would like some fresh air myself." She was not used to sitting around with nothing of importance to do. "And Lady Edward is coming with me."

She'd like to tell Sam to stay inside. Ellie had managed to get free of *her* shadow—well, that was because Ned had finally decided the boy was too much in the way, especially when Ned wished to steal a kiss. And since Ellie rarely went out without Ned at her side, the poor lad had been bored. He'd got into a bit of mischief, so everyone agreed it was better if he went off to do something else.

Frances could well understand his boredom.

She watched Sam shake hands with Shakespeare. It was kind of Jack to look out for her, but it was also wearing to have the boy at her heels all the time. It wasn't as if there was any real danger.

Sam laughed at something Shakespeare did and then

grinned at her to share the joke. She'd no idea what was so funny, but Sam's smile was infectious. She grinned back.

Had Frederick ever been happy like this when he was a boy? She didn't remember it if he had.

She rubbed her forehead. Damn it, Frederick's words from that dreadful day in the yellow parlor still haunted her. They'd lodged in her heart and ambushed her at odd times: when she was falling asleep or woolgathering at some dull society event or doing mindless tasks like dressing or bathing. She couldn't escape the regret and guilt.

Viola *had* criticized him at every turn, and worse, Frances hadn't questioned her cruelty. In fact, she'd taken great pleasure in bettering him whenever she could—and then crowing about it and lording it over him.

And she should *never* have called his wife a prostitute.

She'd written to him, begging his pardon for all of it, but it remained to be seen if he'd accept her apology. She'd sent the letter over a week ago, and she'd yet to have a reply.

"I'm sorry to have kept you waiting, Frances," Ellie said, hurrying up from the back of the house. "I was a little delayed. Mary wanted to give me some advice."

"About what?" Frances asked as she and Sam and Shakespeare followed Ellie outside.

"About—" Ellie looked at Sam and blushed.

This was never going to work.

"Sam, I'm afraid you are very much in the way," Frances said. "Why don't you sit out here on the front steps? If we run into any difficulties, we'll call and you'll be able to hear us clearly." She smiled. "And Shakespeare will be with us as extra protection."

Sam frowned. "I dunno, madam. Lord Jack said to stay with ye whenever ye went out."

"Yes, but I'm quite sure he didn't mean when I'm only going to the little park across the street with Lady Edward."

Sam looked at her doubtfully, but then heaved a large sigh and reluctantly sat on the steps.

Once they were safely out of his hearing, Ellie laughed. "Thank you. I feel able to talk much more freely without Sam's young ears listening in."

"Yes." Sam was from Jack's foundling home, so he'd probably heard and seen things she and Ellie couldn't even imagine, but Frances felt much freer without him listening, too. "So, you were saying?"

"That it's amazing how everyone—and I do mean everyone—feels compelled to offer an opinion or two or three when they learn I'm increasing. I shudder to think what my sisters will say when I get home."

Ellie paused, a bemused expression settling over her features. "But I won't be going back to the vicarage, will I? My home is now with Ned at Linden Hall." She smiled, clearly delighted.

Damn it, *her* home was going to be with Viola in some small house near Bath. Could there be a more succinct definition of hell?

Shakespeare found an interesting scent by the park fence and stopped dead.

"I know nothing about babies." Frances tugged at the leash—it was as if Shakespeare's nose was glued to the spot. "You don't have to worry that I'll give you any advice."

"Oh, I don't mind. People mean well, though I do wish they'd keep their horror stories to themselves." Ellie frowned. "But if they must share them, I'd much rather they tell me than Ned. He is a bit"—she looked back at the house and her frown deepened—"anxious."

"I think it's rather lovely that he's worried." Frances tugged on Shakespeare's leash again. Finally! He lifted his head, sneezed, and agreed to continue to the park. "I thought men didn't care much about babies after they'd planted the seed."

She flushed as soon as she heard what she'd said. How bold! Ellie must think she had no manners at all. And it wasn't as if she had any sort of idea what the *planting* entailed. "I'm sorry. I shouldn't have said that."

Ellie's expression was serious as she held the gate open. "Not all men are like your father, Frances."

"No, of course they aren't." She did not want to talk about her father. She unfastened Shakespeare's leash so the dog could follow any scent he liked without dragging her along after him.

Ellie started walking toward the spot where Frances had danced with Jack. Oh no, there were too many memories there. Frances turned in the other direction. "Let's sit on this bench in the sun."

"Oh yes. Our bonnets will shade our faces, won't they?" Ellie joined her. "It's amazing to think we had a blizzard at Valentine's Day, and now everything is starting to turn green. It happens every year, and every year it seems like a miracle."

"And next year you'll have a baby." Next year Frances would be . . . what? Living with Viola in some little house where they'd be tripping over each other constantly.

It wouldn't be so bad. She'd lived with Viola all these years—surely no house was so small that she couldn't find some way to avoid her aunt.

She wouldn't have an estate to manage, but perhaps she could put her talents to some other use. Jack spent his time helping the less fortunate. Maybe she could do that, too.

But Jack had his Bromley houses only to care for his by-blows and their mothers . . .

No. She no longer really believed that. She wasn't certain when her opinion had changed, but it had.

"Yes," Ellie said. She sighed with happiness. "Just a month ago, when I arrived at the duchess's house party, I'd given up all hope of marrying Ned and had decided it was time to settle for some other man. I wanted children, you know, and I wasn't getting any younger. And now I have Ned *and* a baby on the way."

Frances felt a piercing, unexpected stab of envy.

What was the matter with her? She'd never wanted a husband or a baby.

Not until she'd met Jack.

Ever since he'd kissed her in this park—just over there, under those trees—she'd felt like a stranger in her own skin. She'd wanted him to kiss her again.

She still wanted it.

Her heart leapt when he came into a room, her palms grew damp, and her stomach churned with nerves and excitement and a kind of frenetic happiness; it was very exhausting. She'd even wondered in the beginning if she was sickening, but she was fine when Jack wasn't around.

And when she'd been crying in the yellow parlor after Frederick had left, feeling more miserable than she could ever remember feeling, all it had taken to send her spirits soaring was Jack walking through the door.

"I hope you find someone, too, Frances. Has any man caught your eye?"

Only Jack.

No. She wasn't herself when she was around Jack. She felt far too agitated. She wasn't in control.

And she didn't want a husband anyway. She didn't want to be subject to some ignorant male.

Not subject, but a partner?

Oh, everything that had once been so clear to her was now murky. She didn't know what she thought.

"I suspect I'm meant to be a spinster. I can knit booties for your babies." She didn't know the first thing about knitting, but if she was going to be consigned to live the rest of her life with Viola, she'd have to learn to do something with her hands or she'd strangle the woman.

"Oh no, Frances." Ellie leaned forward and touched her arm. "Don't give up on love. I felt *exactly* that way after I realized I just couldn't care for any man other than Ned, no matter how much I wished otherwise. I'd resigned myself to being just Auntie Ellie, helping with my sisters' children, and then that very day Ned, er,"—her face suddenly turned red—"asked me to marry him."

Shakespeare trotted up then, his tongue hanging out, and Frances leapt to her feet, hoping her relief wasn't *too* evident. "It looks like it's time to go in." Ellie might be her friend, but she wasn't ready for any more confidences.

She paused as she attached Shakespeare's leash. Ellie *was* her friend, wasn't she?

She'd never had a friend. She'd never played with the other girls in the neighborhood; she'd thought them silly, with their dolls and then their talk of boys and dresses and parties and marriage and babies. She'd had more important matters to concern her: her studies and the management of Landsford.

How had she become so arrogant?

Ellie got up, too, and shook out her skirts. "Thank you so much for inviting me to come with you, Frances. The fresh air and sunshine—and our talk—have put everything in perspective. I feel so much better." She touched Frances's arm again. "I do wish you would look around you for a husband, though. Pardon me for saying it, but you don't seem happy with your current situation. It's no secret that your brother's visit reduced you to tears."

"Ah." Frances looked down at Shakespeare, who tilted his head as if to ask why they weren't moving. An excellent question; she started back toward the gate at once. "My brother and I do not get along."

Frederick had told her to stop trying to be a man. Was that truly how people saw her?

Perhaps. Certainly the people back at Landsford had long said she was mannish. She'd marked it down to jealousy, but perhaps she should have paid more attention. Not that there was anything wrong with being confident and determined, surely, but she might have got people's backs up, too. She could have been more diplomatic. More like Jack.

"I thought you were interested in Jack."

Her fingers tightened on the gate, and then she pushed it open. She couldn't talk about Lord Jack. "Mr. Pettigrew has been paying me some attention."

"Yes, I've noticed that." Ellie's eyes lit with mischief. "He's been trying to get you into the garden alone, hasn't he?"

Frances flushed. "Yes." Especially now that the weather was warming up. She hadn't been tempted to accept any of his offers, but perhaps she should, if only to find out if kissing another man would make her feel the same things she'd felt with Jack.

No, of course it wouldn't—at least not with Mr. Pettigrew. The man was still large and unpleasantly odoriferous, and his breath still reeked of whatever his last meal had been.

And even disregarding the challenges to her nose, she didn't like him. His conversation was dull, and he had no sense of humor or any entertaining insights. The only thing he had in common with Jack was his gender.

"But getting back to Jack," Ellie said.

Oh God, no. Let's not get back to Jack!

"Ned and I think he cares for you."

Panic made her thoughts run in circles like drunken mice. "Oh. Well. Jack likes all women, doesn't he?" It was certainly true all women liked Jack.

Shakespeare stopped in the middle of the road to sniff. If she were lucky, a runaway carriage would come flying round the corner and flatten her, putting her out of her misery.

Ellie was frowning at her. "What do you mean?"

What *did* she mean? "I've, er, heard all the talk." And seen for herself in London's ballrooms and salons. "Lord Jack is a favorite of the ladies—both those in the *ton* and those very much outside of it."

But that wasn't quite fair. She knew much of the gossip was untrue. Jack had told her about his house for women in Bromley. His interest in prostitutes wasn't limited to joining them in bed.

Still, there were all the society women vying for his attentions.

"I don't care to be another on his list of conquests."

"Frances! Jack's not like that."

Shakespeare was finally ready to move. Sam had stood up and was jiggling his foot rather impatiently. If she hurried, she could bring this conversation to an end—

Ellie caught her arm, pulling her to a stop just outside Sam's hearing. "You can't listen to the gossip. Jack is not the careless fellow people think him—or which he often pretends to be. He's thoughtful and kind. I will be forever grateful to him for some things he said to me at the duchess's Valentine party, things that made me see what I needed to do to ensure my happiness."

"Oh. Then I am just another of his charities. Just another lost soul to save." She'd not thought of it that way before, but it made perfect sense.

Ellie was staring at her, her brow wrinkled in puzzlement. "His charities? What do you mean?"

Oh, damn, she'd forgotten his family didn't know about his Bromley houses, though she couldn't understand why he'd keep his activities secret. Still, it was not her place to say anything. In fact, she'd promised him in so many words that she'd hold her tongue.

"Nothing. Just that, as you say, Jack *is* thoughtful and kind. I'm just a poor stray, like Shakespeare, who needs help. That's all I mean to Jack."

"I don't think that's the case at all. I think you're just refusing to see what's right under your nose." Ellie shook Frances's arm a little to emphasize her words. "Don't be afraid of love, Frances. Go after it with all the courage you used to come to London."

Frances did not feel at all courageous at the moment. "Er, yes. Of course." She tore free and almost ran to join Sam.

Bloody hell. Three more girls had been murdered in the last two weeks, but since they were light-skirts, none of the *ton* cared. Well, that wasn't completely true. Some idiot had written in the *Morning Post* that society should be happy the Slasher was cleaning out London's underworld like a gardener pulling weeds.

Jack jerked open the door to Greycliffe House. Jacob, the footman, leapt up.

"Milord, Mr. Braxton has been looking for you."

"Oh?" He tried to sound pleasant. "Why?"

"It's about Lord Ned, milord. He's in the library. Mr. Braxton says he needs you."

"Very well, I'll go there directly." He could stand to have a glass of brandy or two before he went upstairs to change for whatever god-awful event they were promised to this evening. Ah, right. Easthaven's ball—that was it.

He strode down the corridor. *Zeus!* Why the hell couldn't he figure out who the Slasher was? It was beyond maddening. He had the man's watch, but that was almost worse than having nothing.

He'd swear he'd seen the bloody timepiece in someone's hand, but he was likely fooling himself. Watches all looked alike. And he couldn't go through London checking men's pockets to see if they were missing theirs, though he had gone so far as to ask both Botsley and Ruland for the time. They'd each been able to pull out watches. Of course, that proved nothing. They could have bought new ones; if he lost his watch, he'd be quick to replace it. A man needed to be on time.

He jerked open the door to the library.

"Bring the brandy here, Braxton." The slurred voice was Ned's.

"I'm not Braxton," Jack said, closing the door behind him. It didn't take a genius to discern that this conversation wasn't going to be pleasant. No need to encourage an audience. "And I don't have any brandy."

Ned looked around from the wing chair by the fire. He was slumped down and his cravat was half untied. His hair looked as though he'd been caught in a very nasty windstorm. "Go 'way."

Jack got himself a glass and walked over to his brother. The decanter by his elbow was almost empty. "I see you saved me some. Thank you."

"N-no, I didn't."

Ned reached for the bottle, but he was far too slow and clumsy. Jack picked it up before his brother was even close to touching it.

Ned scowled at him. "Give it back." He lunged for the decanter, but Jack held it out of reach. "Damn it, get your own bloody brandy. Braxton!"

"He can't hear you. I've shut the door."

"Then I'll ring for him." Ned tried to get out of his chair to reach the bellpull.

Jack watched his drunken attempts. "You know you're going to feel like the very devil in the morning."

Ned flopped back into the chair, defeated. "Ring for the bloody butler, will you?"

"Braxton's worried about you, Ned. That's why I'm here."

"Damn it, I'll go to W-White's, then."

"I should like to see you try. If you can't manage to stand long enough to reach the bellpull, you won't make it to the library door, let alone White's."

Ned glared at him a moment longer, and then groaned and dropped his head into his hands. "Father's already been in, you know. You may as well save your breath."

Jack regarded the back of his brother's head. He had a good idea what had put Ned in such a state, but it was never wise to assume anything. "Why don't you tell me what sorrow you're drowning? It's not like you to search for solace in a decanter." Ned had been drinking far more than his custom during the Valentine house party, but that had been before he'd recognized his feelings for Ellie.

A shudder racked Ned's body. "Ellie's increasing."

"Ah." That was exactly what Jack had suspected. The pregnancy was not precisely a surprise. The entire household knew Ellie had been sharing Ned's bed since the night they announced their betrothal.

"What if Ellie dies, too, Jack?" Ned's voice was raw with despair. He looked up, his eyes so full of pain, Jack almost winced. "What will I do?"

Ned did not need false promises. He wouldn't believe them. While it was true most women survived childbirth, Ned had learned all too well the agonizing difference between *most* and *all*.

"You'll mourn again. We all will."

Ned's eyes widened, and he jerked his head back as if punched.

"No one can predict the future, Ned. Not even you."

"I know that. I—"

"But just as I can't say Ellie will be fine, you can't say she won't be." Jack wouldn't give Ned empty promises, but he wouldn't listen to needless worry, either. "You don't know what will happen. You can only live each day as it comes and hope for the best."

Ned stared at him while his drunken mind processed his words. "But I feel so damn helpless."

"I know." He *did* know, all too well, the frustration, fear, and anger of having no control over life. He'd come to terms with that, at least to a point.

He knew not all the babies he rescued from the stews would live, though thank God Ursula had written just this morning to report baby William Shakespeare was flourishing.

He needed to get out to Bromley again soon to see how William and the other children went on. If he hadn't been so blasted busy, he would have been there a week or more ago. He'd written Ursula back, asking her to tell the children he'd visit as soon as he could.

But when? He'd been spending every spare minute rushing futilely around London trying to identify the Slasher before the blackguard killed any more women. He felt like he was chasing his damn shadow.

And what if the madman got hold of Frances?

Panic slammed into his gut. He should—

He clenched his teeth. He should stop panicking.

"Panicking never helps," he told Ned—and himself. "Nor does despair." He put his hand on Ned's shoulder. "And you certainly can't spend the next eight months in a drunken stupor."

"I know." Ned closed his eyes and dropped his head back against the chair. "But what am I to do?"

"Tell yourself all will be well, and then act as if you believe it."

Ned kept his eyes closed. "I can't."

"You *can*." Jack tightened his grip, and Ned glared up at him. "You have to. Ellie's depending on you."

Ned's face stilled, and then his jaw hardened. "Yes,

you're right." Disgust crept into his voice. "I'm being a coward."

Oh God, Ellie didn't need Ned flogging himself. "No, you're being human. But now you've got to pull yourself together for Ellie's sake." Ned loved Ellie intensely; he'd do anything if it was for her.

Ned nodded and then shook off Jack's hold, hauling himself upright. "I shall go b-beg Ellie's pardon immediately."

"Just go tell her how happy you are about the baby. You *are* happy, aren't you?"

Ned's face held an arrested expression for a moment, and then he grinned. "Yes. Yes, I am. I'm terrified, but also very happy."

"Then tell Ellie that."

"I will." Ned wove his way across the room and out the door.

Jack smiled, poured himself the last of the brandy, and sat in the chair Ned had just vacated. So Ellie was increasing. It might be fun being an uncle. Would the baby look like Ned or Ellie?

He hooked one leg over the chair arm and cradled his glass in his hand. Ellie would be a wonderful mother.

He took a sip of brandy and swung his foot back and forth. What sort of mother would Frances be? He chuckled. She'd acted as if he were handing her a poisonous snake when he'd given her baby William to hold on their mad dash to Bromley, but by the time they'd arrived, she'd been cradling the infant securely in her arms. And she'd been wonderful with little Eliza, who normally didn't take to strangers.

She might be a bit awkward at first, but Mama would help—

He sat up so abruptly, his brandy almost splashed out of his glass.

Good *God*, what was he thinking? He'd exchanged a few chaste kisses with the woman, and now he was imagining her the mother of his children?

His cock jumped with enthusiasm.

He glared at his cock. Marriage was more than a physical union.

His cock argued that, yes, of course it was, but it was still very physical and Frances had splendidly long legs.

Yes, she did. He hadn't been able to erase the memory of those legs clad in breeches. And she had big green eyes and wavy red hair that was just beginning to grow out.

And a voice that made him think of twisted sheets.

And a rare but lovely smile.

A brave, indomitable spirit.

And . . .

And she needed him.

He couldn't quite explain it. She wasn't anything like the Covent Garden girls, of course, but in some way she was. She was wounded, lonely, and alone. He wanted to share her burdens and bring her joy.

He no longer had to marry her. His parents and her grandparents had seen that her reputation was well on its way to being fully restored. He was free—as she was.

But perhaps he *wanted* to marry her. He hadn't thought to set up his own nursery so soon, but it might be nice for Ned's child to have a cousin to play with . . .

No. He should not be thinking about marriage. He was only twenty-six, far too young for such things.

But he was older than Father had been when he'd married. Older, too, than Ash and Ned when they'd first stepped into parson's mousetrap. Perhaps he was old enough. He certainly felt old. He'd seen so much of the darker side of life these last four years.

A man couldn't schedule when love walked into his life.

If he loved Frances—and he wasn't sure yet that he did—he would just have to amend his rational matrimonial plan.

But first he had to take care of the Slasher; then he could see what Frances thought about weddings and babies.

Well, he knew what she thought; he needed to find out if she could be persuaded to change her mind.

His cock pleaded with him to persuade her now, before he found the Slasher. If they were married, if she was in his bed, he could keep a close eye on her.

A *very* close eye.

And if what he'd told Ned was true and the Slasher was only targeting women with damaged reputations, marriage would remove Frances from danger.

He stood and adjusted his pantaloons so his thoughts would be a little less obvious. There was no reason he couldn't take a moment this evening to stroll with Frances in the shrubbery at the Easthaven ball. The weather was warmer, and if he remembered correctly, Lord Easthaven had a pleasantly overgrown garden with an assortment of well-placed evergreens perfect for stealing a kiss or two.

Chapter 17

Caution is good, but sometimes courage is better.
—Venus's Love Notes

"Thank you for persuading your brother to visit us, Frances." Lady Rothmarsh squeezed Frances's hand. "You can't know what it means to me and your grandfather to finally meet you both."

They were sitting on a settee in a corner of Lord Easthaven's very crowded ballroom—Frances had to lean close to Lady Rothmarsh to hear what she was saying.

She squeezed her grandmother's hand in return. "I doubt I had anything to do with Frederick's decision, Grandmamma." The word still felt odd on her tongue. "I suspect his wife was the one who convinced him, but I'm very glad he came."

At the beginning of the ball, she'd seen Frederick for the first time since that dreadful meeting in the yellow parlor. He'd introduced his wife grudgingly, glaring at Frances as though he expected her to say or do something rude.

A few weeks ago, she *might* have said something cutting. Now she just felt sad. Not at Frederick's marriage—Maria, his wife, was rather meek and a bit plain, but she clearly loved Frederick and he loved her—but at the mull she'd made of her own life. She wasn't certain she could ever mend things with her brother, but she found she'd like to try.

Her grandmother shook her head, sending the impressive selection of ostrich feathers on her turban bobbing. "Nonsense. He told us it was your letter that swayed him."

"Really?" When she'd written her apology, she'd mentioned how kind Lord and Lady Rothmarsh had been to her, but she hadn't urged him to visit them. She was done with giving advice—or, as it likely would have sounded to him, orders. "I'm glad of it."

"As are we." Her grandmother sighed. "We've had this huge hole in our lives ever since Diana ran away. Meeting you and your brother has mended it a bit. It's as if we have a very small piece of our beloved daughter back." She squeezed Frances's hand again. "Family is so important."

"Y-yes." *Her* family—or at least the family she'd known before this trip to London—was hopelessly broken. Even if she could reconcile with Frederick, she couldn't imagine ever being able to heal the breach with her father and her aunt.

She'd written to Aunt Viola before she'd written to Frederick, asking why she'd lied to her about her grandparents, and Viola had sent back a very unpleasant, self-serving note saying she'd known that if Frances went to London, she'd be blinded by the wealth and rank of her mother's family. The only good thing about the letter was that it had shown her what *not* to write in her apology to Frederick.

And as for her father—it wasn't possible to heal something that had never existed.

"Don't look so woebegone," Grandmamma said, patting Frances's knee. "Lady Amanda has been chasing Lord Jack for years. She won't catch him."

"What?" Her grandmother hadn't seemed prone to demented moments, but she *was* getting along in years. "Who is Lady Amanda?"

Grandmamma nodded toward the dancers. "The woman with Lord Jack, the one you were just staring at as if she'd stolen your most precious possession." Lady Rothmarsh's eyes twinkled and her brows danced suggestively.

Frances blushed and scanned the ballroom floor with more attention. Oh. Jack *was* there, dancing—and smiling and chatting—with a beautiful blonde.

Her spirits sank even lower. Grandmamma might believe the woman wouldn't catch Jack, but Jack looked quite amenable to being caught.

"The duchess told me she thinks you two might make a match of it." Her grandmother winked. "And Jack's mother is the Duchess of Love, you know."

If the blonde batted her eyelashes any faster, Jack's hair would begin to stir.

"Oh no, I think you must have misunderstood, Grandmamma. Lord Jack was afraid we'd have to marry because of the scandal. That's why the duchess came to London. She and the duke—and you and Grandpapa—have done a wonderful job repairing my reputation. Her Grace was saying just the other day how no one has excluded me from any invitations."

Her grandmother's eyes were now laughing. "Oh, I've seen how Lord Jack looks at you."

"Like I'm a sticky problem in need of a tidy solution?"

"Not at all. He—" Lady Rothmarsh's attention was taken by something over Frances's shoulder. "Oh dear, Lord Ruland is coming this way."

Lord Ruland hadn't approached Frances since Ned's and Ellie's wedding ball, though she'd caught him looking at her from across a crowded room more than once. "He's probably just walking past."

"No, I'm afraid we are not to be so fortunate." Lady Rothmarsh tsked disapprovingly and leaned forward to whisper loudly. "I don't know why he is still accepted in polite company."

Since Lord Ruland had stopped by their settee at precisely that moment, he must have heard Lady Rothmarsh, but he gave no evidence of it. He bowed. "Lady Rothmarsh, Miss Hadley, good evening."

Grandmamma sniffed. "It *was* a good evening, and I assume it will be again"—she raised her brows—"after you move along."

Lord Ruland looked almost amused. "I will once I've collected your granddaughter. I've come to ask her to dance." He turned to Frances. "Will you, M-Miss Hadley?"

Had Lord Ruland imbibed too freely? His words were faintly slurred, and his eyes looked a little bloodshot and overbright.

"My granddaughter and I were conversing, Lord Ruland."

"Yes, but I want to dance with her." His smile was a bit too wide.

"You are disguised, sirrah."

"No." Lord Ruland tugged on his sleeve. "Only slightly in my altitudes."

Her grandmother straightened and looked to be on the verge of sending Lord Ruland off with a flea in his ear. But if the man was slightly foxed, he might be careless and say something to prove he was the Silent Slasher.

Jack would be delighted—and relieved—to have found the villain out. And if he was also impressed with Frances's cleverness, that would be all the better. It wasn't as if there was any danger. Lord Ruland couldn't harm her in the middle of a crowded ballroom. "It's all right, Grandmamma. I will dance a set with Lord Ruland."

She stood before her grandmother could protest and put her hand on Lord Ruland's arm. The fat rogue smirked, bowed to Grandmamma, and led Frances toward the dance floor.

She could hardly wait to trick some telling detail out of him.

"That's a fetching frock," he murmured as they promenaded around the room. "Shame to hide your legs, though."

"Don't be impertinent." She gave him her coldest stare. How could she get him talking about the murders?

Killed any women recently, my lord?

No, that wouldn't work.

He giggled. "Me, impertinent? That's rich. You were the one t-traipsing about Town in breeches with the *ton*'s most n-notorious rake."

"If you are going to be insulting, I shall have no more to do with you." How dare the man! The fingers on her free hand tightened into a fist, but she forced them to relax. She must hold on to her temper if she wished to get any information out of the drunken scoundrel. Though it was hard to imagine how Ruland could be the Slasher—no woman in her right mind would spend five seconds alone with him.

Ruland was smirking again. "At first I thought Rothmarsh would demand Jack marry you, but then I realized that was the last thing he'd do. Marrying a rake didn't work out so well for your mother, did it?"

It hadn't, but bloody Lord Ruland had no place saying so. "My mother never said she regretted her marriage." She had looked as if she must regret it, but she had never breathed a word against her despicable husband that Frances could remember.

Ruland grunted. "No, she wouldn't admit that, would she?"

They'd reached the side of the room that opened onto the gardens. Ruland turned in that direction. "It's infernally hot in here," he said. "Dancing will just make us hotter. Let's stroll outside instead."

Oh no, she was *not* going out into the dark with him. "I am happy to forgo dancing, my lord. If you are warm, we can stand by the windows."

He stopped and raised his eyebrows. "Are you afraid of me, Miss Hadley?"

"Don't be ridiculous." She was not afraid of him as long as she stayed in this well-lighted ballroom. "You're old enough to be my father."

His face darkened. "Yes, I *am* old enough to be your bloody father, and if your mother had had any sense, I would have been."

Frances didn't know whether to gag or laugh. The sound she did make was a cross between a gasp and a hiccup. This fat little man married to her mother? Perhaps he'd been more attractive twenty-five years ago. She tried to picture him with hair and a smaller belly.

But what did it matter how he'd looked? Any man would make a better father than her own—

Well, perhaps not Ruland. Her father hadn't slashed any throats that she knew of.

Lord Ruland suddenly looked smaller and older. He ran his finger around his cravat and cleared his throat, turning to stare out the window.

"It's my fault your mother fled London, you know. I, er, pressed my case a little too ardently."

What? Ice spilled through Frances's veins. "What do

you mean?" She narrowed her eyes. "Did you force yourself on her?"

His jaw dropped. Shock and anger colored his words. "Good God, no! What do you take me for?"

She couldn't very well tell him she suspected he was a murderer, so she said nothing.

He frowned. "Hell, it might have been better if I *had* forced your mother. That would have saved her from Hadley. At least I loved her." He glared at Frances. "Even though she was as headstrong and wild as you are."

Arrogant toad. "You mean you loved her in spite of herself."

His brows shot up and then slammed back down into a scowl.

"You know nothing of the matter."

"Oh, come, Lord Ruland. What were you going to do with a 'headstrong and wild' woman? Keep her in a cage?"

His scowl deepened. "Of course not. She would have settled down once we were married. She just needed a firm hand on the reins. Her father never tried to restrain her—he and her brothers spoiled her dreadfully."

Frances's hand curled into a fist again. Perhaps she *would* step into the garden with him. She'd like to practice some of the defensive techniques Lord Jack had taught her, beginning with the one that required her to thrust her knee up hard between—

"Miss Hadley." Jack had come up next to her. "Ruland."

Ruland turned his scowl on Jack. "Have you come to take the girl away, then?"

Jack's brows rose and he looked vaguely amused. "Actually, yes."

Ruland snorted. "I wish you joy of her. I suspect she's as bad as her mother."

* * *

"What was that about?" Jack struggled to keep his voice even as he led Frances onto the terrace. When he'd seen her by the doors with Ruland, it had taken all his control not to literally run across the ballroom to reach her. That would certainly have got the gossips' tongues wagging. And now he wanted to shake her for taking such a risk—or kiss her because she was safe.

Clearly he was no longer fully in control of his emotions with regard to the angry woman walking—no, striding—next to him.

There were three other couples on the terrace, so he headed for the stairs down to the gardens. Given Frances's current, barely restrained temper, they did not need any witnesses to their conversation.

Easthaven, anticipating the mild evening and the desire of his guests to escape the ballroom, had hung lanterns here and there to light the way. Not *too* many lanterns, of course. The earl understood the allure of well-placed shadows. Too bad Jack wouldn't be able to put them to their best use.

He'd wanted to take Frances into the shrubbery the moment they'd arrived, but he hadn't. Besides the scandal that action would have provoked, he wasn't entirely certain she'd welcome his advances.

He thought she would. After all, she hadn't slapped him when he'd kissed her in the park, and he'd swear that ever since that interlude, her eyes followed him when she was in the same room with him. Whenever he caught her gaze, she blushed and looked away.

He'd been chased by legions of females; he knew the signs of a woman's interest.

But now that they were finally headed into the gardens, Frances was furious, blast it. It was not the time for amorous activities, though perhaps he *should* try to kiss her. Slapping him—or kneeing him—might give poor Miss Hadley a way to release her spleen.

"Lord Ruland is an idiot." She just about hissed the words.

"He is indeed. Did he do something especially idiotic just now?"

Fortunately they were far enough away from the terrace that he thought Frances hadn't been overhead. Still, it paid to be cautious; he urged her deeper into the bushes. The shrubbery was good for many things, including muffling an irate Miss Hadley.

"Yes." She glared at him. "He said he'd loved my mother *even though* she was headstrong and wild. That she just needed a firm male hand to bring her to heel. Can you imagine?"

"Er." He was suddenly imagining *his* hand moving firmly up Frances's long legs—

He stumbled. Good God, he really had decided to marry her, hadn't he? He wouldn't be entertaining such salacious thoughts if he hadn't.

"Mind the tree roots."

"Thank you. I'll pay more attention to where I put my feet in the future." Did she even like him? There had been that kiss in the park . . .

He steered her down a side path. He *would* kiss her. He'd risk a slapping, but his reactions should be good enough to avoid any serious injury. He stopped in the deep shadows and turned so he could see anyone approaching.

"If he'd wanted some meek woman, he should not have been courting my mother." She paused, and when she spoke again, her voice sounded bleak. "Though when I knew her, my mother wasn't wild or headstrong. She was broken and sullen"—she glared at him and her voice got stronger and rather accusatory—"all because she married a rake who got her with child—with *children*—and abandoned her to make his merry way from one whore's bed to another's."

His passion cooled. Damn it, was she calling him a rake again?

Frances sniffed and looked away. "I was just going to tell Ruland exactly what I thought of him, but then you came up and interrupted me."

Thank God he had. That was exactly why he'd hurried over to her. "The gossips would have enjoyed watching you take the man to task." The old cats who remembered that Ruland had courted Frances's mother had already started whispering.

She raised her chin. "I imagine your precipitous dash to my side got the tongues to wagging more than anything I did."

He'd tried to be discreet, but she was likely correct.

"But in any event, I was going to step outside before I—"

"What?"

Bloody hell! Did the woman have a death wish? He'd demonstrated in the yellow parlor how she couldn't hope to win a fight with a man, and here she was planning to go outside with a fellow who might be a deranged murderer. "That is the stupidest, the—" He pressed his lips together.

She wouldn't meet his gaze. "I wasn't going to go far."

"One step would have been too far." He kept from shouting, but only just. He clasped his hands behind his back so he wouldn't throttle her.

She sniffed in obvious annoyance. "Oh, why don't you just say it? You think I'm headstrong and wild, too, don't you?"

Yes.

He knew better, even with anger—and frustrated

desire—pounding through him, than to answer truthfully, so he didn't answer at all.

"You're just like Ruland. Like all men. You do all your thinking with your co—"

She slapped her hands over her mouth.

His cock jumped, pleading with him to show Miss Hadley exactly what it was thinking.

Damn cock.

He was still too angry to speak, so he just looked down at her.

Her eyes were huge in the darkness. "I'm sorry," she said. "That was rude." She lifted her chin. "But it's true, isn't it? You're a rake just like my father."

His anger turned suddenly to despair. "Do you really believe that?" If she did, then there was no hope for them.

She opened her mouth as if to agree, but then she shook her head. "No." Her voice caught slightly. "Not really."

Ah. He heard her pain. She needed him.

He cupped her cheek. "I'm nothing like your father, Frances." Thinking of her father always made him furious, but he tried to keep the anger out of his voice. "I would never abandon you."

She shrugged as if it didn't matter. "Frederick said our father left Landsford because Viola was cruel to him growing up, just as she was cruel to Frederick."

What a sniveling, lily-livered excuse. "And your brother thought your aunt's behavior justified your father's? It does not. Frances, your father ran away and left his wife and his children with a woman he knew to be cold-hearted. *That's* cruel."

Frances's eyes widened. Clearly that aspect of the matter had not occurred to her.

He gripped her shoulders gently so she couldn't turn away from him. "Your father's actions are unconscionable,

Frances. As you are so fond of telling me, society gives men powers that women do not have. He could have sent Viola packing the moment he inherited. He should have made other arrangements for her when he brought your mother home. And he should never, ever have let her raise his children."

"But . . ."

He rested his fingers on her lips. "No. If nothing else, he could have sent you to your mother's family. Surely he knew that, no matter what they thought of him, Rothmarsh or Whildon or any of your mother's relatives would have taken you in and loved you."

"That would certainly have been better for Frederick."

"And for you, too." He stroked her cheek with his thumb. Her skin was so soft. "Frederick is not totally blameless here, you know. Yes, he may have had an unfortunate time of it as a boy, but he's a man now. He should have insisted your father write to you and come to see you. But, in the end, it is your father I most fault, as I shall tell him when I meet him. He has much to answer for."

Her lips twisted into the slightest of smiles. "I can't imagine you would want to meet my father."

"I don't, but as I intend to wed his daughter, I fear I must."

She blinked. "You're going to marry . . ."

He saw the moment she comprehended his words. Her mouth dropped open, which was all the invitation he needed.

Jack's lips brushed lightly over hers. Their touch felt as good as she remembered—no, better. She pressed against him.

And then his mouth came back. This time it clung, and

the fire that had raged in her the first time he'd kissed her returned tenfold.

His tongue touched her lips. Did he want her to open her mouth? She did.

Ohh.

He slid deep inside, stroking . . .

She arched against him. She wanted him even closer. She slipped her fingers under his coat and waistcoat, tugging on his shirt—

Jack lifted his head, catching her hands and bringing them around to rest on his chest. He was slightly breathless. "We need to go back into the ballroom, Frances. We've likely been out here too long as it is."

Go back to the ballroom? Stand quietly among all those prim, superficially polite people for another hour or two? She wanted to scream.

"Think about something else," Jack said.

She'd been staring at his chest. Now her eyes snapped up to meet his. "You know what I'm thinking?" Oh God! A hot flush exploded over her face—and probably every other part of her body.

He chuckled, though the sound was a bit strained. "Yes, because I'm thinking the same thing"—his lips turned up in a tense smile—"except in much more detail."

So he knew what this madness was? "Tell me."

His eyes widened before his lids dropped down to shield his expression. "Tell you what?"

She was certainly breaking a thousand spoken and unspoken rules of polite discourse, but she didn't care. "Tell me what is happening to me, why I feel so . . . unsettled."

She saw honor battling desire in his eyes—and honor won, blast it. His mouth hardened. "I should not have brought you into the garden, and I definitely should not have taken you down this dark path."

"But you did bring me, and now I want you to finish what you started." She pressed against him again, against the large bulge that had grown in his breeches. "Finish what you started, my lord. I shall never be able to sleep in my current state."

He held her away from him and snorted. "You'll fall asleep sooner than I will." He stared down at her. "But what are you really asking, Frances? Are you ready to give up your fierce independence and your dream of living alone in a cottage to marry me?"

The heat of passion suddenly cooled. What was she thinking?

"Frederick won't let me live by myself," she heard herself say. "He's going to condemn me to share my cottage with Viola."

She'd discovered in the park when Jack had taught her to dance how potent a man's kisses were. They scrambled the female brain. This must be the way her father had cozened her mother into eloping with him.

She understood her mother's error so much better now.

"Oh?" Jack frowned. "So I would be the lesser of two evils?" He stepped back, and his voice sounded almost cold. "It may be selfish of me, Frances, but I find I do not wish to be merely an alternative to your very disagreeable aunt. I want you to marry me only because you love me."

Heavens! Now he was behaving like a typical male, his masculine feelings offended because she didn't swoon at his feet. He—

Her heart twisted, interrupting her head.

That wasn't what she truly felt. This wasn't some anonymous man, and it certainly wasn't her father. It was Jack who had been patient and kind and loyal. He was her friend . . .

But did she love him? Was she willing to give up her freedom to become his wife?

What if she married him, and he left her? What if he didn't? What if he stayed but grew to hate her? She knew nothing about men or marriage.

She shivered.

"Come, you're cold. We've been out in the garden too long. We'll be missed." He took her arm and started back toward the ballroom.

She shouldn't leave it like this. She should explain, but what could she say? She didn't understand herself.

She'd always known her own mind, but now her mind was a confusing jumble of emotions.

"I'm sorry."

"Don't be." Jack squeezed her fingers gently. "You're just feeling overwhelmed. You'll figure things out in time. There's no hurry."

Except it seemed she could not be near him without experiencing this strong attraction. It still simmered under her skin. And she found she did not at all like the new friendly but remote tone of his voice.

"Do you truly want to marry me, or were you just overtaken by your male instincts?"

He chuckled. "Frances, I've been managing my 'male instincts' for years, and I've never yet discussed marriage with a woman."

"But why would you want to marry me? You don't need a wife."

"But I seem to want one. I seem to want you." He smiled down at her. "I like you. You're beautiful and passionate, intelligent and brave"—he winked—"and it turns out you kiss very well."

Her mouth fell open.

He tapped her chin, and she snapped her lips together. "Now go into the ballroom. I'm going to stay outside a few more minutes to cool my, er, overheated blood."

She glanced down at his fall. Yes, he did look rather overheated.

"Go, Frances, before you cause me to embarrass myself."

She went. She almost bumped into Mr. Pettigrew by the door.

"You were out in the gardens with Lord Jack, weren't you?" he said, glowering at her.

"I was outside." Where she'd been and with whom was certainly none of Mr. Pettigrew's concern. She brushed past him. Who else had noticed her whereabouts? Had Lady Rothmarsh and perhaps Jack's mother? She glanced around.

Oh dear.

Grandmamma was with the duchess. They smiled and waved.

Chapter 18

Trust your instincts.

—Venus's Love Notes

"You may stay here, Sam," Frances said, tying her bonnet strings in the entryway while Shakespeare sat waiting. "I'm only taking Shakespeare across the square to the park."

Sam twisted his cap in his hands. "Lord Jack said when he left this morning to stick to ye like glue."

Her heart leapt at the sound of Jack's name. *Stupid!* "But I'm sure he didn't mean when I'm so near at hand. Remember nothing happened when I went out with Lady Edward the other day."

She wanted rather desperately to be alone. She'd pleaded the headache—not that the duchess was fooled by that excuse—and hidden in her room until she'd seen everyone leave. At least Jack had departed quite early. He probably hadn't wanted to encounter her. Was he regretting last night?

She was tired and on edge. She'd hardly slept a wink,

and the few times she'd managed to drop off, she'd seen Jack's face—and felt his body, his hands, his lips, his tongue—

Damn it, the hot, frantic feeling was churning in her gut again. "Shakespeare will protect me from any villains, won't you, Shakespeare?"

Shakespeare barked his assent, sweeping the floor with his tail to emphasize his willingness to keep all blackguards at bay.

"But his lordship said I was to stay with ye."

She *had* to be alone. She bent down to fasten Shakespeare's leash. "I hear Cook is making gingerbread." Frances had just been in the kitchen, fetching Shakespeare from under the worktable where he'd taken to stationing himself. It was an excellent location for gobbling up any bits of food that fell to the floor.

A look of yearning bloomed on Sam's face. "She is?"

"Yes, and I believe she was just getting ready to take a pan out of the oven." She wasn't playing fair. Sam loved gingerbread above all else. "If you hurry, you can get some while it's still warm."

"Oh." He looked in the kitchen's direction. The poor boy was clearly torn.

"I'll likely not be in the park more than half an hour. Lord Jack will never know."

Sam bit his lip. "But Lord Jack said—"

"Yes, but I'm sure he *meant* for you to come with me when I was away from home. Going out to the park in the square can't be considered away from home."

Sam began to look hopeful. "Ye think so?"

"I know so." She delivered the final blow. "And should Jack mention it, I'll tell him how valiantly you tried to accompany me and how vehemently I insisted you stay here."

That did the trick.

"Ye promise to tell him?" The boy was already edging toward the back of the house.

"Yes indeed." She smiled. "And he'll understand completely because he knows how determined I can be."

Sam nodded. "Aye. Everyone says yer pighead—" His eyes widened as he heard what he was saying, and he coughed, eyeing her warily. "Er, everyone does say yer determined."

"Exactly." She was not about to get into an argument about that; freedom was at hand. "Off with you now."

He didn't have to be told twice. He vanished down the corridor in the direction of the kitchen before she'd finished speaking.

"Finally!" She looked down at Shakespeare. "Let's go before someone else comes along to detain us."

Shakespeare barked and leapt to his feet, putting his nose to the door, so she had to push him aside to open it. Then he tugged her out into the March sunshine and across the road to the park.

She took a deep breath of the cool, crisp air and immediately felt better. This was what she needed. The four walls of her room had been closing in on her, and the house felt too much like Jack. She needed to be out in the open, away from everything that reminded her of him.

Once she shut the park gate, she took off Shakespeare's leash. As soon as he was free, he raced after a squirrel, of course. She smiled. Did he realize how futile his efforts were? He was never going to catch one.

She walked deeper into the park to the spot where Jack had waltzed with her, where he'd kissed her for the first time, and sat on the bench. It was quiet—except for the sound of Shakespeare tearing through the bushes and barking—and peaceful, all things considered. She closed her eyes, letting the memories flow through her: Jack comforting her when she'd tripped over Frederick's boots in the inn, and again in Hyde Park after that dreadful meeting with Puddington; Jack carrying baby William so confidently through the dirt and muck of Hart Street; Jack surrounded by a bevy of happy, chattering little girls at his Bromley house. Those were not the images of a callous rake.

But men were overbearing and selfish and condescending and unreliable.

Not Jack.

She wanted to live by herself.

But she'd miss Jack.

She cared too much for him. If she married him, she'd lose herself. She'd turn into someone she wouldn't recognize.

Perhaps that wasn't such a bad thing. Maybe she'd become someone better.

Ellie was happy with Ned. Jack's mother and her grandmother—they were happily married to men who gave every appearance of loving and valuing them.

Perhaps she'd only lose herself if she let herself be lost.

But why did Jack want to marry *her*? Frederick had been right that day in the yellow parlor. She was mean and hateful and cruel, or at least she had been. What could Jack possibly see in her?

Her thoughts were still going round and round like a dog chasing its tail.

Shakespeare bounded out of the underbrush just then and ran past her.

"Tired of chasing squirrels?" She got up to follow him. "If you've attended to your business, we can go back inside. I'm not finding the park as calming as I'd hoped."

Neither was Shakespeare. He'd stopped and was growling low in his throat, facing the gate. A large man was letting himself in. He had his head down, fumbling with the latch, so she couldn't immediately identify him.

"What is it, Shakespeare?" She paused as she fastened his leash. Perhaps she should leave him free so he could defend her better.

Silly! She was letting her imagination run away with her. What sort of villain would appear in this peaceful park in London's best neighborhood? The man was well dressed—he clearly wasn't some vagrant or a denizen of the stews. Likely he was one of the neighbors.

"Stop it, Shakespeare." She kept her voice low so the fellow wouldn't overhear as she finished with the leash. He'd probably be mortified to discover he'd caused anyone the least concern. "Where are your manners?"

Shakespeare's hair was now standing on end, and his growl had gotten louder. It was more of a snarl.

It was definitely time to depart. Her privacy had already left anyway.

The man looked up and smiled. "Miss Hadley," he said, bowing.

She relaxed. "Mr. Pettigrew, I didn't know you lived in this square." Why wouldn't Shakespeare stop snarling? It was most impolite and completely unlike him.

"I don't." He closed the gate behind him. The click of the latch sounded unnaturally loud.

Silly! Now she was allowing Shakespeare's peculiar behavior to unnerve her.

"Then you're visiting?" Shakespeare forgot himself so far as to bare his teeth. She would admit Mr. Pettigrew looked a little . . . odd. Something about his expression—his eyes, perhaps—was rather strange. "Do you feel quite the thing, sir?"

He ignored that question to answer her first. "Yes, I'm visiting."

The man was still about ten yards away, but he was blocking her path to the gate. "And whom do you wish to see?"

He smiled, if that was what one should call the rather grotesque expression.

"You."

Jack turned onto Southampton Street. He'd not been able to sleep last night for an obvious—a painfully obvious—reason. On more than one occasion, he'd been on the verge of creeping down the corridor to Frances's room to continue the "conversation" they'd started in Easthaven's garden. He could easily have seduced her and likely made them both feel better.

But it would have been the wrong thing to do. Frances had endured one betrayal after another—her father, her aunt, her brother. She did not need him persuading her to do something she might regret later. She would have to come to him on her own.

But, blast it, it was bloody hard—in all respects—to be noble. His head might assure him he was wise, but his heart—and a much more insistent organ—called him every sort of fool. He'd tossed and turned all night and had had to get out of the house first thing this morning. He didn't wish to encounter Frances again until he'd better control of this raging lust.

It was far more than lust.

Damn it, he had other things to occupy his mind besides Frances's soft curves and fiery temper and sweet, vaguely lemony scent.

Mmm. Her mouth had tasted—

Bloody hell, he was here in Covent Garden to consider murder, not marriage. Two more women had turned up with their throats slashed, but since they were both prostitutes, the newspapers had barely mentioned the deaths. He had the Slasher's gold watch in his pocket. He'd shown it around when Nan had first sent it to him and no one had recognized it, but there was always someone new to Town. He'd try again.

He had nothing else to go on.

He skirted the square, ignoring the people trying to sell him all manner of things, and turned up James Street.

Henry came running when he pulled into the Nag's Head. "Morning, milord," he said as he took hold of the horses.

"Good morning, Henry." Jack swung down. Henry saw everyone come and go and knew Jack was trying to discover the Slasher's identity. "Any news?"

"Maybe." The word came out in a whisper.

"Oh?" Excitement shot through him, but he kept it out of his voice. It was probably nothing—and he didn't want to upset Henry. The boy was obviously nervous. "What have you learned?"

"Nothing, really."

Jack waited, trying to appear patient. Sometimes silence worked better than words in getting a person to talk.

Henry glanced at him and then back to his horses. "Dick Dutton's back. He was asking after Shakespeare."

"I see." Was that all? No, Sam wouldn't be acting this way if that was all he had to say. "Perhaps I could meet Mr. Dutton to assure him of Shakespeare's well-being?"

"'E's afraid." Henry looked around the innyard, but it was too early in the day for anyone else to be about.

"Of what?"

Henry shrugged. "'E wouldn't say, but I think 'e saw something to do with the Slasher."

"Ah." It was probably nothing. He'd had his hopes raised before only to have them dashed. "I'd like to speak to the man. Can you take me to him?"

Henry shook his head. "Can't leave yer horses."

"You could stable them." Though that might raise everyone's suspicions. He was never in the area that long.

Henry thought about it for a moment and then must have come to the same conclusion. "Nay. Just go down toward the theater and knock on the red door. Tell the lady who answers ye want to speak to Romeo."

"Romeo? I thought I wanted Dick Dutton."

Henry nodded. "Aye, but 'e's afraid to use 'is own name. Thinks someone's out to kill 'im, 'e does."

Interesting. "And what do you think?" Henry was only the boy who held the horses, but in Jack's experience, the most insignificant people generally saw the most.

Henry shrugged. "Could be. Don't take much to make a man want to kill another sometimes."

Unfortunately that was too true, especially in this neighborhood. "Very well." He slipped Henry a shilling for his help. "Take care of my cattle while I go off to pay a visit to Romeo."

The red door was easy to find. He rapped on it sharply.

Nothing.

He rapped again. Again nothing.

He was raising his hand to knock once more and harder when the door finally swung open to reveal a tiny, wizened old lady with a cane and a powerful voice.

"What do you want?" She looked him up and down, and then grinned, revealing several large gaps where teeth should have been. "Fifty years ago, young bucks like you were knocking at my door at all hours, and I could take care of three or four in an evening. Sadly, those days are over." She wheezed in apparent laughter and batted her eyelashes. "But I can try. I've learned a number of tricks over the years, you know."

He bowed. He'd long ago learned to control his expression, so if she'd hoped to see horror or shock, she was disappointed. "Alas, my betrothed has forbidden me to engage in such activities." Frances wasn't formally his betrothed yet, but that was just a matter of time, he hoped.

The woman snorted. "And you allow a woman to dictate your behavior?"

He nodded. "I confess I tremble at the thought of her wrath." Frances did have a prodigious temper. "I fear I am here on business, not pleasure. I need to speak to a man who calls himself Romeo."

In a flash, her face turned wary. "There's no one here by that name." She started to close the door.

He stuck his foot in the way. "I have his dog, Shakespeare."

Her eyes widened for a moment, and then she got control of herself again. Her eyebrows rose. "A dog named Shakespeare? That's ridiculous."

"He's brown, about average size, with a notch out of one ear. Very talented, too—can do all sorts of tricks."

She frowned at him. "If there were a man named Romeo here—which there isn't—whom should I say was looking for him?"

"Lord Jack Valentine."

Some of the distrust left the woman's face. "Oh, Lord Jack. I've heard of you, of course." She leered at him again. "Never had the pleasure of seeing you up close—and quite a pleasure it is. Come in, and I'll see if there happens to be a Romeo about."

Jack stepped inside, and the woman bolted the door behind him.

"Can't be too careful," she said.

"No indeed."

She shuffled off down the corridor and disappeared through a doorway. He heard a rather spirited, but whispered, exchange, though he couldn't quite make out the words, and then the woman poked her head out of the room.

"Come on," she said, gesturing. "*Romeo*"—she rolled her eyes—"will see you."

"Thank you." He stepped briskly—no use giving anyone a chance to change his or her mind—and crossed the threshold into an extremely cluttered, musty-smelling study. Books and papers covered all the horizontal surfaces, including the floor, while paintings of a lovely woman—likely the old woman in her youth—in various forms of theatrical dress adorned the walls. A teapot and cup sat on a cart, and an empty mug and a half-eaten sandwich were abandoned on a table by a wing chair, around which two bespectacled, watery, rather bloodshot blue eyes peered.

"Mr. Dutton?"

"*Romeo*," he said, glaring at Jack and then the woman as he stood, revealing a slightly stooped, paunchy, balding figure. "My name is Romeo."

"Oh, don't be ridiculous," the woman said. "Lord Jack knows your name isn't Romeo. No one is named Romeo."

"Romeo was one of my most memorable roles, as well you know, Olivia."

"Which you only played because Jasper ate some bad fish and was puking up his guts."

This did not sound like a productive conversation. "I believe I saw you in *The Merchant of Venice* with Mr. Kean, didn't I, sir?"

Dutton straightened and puffed out his chest. "I was rather good in that play, wasn't I?"

"Yes indeed."

"And now you've admitted you're Dick Dutton," the

woman said, "so you can leave off pretending to be Romeo, which I said was a stupid idea from the beginning."

Dutton's jaw clenched. "Damn it, Olivia, I—"

Jack cleared his throat. He did not have time to listen to these two brangle. "Perhaps it would be better if you left us alone, Miss . . . ?"

The woman flushed. "Mrs. Bottomsley," she said.

Dutton snorted and opened his mouth, likely to contest her married title—which would certainly lead to more squabbling.

"Thank you, Mrs. Bottomsley," Jack said, gesturing toward the door.

She sniffed at Dutton, smiled at Jack, and then swept out of the room as well as an aging woman with a cane could sweep.

Jack turned back to Dutton. "What are you so afraid of, Mr. Dutton?"

Dutton slumped down again, keeping the chair between them. "Olivia said you had Shakespeare."

"I do. He's well. I was going to bring him with me, but decided it was wiser to leave him with my betrothed. I confess I'm concerned for her safety with the Slasher still at-large."

Dutton nodded. "Shakespeare's smart. He won't let the blackguard hurt your lady if he can do anything to stop him." Dutton collapsed further into himself. "I just don't know if poor Shakespeare can stop the villain."

Perhaps he was finally going to learn something. "Do you know who the Slasher is?"

"No."

Damn.

"But I saw him—or I sort of did." Dutton sighed, shaking his head. "I was leaving the Bucket of Blood after having a few pints one night about a month ago, when I heard an odd noise coming from the alley. Shakespeare was with me, and he started barking and growling. He would have run down to investigate if I hadn't caught his collar. I saw a big shape, like a bear, and then I ran. It wasn't until the next day that I learned Martha had been found dead there."

Blast it all, he'd gotten his hopes up, and this was worse than nothing. A big bear? Ridiculous. Dutton had likely been thoroughly drunk at the time. "So why did you lope off and leave Shakespeare?"

"I couldn't see the Slasher, but I'm sure he saw me. I was standing by the public house's light, and I had Shakespeare. Lots of people know Shakespeare." He looked down at his hands. "I was afraid he'd think I *had* seen him and so would slit my throat. I had to leave quick, and I knew the dog would land on his feet." He snorted. "More than that—he's landed in the lap of luxury, hasn't he?"

Greycliffe House *was* markedly better than their current surroundings. "Do you want him back? I'm afraid we've gotten rather attached to him."

"No no, that's all right. You can have him. We were mates, but of a professional sort, you see. He wasn't a pet; he worked for his keep. I just thought I should come back to see how he went on."

Dutton didn't sound bereft, but he *had* come back to check on Shakespeare. "You may visit him, if you like. Or I can bring him here."

Dutton shook his head. "No, best not, since the Slasher is still roaming the streets. I think I'll leave London again. Perhaps go to Brighton . . . or maybe York. The farther from Town the better, I wager."

"Very well. If you remember anything—even the smallest detail—do send word to me. I'm determined to catch the madman." Jack turned toward the door. He'd been so hopeful when he'd spoken to Henry. Now . . . wait a moment. He still had the watch. It was unlikely Dutton would recognize it, but it certainly wouldn't hurt to ask. He turned and pulled it out of his pocket. "Have you ever seen this before?"

Dutton took it and turned it over to look at the initials. "Oh yes. It's Pettigrew's. What are you doing with it?"

Jack's stomach twisted into a hard, icy knot, and dread made his arms feel like lead. "Pettigrew's?" The man had been talking to Frances just last night. "But the initials on the watch are H-E-B. It can't be his."

"Oh, it's his, all right. He had it at the Bucket of Blood that last night I was there. I asked him the time, and when he pulled his watch out of his fob pocket, he almost dropped it. Said he needed to get the chain fixed, that he didn't want to lose the watch because he'd inherited it from his maternal grandfather, Horace Edgar Blant, a dashing—and from the tales Pettigrew tells—violent army officer."

Bloody hell.

"And where was Pettigrew when you left the pub?"

Dutton stared at him, comprehension beginning to dawn on him as well. "Gone. He left about ten minutes before I did. I still had half a mug of ale to drink when he got up, but it didn't take me long to finish it. It was getting late . . ." He ran his hand over his balding pate. "Pettigrew does look a bit bearlike."

"Yes, he does." Jack had to go home. He had to be sure Frances was safe. "If you'll excuse me?"

He was out of the room and down the corridor before he heard Dutton's faint reply.

"Good luck."

"Why do you wish to see me, Mr. Pettigrew?" Frances asked. This was the most stilted conversation she'd ever engaged in. In truth, it hardly qualified as a conversation—it was more of an inquisition, though she didn't care what he answered. All she wished to do was leave, but he was still standing in her way. "Shh, Shakespeare."

Mr. Pettigrew dropped his gaze to Shakespeare. "Why do you have Dick Dutton's dog?"

"Mr. Dutton left London, and Shakespeare was in need of a home."

"Ah." Mr. Pettigrew nodded. "I thought he'd seen me."

He was making no sense, and Shakespeare was now interspersing his snarls with barks and tugging on the leash. It was definitely time to leave. "Yes, well, as you can see, Shakespeare wishes to depart. If you will excuse us?" She hesitated to proceed until the man had stepped out of their way. If Shakespeare decided to go beyond the pale and try to bite Mr. Pettigrew, she'd be hard-pressed to restrain him.

"No."

"Pardon me?"

"I said no, I will not excuse you." He stared at her, his eyes oddly flat. "I've been waiting for weeks to get you alone." His voice sounded flat, too. "You would never go into the gardens with me."

"Of course not. That wouldn't have been proper." She looked around. The square was deserted. All the nursemaids and their charges must be inside, the children taking naps, the maids propping up their feet and having a cup of tea.

Oh, *why* had she persuaded Sam not to come with her?

"You went into the gardens with Lord Jack last night. That wasn't proper." He took a step closer; she would have taken a step back if Shakespeare would have let her. At least Mr. Pettigrew was keeping a safe distance from Shakespeare's jaws. "And what you did with him out there in the dark wasn't at all proper, was it?"

She must remember Mr. Pettigrew had no idea what had happened in Lord Easthaven's shrubbery, and even if he did know, he had no business caring about it one way or the other. "What I did or didn't do is between me and Lord Jack. Now please step aside. I wish to go back to Greycliffe House."

He chuckled—at least, she thought he intended the sound to be a chuckle. Given the circumstances, amusement was highly inappropriate.

"You must be a very hot-blooded whore. Couldn't even wait until you got back to Greycliffe House, could you, to have Jack scratch your itch? I'm surprised the duchess hasn't seen through your ruse, but I suppose she thinks her precious son can do no wrong. Well, you won't be spreading your legs for him any longer."

Her stomach twisted at the ugly words. Shakespeare took exception, too, and began to bark in an even more threatening manner. She could barely hold him back from attacking the man. "Step aside immediately, sir, and let me leave."

He shook his head, reaching inside his coat. "Oh no. You're not leaving."

"Mr. Pettigrew, Lord Jack—and his father, the Duke of Greycliffe—will be very angry if you don't move aside at once." He was pulling his hand out from his coat.

Good God! Was that a hunting knife?

"Put that away, sir." Shakespeare was barking so loudly, she had to raise her voice. If only there was someone nearby to hear them and come to their aid.

"I will, once I've slit your throat. You are putting me to some inconvenience, you know. I prefer to kill at night, but I haven't been able to get you alone. Thank God you are finally without that boy who shadows you."

"Sir, God has nothing to say to this matter, except to condemn you to burn in eternal flames." This couldn't really be happening. Mr. Pettigrew was unpleasant, but not *this* unpleasant.

He laughed. "Then thank the devil. Give him my regards when you meet him, whore." He jerked the knife free of its sheath; the sun glinted on the curved steel of its blade.

The time for conversation was clearly over. What had Jack told her? Don't be overconfident. Don't hesitate. Move fast and intend to injure the bloody blackguard.

It was time to give Shakespeare his wish. She dropped the leash.

Shakespeare leapt straight for Pettigrew's knife. She watched in shock as the dog's teeth closed over the madman's wrist, and then she picked up her skirts and ran. If she could just make it out of the park, surely someone would see her and help her capture the villain.

Pettigrew was screaming and yelling behind her—she hoped Shakespeare had managed to sink his teeth in all the way to the bone. And then she heard the dog yelp, followed by the terrible sound of something hitting the ground hard. Oh, dear God—Shakespeare! But she couldn't stop; she was almost at the gate—

A large, hard hand wrapped around her arm, jerking her back. Terror surged through her, taking her breath. For a moment, she was blind with it—and then she saw Jack's face, heard him telling her what to do if a man ever grabbed her.

Damn it, she was *not* going to let the blackguard win. She wanted to see—and hold—Jack again.

All the emotions that had churned through her since she'd come to London—all the guilt, the frustration, the anger, and the pain—coalesced with the love she had for Jack. Fear and hesitation burned away. When Pettigrew swung her around to face him, she put all that energy into her arm as she slammed the heel of her hand up into the underside of his chin.

His head snapped back, and he grunted in pain, loosening his hold on her arm. She jerked her knee up into his groin, and he screamed. When he bent over—in agony, she hoped—she linked her hands and swung them down as hard as she could on the back of his head.

He went down and stayed down.

If she'd been wearing Frederick's nice hard boots, she'd have kicked him.

"Frances!"

She snapped her head around. Jack was leaping down from his curricle, leaving his horses standing in the street, and running to the gate.

He was here. Everything would be all right now.

Chapter 19

Love is always worth the risk.
—Venus's Love Notes

He never wanted to live through this day again. Jack stretched his slippered feet toward the fire and took a large swallow of brandy. Usually being alone in his room relaxed him, but tonight he felt as tight as a bowstring.

Thank *God* he'd come straight back to Greycliffe House after he'd spoken to Dutton. It was a little surprising that he had. He'd been in Covent Garden. It would have been reasonable to let Nan know and send Jeb to take word to Trent and the others who were helping him look for the Slasher. But something had told him to go home. All he'd been able to think about was Frances.

He rubbed his hand over his face. Frances. When he'd heard Pettigrew's shouts and then Shakespeare's yelp as he'd turned into the square, he'd thought his heart would leap from his chest. He'd whipped his poor horses to a lather, racing them to the park gate, and then he'd jerked them abruptly to a stop.

He'd arrived just in time to see Frances fell Pettigrew, a man almost twice her weight. She'd been spectacular, truly an avenging Fury.

But how was she now?

He took another mouthful of brandy.

Fortunately, Sam had been watching out the window—Jack had had a few choice words with the lad later about allowing Frances to go out alone, but he couldn't come down too hard on him. Frances *was* an extremely strong-willed female. When Sam saw him abandon his curricle in such a precipitous fashion, he'd raised the alarm, and the entire male staff had rushed to the park, arriving just minutes after Jack.

A good thing—he'd needed some help as he hadn't wanted to leave Frances. He'd put Richard and William, the two strongest footmen, in charge of Pettigrew with instructions to sit on him if he regained consciousness. He'd sent Sam to fetch the authorities and Jacob to get the doctor. Braxton had carefully lifted Shakespeare and carried him into the house—the dog was now sleeping soundly on Jack's bed. And Frances . . . After a brief argument—Jack had wanted to carry her and she'd insisted on walking—he'd escorted her to her room.

He scowled at the fire. And that had been the last he'd seen of her. Mama and Ellie had rushed upstairs the moment they'd returned from shopping and insisted on keeping Frances company. The doctor had come while Jack was dealing with getting Pettigrew carted off to the gaol and dosed her with laudanum.

He should check on her. Laudanum sometimes gave people bad dreams. The damn doctor had said she'd be fine, that no one need sit with her, and Mama had told him about an hour ago that Frances was indeed resting comfortably, so she was going to bed. Ellie couldn't stay up, of course, since she was increasing.

He shifted in his chair. Frances didn't need laudanum to give her nightmares; Pettigrew's attack would do that.

He put his brandy glass down so forcefully a few drops sloshed out on the table.

Blast it, he was going to her room. He'd almost lost her today. Even if she was sleeping soundly, he needed to see her.

Frances's room wasn't next to his—for once Mama hadn't been matchmaking—but it wasn't far and the corridor was deserted. Ned and Ellie were asleep—they planned to return to the country in the morning—and even Mama and Father appeared to have retired for the night. It took only a moment to reach Frances's door.

He eased it open and slipped inside. The room was dark; the only light came from the hearth. "Frances." He spoke quietly so he wouldn't wake her if she was asleep. "It's Jack."

He heard her covers rustle, and then she whispered, "Jack, what are you doing here?"

"I had to see how you were." He came closer. "I had to be sure you were all right."

"I'm f-fine."

She didn't sound fine. He took her bedside candle and lit it from the hearth fire. He wanted to see her clearly.

Her hair, still far too short to braid, stood out at odd angles as if she'd been tossing and turning on her pillow. Her face was pale; her eyes, huge.

"No bad dreams?"

"N-no."

He raised his eyebrows and waited.

She looked down at her tangled sheets. "Perhaps a few."

"Laudanum can do that."

She shivered. "Yes." She looked back at him. "Would you . . ." She bit her lip. "No, never mind."

"Would I what?" He came closer. "Would I stay and listen to you talk about it?" He smiled. "It often helps to talk, you know."

She plucked at her covers. "No . . ." She paused and then whispered so low he would never have heard her if it wasn't so quiet in the room, "Will you hold me?"

She was afraid to look at Jack when she said the words. Was he shocked? But he'd come to her room; he must know she needed him. And she *did* need him. He was right—she'd had horrible nightmares. She'd kept seeing Mr. Pettigrew's face, kept feeling his grip on her arm and the jolt when her hand slammed into his chin.

She shivered. She'd been shivering a lot, but blankets didn't help—the cold was a hard, icy knot inside her.

She felt the mattress depress, and then Jack's arms came round her.

"I'm here," he said, pulling her close.

He piled the pillows up against the headboard and propped himself there. Then he cradled her against his side. She threw one arm over his chest, buried her face in his banyan, and took a deep, shuddery breath. He smelled of soap, brandy, and Jack.

One of his broad hands stroked comfortingly up and down her back. A sob bubbled up from deep inside her, and then another and another, harsh and racking, sometimes gripping her so tightly she made no sound at all.

She hated crying. Tears were for weak females. But she couldn't stop these. These tears—she felt as if they were ripping her apart.

She cried first because of her horrible encounter with Mr. Pettigrew, but that quickly became the crack that caused the entire dam to fail, letting a dark pool of hurt spill out. She cried because of her aunt's betrayal, her estrangement from her brother, her mother's death, her father's rejection. She cried until she had no more tears left.

"I'm sorry for being such a watering pot," she said finally, exhausted. Ha! Hardly a watering pot—more a typhoon. She wiped her face and nose on her nightgown sleeve. "I've soaked your banyan."

Jack's fingers combed through her hair. "You needed to let all of that out."

She rested her head on his chest and listened to the steady beat of his heart. "I'm so lucky you came when you did this afternoon."

"You didn't need me. You'd already saved yourself."

She had, hadn't she? She felt a small spurt of pride. "But I couldn't have done so if you hadn't shown me what to do, and if Shakespeare hadn't bitten Mr. Pettigrew and made him drop his knife—" Her stomach lurched, and she jerked her head up to stare at Jack. The sound of Shakespeare hitting the ground had been terrifying. "Is Shakespeare all right?"

Jack grinned. "He's fine. Probably a bit sore—he likely got the wind knocked out of him. But Cook rewarded his bravery with any manner of treats—including a nice piece of meat that was supposed to be *my* supper—and now he's snoring happily on my bed."

"Thank God." She put her head back down on his chest and closed her eyes. His warmth was melting the icy knot inside her. Could she persuade him to stay all night? She didn't want to be alone.

His fingers moved through her hair—a lazy, almost sleepy movement—but she didn't feel relaxed or sleepy. She felt drained and empty. Dead.

No. She'd almost died in truth today; she wanted to live

now. She wanted to feel something besides sorrow and regret.

When she'd fought Pettigrew, it had been her love for Jack that had given her strength.

She couldn't foretell the future; she could only live in the present. She needed the courage to choose today, knowing that everything could change tomorrow.

And today she knew she loved Jack.

She wanted him to fill her empty places. Her body hummed. *All* her empty places. And she wanted to be part of his life until death parted them.

"Remember when we were in Lord Easthaven's garden the other night?"

His hand froze. "Yes."

"Remember what you said?" She lifted her head to look at him. He looked somewhat wary.

"Which bit?"

She was afraid to say it—

No, she was *not* afraid. "Do you still wish to marry me?"

He smiled. "Yes." He cupped her face so she couldn't look away. "But do *you* wish to marry me?"

"Yes." Perhaps her mother had been foolish to wed a rake—but Jack wasn't a rake. Still, he might fall out of love with her. The future might hold any number of sorrows. But it also might hold joy, the joy his parents and her grandparents had. She couldn't hope for the joy if she was afraid to risk the sorrow.

She wasn't going to be afraid any longer.

"I love you, Jack." She should be completely truthful. "At least I think I do. I never learned how to love. You'll have to teach me, like you taught me to dance." She searched his eyes and saw only kindness and love there. "You will teach me, won't you? I want to learn."

* * *

"Of course I will." He stroked her cheeks with his thumbs. Happiness of a sort he'd not felt before flooded him. Frances was finally stepping beyond her past, and she had chosen to let him share her present and her future. She was offering him the gift of her love.

She'd been alone for so long, but he'd been alone, too, even though he had brothers and parents. Now he would have a wife, a woman to share his life with, a companion, a friend, a lover. "And you'll teach me."

"But—"

"I think you do know how to love, Frances, but loving, like anything, gets stronger with practice." He smiled. "Let's practice together for as long as we both shall live."

She didn't smile back. "Are you quite, quite certain you wish to marry me? I'm not the bride your mother would have chosen for you."

She might be right, but one never knew with Mama. Mama was devious—and wise. "Mama just wants me to be happy, Frances. Since you make me happy, you are precisely the bride she'd have chosen." He brushed a kiss over her forehead. "She's so successful as the Duchess of Love because she realizes people need to select their own mates. She just makes sure they meet each other."

Frances did not look completely convinced. "And what about my father and Aunt Viola?"

It *was* too bad about them, but they were part of Frances's family, and he intended to share all of her life. He couldn't pick and choose. "Well, I'm not marrying either of them, am I?"

She giggled. "No, but you can't escape the connection."

"True, but I doubt we'll be seeing them often—and I promise to *try* to be polite at our wedding and the christenings of our children."

"Oh," she said. He felt her swallow. "Children?"

"Yes." He moved one hand slowly down her back as she

rested her cheek on his chest. "I'd like several children, I believe. A son or two and a daughter. How many do you want?"

"I-I don't know. I've never thought about it."

His cock was painfully eager to begin the process of getting the first of those children. In fact, it was so insistent, it was getting increasingly difficult to concentrate on anything else.

He'd best find out now if Frances was willing to proceed in that direction; if she wasn't, he'd keep her company as he'd promised, but in a nice hard chair with a block of ice in his lap. "Would you like me to show you how babies are made?"

Her face was almost as red as her hair. "Does it involve kissing?"

"Yes. A lot of kissing. Everywhere." He smiled somewhat tightly. "Even in places you might not expect."

"Oh." Nerves fluttered in her chest. Once she took this step, she couldn't turn back . . .

But she didn't want to turn back. Whatever happened in the future, she loved Jack now.

Her body was certainly eager to proceed. It remembered the kisses in the park and in Lord Easthaven's garden—especially in the garden. Her lips, her breasts, even the place between her legs begged her to tell Jack to get on with it.

"Or I can just hold you. I won't force you, Frances. Ever."

But she heard the thread of disappointment in his voice. There were two people in this bed. She should stop thinking only about herself.

Well, but she wanted this, too. She was only being

cautious—and caution was sometimes just another name for fear.

She was going to be brave. She started unfastening his banyan.

He grabbed her hands. "Frances, you are crossing a line from which there is no return. Are you sure you want to do this?"

Happily, he wasn't wearing a nightshirt. Any remaining wisp of caution or fear burned away, incinerated by the intense need building in her. "Yes, I'm sure."

She opened his banyan, and his male member stood up, begging for attention. How odd it looked. She reached for it—and paused.

"Will it hurt if I touch it?" Jack's poor thing was terribly swollen.

"No."

He sounded as if he was in pain already. Well, she would be gentle. She touched it with just a fingertip. It bobbed. She glanced up at Jack.

He smiled, though his expression looked tight. "Go on." He cleared his throat. "It's all right if you want to wrap your . . . hand . . . around it."

She did. It was both hard and soft at the same time. She ran her hand up and down its length, stroked the odd little sacks at its base, glided the tip of one finger over its head.

It jumped. She laughed and, on some odd whim, leaned forward to kiss it.

Jack's hips bucked up, and he made a very odd sound. "Are. You. Finished?" He bit off each word.

"You said I wouldn't hurt you. You should have told me I was—"

"You weren't hurting me; you were *torturing* me. Another time I would welcome it, but not tonight. Tonight my control is hanging by a thread. I don't want to be done before I've begun."

Now the annoying man was speaking in riddles. "I have no idea what you are getting at."

"Just trust me on this. Now will you kindly remove your nightgown? I believe it's my turn." He sat up and pulled off his banyan, tossing it on the floor.

"Maybe I'm not finished with my turn." But maybe she was. She bit her lip as she looked at his splendid chest and back.

"Please, Frances? I really do beg you."

He looked rather desperate. And she felt rather hot, but she hesitated. She wasn't at all as impressive naked as he was. "Are you sure?"

"Yes. I am very, very sure. I've never been so sure of a thing in my life. May I help you?"

Her body seemed to think that was a good idea. Her breasts . . . and other places . . . throbbed encouragement. "Very well, I—oh!"

Jack didn't wait for her to say more. He pulled her skirt out from under her knees and then slowly slid his hands up her body, taking the nightgown along. Up her thighs, over her hips, along her waist to her breasts, leaving a trail of heat and need behind. Any hesitation or embarrassment she had, burned away.

Desperate didn't begin to describe what she felt.

He dropped her nightgown, and his hands—and lips—returned to her small, unremarkable breasts, which suddenly felt oddly large and swollen. Her nipples tightened to aching points. She lay back against the pillows, arching a little to encourage his further explorations. She needed him to touch—

He must have read her mind. His thumb flicked over a nipple. Her hips twisted on the bed as sensation shot straight to another tight point she hadn't known existed until this very minute.

"You're so beautiful, Frances."

Her mind was too fogged with desire to debate the point. She even *felt* beautiful.

And then his lips latched on to her breast and sucked, and she couldn't think of anything at all.

His hand moved down her body, his lips following. Each touch, each kiss, brought her closer to . . . something.

Stop. You'll lose control. You're giving yourself into a man's power. You'll never be the same.

Whispers of worry, but the needs of her body shouted them down. Her body and her heart. She loved Jack. She might not know how to love, she might not love as well as other women, but she loved him as best she could. She *wanted* to give herself to him. He would hold her safe. He would stay with her—by her side and in her heart. She knew it as surely as she knew her own name.

But even if he didn't, if the future brought something else, she was choosing him—and this—now.

He'd reached the aching point between her legs. She closed her eyes—the sight of his head between her thighs was too embarrassing—but that only served to narrow her focus to the sensation of his warm breath against her and then—

She gasped, and her hips jerked. Jack's tongue had touched . . . was touching . . . oh! With each teasing flick, he was drawing her closer to wherever it was he was taking her. Closer and closer until she could no longer stand it—

And suddenly she was there. Wave after wave of pleasure rushed from that tiny point to her womb and her breasts and her heart.

And then Jack's body was over hers. She felt him pushing slowly into her, opening, stretching . . .

She caught her breath as something deep inside her gave way with a burning pain, and then he was there, filling her completely.

"Are you all right?"

"I'm wonderful."

Wonderful? You are completely in a man's control, trapped by his weight, impaled by his body.

And he was in her control. His face was tight with a need she recognized all too well. She was giving him love, the love he'd given her. This was a gift of bodies, but also of hearts and minds.

She ran her hands from his narrow waist to his broad shoulders and back to his buttocks pressed against her.

"I love you, Jack."

He looked into her eyes, his passion receding for a moment, so she knew he was speaking to *her*, not some convenient female. "And I love you, Frances." He kissed her. "Soon to be wife and perhaps mother."

His hips moved. In and out, in and out, and then in one last time, deep, as deep as he could go, all the way to her heart. He stilled; he made a small noise—a gasp or a moan, she couldn't tell; and then she felt the warmth of his seed pulse into her, perhaps beginning a child, a child who would be loved and cherished and cared for and never, never abandoned.

They lay together, his weight pressing her down into the mattress, her arms holding him close. The doubting voice in her head was completely silent, perhaps as stunned as she was by the intense intimacy of what had just happened.

Jack started to lift himself away; she clutched him tighter. "Don't go."

He chuckled. "I'm crushing you—and I'm not going far."

His weight *did* make breathing a little difficult, but she felt chilled and bereft when he left her—until he settled next to her on the bed, gathered her close, and pulled the coverlet over them.

"Are you all right?"

"I'm wonderful," she said again. It was true. She *was* wonderful.

He kissed her forehead. "Yes, you are." He ran his hand up her naked back. "Go to sleep now."

"You'll stay here with me?"

He laughed again. "Yes, though I'm afraid I may shock the maid in the morning." He cupped her breast. "I'll try to leave before she comes in. I need to be up early anyway—I want to see about getting a special license."

"Oh." Frances found she didn't care about the servants' opinions. "There's no need to rush for the license, is there?" She trusted Jack would marry her.

He kissed her. "Yes, there is. My parents are very understanding, but they'll expect a prompt wedding if I'm sleeping in your bed, which I fully intend to keep doing."

And she wanted him to keep doing so, but—

"Oh, dear heavens, do you think they know you're in here with me?" His parents would be scandalized!

"I wouldn't be surprised—Mama seems to know everything that happens even before it does. And if she doesn't know now, she will by noon tomorrow. I learned as a child that there's no hiding things from her."

"Ohh." She buried her face in his chest. "They will throw me out of the house—and with good reason."

"Nonsense. Mama and Father will be delighted. Mama will be happy that her last son is safely wed, and Father will be happy Mama need no longer subject him to the annual Valentine house party, whose main purpose was to find brides for Ned and me." He rested his hand on her stomach. "And they will both be thrilled that they may have another grandchild to spoil."

She put her hand over his. "Do you think we made a baby?" The thought was both thrilling and terrifying.

"Perhaps." His smile turned seductive. "I plan to keep

trying—which is why I need that marriage license. Now go to sleep."

"All right." She smiled and closed her eyes. "You are very wise."

"Of course I am."

Someone was moving around in her room. Venus reached over to poke Drew, but his place in the bed was empty. That's right. He was going for an early-morning ride. So who was here?

She cracked one eye open. It *was* Drew; he hadn't left yet. Or was he back? She sniffed. No horse smell—he hadn't yet left. But he had a very odd expression.

As if he had a secret.

She popped up, and then pulled the covers up over her. It was chilly. The maid hadn't yet been in to make up the fires.

"You're awake," Drew said.

Brilliant deduction—but she swallowed the words. She knew better than to start with sarcasm when she wanted something from her dear duke. And she was only tetchy because he wasn't in bed with her. She knew he enjoyed his early rides—he hated Town enough as it was, but if he got no exercise, he was unbearable—but she preferred early-morning rides of the bedroom sort.

"Yes," she said. "You look as if you have something to tell me."

He also looked as if he couldn't decide whether to scowl or grin.

He decided to grin.

"I ran into Jack in the corridor."

"Oh?" Why was that newsworthy?

"He wasn't coming out of his own room."

"Oh!" Damn the cold. She leapt up to kneel on the

bed and grab Drew's lapels. "Whose room was he coming out of?"

"Not Ned's."

She was going to strangle him; she contented herself with just gripping his coat tighter. There could be only one possibility. "Did he spend the night with Miss Hadley?"

"It would appear so."

"Ah." She forced down her excitement; she must not jump to the obvious conclusion. "He likely was concerned for her well-being. She had a very upsetting experience yesterday."

"Indeed she did. I suspect he comforted her most thoroughly. So thoroughly, in fact, that he advised me he'd be making arrangements for a special license today."

Venus so forgot herself as to squeal.

Drew looked slightly pained. "I hope that is a sound of joy, my dear duchess."

"Of course it is." She sat back down on the bed. There were so many things to do. "I know I didn't select Frances for Jack, but that makes no difference. They clearly have strong feelings for each other. Lady Rothmarsh will be so pleased. And Jack will be married!" She started to climb out of bed. "I must get dressed and go welcome the dear girl into the family."

Drew caught her arm. "I suspect that would not be a good idea, Venus."

She frowned at him. "Why not? We don't want Frances to think we aren't delighted she is marrying Jack."

"Yes, but I think we can convey that sentiment later. Miss Hadley might be a little, er, distressed to have her future in-laws burst into her room because they know exactly what she'd been doing with their son the night before."

"Oh. Yes, I see your point. That might be a trifle awkward."

"A little more than a trifle." Drew smiled and slid his

hand slowly up her arm. "And I have another reason you should delay your visit to Miss Hadley."

"And what is that?" Drew's fingers were now toying with the neck of her nightgown. It was most distracting.

"I missed my exercise this morning by coming back to give you this news," he said.

"Oh, I see. I'm sorry, but—"

He interrupted. "So I think you should help me rectify that problem."

Now his hand was skimming her side, his fingers so very close to her breast. She wet her lips. "Ah. Perhaps you can still get a ride in."

"That's exactly what I was hoping."

The Duchess of Love and her duke did not arise until noon.

If you enjoyed SURPRISING LORD JACK,
don't miss the first book in Sally MacKenzie's delightful
"Duchess of Love" series:
BEDDING LORD NED.

Read on for a special excerpt . . .
Available as a Kensington eBook
and mass-market paperback,
on sale now!

A man's pride needs careful handling.
—Venus's Love Notes

Miss Eleanor Bowman stood in the Duchess of Love's pink guest bedroom and stared at the scrap of red silk spilling out of her valise, her heart stuttering in horror. That wasn't—

Her brows snapped down. Of course it wasn't. She was letting her imagination run away with her. The red fabric was merely her Norwich shawl. She distinctly remembered packing it, as she did every year. It was far too fine to wear to darn socks or mind her sisters' children, but it was just the thing for the duchess's annual Valentine party. It was her one nod to fashion, the small bit of elegance she still allowed herself.

She snatched the red silk up again, shook it out—and dropped it as if it were a poisonous snake.

Damn it, it *wasn't* her shawl. It was those cursed red drawers.

She closed her eyes as the familiar wave of self-loathing

crashed over her. She'd made these and a matching red dress to wear to Lord Edward's betrothal ball five years ago, desperately hoping Ned would see her—really see her—and realize it was she he wanted to marry, not her best friend, Cicely Headley. But Mama had seen her first, when she'd come downstairs to get into the carriage, and had sent her straight back to her room.

She glared down at the red cloth. Thank God Mama had stopped her. If she'd gone to the ball in that dreadful dress, everyone would know she wasn't any better than a Jezebel.

It was no surprise Ned had chosen Cicely. She'd been everything Ellie wasn't: small, blond, blue-eyed—beautiful—with a gentle disposition. And then when Cicely and the baby had died in childbirth . . .

Ellie squeezed her eyes shut again, the mingle-mangle of shame and yearning twisting her gut. She'd mourned with everyone else—sincerely mourned—but she'd also hoped that Ned would turn to her and their friendship would grow into something more.

It hadn't.

She snapped her eyes open. Poor Cicely had died four years ago; if Ned were ever going to propose he would have done so by now. She'd faced that fact squarely when she'd turned twenty-six last month. It was time to move on. She wanted babies, and dreams of Ned wouldn't give her those.

She picked up the drawers. She'd dispose of this ridiculous reminder of—

"Ah, here you are, Ellie."

"Ack!" She jumped and spun around. Ned's mother, the Duchess of Love—or, more properly, the Duchess of Greycliffe—stood in the doorway, looking at her with warm brown eyes so like Ned's.

"Oh, dear, I'm sorry." Her Grace's smile collapsed into a frown. "I didn't mean to startle you."

Ellie took a deep breath and hoped the duchess couldn't see her heart banging around in her chest. "You didn't s-startle me." If she looked calm, she'd be calm. She'd been practicing that trick ever since her red silk disgrace.

And what was there to be anxious about after all? The duchess's house parties were always pleasant.

Ha! They were torture.

"I was going to look for you later." Ellie tried to smile.

"Then I've saved you the trouble." The duchess had an impish gleam in her eye. "I thought we might have a comfortable coze before everyone else arrives."

Ellie's stomach clenched, and all her carefully cultivated calm evaporated. There was no such thing as a "comfortable coze" with the Duchess of Love. "That would be, ah"—deep breath—"lovely."

"Splendid! Come have a seat and I'll ring for tea." Her Grace grasped the tasseled bellpull and paused, her gaze dropping to Ellie's hands. "But what have you there?"

"W-what?" Ellie glanced down. Oh, blast. "Nothing." She dropped the embarrassing silk undergarment on the night table; it promptly slithered to the floor. Good, it would be less noticeable there. "I was unpacking when you came in."

The duchess frowned again. "Should I come back later then?"

"No, of course not." There was no point in putting this interview off. The sooner she knew the woman's plans, the sooner she could plan evasive—

She clenched her teeth. No, not this year.

"You're certain?"

"Yes." Ellie moved away from the incriminating red fabric.

"Excellent." Her Grace tugged on the bellpull and sat in the pink upholstered chair, her back to the puddle of silk. "I told Mrs. Dalton to have Cook send up some of her special macaroons. It will be a while until dinner, and we need to keep up our strength, don't we?"

"I'm afraid I'm not hungry." Ellie would almost rather dance on the castle's parapets naked—or wearing only those damn red drawers—than put anything in her mouth at the moment. She perched on a chair across from Ned's mother.

"Oh." The duchess's face fell.

"But, please, don't let me keep you from having something." It was a wonder the woman stayed so slim; she had a prodigious sweet tooth.

Her Grace smiled hopefully. "Perhaps you'll feel hungrier when you see Cook's macaroons."

"Perhaps." And perhaps pigs would fly. Ellie cleared her throat. "You had something of a particular nature you wished to discuss, Your Grace?"

"Yes."

Damn.

No, *good.* Very good. Excellent.

The *ton* hadn't christened Ned's mother the Duchess of Love for nothing; she'd been matchmaking for as long as Ellie could remember, usually with great success. Ellie was one of her few failures, but this year would be different. This year Ellie was determined to cooperate.

"I was chatting with your mama the other day," the duchess was saying, her eyes rather too direct. "She's quite concerned about your future, you know."

Ellie shifted on her chair. Of course she knew—Mama never missed an opportunity to remind her that her future looked very bleak indeed. She'd been going on and on about it while Ellie packed, telling her how, if she allowed herself to dwindle into an old maid, she'd be forced to rely on the charity of her younger sisters, forever shuttled between their homes, always an aunt, never a mother.

Perhaps that's why she'd brought those damn drawers

instead of her shawl; she'd been so distracted, she could probably have packed the chamber pot and not noticed. "I believe Mama likes to worry."

The duchess laughed. "Well, that's what mothers do—worry—as I'm sure you'll learn yourself someday."

"Ah." Ellie swallowed.

Her Grace leaned forward to touch her knee. "You do want to be a mother, don't you?"

Ellie swallowed again. "Y-yes." She wanted children so badly she was giving up her dream of Ned—her ridiculous, pointless, foolish dream. "Of course. Eventually."

The duchess gave her a pointed look. "My dear, you are twenty-six years old. Eventually is now."

Ellie pressed her lips together. Very true. Hadn't she just reached the same conclusion?

"And to be a mother, you must first be a wife." Her Grace sat back. "To be a wife, you need to attach some gentleman's—some *eligible* gentleman's—regard. I believe you spent a little too much time with Ash last year. That will never do."

"I like Ash." The Marquis of Ashton, the duchess's oldest son, was intelligent and witty . . . and safe.

"Of course you like Ash, dear, but I must tell you more than one person remarked to me how often you were in his company."

Ellie narrowed her eyes. "What do you mean?"

"Only that you appeared to be ignoring all the other gentlemen."

She'd been trying so hard to ignore Ned—to hide how much she longed for him—that she hadn't noticed the other gentlemen. "Certainly you aren't insinuating . . . no one thought . . ." She shook her head. "Ash is married."

The duchess sighed. "Yes, he is, at least according to church and state."

"And according to his heart." Ellie met the duchess's

gaze directly. "You mustn't think he encouraged any kind of impropriety. He still loves Jess; I'm sure they'll reconcile."

The duchess grunted. "I hope I live to see it. But in any event, I don't believe anyone truly thought there was something of a romantic nature between you—"

"I should hope not!"

"However people are so small-minded, you know, and they love to gossip, especially about Ash's awkward situation."

"I know." Ellie hated how the marriageable girls and their mamas clearly hoped Jess would magically vanish and thus cease to be an impediment to Ash's remarriage. Some had actually said they doubted Jess existed. "It makes me so angry."

Her Grace waved Ellie's anger away. "Yes, well, Ash can take care of himself. What really matters is the fact you *were* ignoring the other gentlemen, Ellie. It quite discourages the poor dears."

Ellie snorted.

Her Grace gave her a speaking look. "I assure you most men . . . well, I wouldn't call them timid, precisely, but they hate to be rejected. If you wish a gentleman to court you, you must give him some encouragement—a smile, a look, something to let him know you would welcome his attentions. You cannot be forever scowling and dodging."

"I don't scowl or dodge."

The duchess's brows rose. "No? What about Mr. Bridgeton last year? I was certain you two would be extremely compatible and made every effort to throw you together, but whenever I looked to see how things were progressing, you were chatting with Ash, and Mr. Bridgeton was crying on Miss Albert's shoulder."

Which one had been Mr. Bridgeton? The sandy-haired man with the receding chin or the tall, thin fellow with the enormous Adam's apple? "There was no one crying on anyone's shoulder."

"Figuratively speaking, of course." The duchess shrugged. "I confess Miss Albert was my other choice for him. I do usually have more than one match up my sleeve, you know, since I've found young people can be somewhat unpredictable." She smiled rather blandly. "They married last summer, by the by, and are expecting an interesting event this spring."

Ellie felt a momentary twinge of envy. Mr. Bridgeton—she was almost certain he was the sandy-haired one—had been pleasant. His only fault was he hadn't been Ned.

Well, whomever she ultimately married wouldn't be Ned, either. "Whom have you invited . . . I mean, have you invited any gentlemen that I might . . . er, men who might . . ." Oh, blast, her face felt as if it was as red as those damn silk drawers. "You know."

Her Grace beamed at her. "Of course I've invited some gentlemen who might be suitable matches for you."

Ellie willed herself to keep smiling. It would get easier with time . . . it had to. She cleared her throat. Her mouth was infernally dry. "Who?"

The duchess leaned forward. "First, there's Mr. Humphrey. He's a little younger than you and very, ah . . . earnest. He's just inherited a small estate from his great aunt; rumor has it he wishes to start his nursery immediately."

"Ah." Mr. Humphrey sounded terribly dull . . . but dullness was fine. She wanted babies, not conversation. And he apparently wanted babies, too. Excellent.

"And then there's Mr. Cox. He's one of the Earl of Bollant's brood, the fourth—or perhaps the fifth—son. He's very popular with the ladies and a trifle wild, but he's shown some signs of being ready to settle down. He's to go into the church, so you could be very helpful to him, your papa being a vicar."

"I see." Taking charge of some silly sprig of the nobility was not especially appealing, but the man did have a number of brothers. With luck he would be equally skilled at procreating, though it would be nice to have a daughter or two as well.

The duchess was smiling at her, a rather expectant look on her face. Did she want her to pick one right now?

"I . . . er, they both sound very . . . pleasant, but . . ." *Remember, she wanted children.* "Well, I suppose I will have to meet them."

"Yes, indeed." The duchess glanced at the door. "Ah, here is Thomas with the tea tray."

One of the footmen came in, a large ginger cat, tail high in the air, strolling along behind him.

"Reggie!" Ned's mother bent to scratch her pet's ears. "Did you come for a treat?"

Reggie meowed and butted his head against her hand.

"Cook sent up Sir Reginald's dish, Your Grace," Thomas said, putting down the tray.

"Excellent. Please give Cook my thanks."

"Very good, Your Grace." Thomas bowed and retreated while the duchess poured Reggie a generous saucer of cream and put the dish on the floor.

Ellie kept one eye on the cat, lapping delicately, as she prepared the tea. Reggie looked harmless, but he'd caused quite a commotion last year, stealing feathers and other items from the ladies—and at least one of the gentlemen—and hiding them under Ned's bed. He'd even snatched the stuffed pheasant from Lady Perford's favorite hat. Lady Perford had not been pleased.

"Has Reggie given up his thieving ways, Your Grace?"

"I don't know, as he hasn't had another opportunity to misbehave." She snorted. "As you well know, Greycliffe hates having any of the *ton* underfoot and grumbles from the moment they arrive until the last one departs."

It was true the duke rarely looked happy during the Valentine house parties. "How does His Grace bear your London balls?" Ellie asked, handing the duchess a cup of tea. She used to read the London gossip columns, but as she only ever saw Jack, the youngest of the Valentine brothers, mentioned, she no longer bothered.

"With as much patience as he can muster which is not very much, but since people expect dukes to be annoyingly haughty, it just adds to his consequence." Her eyes twinkled as she sipped her tea. "And it makes people toady him all the more which infuriates him further. No, once a month for four months a Season is the very limit of what he can tolerate. And a ball is only one evening. This . . ." She shook her head and sighed. "But it is my birthday as well as the boys', and he knows how important it is to me, so he grits his teeth and endures. You can imagine how much he's hoping Ned will remarry and Jack will wed soon so I have no more need to have these gatherings."

"Ah." Ellie forced a smile. "Yes." She knew the main point of the damn party was to find Ned—and Jack, of course—a suitable wife. "I can see that."

The duchess glanced down at Reggie who was now cleaning his paws. "Greycliffe is actually hoping Reggie pilfers things again. He thought it made the gathering much more interesting."

Interesting was one way to describe the screaming and tears Lady Perford had treated them to upon finding her mangled pheasant.

Ellie took a sustaining sip of tea. She might as well know everything now; it would make it easier to appear composed in company. "And whom have you invited for Jack"—she swallowed—"and N-Ned?"

Damn, her voice cracked. Perhaps the duchess hadn't noticed.

And perhaps Reggie would leap upon the tea table and sing an aria.

At least Ned's mother didn't comment beyond a raised eyebrow. "I'd originally had Miss Prudence Merriweather in mind for Jack," she said, "however the girl eloped with Mr. Bamford three weeks ago. Quite a shock to everyone, but of course I must take it as a blessing. She clearly would not have done for Jack if she was in love with another man."

Her Grace sent her a significant, if obscure, look. Ellie took another sip of tea.

"I had to scramble a bit," Her Grace continued somewhat dryly, "but I found Miss Isabelle Wharton to take her place. I've never actually met the girl, you understand, but my friend Lady Altman says she is quite striking. I imagine Jack would appreciate a lovely bride." She shrugged slightly. "And if the match comes to nothing, well, Jack is only your age. He has plenty of time."

"Yes." Twenty-six was young for a man; it was firmly on the shelf for a woman.

"And as for Ned"—Her Grace shot Ellie another indecipherable look—"I invited Lady Juliet Ramsbottom, the Duke of Extley's youngest daughter, with him in mind."

A vise clamped around Ellie's heart. Stupid. A duke's daughter was an excellent choice for a duke's son. She nodded and took a larger swallow of tea. If only there was some brandy at hand to flavor it.

"Frankly, I hope to see you and Ned married this summer."

Ellie choked—and made the unpleasant discovery that it was possible to snort tea out one's nose.

"Oh, dear." The duchess leapt up and slapped her on the back. "Are you all right?"

Ellie, gasping, fished her handkerchief out of her

pocket and waved her hand, trying to get the duchess to stop pounding on her. She would be fine if she could just catch her breath.

Of course Ned's mother hadn't meant she hoped to see Ellie married *to* Ned, only that she hoped both their nuptials would happen this summer.

The duchess pounded harder.

"Please," Ellie gasped, "don't—"

Through watery eyes, she watched Reggie abandon his ablutions and head toward . . .

"Ah, ah, ah."

"What are you trying to say, dear?" The duchess paused in her pummeling. If she happened to glance in the direction Ellie's horrified eyes were staring, she'd see Reggie sniffing a pair of red silk drawers.

Ellie sprang to her feet. Panic miraculously cleared her throat. "I'm fine," she croaked. "Wonderful. Fit as a fiddle." She glanced over her shoulder. Now Reggie was batting at the drawers with one paw.

She shifted her position to block the duchess's view.

"I shouldn't tease you, I know," Her Grace said. Her eyes dimmed and she sighed, shoulders drooping. She suddenly looked every one of her fifty years. "I've certainly learned harping on a subject doesn't get results. If it did, my boys would all be happily married."

"I'm sure they will be, Your Grace." Ellie impulsively laid her hand on the duchess's arm. She hated to see her so blue-deviled. "Just give them time."

"Time." The duchess bit her lip as if she'd like to say more on that head. She let out a short, sharp breath and shrugged, smiling a little. "It's only . . . well, I'm so happy with the duke. Is it wrong to want that happiness for my sons?"

"Of course not, Your Grace, but your situation *is* rather extraordinary." The duke and duchess had fallen in love at first sight when they were both very young. Even more unusual, they'd been happily married for over thirty years and, by all accounts, completely faithful to each other. There was probably not another couple like them in all the English nobility.

Ellie glanced at Reggie again. Damn it. Now the drawers were over his head. If he got caught in them . . .

"I know," Her Grace said. "When I look around the *ton*, I see so many unpleasant unions." She shook her head. "Well, just consider Ash and Jess. They've been separated for eight years now."

Ellie wrenched her gaze away from Reggie's activities. "I'm certain they will reconcile eventually."

"But when?" The duchess's voice was tight with frustration. "Ash will be the duke; the duchy needs an heir, and neither he nor Jess is getting any younger." She frowned. "And I want a grandchild or two before I'm completely in my dotage."

Damnation. Reggie was now coming their way, the silk drawers in his mouth. Ellie took the duchess's arm and started to walk toward the door with her.

"Ash—and Ned and Jack—can manage their own lives, Your Grace. You must know you've raised them well."

The duchess sighed. "And there's nothing I can do about it anyway, is there?" She paused and glanced around. "Where has Reggie got to?"

"Likely he finished his cream and left," Ellie said. The blasted cat had just passed behind the duchess's skirts and out the door. Where the hell was he going? Certainly not . . . last year he had . . . but he wouldn't this year, would he? "Has Ned"—Ellie caught herself—"and Jack arrived yet?"

"Oh, no. I don't expect them for a while."

Ellie almost collapsed with relief. If Reggie was taking her undergarment to Ned's room, she'd have time to get it back before anyone—especially Ned—found it. "I hope they reach the castle before the storm. Mrs. Dalton was just saying her rheumatism is acting up."

"Oh, dear. Mrs. Dalton's rheumatism never lies." The duchess stopped on the threshold and smiled, her good spirits returning. "Just think! You young people can go on sleigh rides."

"I'm hardly young." At the moment she just wanted to chase down one misbehaving cat.

"Oh, don't be such a wet rag; you'll freeze stiff in this weather." The duchess laughed. "You can make snow angels, and I'm sure the men will get into a snowball battle."

"Everyone will be cold and wet." Ellie did not want to play in the snow. Such activities were for children.

"And there are ever so many games and things we can do inside." Her Grace clapped her hands. "You know, I have the greatest hope this will be a wonderful party."

"Er, yes." Just wonderful, though perhaps snow would be better than rain or general February dreariness.

The duchess patted her arm. "And I have great hopes for you as well, dear." She stepped into the corridor. "I'll expect you downstairs in the blue drawing room before dinner. Don't be late."

"I won't."

Ellie watched the duchess walk down the passage—and the moment she turned the corner, she bolted for Ned's room.